THE MALICE OF MOONS & MAGES

THE MALICE OF MOONS & MAGES

N.V. HASKELL

Cursed Dragon Ship
PUBLISHING

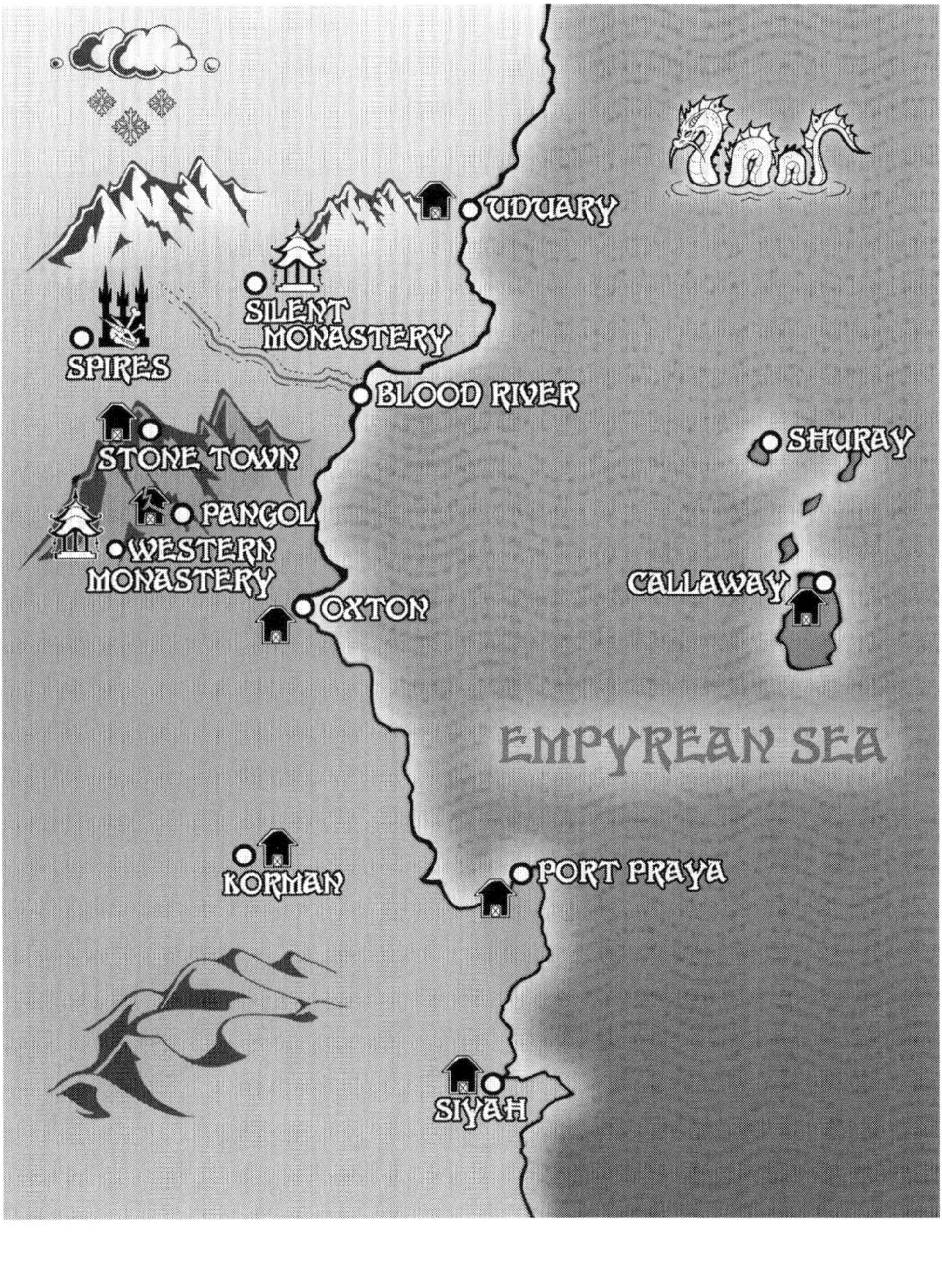
UDUARY
SILENT MONASTERY
SPIRES
BLOOD RIVER
SHURAY
STONE TOWN
PANGOL
WESTERN MONASTERY
CALLAWAY
OXTON
EMPYREAN SEA
KORMAN
PORT PRAYA
SIYAH

Copyright © 2025 by N.V. Haskell

Cursed Dragon Ship Publishing, LLC

6046 FM 2920 Rd, #231, Spring, TX 77379

captwyvern@curseddragonship.com

Cover design © 2025 by We Got You Covered Book Design

Developmental Edit by S.G. George

Copy Edit by Kelly Lynn Colby

ISBN 978-1-951445-88-1

ISBN 978-1-951445-89-8 (ebook)

All rights reserved

No part of this book may be reproduced in any form or by any electronic or mechanical means, including information storage and retrieval systems, without written permission from the publisher, except for the use of brief quotations in a book review.

No part of this book may be used to train AI or to generate AI content without express written permission from the copyright holder.

This book is a work of fiction fresh from the author's imagination. Any resemblance to actual persons or places is mere coincidence.

For those whose voices were silenced, may you find your words once more.

One

Audra
Western Thief

With its clean, tiled floors and bland but edible food, this was by far the most luxurious jail Audra had ever been in, and she'd sampled several. Even the guards were decent; none had raised a hand to her yet. Yet despite those small luxuries and the island's temperate climate, Audra hated Callaway.

A small, gray shape skittered across the cell floor. Audra caught the thin mouse by the tail and held it aloft. Its broken whiskers danced, small teeth gnashing as it squirmed at the insult. Gently stroking its head, she pursed her lips. Maybe they weren't that different. She released it, watching it dart toward the cracked mortar between the wall and the floor. The mouse flattened itself and disappeared with a small flick of its tail, as if it had never been there at all.

"Fine. That's fine. Just like everyone else," she whispered. "Leave me to find my own way out. Coward."

She rolled onto her back. Starling's bright morning shine cascaded through the window high above, ushering in a mild sea breeze that failed to clear the stench from the adjacent cell. Though she was only a short distance from the dock, getting there would be a challenge.

Traq, her oldest friend, had sailed away on a Starling ship before dawn, taking any evidence of what she'd stolen across the Empyrean Sea in his safekeeping. As a mage, he'd escape the usual scrutiny that the soldiers experienced. And thanks to the mage wind, the ship would reach Oxton in a few days, though the journey might take a standard vessel twice as long.

The Callaway guards had no evidence to hold her, and they knew it. Only an old man's accusations kept her where she was, but authority on the islands moved notoriously slow unless you had coin to hasten it.

While the archipelago's other islands were small and sparsely populated, Callaway was ruled by merchants loyal only to coin. Their wealth stemmed from other tribes' stolen art and history. That they'd had a hand in taking nearly all that remained of the Western tribe's dragon-eye jade was what had brought her to this wretched place. And though it would be easy to blame the southern Starling tribe for pilfering her culture's treasures, the northern Moon tribes were certainly no better.

There wasn't any need to rush for a drab Westerner such as herself. Which was unfortunate since the smuggling vessel she'd been counting on to take her back to the mainland was due to disembark in the morning, and she needed to be on it.

The cell to her right had been empty since they'd dragged Audra in the day before. The cell to her left, however, housed a Starling tribe couple brought in for drunken brawling late in the evening. They'd refused to be separated, promising the arresting guards they'd settle. Then they proceeded to spend several hours hurling accusations of cheating at each other before their dispute dissolved into tears and apologies too garbled to quite make out. Eventually, they'd passed out in each other's arms as the flicker of the all'ight dimmed, their backs pressed against the bars shared with Audra's cell. One of them had vomited sometime later, and the stench of piss and excrement grew stronger with every passing hour.

They'd died while Audra slept. She hadn't realized it at first. It wasn't that she was unaccustomed to death, more like she didn't expect it to come quite as often as it did.

The Callaway islands' best export were their wines—rice, blackberry, hibiscus, and the infamously daring and insultingly expensive liger's bane. Liger's bane was a poisonous flower, but the islanders had deduced a way to remove the concentrated poison for wine because, Audra supposed, there must have been little else to do while their neighbors warred. The real danger with that wine was that its toxicity returned about four hours after it was uncorked.

The islanders had spent generations building up a solid resistance to the poison and sometimes neglected to emphasize that information while the less worldly foreigners didn't pay attention to this small—but incredibly relevant—detail. Since the jugs were small and went down so smoothly, there wasn't usually any threat of it not being consumed before it turned. Unless, of course, there were several bottles open at a time and people were already drunk. Then time was lost as well as lives. There was an antidote that barkeeps held, but it was three times the cost of the wine.

The couple's lifeless arms were drawn tight around each other. At least they'd made amends before they died, and they'd be able to do one last good deed with their deaths.

Thick brown hair hung to her waist. She considered pulling it back, but it was important they remembered her this way.

The guards, Hana and Lot, were talking across their desks. Having already discussed their welfare, woes, and wages they now sank into gossip. Their voices lilted toward Audra as she stared longingly at the cracked mortar where the mouse had gone. Her escapes were never so easy.

"I'm telling you, he said the tyrant was dead. Insisted the Moons were keeping it hushed until the dual eclipses or until they caught the murderer." Lot was the youngest of the guards and spoke with an overconfidence that took an obvious toll on his companion.

"You'll believe anything. And who would trust you with such information?" Hana asked.

"A captain. Said they'd just come from Uduary with a shipment of silks. Heading to Oxton tomorrow."

Audra had listened to the gossip with half an ear but stiffened at the mention of the Moon tribe's capital. The *Requin*'s captain was a crooked trader named Chon Gioni who'd returned from Uduary and the northern tribes two days ago and was set to sail in the morning. Knowing Chon kept several guards on the payroll to get through customs made her plan to stowaway only slightly inconvenient. Still, she was small enough to squirm into tight spaces and go unnoticed, much like the mouse.

"And who did they theorize could kill someone so high and mighty?" Hana asked.

His nails scraped across his patchy beard. The length of Lot's pause defeated the conviction of his next statement. "Maybe one of the bastard's children?"

Hana shook her head. "Don't believe everything those swindlers say. Next thing you know, you'll lose a month's wages thinking it's going toward the promise of a spouse. Besides, you can never believe the mages. Everyone knows that. Not the Moons or Starlings. They probably spread those rumors on purpose." She glanced guiltily toward the cell and lowered her voice. "Just look at how they destroyed the Westerners."

Audra shifted awkwardly at the truth of that statement. Her people had been crushed between the Moons and Starlings for centuries.

Alver, the third guard, returned with an older man nagging at his footsteps. Audra licked her teeth, watching the antiquities dealer storm in. Claude Suna was in good health for his years. His white hair contrasted pleasantly with his oaky complexion and fanciful orange and yellow silks. The garments were meant to flaunt his wealth but only made him appear somewhat ridiculous when contrasted with his surroundings, like someone who required a good deal of attention. He had the smooth hands of those unaccustomed to labor and the dour expression of one used to obedience.

"What do you mean you haven't found it?" Claude's husky voice rose indignantly. "Do you know how much it's worth?" Alver gave nothing away in his look as Claude continued. "More than you three make in a year combined."

The other guards rose to their feet with a sudden need to be busy. Audra stood and stretched while the old man rattled them. Her naked feet chilled against the tile. They'd taken her boots when they brought her in. Just as well, they'd be useless where she was going.

Sometimes opportunity came in unexpected ways, especially when combined with a host of lies, opportunities like poisoned wine and bright colors that sung with audacity.

"I need to use the latrine," Audra said loudly. All eyes turned to her. She made a point of meeting the old man's gaze before turning to the guards.

"You!" Claude shook his fist in the air. "Where did you hide my jade, you filthy bitch? You don't know who you are trifling with. My husband—"

"I need to use the latrine," she repeated louder. Hana squirmed beneath Audra's stare while the merchant's face darkened with affront.

"There's a bucket in the corner," Lot said.

"Where is it?" Claude started forward, but Alver held him back with a light hand on his chest.

Audra turned to Lot. "Not for this. And I'd rather a woman escort me if it's all the same. Unless Callaway men are more comfortable with feminine issues."

Color crept up Lot's cheeks and reddened the tips of his ears. He looked sheepishly at Hana. She pursed her lips and moved toward Audra's cell.

"Make her tell where it is! Give her a sound whipping if you must," Claude said.

Alver sighed with more patience than Audra had given him credit for. She liked Alver. He seemed to hate the Callaway merchants almost as much as she did. "We don't torture prisoners here, Mirz Suna. You'd have to return to the southern lands for that."

Hana opened the door enough for Audra to wriggle through. The guard's eyes darted toward the couple. Audra nudged her.

"Please." Desperation oozed through Audra's voice.

With a last glance at the couple, Hana gripped Audra's elbow and hauled her through a rear door to a small outside enclosure. Claude's threats followed them into the bright Starling light. The walls were disappointingly flat, too smooth for handholds, and rose twelve feet high, where iron spikes jutted inward at the top. Two stone seats with hip-sized oval holes were set along the perimeter. At the bottom of those holes, the drainage system connected to the rest of town and, eventually, out to sea. She went to the one furthest away, closest to the main drain.

Audra undid her breeches and sat, massaging her abdomen, and working a dramatic grimace. Hana sighed and looked away.

"They're dead, you know," Audra's voice trembled in feigned fear.

"What?"

"That couple. Before you came on shift, the guards last night made a bet."

Hana's eyes narrowed. "What bet?"

"The big guy with the beard bet that the man would die first. The smaller guy put his money on the woman." The story sold itself. They had been gambling, and it was safe to think they were known for it, but it was not over a game of death. "I think the bigger guy won."

Hana blanched. Larceny or drunken violence wasn't rare on the island, and the unintentional poisoning of tourists was an occasional issue, but guards betting on tourist deaths went against all the islanders' beliefs of their moral superiority.

Audra watched the options ripple across Hana's face. She couldn't leave a prisoner alone out here and didn't want to call to the others since the old man was there. If Audra was telling the truth, then it would need to be kept quiet, and Claude Suna lacked the personality for discretion.

Audra groaned and clutched her lower belly, squeezing her eyes hard enough to create tears that trickled from the corners. Hana's gaze darted from the door to the prisoner.

"I should have said something earlier, but I was so scared. I think she, that woman might still be alive."

Hana reached for the door.

"But her breathing was so . . ." Audra's voice broke.

Hana leveled an authoritative finger at her. "You stay right there." The door closed behind her.

Audra cinched her pants tight and tied her hair back with a bit of string yanked from her hem. She stared into the hole and shuddered.

It would be a tight and disgusting fit.

She perched on the seat's edge and dangled her feet inside. The stench made her gag. It didn't matter if swimming through shit would be justifiable for what might be nothing more than another fool's mission. The jade was already on its way to Oxton, and getting it to her brother was imperative. Even if she wasn't wholly responsible for Ferin's injury, their well-being was connected.

Auntie Zin was waiting for the jade in another attempt to heal Ferin. Plus, Traq would worry if Audra didn't show in Oxton within a couple of weeks. She'd had a plan. Crawling through sewers hadn't been part of it, but she'd survived worse.

Taking a deep breath, Audra squirmed down into the muck, scraping the backs of her arms and shoulders in the narrow descent. Slime oozed between her toes as her feet hit the bottom. The drain's ceiling was low, forcing her onto hands and knees. As bile burned her throat, Audra crawled. Filth seeped through the linen shirt to coat her skin. She barely kept her chin from skimming the muck when she vomited.

Three hours later the tunnel widened. She sucked in a breath of fresh air as the sewer opened onto the cliff side. In the sky above, the remnants of Raia's broken moon ringed the planet, illuminated by full Starling light. Parts of the ring shone like the brightest emerald in places and the darkest moss in others, shifting as it rotated slowly with occasional gaps. No one valued the ring as much as Starling or the Song and Silence moons. People always seemed inclined to deny the power of broken things.

It was a thirty-foot drop to the bay, and, from this height, impossible to tell the depth of the water below.

Audra crouched, letting the liquid flow past her feet and fall to the sea. Scaling the cliff wasn't an option. The handholds were too loose, the face too steep. She'd tumble backward and probably break something on the way down, leaving her body for the crabs to feast on.

"Shit." The irony of the curse wasn't lost on her. She'd have to jump. At least she'd be clean. Or her corpse would be.

Her dive was graceless. The water broke like a pane of glass, equal parts sharp and brittle. The landing punched the breath from her chest, but the water was cool and deep.

Gasping, she broke the surface a few moments later. Audra

scrubbed the filth from her skin before dragging herself to a pebbled shore. Thick trees grew bent by the eastern wind, providing a curtain of lush foliage as she moved inland. The nearby homes belonged to the island's poorest inhabitants, most of whom were scraping for coin to feed their families at this time of day. Save for a few small children and their elderly caregivers, the huts were empty.

To reach the *Requin*, she'd have to move unnoticed back through town.

After donning a set of men's breeches and two linen shirts pilfered from a line, she slipped on a pair of abandoned straw shoes. Guilt churned her stomach. Stealing from the poor wasn't something she'd done in a long time, and there was nothing to leave by way of compensation. She'd just have to add this place to her growing list of those she owed favors to.

Inside another hut was a set of shears gone nearly dull. Placing them at the base of her ponytail, she hesitated. Traq would be disappointed, but his opinion didn't matter as much as he wished it did anymore. Mages never cut their hair, but Audra had no magic of her own to speak of.

It was just hair.

The shears shook as she cut too close to the scalp, nicking her head in places. Everything would be worth it if she could get home.

Months of malnourishment finally came in handy. No one spared her a glance as she walked through town: another young man looking for work, too poor to afford a proper pair of shoes. His collar bones jutted through his shirt.

There was commotion in the streets of the merchant district. Claude Suna was yelling as guards ran past, his cheeks deeply flushed. Audra hoped that Hana's punishment wouldn't be too harsh.

She ducked her head and angled quickly away from the crowd. It was too early to think she'd gotten away with anything. Chances were all departing vessels would be searched before dawn. However, the *Requin* was carrying reams of northern silk, and they'd avoid damaging such finery. If they did more than glance at it, they'd be careful in their handling. The captain might even slip them some extra coin to avoid the mess entirely.

Getting on board was easier than expected since nearly the entire crew seemed to still be sleeping off the previous night's booze in the late afternoon. No one on the *Requin* ever expected stowaways, not unless those people were looking to feed the sea dragons.

The silks lay neatly folded in two large chests in the cargo hold. The fear of being trapped made her breath quicken. When a heavy voice spoke with a familiar one—Lot—above, she scrambled inside and tugged the lid closed. Audra burrowed beneath the cloth, flattening herself like the mouse had earlier, and waited for the voices to pass.

In the darkness she allowed herself to imagine a future outside of stealing and jails. If the jade broke Ferin's spell, it might change everything. Maybe restore her tribe to their former glory and return the dragons to the skies. But first, she had to reach Oxton. And no one would stop her.

Two

Lua
Moon Tribes Oji

Lua lay curled on his side, planning the murders of each person aboard the *Mirren*. For two days, he'd languished in the bowels of the ship, encouraging his captors to believe he was defeated while gathering strength enough to manage the spells necessary for escape.

"*It's nearly time.*"

The moon's voice pulled him from his musings on the cell's musty floor. Salty air burned his throat, distracting him from the nausea brought on by the rocking sea and the tearing of flesh where the constraint bolt burrowed deeper into his back. It squealed like a wounded cat when he resisted it—high-pitched and furious.

It would take everything to sever his anchor, but Dain's betrayal left Lua no other option. If Selene, his sister, took him back to Uduary, their tribes were doomed. With the Rajav dead, the people needed a stable leader, not a darker shadow of the man who'd just been assassinated. And the Song tribe was too desperate to maintain control. It was time for Silence to rise again.

Whispering prayers to the Silence moon god, he didn't deserve the blessings asked for, not after everything he had done. Even less so if he survived this day. With that thought in mind, Lua tugged off his stained gloves.

He reached down the magical threads connecting him to Dain, his anchor, trying to draw energy from him. But the way remained blocked, as it had been for the last three days. If Lua waited any longer, he'd be too weak to manage the task before him, whether the Song and Silence moons favored him or not.

On the ship's deck, sheltered beneath silk canopies from the harsh Starling rays, mid-level mages cast steady winds that pressed the sails northward. Their magic whispered to him through the air. Lua would need to take it all, down to their very lives, to survive.

All Moon mages knew where Starling was in the sky, since its light diminished the powers of the moons and their magic. The star would set in a few hours, and then Song moon would rise in a parallel trajectory beside Raia's emerald ring. Lua needed to act before Starling passed over the horizon. Well before they travelled into northern waters, where his sister's collection of Song tribe soldiers and more powerful mages awaited his delivery.

Xiang, his sister's favorite general, was on his way to intercept the *Mirren*, likely accompanied by another triad of mages. This was further proof that Selene didn't want him dead yet. She had plans for him, or, more specifically, for his magic. Lua needed to disappear before Xiang arrived.

There was a small knock on the cell's door a breath before it opened. Rayan, a six star mage, carried a tray of food. Lua had taught her the spell that got her that ranking and relied on those nostalgic emotions to bring her nearer. He'd been in the same position for days, each tray she'd kindly delivered went untouched. Her footsteps paused, as they had before, and she settled the tray slowly on the floor.

Rayan's voice was soft with natural concern and empathy. "Oji, are you awake?"

He kept his breath shallow. The movement of his chest was barely visible beneath the layers of black silk and the long shroud of ebony hair surrounding him. Dried blood pooled on the oaken planks beneath him, a consequence of the bolt's damage. Lua had smeared that blood down the sides of his face, pasting his locks to his skin so that the hair wouldn't inhibit his movement or vision when the time came.

Rayan hesitated before stepping cautiously forward. "Oji?" But she'd come too near.

Lua gripped her ankle and yanked her to the ground. The struggle was short and quiet. Only a small cry rang in the air before Rayan's voice dried. Her muscles clamped tight in protest as they shriveled. Skin withered on her bones. Her dark eyes dulled and emptied as his magic consumed hers.

The bolt whined, twisted, and squealed as it fought to restrain him. He grimaced, accepting the pain while continuing his resistance.

Lua pulled himself to standing and shook the stiffness from his limbs. Rayan's husk lay at his feet. He closed her eyes, her skin already fragile and ashy. She'd known better than to get near him. Avoid contact with any mage over ten stars, only their anchor was made for it. Rayan's foolish concern had been a mistake that she'd paid for with her life.

The food's enticing smell caught his attention, but he wasn't hungry yet. Dain, like all other anchors, had no magic. An anchor's sole purpose was to act as a robust repository for their mage's power. However, ever since their capture, Lua hadn't been able to reach or control Dain. These offensive limitations on their connection prevented Lua from drawing more than the essentials for life. If Lua managed to siphon all the mages' magic, he'd be able to cut the strings between Dain and himself. If the Silence monastery sent aid and another anchor with them, perhaps he'd live. But there were too many ifs.

The *Mirren* was too far from land, and unless the Silence monks had anticipated what Selene would do, it wasn't likely they'd arrive in time. Lua was on his own, and he'd rather take his chances with the ocean than his sister's mercy.

The Oji's lethargy had made the guards in the hall too complacent, believing in their victory. The bolt's frantic whisper startled them a moment before Lua's fingers brushed their arms. As they stiffened and fell backward against the wall, he claimed one of their poleaxes and hauled them into the cell with Rayan. The crude weapon felt awkward, but it would do until he was stronger.

Lua siphoned the lives of four more guards, stuffing their bodies into rooms as he went. He stood outside Brav and Elicia's door, listening to the soft snores emanating from within. Elicia would be sleeping with a weapon at the ready. If Lua's preference ever had any weight, he'd have been bonded with Elicia rather than Dain. But the Rajav had never given any bearing to his son's desires.

Lua's hand paused on the door handle, sending a sliver of magic to release the gears of the lock. He held his breath at the small click. Pressing the door slowly open, he winced as the bolt squirmed deeper.

Elicia's sword sliced through the air, severing a lock of his hair as Lua ducked sideways. His poleaxe caught her blade on the second swing. A thin silver thread of magic wound from his fingers, strengthening his weapon under her assault.

Brav roused with a start, flinging the covers from an abdomen so thick it hid his genitals. He stood, naked, spanning his arms like a fool, and began a low chant. He'd never been a subtle man, too obvious in his choices for Lua's liking, but he had talent. His spell would land hard if Lua didn't disarm him the easiest way possible.

Lua thrust the poleaxe's spike toward Elicia's arms, catching her hand on her hilt. He jerked the spike back, dripping her blood across the floor. Brav cried out, his hand bled a matching insult. His spell fumbled.

Silence mages knew to embrace pain if they wished to survive it. Those of the weak and unfocused Song tribe lacked fortitude.

Elicia shouted for guards as she thrust the sword forward and slid away at his counter move. Lua twisted his weapon, sliding it down to the hilt of her blade as it neared. The curve of his poleaxe hooked her thumb. She screamed as he severed it from her hand.

Brav yelled, his dismembered thumb thudding on the dark floor. But this time the pain focused him. His spell strung tight and strong. It lashed across the room, heating Lua's back as he spun away, and the magic crashed through the wall. Chunks of wood sailed through the air. Voices and boots careened down the stairs from the deck above.

With the aid of Brav's bond, Elicia's energy swelled. She gripped the blade with the other hand and feinted, swinging high, before dropping the blade mid-swing. Her thrust nicked Lua's chest. Though her blood still dripped to the floor, her wounds were already mending, fresh skin stitching over her knuckle. With enough time, Brav's magic could regrow the thumb completely. But that was a kindness Lua had no intention of giving them.

Lua darted from her sword's path as magic lit Brav's hands. Gray threads lashed out, a hungry whip. Lua ducked and deflected the spell, though that took half of what he'd siphoned from Rayan. He'd fall if the fight lasted much longer.

Lua blocked Elicia's next blow and glided in close. They locked eyes as Brav's spell threaded together and strengthened. Elicia gasped as one of Lua's fingers skimmed her forearm.

"No!" She tried to jerk away, but Lua's touch stayed her. Her mouth hung open, frozen in disbelief. A soft groan escaped her lips.

Behind them, Brav's words faltered. He struggled to throw the remnants of a spell as his legs failed him. Elicia's eyes slid to her mage as her muscles shriveled toward her bones.

"*Please* not her . . ." Brav's voice faded. His thick body struck the floor while Lua drained their lives away.

Lua lowered Elicia gently to the ground before siphoning the rest of Brav's magic. He took a deep breath. Their energy swelled inside him while he ignored the weight of guilt. Emotions like that would only get him killed.

Lua draped a scarf over Elicia's face as the thundering footsteps neared. Would that he had as good and honorable an anchor as Elicia had been to Brav. He hoped it was just one regret the Rajav had before he died. But for regret to occur, someone had to feel something for others, and his father never cared for anyone other than himself, not even his Raani.

A surge of emotion distracted him, and the bolt burrowed deeper. He staggered, adding a stronger thread to hold the bolt at bay, then stepped into the hall to meet the soldiers.

Some died beneath a silver whip of magic, others he drained for their strength. A blessed few took the point of the poleaxe to their head for a quick end but not before landing hits to his arms and torso.

The *Mirren* slowed as the mages abandoned their wind spells above. They raced down the stairs to confront him. Despite the protective silk screen and robes covering their fair skin, Starling had weakened them.

They fought heartily, but the four and eight star mages lacked experience and had no anchors to draw from. Though Lua would have killed those anchors, too, if they'd had any.

Blood splattered his face, dripped down his fingers from the cuts on his arms as he stood before a cabin door. Dain's energy pulsed on the other side. Lua focused on the thick threads still connecting them, that sacred spell that guaranteed mutual survival or death. At eleven stars, Lua had lost and replaced anchors, but always with the help of other mages. He'd never had one betray him, never heard of it happening before. An anchor made their vows young, committed to a lifetime of selfless service. If he'd only been a ten or an eleven star, Dain's betrayal would have been a death sentence for them both. At thirteen stars, the chances of Lua surviving were slightly higher, but not guaranteed.

Lua placed a hand on the door. Dain's fear swept toward him, though his thoughts were still cut off. Lua's influence remained blocked. The bolt writhed, emitting a pungent scent that drifted through his clothing, like the incense of the Western tribes before he'd helped slaughter them.

Lua sighed. Dain was trapped. Death was inevitable. Best to draw the storm first and wait for his anchor to come to him.

He donned one of the dead mage's robes, pulling up the hood to shield his skin from Starling before heading onto the deck. Standing beneath the dark silk screen, he chanted and called on the strength of his gods. Silver threads spun from his hands, reaching for the clouds above.

He'd only drawn this spell once before, over a small Western village and monastery fifteen years prior. That memory was a bitter taste in his mouth, a foulness he'd never managed to swallow. The Westerners had fought hard, died with dignity, and their deaths had lacked satisfaction. It was only later that he understood how pointless it had been. The moons hadn't spoken to him for a long time afterwards.

His hands moved faster, words slipping past his teeth in a succinct rhythm as the spell grew.

The wispy clouds above thickened, darkened, lashing together until they covered the sky. A sudden chill sent the sea to roil as thunder vibrated the air. The spell would linger well into the night unless Lua died. He only hoped to find land or another vessel before the clouds parted tomorrow morning. If not—

Heavy steps broke through the pattering of rain on the deck behind him. Dain was a quiet man by nature, but tethered to such a powerful mage, he'd never had to learn the light step.

His blade missed Lua's heart by an inch when he spun backward. A strip of his robe sailed away in the mounting wind as they stared at each other. Dain's bloodshot eyes narrowed as the storm broke above. Hard rain wept through the silk screens, dripping down their faces.

Dain's shirt clung to his chest, pulling the wet fabric open. A dull stone peeked from beneath, its black and red color disturbingly familiar: bloodstone. Lua's lips pressed into a thin line.

"Take that off," Lua said, nodding to the necklace. "We could still escape together."

Dain wiped the water from his shorn head. His voice broke. "She took Maya."

Lua's jaw clenched in resignation. He should have expected no less from his sister. Dain chose his death when he'd twisted the bolt into Lua's flesh. He offered his anchor no words, taking strength in silence as they danced around each other.

Without Lua's magic, Dain's long sword looked suddenly graceless. Lua batted it away with the poleaxe, taking his time. They parried as he started another spell. He brought it down as the poleaxe speared Dain's shoulder.

Dain grimaced while Lua winced at the matching pain. Lua had hoped that the bloodstone weakening his control over Dain would also prevent him from sensing his anchor's suffering. Yet, although his skin did not break or bleed, he felt the stab. He'd feel Dain's death just as he had with his previous anchors.

Lua sharpened and honed the spell before bringing it down again as Dain advanced. Despite the spell cutting some of the silvery threads, the knots formed over the years remained too entangled to be cleanly severed. Their connection stubbornly held.

The bolt twisted furiously, grinding deeper into his back. Lua stumbled, accepted the pain, let his resistance to it lapse as he gathered his full power.

Dain loomed, sword raised high. The poleaxe met the blade and wrenched it away. It spun across the slippery deck as the poleaxe plunged into Dain's gut.

Lua's spell slammed down between them. They flew in opposite directions as the bond snapped and unraveled.

The sharp pain in Lua's stomach faded quickly, leaving the sensation of a deep bruise. With labored breath, he drew the dregs of his magic around the bolt and slowed its movement again. The unspooling threads of Dain's life force lashed desperately toward Lua, but he shielded himself and batted it away.

He drew the spell that he hoped would keep him alive without an anchor until the Silence monks found him. But he didn't know how long he'd last. He stood on trembling legs.

Dain was sprawled on the deck in a pool of blood and pelting rain. One hand gripped the handle that jutted from his stomach. He moaned pitifully as Lua moved closer. Dain mouthed soundless words until he fell still. Lua closed his eyes gently and said a small prayer.

Grief would have to wait.

Thunder cracked as the storm gained strength with the violence necessary to sink the *Mirren*. There was no time. Darting below deck, he found his ebony robes neatly folded in Dain's rooms. That the man had cared for them so tenderly sickened him further.

Ominous, green-tinged clouds swirled above as Lua tumbled into the small rowboat. His hands slipped on the ropes and gears as he tried to loosen them. He cursed. There was no magic left unless he relaxed his hold on the bolt, and that would hasten his demise. He struck the winch repeatedly until his knuckles bled.

The ropes released at the same moment a lightning bolt split the ship in half. The rowboat slammed into the water. It tipped, hovering on its side for a long moment before toppling over and trapping Lua beneath it.

Ducking under the side, he sucked in sea water while gasping for air. Lua clung to the overturned boat as angry waves beat their wrath. Starling was setting. The star's power waned behind the clouds. It was no night for Silence, the larger, slower moon, but perhaps if he prayed, Song would watch over him.

"Are you worthy of being Rajav to the Moon tribes, little Oji? After everything you've done?" Song asked.

Something brushed his feet beneath the water. It slithered past, working its way to the corpses from the ship. A long thick tail flicked upward, silver scales gleaming, before it crashed down on the moon mage and the boat. He flailed, grasping at water and finding nothing to hold.

The next wave took him under and dragged him deeper to sea.

Three

Audra

"Get him up!" Chon cried. He leaned over the *Requin*'s bow as rain dripped from his hooked nose, studying the figure floating in the water. His voice was barely audible over the gusting wind and crashing waves.

The sudden storm had dragged the boat east, past the furthest charted islands, where it balanced precariously at the edge of safe waters. Another few miles and they would never be seen again. Nothing returned from the edge of the world. Out there lay only hungry mouths waiting to swallow vessels whole.

The boat lurched dangerously. The crew yelled with concerns that the water was too rough, the ship's rocking too violent to warrant saving a stray. And Munk's whispers of a cursed storm had set everyone on edge.

"Where's the boy?" Chon said before spying Audra holding tight to the mast. "Time to earn your keep, Alver."

Audra's grip slipped on the slick wood. Her stomach churned a moment before she retched on the deck for a third time. The vomit mixed with the water and slid toward Toman's approaching feet. Pleading would be useless, and she had yet to prove her worth.

The only positive was that they still believed her to be a boy. The rags she'd stolen and the short, cropped hair had done its job. But it was just a matter of time until someone in the crew decided boys had other uses. Toman was a beast of a man, and his looks already lingered too long. The less reason he had to put hands on her, the better.

When Toman reached for her, she lunged sideways, avoiding his grasp. "Piss off. I'm going."

Chon tied the rope around her waist as a white-capped wave soared high, momentarily blocking the view of the body.

"What if he's already dead?" Audra asked. The boat tilted again, bringing her stomach to her throat as her knuckles blanched upon the rail.

"Then we pick through the pockets and toss them back to the sea." He gripped her shoulder. "Might be someone important, worth a reward."

Her brown eyes met Chon's. "And if I can't hold him?"

He shrugged. "Then we'll have one less stowaway to feed." With that, he hoisted her over the edge into the rocking sea.

She broke the surface, choking on frigid salt water as another wave crashed on her head. Audra flailed for a moment before well-practiced survival instinct took over. There was a shout from above as the rope around her waist pulled taut. She fixed her gaze on the surrounding water.

A glimpse of pale skin caught her eye when the sea dipped. With his black hair and robes, it was a miracle the lookout had spied him at all. And another miracle that Chon had chosen to save him. Audra swam toward the figure. The next wave nearly propelled him past her, but she grabbed a floating sleeve and held on. Another wave brought him crashing into her. She secured her arms around him, her skin stinging at the sudden connection.

The man moaned. His fingers clenched the thin fabric of her shirt, changing the sting to a tingle that made her shiver. His long black hair waved atop the water's surface, wrapping around her shoulders along with his lean arms. His silver eyes widened in panic. Nails dug into her shoulders and neck. The bastard would drown them both. Audra struggled, trying to break free, but he went wild. She cursed, brought one arm up to break his grip, but he was too strong.

"I'm trying to save you!" she yelled. He pressed her down, and she inhaled a mouthful of water. Lightning cracked the sky, illuminating his terrified features.

Audra cursed again while the men on the *Requin* shouted unhelpful advice. She bit his wrist hard, hoping a dash of pain would sharpen his senses. His eyes narrowed, but the panic continued.

Why was nothing ever easy? Audra punched his stomach. Her weak strike was enough to startle him. His grip eased. When her knee connected to his groin, he pushed her away. His flailing caused him to bob beneath the water's surface. Audra balled up her fist, drawing as much strength as she could before knocking his head sideways. Finally, he stopped struggling.

She hauled him backward toward the ship, wrapping the slack of the rope twice around his torso before raising an arm to let the crew know they were ready.

"You better be worth it," Audra muttered as his head found purchase on her shoulder.

Another streak of lightning skittered across the clouds. He groaned.

The rope jerked them upward. Suspended in the air alongside the rocking boat, a sliver of Song's light broke through the storm clouds and shone upon them. Cold, silver eyes opened and focused on her. His arms encircled her. She considered what another punch might do, but his hands warmed her back. The heat moved through her limbs and settled in her chest. He closed his eyes, mumbling unfamiliar words that were lost in the wind. She tried to pull away, but he clung to her even as the crew hauled them over the ship's rail.

Audra dropped to the deck on top of him, gasping like a fish. She lay there for long minutes before wrestling him onto his side as the crew looked on. He writhed, coughing sea water, his hair and sodden ebony robes spread around him. That much fabric should have dragged him to the ocean floor. This bastard's luck bordered on insult.

Chon stood over them with a cautious expression. He spread his arms wide to keep the crew away then nudged the man with his boot.

The man coughed up another round of water then lay still. Chon rubbed the silk robes between his fingers, avoiding touching the man directly. He chewed his lower lip, brows worried together.

"Man your posts," he ordered before backing slowly away.

Another wave spilled over the bow; water slid across the deck as men held on to whatever they could find. Chon scowled, coming to some decision, before addressing Audra. "Put him in the drunk tank."

"Me? But . . ." Her arms burned, and her lungs were tight, like she'd inhaled half the sea. Still, the last thing she wanted was to be delegated to the role of caregiver.

"You'd rather work the ropes?" Chon asked. The other men scurried about the ship. Several disappeared below to work the rowers.

She struggled to her feet, pulling the wet fabric of her shirt away from her skin. Chon's eyes narrowed. Audra slouched too late. He knew.

Chon coughed and looked away. "There are spare clothes in the infirmary. Get some dry clothes on him. And yourself." He glanced at the clouds above. The rain was lighter than it had been moments ago. "We'll be past the storm soon, then we can figure out what to do with him." His eyes slid down her body. "With you both."

Audra pulled the man onto feet that tried to plant. She barely came up to his armpit. Dragging him over her back, they stumbled across the deck and down the small ramp. A purple bruise bloomed around the eye she'd struck. Entering a small door, she dumped him on the filthy blanket leftover from Toman's last alcohol induced rampage. There was still a spot of something on the fabric.

The spare clothing in the infirmary was piled in a small chest atop a couple of rusted swords. Yanking the wet shirt over her head, she donned a fresh undershirt and a dark green top. The only pants that wouldn't fall over her hips at a quick pace were striped, but they'd have to do. She grabbed a set of clothing that looked like they'd fit the stranger, then paused. It was a rare opportunity that presented itself. She'd been under close scrutiny since they'd found her.

Below the clothing and rusted swords were a few smaller knives, sheathed. One fit her hand perfectly. Its handle was dull, but the blade was sharp. She secured it in her pocket in case Toman's gaze turned to more than casual interest. She'd have to come back for anything else when they were closer to Oxton.

The man lay exactly as she'd left him. Black hair strewn around a pale, sickly face. His layers of silk were an expensive rarity no matter your class. Chon had been right to grab him. Someone might pay a good price for this man. His outer robe was obsidian black, but the inside was speckled with silver, like the night sky. Thirteen stars were stitched in silver thread into the black interior.

Audra bit her lip. The number of stars showed a mage's ability, but she'd always heard that ten was the upper limit. Though that rule may have only applied to the Starling tribe. Her mother told her that the Western mages never needed such a system.

The Moons hadn't ventured this far south since the assault on Oxton seventeen years ago and hadn't crossed the northern border for fifteen years. Not since they'd demolished hers and several other villages and the last western monastery hold out, killing the last of the Western mages in the process. Their sudden retreat had indicated that they'd either finally been satisfied with the slaughter or deemed it too costly to fight when the Starlings intervened.

The crumbling Western government had desperately trusted the Starling's offer of aid in exchange for crops and servitude. No one could have predicted the ongoing destruction that was still occurring. The Starlings rounded up every westerner with a hint of magic and dragged them into the southern sands. The ultimate example, Zin had said, to never hand your fate over to another.

Audra studied the stitching. Thirteen stars was unprecedented. How had someone so powerful ended up floating in the Empyrean? This wasn't good.

She dropped the robe in the corner where it landed open. Blood darkened the space around the stars, turning three a pinkish hue. She rolled him over, running a hand over his shirts. Her palm came back streaked red.

Not good at all.

Chon could figure this out. She had no desire to invest in an injured Moon mage. They could all end up at the bottom of the sea for all she cared. Audra backed toward the door. This was absolutely *not* her problem.

The man moaned, limbs flexing into a fetal position as something in her chest contracted and took her resolve with it. She hesitated as he groaned again. There was pleading in his cry.

"Shit," she hissed. "Fine."

She drew the dagger and knelt beside him, cutting through one layer of fabric at a time. Dozens of silvery scars and fresh wounds crisscrossed his lean muscles. Blood pulsed from a deep triangular shaped gouge slightly left of his spine. The lines were unusually sharp. He whimpered as a puff of sweet-scented violet smoke eased out. It tugged at a memory, but Audra waved it away before leaning closer to examine it.

Buried deep in his muscle, an object shone brightly. Audra gasped as it burrowed deeper, and the mage grimaced pitifully.

"Get it out," he mumbled.

She shook her head. "I'm not . . ." But her hands moved toward him before she could stop them. Her dagger cut into his flesh, striking something hard that squirmed at the attack. Nausea churned her gut, but there was nothing left to vomit. The storm and Munk's foul cooking had seen to that.

He hissed as she moved the blade to the side. The point of the dagger caught on the object. She angled further, cutting deeper, and pressed the blade underneath it. As she pried it upward, more violet smoke spewed out. A squeal pierced her ears.

A small gold object popped to the surface, perfectly matching the shape of the wound. The barbs that jutted from its sides sliced her fingers as she pried it out and tossed it aside. It clattered along the boards, spewing purple haze and emitting a high-pitched whine.

The man sighed in relief. His bleeding ebbed. Beneath her gaze, the wound slowly stitched itself together.

A wave of exhaustion overwhelmed her, and she leaned back against the wall. She slid the blade back into its sheath. Running a bloody hand through her jagged hair, she took a deep breath against the steady pulse thrumming inside her skull.

"I should have stayed on Callaway," Audra said.

Four

Xiang
General of the Song Moon Tribe

General Xiang stared over the *Bulou*'s prow and studied the boards floating atop the water's surface. He counted twelve bodies littered in the waves, most in pieces. The others had become food for the sea, or worse, turned to ash.

Lua must have drained the entire crew to sever Dain and survive. Knowing the Oji, he shouldn't have been surprised. Even though these mages were once Lua's comrades, Xiang didn't expect to find much left. He'd seen it before. Mercy had no place in the Oji's nature.

Whatever dark spells Lua had cast or bargains he'd made with his moon god in order to escape would remain a mystery until they recaptured him. Though the sky remained overcast, the brunt of the storm was southeast. That it hadn't faded completely meant Lua still lived.

Xiang was an imposing man, tall for a westerner, whose darker coloring made him stand apart from the pale northerners on the ship, something he'd grown accustomed to over the years. With the traditional shorn head of a lifelong soldier, he was attractive in a fearsome way, as if scars had formed in his deepest recesses.

He clenched his hands behind his back.

More would die attempting to bring the Moon Oji back north. If Xiang had been on the *Mirren*, this wouldn't have happened. Everyone else believed better of Lua than he deserved, or perhaps their fear kept them respectful. But the general didn't give a shit about the Oji. Not after witnessing the atrocities committed during the attacks on the Western tribes. Xiang hoped to prevent any further threat to Selene and Bolin. But Oja Selene had held him back until it was too late.

You're too valuable, she'd said, her usual lie. Xiang was a blade kept sheathed, because Selene feared his death would affect Bolin, her anchor, and therefore herself in ways she wasn't equipped to deal with. In some ways, she and Lua were very similar. Two branches of the same wicked lineage that needed pruning. Yet no shears had ever seemed sharp enough.

Fifty-three soldiers and seven mages died capturing Lua. If not for Dain's cooperation, it would have been more. Selene's constraining bolt should have either disabled or killed him. When word reached her about Lua's escape, people would pray to their moon gods for mercy. The Oja was temperamental on a good day, and she'd had very few of those in the many years he and Bolin had been in service to her and the Song tribe.

"Sir." Galia stood behind him. Slivers of Starling light broke through the thinning clouds and dappled her square face. The long scar that ran from her brow to her cheek gleamed white. "The mages have tracked the remains of his thread." She pointed southward, where the clouds were thickest.

"Dain?"

She shook her head, hesitated. "Just pieces." She raised a cord, the bloodstone still attached. Selene had given it to Dain to break Lua's control. "Do you think . . . ?"

Xiang rubbed his stubbled chin. He knew her thoughts. If Dain was dead, then Lua must be too. The connection was not easily split, and all mages over nine stars must have an anchor to properly harness the strength of the magic. But a sliver of thread remained, enough for the mages on board to track. And the storm still raged to the south. He was protected beneath the clouds for now. "No. The Oji still lives."

"Won't he need another anchor, sir?" Galia asked. Her gaze shifted to Jayna, the lone mage on deck. Jayna met the lieutenant's eyes shyly from beneath the shadow of her hood.

Their attachment was a distraction at times like these. He pulled the bloodstone from Galia's hands, startling her back into proper form. It would be difficult for Lua to find an anchor before the bolt overwhelmed him.

The western regions had been under Starling control for decades and, though the indigenes held no love for them, they remained rightly wary of the Moon tribe. This might give Xiang a short advantage. If they could find Lua soon, they could still capture him. He placed the stone in his pocket, fingers lingering on it a moment longer.

"Raise the sails. Head us toward the storm."

Galia hesitated. "We'll be moving into Starling territory, sir."

"I know the implications, Lieutenant." He glowered down at her. "Or would you rather return to our Oja empty-handed?"

Galia paled. "I meant no offense, sir."

Xiang turned away. "Ready the sails. I'll tell the Oja myself."

Five

Selene
Moon Tribes Oja

Selene's pacing steps echoed off the stone walls. Every few rounds she paused to gaze through the long window at the dark sea. Two trays of untouched food lay on the table, but she hadn't let anyone clear them away. Her floor-length ebony hair was tangled, and her body reeked from neglect. She should have been wearing mourning clothes but that would have to wait for an announcement that couldn't be made until Lua was secured. Her brother had always been difficult.

Outside of a few trusted staff ministers and the Council of Moons Mages, no one knew that the Rajav Li-Hun Koray and Raani Amala were dead, murdered at almost the same moment at opposite ends of the castle—one death born of mercy, the other opportunity. She'd always wondered if, left to their own devices, she and her brother would work well together.

Lua and Dain had set sail a couple of hours after the murders, leaving her to spin the crimes as she chose. If he'd been less arrogant, he'd have considered what she might do and insisted that they leave together. Instead, he wanted them to go to the islands because Silence had told him to. He'd forgotten that Selene hated leaving Uduary. This was where Song's power was greatest and where her rule would start. A rule she had no intention of sharing.

By manipulating the Mage Council's inherent dislike of Lua, blame shifted easily his way. The wicked Oji must have killed them both or killed one to kill the other. Whatever people believed was fine. The truth was their father was strong enough to survive quite a while without an anchor. It was Selene and Bolin who saw to it that he did not. With Dain's death only she, Bolin, and Lua knew the truth. And Xiang, who was a bit too observant for his own good.

She stepped onto the balcony, ignoring the cold air that breezed through the single layer of silk wrapped around her. Full Song flitted overhead, pale yellow light glittering upon the water. Raia's ring spanned from one horizon to the other, glowing softly. Though the ring was more visible at night, the planet's shadow was darkening it closest to the horizon.

The scholars had predicted that Song's quietude would begin before the cycle toward the eclipses. With the Rajav dead, the moons would have to bestow their blessings on one of his children, and Selene had faith that Song would choose her.

It must be her. Lua was, well, himself. And that was bad enough. He was cryptic and aloof but not stern enough to be an adequate leader of both Moon tribes. He'd never hold them together. If she could siphon him, she'd be more powerful than their father had ever been.

Beyond Uduary's sea wall to the south, a silver tail arced in the water. White scales shimmered in the song-light, an auspicious sign. The sea dragons hadn't visited the bay for decades, not since Amala had been strong enough to see them from the highest balcony. Sixty years, perhaps more. But not less. Their mother had been mostly bedbound for at least fifty years. Selene leaned on the marble rail and watched the rippling water, fighting a flicker of nostalgia and sorrow.

Lua couldn't have imagined his anchor betraying him. After Dain bolted him, Selene's people secured him. The bloodstone should have cut him off from drawing on Dain's energy. The bolt should have kept him weak enough to bring home. He was defeated. They'd held him.

Yet, they'd still failed.

Xiang's report, given through the mirror he shared with Bolin, left no doubt. The Oji had destroyed the ship and still lived.

The small angry threads of her bolt had yanked her from sleep when they recoiled. Someone had removed it, which meant her plans needed to change. Lua would head to the Silence monastery with hopes of the moons choosing him as Rajav at the eclipses. Selene had to ensure that didn't happen.

A familiar knock shook her door. She strummed the connection between them a moment before Bolin pressed in bearing a tray of food in his arms.

"You need to eat." His voice warmed her.

"I'm not hungry."

He shoved the other trays aside to set the fresh one down. "Liar."

She turned to him. "Did you see the dragon?"

He shook his head and stepped onto the balcony, taking her hand. His skin was tan against her pale flesh. Warm against her cool. His touch was a rare treat offered more frequently when Xiang was away. Even though their relationships were very different, she didn't like sharing her anchor. But Bolin had belonged to Xiang before her magic had claimed him.

"You've been draining my energy since yesterday. Eat," he said.

Selene settled on the small lounge and sipped the spiced broth he fed her. He offered the rosemary flatbread she liked and poured a glass of wine. She relished the moments when Bolin tended to her like a lover. He loved her, she knew that. But not as much as he loved Xiang, never as much as that.

"Any word?" she asked.

"No. I may have missed him earlier." He raised the spoon to her lips again. "I was trying to replicate one of my mother's recipes. It's not quite right; we don't have the spices."

With his rich tawny skin, warm brown eyes, and ready smile, there was something compelling about him. People gravitated toward him, even those who hated foreigners.

He studied her face. "You should rest."

"I'm not—"

"There's nothing to be done until Lua is found. And the ministers will demand a plan for the upcoming winter. I've already delayed them as long as I can. You have obligations to fulfill now." He set the bowl on the table and unraveled a lock of her tangled hair before tucking it behind her ear. "Your parents are dead and, though you may deny it, I know you grieve. You need to sleep."

She brought a hand to his cheek, enjoying the intimacy of their connection. "I'll rest better with you beside me."

His face altered just enough to reveal his answer. "I'll lay with you but nothing more tonight."

"You're worried."

He sighed, small and controlled. "Of course."

"Xiang'll be fine. He's got his mages and a solid crew."

"Lua killed a ten star and everyone on the *Mirren*. Why do you think Xiang has a chance of succeeding? He only took two mages, neither over ten stars."

Selene patted his arm. "Lua must have depleted his magic to accomplish everything he's done. Even if he's found another anchor, which is unlikely, it'll take him months to recuperate." She kissed his knuckles lightly. "Besides, he'll never find an anchor as perfect as you."

Six

Audra

Audra tugged fresh clothes onto the unconscious man. He was heavier than he looked, and his pockets had been disappointingly empty. She piled the bloody clothing in the corner before brushing the hair from his face. He was, by general standards, attractive with a straight nose, sharp jaw, and high cheekbones set in an oval face. There was something familiar about him, though she swore she'd never seen him before. But, even in sleep, his expression was disagreeable.

She'd already decided to hate him.

From his Moon robes to his finery, there were multiple strikes against him. And the length of his hair and smoothness of skin must have come from years steeped in magic. It reminded her of her mother, difficult to tell their true age.

Don't trust anyone not of our tribe, her mother, Lorah, used to say. *No matter if they're southern or northern. They'll want to control or destroy you eventually. We can only trust our own.*

Or a dragon. Zin added after Lorah died.

As Chon predicted, the storm passed by mid-afternoon. Audra

would have to bargain with him, offer a deal that wouldn't involve him putting anything anywhere. She was dozing against the wall when the door flew open, barely missing her shoulder.

Toman's hulking figure filled the doorway. The combination of waning adrenaline and ensuing exhaustion made his thick face uglier. His eyes raked over the sleeping man before settling hungrily on her.

"Captain wants you in his office. Said to bring his clothes."

She wrapped the garments in her arms and stood. Toman braced himself in the narrow doorframe, forcing her to duck under his arm and scrape against his side. He sniffed and chuckled in a way that made her skin crawl. "You smell good, boy."

"All I smell is rat." She'd intended it as an insult, but Toman only chuckled.

Chon waited behind his desk: wan face illuminated by the yellowish hue of the all'ight that warmed the wood interior. She placed the clothing on the desk.

"Has he said anything?" He flipped the shirt over and back, pretending to examine it.

Any decent thief knew a test when it appeared. Every job was a test of skills, survival, and success. This was no different, and Audra's instincts cautioned against mentioning the mage's wounds. "He's still sleeping."

Chon frowned, continuing to rifle through the man's garments. She'd buried the bloody bits inside the dryer ones. Thankfully, Chon chose to focus on the robe. He traced the inner lining, pausing on the top star, and refolded them without examining the others.

"Anything in his pockets?"

Audra shook her head.

"Do you know who he is?"

Again, with the test. It was just terrible luck that she'd had a bit more experience with the Moon tribe than anyone should ever want, but when Chon asked, only one answer would do: ignorance. "Should I?"

He licked his teeth before giving a small shrug. "He's probably of no great importance."

The test continued. "Those are the finest silks I've ever seen. He's a rich man somewhere." She paused, letting her words settle. "We can get a good ransom for him."

He chuffed. "*We*? Me, my crew, yes. You?" He walked around the desk toward her. "How long did you think to deceive me?"

Her hand hovered above her pocket where the dagger pressed against her thigh.

Chon's expression was grim. "Little thief, what should I do with you?"

"I haven't stolen anything from you," she lied.

"Only because you've nowhere to hide it," he said, tilting his head. "I should've known when we found you. The guards had swept through the night before we disembarked, but they were searching for a woman. The writ they served had a bad sketch and, I must admit, it wasn't a very good likeness."

Never give too much away, better to let people draw their own conclusions and manipulate their assumptions. Audra waited.

"Usually we only get rats on board, didn't know we'd caught a mouse too." Chon winked.

She scowled. The mouse of the Western tribe—it wasn't a nickname she'd have chosen since it combined two seemingly powerless things. But after years of stealing everything from jewels to cattle, the moniker stuck and it was pointless getting worked up about something already done.

"You're lucky those Callaway guards didn't figure out who you were. Pretty sure I saw a similar poster in Port Praya with a hefty reward on your head. Brave of you to delve into Starling territory." He crossed his arms, a glimmer of respect brightened his eyes. "What is the mouse stealing to warrant such attention?"

Her hand relaxed. Better to be a bounty than a target for other things. "Nothing that made it onto this ship. Nothing of value to anyone like you." He frowned as she continued, "I'm worth more alive."

"Maybe, but there's no telling what shape you might be in."

Her fingers trailed to the dagger's hilt. She didn't like violence but knew where a blade should go to silence someone while they died. Of course, then she'd have the rest of the crew to contend with. "If you think I'll let you touch me—"

Chon scoffed. His expression full of genuine offense. "You think I'd ...?" He shook his head. "I'm not that desperate, though some on board might think differently."

"What then?" she asked.

"Could use a decent thief," he said. "Agree to do a couple of jobs and I'll keep your secret."

She crossed her arms. "And after?"

"You can go your merry way."

"You won't tell the crew?"

"That you're the western mouse?" he asked.

"That I'm a woman," she said.

He tapped his fingers on the desk, considering. "Probably best to lock you in with the stranger. Wealthy men aren't used to such tawdry conditions, are they? He'll need tending to."

Chon could turn her in at Oxton or kill her. But his sort always needed illegal things done, and they hated risking their own. Plus, Chon didn't think she knew what the man was and, better for him, she was expendable.

"Fine. I get the key. Come and go as I please that way."

He smiled. "Imagine that? A mouse who hates being trapped."

Seven

Lua

Raani Amala gazed up at Lua from beneath rich burgundy blankets. His mother had been beautiful once, long ago, but her face had become nightmarishly hollow over the decades as the bones beneath her skin crumbled to dust. Tangled white hair was strewn across the pillow, knotted like magical threads. Her cracked lips mouthed soft pleas that the dream wouldn't let him hear again. With trembling hands, he held her as she wept.

Lua sat up, wincing at the protest of his sore back. The world spun and threatened to darken, but he closed his eyes and focused on his breath, the way his mother had taught him when he was a boy. He wiped the guilt from his eyes. No one deserved to suffer like she had.

The bolt spewed soft smoke in the corner. Though its death brought a sense of satisfaction, the knowledge of whom its thread had returned to was concerning.

He had to give Selene credit this time, it was clever magic. He'd never have created something so ruthless. But she'd always been more like their father than either of them would ever say aloud. She was a true Koray, whereas Lua had often been accused of taking after their mother.

Xiang, and whoever else Selene entrusted, would track the bolt quickly once the storm cleared. They'd probably already found threads to lead them. He took a breath and searched for any remains of Dain's bond. Although it had dissipated, he shifted uncomfortably. Something was different. A series of foreign emotions whispered through his skin. An unfamiliar thread spun from him and wound through the ship's interior to settle in an unknown person.

He squeezed his eyes, trying to remember what happened after the sea dragon's tail came down. It was a blur of storms and waves until he met a pair of furious brown eyes. The short-haired woman they belonged to had struck him repeatedly. He grimaced at the humiliating memory.

What kind of audacity does it take to punch an injured man? An Oji of the moon tribe, no less. But she'd touched him and lived. Then they'd been suspended in the air. Lightning dazzled. Song smiled. His magic reached out and—

"*Shit.*"

It wasn't possible. There were time-honored rituals involving mutual consent. The bond had to be specifically woven for stability. It was the same in both moons' monasteries. That was how anchoring worked, so no one could force the bond on another. Even though Lua had suspected that a similar event might have occurred in the past, his sister and the Song moon elders emphatically denied it.

This didn't feel right. *She* didn't feel right. She was weak and, despite the beating she'd given a semi-conscious man, probably useless in a fight. Her spirit was fatigued. A terrible anchor from every angle. He cursed again. This bond couldn't be broken anytime soon. He was depleted and too far from home. This woman would be useful for keeping him alive and nothing more.

When he reached out, her emotions were readily accessible, though her thoughts were strangely silent. He tried again, clawing at the person he'd have to tolerate but only received a name—Audra Shan. An old Western name. Perhaps accessing her mind would improve over time. She'd never trained to be an anchor, obviously. He glanced at the golden triangle on the floor. If she didn't cooperate, he'd have to force her into compliance.

Though her weakness made him vulnerable, her life would at least sustain him until the monks could separate them at the monastery. He'd need to keep her well until then. Pulling on her energy would take restraint to keep from draining her. He rubbed his neck in annoyance.

In contrast with her obvious physical limitations, her will felt too strong. A good anchor was physically tough, their personality pliable, and followed their mages' orders without hesitation. Dread settled in his gut. This wasn't good. Weak and stubborn was a terrible combination. If she grew stronger, maybe they'd survive until they reached the Silence monastery.

Outpacing Xiang would be a challenge. And if Selene and her anchor came for him, he'd be doomed.

His lips were salty, and he closed his eyes again. Thrumming the thread between them, he cursed its strength. Her sharp resistance startled him.

This was going to be like training a feral cat.

Eight

Audra

Audra took two bowls of the worst stew ever made in culinary history back to the small room, and Chon looked over the sleeping man before locking them in. The key secured safely inside Audra's pocket.

The mage lay facing the wall. A curtain of ebony hair concealed his face. His breathing was steady but not deep. She suspected he was awake.

The room smelled sweet, like the incense that burned in the Western temples of her childhood. The memory drew her toward the violet haze that ebbed from the triangle in the corner. The wood surrounding it was charred. It whined softly when she teased it with her toe.

"Leave it," he mumbled, his voice was hoarse. "It's not spent yet." He scowled over one shoulder when she nudged it again. "Back away, fool."

Audra's chest clenched uncomfortably, drawing concern. But it diminished quickly when she rubbed her sternum and sat against the wall, assured that her initial assumptions of him were correct. Setting his bowl on the floor, she pinched her nose while scooping a spoonful of barely palatable sludge into her mouth and choked it down. He didn't move.

"You should eat," she said, shoving his calf with her foot. He grunted, pulling his legs away like an annoyed child. She took another bite. Forcing one after another until she'd eaten most of it. The mage's bowl on the floor had cooled, a skin coated the top. It wouldn't be edible for much longer. The heat at least took the chill from their bones, but once that was gone, the taste overpowered whatever nutrition it held. If any.

"It'll get worse if you wait." She prodded him again.

His sigh was rife with irritation.

"You lost a lot of blood," she said. "Would have died if we hadn't come across you."

He draped an arm over his face before sniffing the blanket beneath him and bolting upright. The disgusted glare he gave it turned to her. He rubbed the side of his head, fingers cautiously tracing the fading bruise around his eye. His scowl deepened, effectively wiping away all his handsome attributes. "Where are we?"

Her spoon scraped the bottom of the bowl. She stuffed the last bite into her mouth with a shudder before replying. "On a boat."

He squared his shoulders and huffed. "Is this how you treat people?"

"Yes, often." Audra set her bowl down before looking back at him. He was easy to measure. An entitled Moon mage that was too weak to do anything about anything. She was glad she'd already settled on hatred. "I see you haven't noticed that I'm sitting next to you in the same situation. Eating the same food, sharing the same small space, and I am a 'people' too." She shoved his bowl at him, her expression one of disgust. "Now eat."

His voice simmered with an authoritarian tone. "Do you know who I am?"

Audra chuckled, hand clenching the stolen blade in her pocket. "Well, I do now." She leaned back and closed her eyes. "You are an asshole. Anyone who asks that question usually is."

The silence was thick. He opened and closed his mouth more than once. After a minute, she heard the bowl slide across the floor followed by him gagging.

"It's only slightly better warm," she said, smirking.

He placed the half-eaten bowl back on the floor after a short time and cleared his throat. "Who did it?"

She opened one eye. She'd been waiting for him to ask. "Saved you?"

He shook his head, his offended look worse than before. "Tried to poison us. They should have their hands cut off for the violations committed to previously harmless chickens."

She snickered. "That wasn't chicken. And Munk is probably the worst cook in three tribes. Lost his sense of taste and smell during the battle of Korman, at least that's what the rest of the crew says. They love him, though, so they eat it anyway. I would say that you'll get used to it, but that'd probably be a lie."

He winced as he leaned against the wall. The worn navy shirt and brown pants looked awkward on him. Even the way he carried himself in discomfort signaled someone used to an entirely different sort of life.

Curiosity finally made her ask. "What's your name?"

His eyelids slit open. "Asshole." He shifted uncomfortably. "And I know it was you who saved me. Unfortunate for both of us. The big guy might have been more useful."

"He would've punched you harder. Rightly so. I saved your life. Twice actually." Some small amount of gratitude would have been expected. But this? He shifted further away as her anger flared. A smaller tug ebbed behind her ribs but didn't last for more than a breath. Her thoughts flicked to her brother before the mage spoke again.

"Now I'm stuck with you." He grumbled.

She snapped. "I should've let you die."

"Too late for that now." His breath deepened as he turned away. "Asshole."

Nine

Audra

The mage's toe dug into Audra's thigh. "Get up, fool. I'm guessing you can get us out of here."

Audra rolled onto her back, wiping the sleep from her eyes. "What?" It was satisfying the way frustration marred his symmetrical features, his long hair dancing around his face.

"I refuse to piss where I sleep." He clasped his hands behind his back and glared.

She rose on aching legs with a groan. The tightness in her chest came again as he gestured impatiently toward the door.

Audra stuck her head into the hall. Munk's notorious snoring drifted in the air, combining with other snorts and grunts to create a chorus of mildly violent sailors sleeping like children. Above deck, two exhausted men rested against the masts. The lookout glanced at them from the crow's nest before replacing the eyeglass to his face and leaning back. She wondered if he slept with it like that.

Audra leaned against the rail, admiring the stars and Raia's emerald incandescence that glittered through a patchy night sky onto the dark sea. Song, the smaller of the moons, would set in another hour, just before Starling rose to begin the day anew. Silence had another night before it appeared.

She struggled to wake from the worst fatigue she'd experienced in years. That combined with the chest tightness, had her worrying about Ferin despite the knowledge that Auntie Zin would keep her brother safe, and nothing could happen while he remained in her territory. When the mage stepped beside her, his presence charged the surrounding air.

"We need off this boat," he said, eyes fixed on the horizon.

"We'll reach Oxton in a few days," she mumbled. "Once Chon gets a ransom, I'm sure he'll let you go. I suspect he's not a killer at heart."

Song light glistened off his hair, tinted his alabaster skin. His gaze shifted to the moon. A small sigh left his lips. "This ship won't make it to Oxton."

She tensed at the assuredness of his tone. He pursed his lips and turned away. Audra gripped his arm, a tingle where her skin met his, and jerked him around. His face was a pale, pretentious mask.

"Why won't we make it to Oxton, asshole?" Audra hissed.

He leaned close. "That bolt you cut out of me is part tracker. If it had finished its job, it would've died happily. That sends a certain energy back to its castor. As it is, it died angry. That also sends energy back to its source. At least one ship will be on us by mid-morning. Afternoon, if we're lucky." He licked cracked lips, gazing back at the moon. "You should have left me to the sea."

He yanked his arm away and stalked back below deck. She followed, relocking the door behind her. He sat in the corner, cross-legged with eyes closed, pouting.

"I apologize for saving you," Audra said. "In hindsight, it was a terrible mistake, and every foul word from your mouth makes me regret it further. Feel free to go back to drowning." The barbed triangle still lay in the corner where she'd tossed it. "Why not just throw it overboard? Won't that solve the problem?"

He snorted, not bothering to look at her. "The tendrils of the spell have filled this ship. Even if the bolt is destroyed the threads will still lead here."

She chilled. There was something in the way he spoke that rang true. "What about the crew? We should warn them."

His teeth glinted in a cruel smile. "So they can kill us and offer my corpse to the Moon tribe? I don't think so."

Her mouth went dry. The last thing she wanted was to fall into either Moon or Starling tribes' hands but, if she helped him escape, perhaps there was another option. If she remained aboard and offered his whereabouts to those chasing him, they might spare her and the crew. Or they might kill them all anyway.

One eyebrow arched as he watched her calculating expression. His jaw clenched. "Is there a rowboat, anything, we can take to get away?"

"There's a dinghy, but we aren't close enough to land. They'd be on us as soon as Starling broke. And I'm not going anywhere with you."

His eyes were bottled storms, silver and grey swirling together. Color flushed his cheeks. "You don't have a choice. Because you saved my life, you're bound to me—"

"If you think that I—"

"—and, as such, we must stay together if we both wish to keep living. Unfortunately, drowning isn't an option for either of us."

She must have hit him harder than intended and knocked his sense out. Or perhaps he'd been in the water too long. For him to think that there was something between them, as if she owed him anything but another fist, was preposterous. Audra's voice was a seething whisper. "You are deranged. You should owe *me*."

"Would that were true, believe me. Pay you. Maybe kill you. Those options would be preferable to the situation before us now. We are bonded, and until we get to the Silence monastery, I cannot undo it." He closed his eyes. "That is how I know that you, Audra Shan, saved me. I feel each of your volatile emotions, the little judgements and assumptions you make. I taste your desperation. It's exhausting."

It was Audra's turn to open her mouth and close it again. She rubbed her sternum, where it tightened again ever since . . .

"Oh no." Audra leaned away from him, noticing a slight tug she hadn't defined before. But no emotions or thoughts came from him, nothing that he'd described. For that, she counted herself lucky. "Listen, I can't help you. I've got to get to Oxton. My family—"

"Whatever you need, wherever you were going, doesn't matter now. We must get to the northern Moon border before the eclipses. Only then can we be separated."

She gripped the dagger in her pocket. "*You* don't understand. I'm going to Oxton, with or without you."

He shook his head. "You have no choice."

She gripped the dagger. He was probably lying, all Moons lied after all. She would injure him enough to put him in his place. Let him know that she wasn't his servant. Force him to release her. But her hand refused to draw the blade from her pocket, remaining securely sheathed despite her efforts. She winced as another constriction in her chest stole her breath.

"I know your intentions," he said, cold eyes glittering. "Remove your hand from your pocket."

Her fingers withdrew, hand trembling against her thigh as she tried to resist. She cursed him, but he didn't respond. When her anger flared sharply against his control the tightness relaxed. Her hand was her own again. She rubbed her wrist. "Who's chasing you?"

A shadow darkened his face. "That is none of your concern."

She spat at his feet. "That's not how this is going to work, Moonie."

He glared. "What did you call me?"

"It's better than asshole."

"Is it?" He grumbled. "Well, I suppose, if you must call me something, Moon is acceptable."

"Who are you running from?"

He crossed his arms defiantly. There was an arrogant lift to his chin her fists ached to punch. He probably wasn't used to being disrespected, and Audra had a natural talent for antagonizing the arrogant.

Her words were a barrage against his haughty manner. "Did you break an engagement? Cheat on someone? You look like the cheating type. Are you a swindler? Abandon a family? You look like that type too. Or is it because you were an ass to the wrong person? Completely feasible given the impression you've made so far."

"Stop your nonsense." He gave her an exasperated look. "It's nothing like that. It's my sister."

"Your sister wants you dead?" Moon glared until she waved her hand dismissively. "I avoid other people's family issues at all costs. Mine are complicated enough. If you could cut this thing between us, I'd be grateful."

"I've told you, it's impossible until we get to the monastery. The monks will help." His voice sounded confident, but she was doubtful. Westerners never fared well at the hands of other tribes, especially not once they crossed their borders.

"Why not sooner? If your stars are any indication, you've got the magic for it. I've never heard of thirteen stars."

His eyes narrowed. "What do you know of the Moon tribes?"

"Your people slaughtered half my village fifteen years ago."

"And you haven't tried to kill me?"

"Give it time. I'm still considering my options." She crossed her arms. "The Starling's killed the other half. I can hate both tribes equally. But I like to think I'm generally a decent judge of character, and you strike me as a true asshole."

Moon chuckled darkly. "I might be the worst person you've encountered in your insignificant life. Unless you've met my sister." He shoved his hair back. "But her bolt siphoned too much of my energy. It'll take time to build my strength. Cutting a bond is dangerous under the best circumstances, and I have no desire to die yet."

She bit her lip. "So you have no magic left?"

"Only enough to get us safely away."

When Traq enlisted with the Starlings several years ago, it had spurned a rift between he and Audra, and he'd acted pleasantly surprised when she found him on Callaway. She'd always had faith that even though their romantic relationship had abruptly ended, Traq's heart was still Western and his loyalty to their people had not changed. He'd been stationed in Oxton for the last year. If he could get her an audience with some of the stronger Starling mages, they might break the bond between Audra and Moon. The Starlings might even pay for the mage outright. Then she could go her own way, untethered, and finish her task. "What do we do?"

He looked at the golden object in the corner as it exhaled a final thin puff of smoke. "I need my robes." He brushed the hair from his face again and sighed. "And a hair pin."

Ten

Lua

Song hovered over the horizon as morning marched toward the *Requin*. When Starling rose, it would rouse the crew and burn Lua's skin. But, for now, the ship still slumbered.

While Audra retrieved his robes, Lua found his way into the kitchen for sustenance of his own. He'd lied when he said he could get them safely away. He was still too weak, and drawing on Audra wasn't much better than starving.

What he found in the galley would have to do. The large man slumbering in the tight closet reeked of onions and burnt rat meat. This must be the infamous Munk whose "stew" was slowly giving the entire crew dysentery and had probably contributed to his anchor's malnourishment. Lua drained him before he could wake. It would have to be enough for them to get away and speed toward land. Audra would have to handle things during the day to ensure their survival.

It was too risky to siphon the other crew members. Waking them was dangerous, and confrontation would likely lead to a quick death. Audra would be little help. He rubbed the sore bruise around his eye.

Of course, he might be underestimating her, though people rarely surprised him.

With his hair secured in a top knot and donned in his robes, they crept onto the deck. Two men stirred momentarily before resettling. The lookout remained silent in his nest.

Six feet below the port side rail, ropes and winches lashed a dinghy to the hull. Lua swept his black robes around him and slid gracefully over the side, landing softly in the small boat. Audra followed, dropping in a crouch.

The boat rocked as she stood, throwing her off balance. He steadied her instinctively. Heat spread through his hands and up his arms as another thread lashed between them. He pulled back at the same moment she pushed him away. Her cheeks flushed, and for a moment he thought she might punch him again. They looked awkwardly away and moved to opposite sides of the small dinghy.

A layer of crusty brine coated the winches. Lua pulled at the gears, picking at the salt while Audra tried the same. His shoulders tightened; his neck cramped. Glancing over, he realized why. Audra was much shorter than him, and the winches were about the height of his head. She strained to accomplish the same task from a much lower vantage while balancing on the balls of feet trapped inside straw shoes that rubbed her toes.

The gears jerked. The boat dropped an inch and stuck. They exchanged a glance before feeding the ropes through again. It lowered another inch as the winches creaked. After six more inches, the ropes ground to a stop and refused to move.

Magic shouldn't be used for such menial tasks. If Dain were here ...

But he wasn't. Dain was dead. Lua motioned Audra out of his way and stood in the middle of the boat.

"Hold on," he said.

Audra crouched, gripping the sides of the boat. His arms swept wide as he drew strength from the remaining moonlight that slipped from the horizon. Tugging on Audra slightly sent silvery light from his fingers. It snaked up the ropes and slithered to the winches. The ropes gave an inch, followed by another.

As Audra groaned, looking green, the lookout's voice shattered the night air.

The rope's sudden release dropped the boat into the water. They landed with a sharp jolt. Audra fell sideways, slamming her arm into the thick wood. Lua hissed, pulling her back. Blood dripped from a new gash down her forearm. Beneath the sleeve of his robe, wetness oozed into the fabric.

Chon's voice rang above. Though his words held remnants of alcohol, his tone was threatening.

"Get the sails up," Lua said. He had to save his magic for the wind.

Audra shook the daze from her head, fumbling with the sails and raising the boom. She untied the oars from the bottom of the boat as Lua kicked them away from the *Requin's* hull.

Chon's yell drew their eyes upward. A small fire cannon angled over the rail and pointed toward the dinghy. The captain held the all'ight lantern, angling the flame toward the wick of the cannon.

"You stealing from me, little mouse?" Chon yelled. The wick caught. It would only take a press of the trigger to rain fire down on them. His voice dimmed for a moment, giving them only a fragment of his question. "—to Munk?"

Lua cursed, but Audra's attention was fixed on the cannon. Chon's words slipped past her.

"They'd never use it. We're too close," she said without conviction.

Toman dove overboard with a blade between his teeth. The dinghy rocked from his waves as he landed only a few feet from them. He broke the sea's surface, water dripping from the blade's edge in his mouth. Lua could either handle the brute or get them safely away. Accomplishing both was not an option.

"Take the rudder," Lua ordered.

"But the oars—"

"Mind the damn rudder!"

Audra cursed at his pull, then scooted to the back and gripped the rudder's handle. Toman reached the side of the boat, rocking it. He hoisted himself up, not enough to get in but nearly enough to tip it.

Lua stood at the front of the boat, legs adjusting with the movement. Magic shimmered from his fingers as he chanted soundlessly. He couldn't break the spell to deal with the brute. Audra's fear and repulsion of Toman swept down their connection and Lua yanked on that thread.

"Get rid of him," Lua ordered her.

Toman leaned on his elbow and pulled the blade from his teeth, beady eyes gleaming. Releasing the rudder, Audra gripped an oar. Her swing hit the side of his head. The blade dropped from his hand, but he didn't release the boat.

She slammed the oar down on his knuckles, hearing the crunch as he wailed. The next swing smashed against his head again. Toman toppled into the water.

Lua's arms rose higher, robes billowing as wind filled the sails. The dinghy lurched forward as the *Requin's* crew screamed above. Audra lunged for the rudder, angling them away from the hull.

The cannon brightened as a fiery blast surged toward their small mast. Lua's wind swelled, sending the flames back the way they'd come. The crew scampered backward as the rail erupted.

The mage wind propelled them into the dawning sky. Lua pulled his robes over his head, turning his back to the dawn until the boat and flames disappeared behind them.

Finally, he collapsed to a seat and surveyed his anchor's status. Audra was paler than her western complexion allowed, turning her almost sallow. The wind ruffled her chopped hair, but her eyes were warm, amber tones intermingled with brown. They reminded him of another westerner he knew. Lua looked away when he felt her discomfort beneath his gaze.

Starling's rays stung the side of his cheek, and he pulled the robes tighter around him. The pull to Audra was like a fresh wound—painfully irritating and strangely compelling. He shook his head, rubbed his arm where it bled beneath his robes, and slowly lowered himself onto his side.

"The wind should last a while longer. Wake me if you see another boat or land." He drew his robe over his head, covering himself completely, and fell asleep.

Eleven

Xiang

Jayna and Nori were sheltered from the morning rays beneath a silk screen hung between two beams. The mages' spells filled the sails with another gust that hastened them forward.

Smoke rose from a mid-grade vessel in the distance. It was built for hauling and storage but had been modified. They'd doused the fire, but one of their sails was browned along the edges. Through the spyglass, he saw several men tending to it. They broke off when their lookout alerted them to the larger vessel approaching.

The *Bulou's* sails died as it drew near the *Requin*. The ragged captain waited at the bow with a small, disreputable looking group of men surrounding him.

Xiang could have yelled over, asked if they'd seen anything, inquired about the fire, but experience told him these men would only respect threats of violence. Twenty archers took aim at the *Requin's* crew as Xiang, a handful of soldiers, and a well-covered Jayna, rowed toward the ship. They lowered the ladder without being ordered to.

The captain was a middle-aged man and, like the rest of his crew, stank of poor hygiene and too much islander wine. But there was a wariness to his expression, a fatigue born of poor sleep and worry. The largest of the men had red, swollen eyes and a deep purple bruise that bloomed across his head and down his face.

The *Requin's* captain cleared his throat nervously. Sweat beaded his brow.

Xiang didn't offer introductions, there was no need. Their black and silver sails were well known, and the tremble in the captain's hands revealed an appropriate fear.

The odor of the burned rail and mast still hung in the air.

The captain feigned bravery. "I'm Chon Gioni, the captain here. What do we—"

"What happened here?" Xiang asked.

"Lightning. Nearly caught the entire ship on fire," Chon said quickly.

The crew stood too stiffly for Xiang's liking. The large man with the bruise glowered at the back of the captain's head. "Have you seen anyone?" Xiang asked.

The men exchanged glances as Chon replied, "Who would we have seen in the storm?"

With a flick of Xiang's hand, the soldiers spread out. Jayna pulled her hood back enough to expose a round face with large eyes that glanced at Xiang before disappearing below deck.

Chon's gaze followed the mage, his hands worried together. "Th-there was someone."

"Who?" Xiang asked.

"I don't know. Truly," Chon said. "We pulled him from the water. His robes were black, like your mage's."

"And where is he now?"

Chon licked his lips and pulled his shoulders back to retain some dignity. "He stole our dinghy before Starling rose."

Xiang stood a full head taller than the captain. His black silks were covered by matching tightly plated armor. "Did he feed on anyone before he left?"

Chon paled. "F-feed?"

Jayna reappeared carrying a bundle of familiar clothing beneath one arm and clutching an object with her other hand. She walked lightly across the deck, stepping through the men's shadows before handing the object to Xiang.

The bolt was heavy in Xiang's hand. "Tell me."

"It was damaged but still working," she spoke softly. "It would have contained him eventually if it hadn't been removed. These are his clothes, but his robes are missing. The bolt was in a separate room. Someone must have helped him."

Xiang held the bolt up for everyone to see. "Who took this out of him?"

Chon glanced at his crew before speaking. "No one so much as talked to him. He was only on board a few hours before..."

"That boy, Alver. They escaped together," the bruised man said. His voice wavered. "After killing Munk."

Xiang stowed the bolt in his pocket, his tone changing to one of sympathy. "What boy? What happened to Munk?" Fearful expressions crossed the crew's faces. "It's all right. Tell us what you know, and we'll be on our way."

Chon ran a hand over his face and sighed. "Alver's not a boy." The men murmured behind him. "She's a thief—ever heard of the western mouse? No? I suppose you wouldn't up north. She stowed away in Callaway. I only realized who she was after we threw her into the water to get your friend. She took care of him. The way the man looked, those clothes, I thought for sure there'd be a reward. I didn't know about that thing." He gestured to Xiang's pocket. "They waited until we were exhausted from the storm to escape."

"And Munk?"

Chon looked ill. "What's left of him is still in his bunk. Whatever they did, it's as if everything was drained from him."

Xiang motioned to a few of the guards, who scampered below.

The bruised man sobbed, one of the others patted his shoulder in consolation. "Our poor Munk."

The soldiers returned with a corpse held between them. Its skin was ashy gray, limbs rigid, and face frozen in wide-mouthed horror. The eyelids were drawn open, revealing papery eyes. There were cries of offense as the soldiers dropped the body none-to-gently on the deck. A cloud of dust spewed into the air. One arm crumbled beside the torso.

The traces of the bolt had doomed these men. The Oji could have tossed it overboard to try and spare them, but Xiang knew that kind of consideration wasn't in either of the Koray sibling's natures.

"Thank you, Captain Gioni. You've been very helpful." Xiang nodded to each of the men in turn. "We'll leave you to your repairs."

He motioned the soldiers back down the ladder and into their rowboats, with the weighted gazes of the *Requin's* crew upon his back.

Xiang stood on the deck of the *Bulou*, Galia beside him. He'd dismissed Jayna to the shade below deck. They didn't need her for this. Nori brought a wind, just enough to move them to a safe distance while the archers lit their arrows with their all'ights. The *Requin's* men couldn't see the flaming arrows from their lower angle. Their deaths would be quick, a mercy Lua should have given them.

Xiang raised a hand to the *Requin*. Misunderstanding, Chon raised one in return, his crooked-tooth smile a deep shade of yellow.

Xiang's arm fell. "Fire."

Twelve

Audra

Audra squinted as she adjusted the rudder. The effects of the mage wind were nearly dizzying. If they kept this pace, they'd reach Oxton in a couple of days. From there it would be a steady climb into the mountains toward home. She was determined to reach her brother, regardless of the mage's threats or manipulations. Getting the jade to Ferin was crucial for everything and her brother needed her.

She cleaned the gash on her arm with sea water, hissing at the sting. Moon grumbled beneath his robes before growing still again. Though he hadn't moved for several hours, the wind stayed hale, hastening them westward.

Audra searched the water's blue-green expanse for any signs of chase and found none, just the occasional ripple of a long silvery tail beneath the distant water. She'd only seen a sea dragon once before: from the bow of the *Requin* a few hours before the storm struck. It was strange to see another one so soon.

She ate a bit of pilfered food. Given that it was Munk's creation, she'd had to force it down with sips of water. It left a sour aftertaste. By midday, just as her lightheadedness eased slightly, exhaustion took hold. Between the merciless burn of Starling on her skin and the boat's rhythmic skimming across the water, her head began to bob. After she jerked awake for the sixth time and Moon showed no indication of rousing, she tied the rudder in place and cautiously stepped over the sleeping man to claim shade beneath the mainsail.

When she woke, Audra's head throbbed. Her limbs were leaden. Moon still slumbered beneath his robes. She considered waking him but decided she preferred his silence to his sullenness. She sipped from the gourd, trying to save the small amount of potable water she'd brought with them, but felt no better.

The thinnest part of Raia's ring rotated slowly above, muted by the setting Starling rays. Moon sat upright and rubbed his neck. He studied the direction they travelled with a scowl.

"Where's your compass?" he asked.

She shrugged. "I never need one if I'm going home."

He snorted with annoyance then nudged her out of his way. Gripping the rudder, he turned them thirty degrees due south. The setting light gave the world a haze that made it difficult for Audra to see anything other than water and clouds.

"Stay on course. We're heading to Oxton," she said.

Moon took a long drink from the gourd and didn't reply. His face was cast in fiery shadows that gave him an eerie appeal.

She stretched to loosen her back, rubbed her sore neck. "I need something there."

He ignored her, maintaining a sharp gaze on the horizon. She gasped as her chest contracted and the wind picked up. Another wave of exhaustion made her slump.

"You're getting weaker. If we don't find nourishment soon, you'll be useless to me." He shoved the gourd at her and watched as she took a long drink. "Finish it." He ordered.

"There isn't much left," Audra said.

"You need it more than I do."

"Where are we headed?" she asked, her voice was hoarse. He pointed toward a small fishing boat bobbing in the distance. Three figures scurried on board, pulling their lines in for the night. Their comfortable laughter bounced over the water toward them.

The hair on the nape of Audra's neck prickled dangerously. She shook her head. "We shouldn't," she said. "Your robes aren't something they'll easily forget."

Another gust of wind took her breath and propelled them forward. The closer they came to the boat, the more her vision blurred. Her head grew heavy. She slumped sideways, unable to fight the fatigue.

Moon stood over her, pressing the back of his hand to her forehead and propping something soft beneath her skull. "Sleep."

She wanted to protest, but slumber claimed her. People were talking, voices raised. As Audra slipped into darkness, a man shouted.

"Where're we going?" Audra asked. Her mother held Audra's small hand while Ferin clutched their mother's pockets. Beyond the walls of their home, screams echoed in the street.

"They've come for us." Lorah's face was fierce, hiding her fear for her children's sake, though Audra hadn't seen that at the time. The long blade that hung above the mantel for all Audra's life, dusty and unused beside the dragon scales, was now secured to her mother's waist. "We need to get to Auntie Zin's."

Audra had only met Auntie Zin a handful of times; the last time was when she'd still worn two braids. But the way mother said Zin's name gave a sense of assuredness, as if this were the only thing to do.

"Stay close," Lorah ordered. She picked Ferin up and opened the door. His small tail curled around her waist.

Though it was midday, the sky was blackened with angry clouds. Snow swirled in the air, reflecting gold and gray bursts. Homes burned as two sets of soldiers clashed, some dressed in dazzling white armor. The other's clothing so black it sucked out the light and gave nothing back.

Magic whipped snow and ice, like daggers that sizzled when met with blasts of silver and gold fiery threads.

"Run!" Lorah twisted the hilt of her sword in her hand and dragged Audra behind her.

They darted down the street and veered right. Their elderly neighbor, Ma-Lu, lay on her stomach, her blood spread across the small path between their homes. Her head was turned at an awkward angle, as if trying to see the spear-sized icicle jutting from her back as it slowly dripped onto her body.

They skirted around Ma-Lu and snaked through familiar, narrow passages. They paused more than once, doubling back, and headed other ways until stumbling into the path of two clashing soldiers. The men's blades sparked as the one in black pressed the other back. His footing slipped. The Moon soldier fell as the Starling's blade plunged into his chest. Crimson sputtered from the wound as the Starling yanked the blade free.

Mother gripped her sword. The Starling caught sight of them. He was a giant man with skin darker than Audra was used to seeing, darker than hers or fathers by several shades. He towered over everything, his thick form terrifying as he advanced. His white braid swung in the wind. Magic sparked from his fingers, tinging the air yellow.

"We've been looking for you." His smile was cruel, face rapt in post kill exhilaration. His eyes landed on Audra. "And your children."

Lorah gently placed Ferin on his feet. Her breath shook as she stood between the attacker and her children. A thin green thread lashed from her fingers, slicing the man's cheek before he could react. "Run!"

"Momma?" Audra cried, but she clutched Ferin's hand obediently.

Lorah stepped forward, dark sword singing in the air. "Protect your brother! Find Auntie!"

Audra ran, dragging Ferin with her as magic clashed behind them.

Audra avoided remembering what happened next, the faces of the dead or the spell that nearly claimed Ferin's life. But whenever she woke, her mind completed the story anyway.

Someone gently lifted her head. Fresh water dripped between her lips. Her skin warmed, eyes blinked open to find the mage holding her. The drape of his loose hair tickled her cheeks, a small line of worry dipped between his brows. Song and Raia glittered in the starry sky behind him.

He tipped the cup to her lips again, but she pushed him away. Frowning, he settled the cup on the deck beside her and stood. His face was fuller, skin dazzling in the moonlight.

Audra's headache was gone, the ache in her limbs disappeared. They were on the fishing vessel. And they were alone. "What happened?" she asked.

He turned toward the bow, gesturing to a bowl on a small table. "Eat. There's fresh fish and rice wrapped in coconut leaves."

A sinking feeling churned her stomach. "Where are the anglers?"

He sighed.

Audra stood, shivering. "What did you do to them?"

His eyes glinted with scorn. "We needed nourishment."

"You killed them." Her breath hitched.

"Would you rather it was you who died?"

"Why wasn't it me?"

He brushed a lock of hair over his shoulder. "I've told you. We are connected, growing strong or weak together." His voice was bitter. "I cannot kill you now, no matter how much I might want to."

She considered his words and the unspoken implications of what might happen to her later. "And the anglers?"

"Stronger magic depends on life force. And right now, I must use others or risk us both meeting death," he said.

Her voice was a whisper. "They didn't do anything. What about their families? What if they had children?"

"It was necessary, believe me."

"Why should I?"

"Because for now, there is no other way to save us." He turned back to her, shadows falling across his face. "Eat. I need you to stay strong."

She licked her lips. "What if I don't? What if I refuse?"

In a flash, he stood before her. Long fingers gripped her throat. Black robes and hair whipped around them. The sneer painting his face marred his good looks. His voice was low, nearly strangled. "Then I will force the food down your throat. It only takes a word to make you sleep, a thought to move your limbs. Make no mistake, if you test me, you will live as I see fit." The thread between them seared behind her ribs. "Be grateful that I killed those men myself. If Dain were still alive..." His words trailed away; a hint of pain swept across his features before vanishing. He released her and took a breath.

Audra stumbled backward as the pull relaxed. "Who's Dain?" she asked but flinched at the hard look in his eyes. "Why me?"

He headed toward the sails like a shadow drifting in the breeze. "I keep asking myself the same damn thing."

Thirteen

Xiang

Xiang watched the Song mages raise their arms beneath the moon. Jayna was already eight stars, becoming an Octra was an impressive accomplishment for someone barely into their third decade. Septra Nori was only seven, and he was her senior by over a dozen years. Yet, even if they'd had Verina's nine-star strength with them, the triad still wouldn't have been a match for the Oji if he were at his strongest. Everyone was keenly aware of the risks that came with fighting Lua. Seeing the remains of the *Mirren* had turned those fears to truths.

Stars weren't necessarily indicative of talent or experience so much as raw magical power, but few mages had ever achieved thirteen. At least that's what Selene had told him. She was eleven stars, would've been more if she'd siphoned the Rajav. But in the end, Bolin had killed her father for her.

Even after all these years being forced to serve it, Xiang still hated magic. It had stolen everything from him during the war: his homeland, his family, and, in a way, his greatest love. If the Moons hadn't wiped out the Western dragons and their mages, he often wondered what sort of life he and Bolin might have had in their homeland. It was a dream, of course. Their country had fallen long before either of them had been born, but he'd used those dreams to get him through the nightmares of their reality.

Thinking of Bolin only brought longing, which was useless. Instead, he studied Galia. She stood on the bow, her eyes returning repeatedly to Jayna. Their affection brought discomfort. It was sweetness doomed, like when worms bred beneath the skin of fruit back home. Galia was too much like himself and Jayna too much like Bolin. Equally stubborn in their affection.

Jayna would hit ten stars in another ten years, and that would be the end of their love. Every ten star needed an anchor, and all anchors were chosen by the Mage Council to ensure the strongest life force and physical strength. It was the best way to guarantee longevity. And though anchors were the force behind an advanced mage's strength, they were ultimately viewed as expendable as their mages' power progressed. When compromised, a mage always sacrificed their anchor to save themselves. It left them weak for months, no matter how strong the new anchor was. There wasn't room for love or attachment unless it grew afterward. Jayna and Galia had to know this.

Inside his cabin, he stripped his armor, thinking of the men on the *Requin*, their dirty lives snuffed in a blaze of fire and screams. He envied them in a way that slumped his chest. He patted the small vials of liger's bane secured in his vest pocket. Someday, when he could stand no more, he'd fall into death's arms. Maybe he'd take Selene with him, but that would kill Bolin as well.

He pulled out the blade that Bolin had given him after they'd first met and settled the small mirror on the desk.

Although Xiang had only a trace of magic to speak of, Lua had taught him this simple trick many years ago—before he understood the Oji's motivations better. It was the only spell Xiang had ever succeeded with, maybe because the reward was so valuable.

The knife sliced his forearm as he repeated a short mantra. A thin stream of blood rose from the broken skin. Bolin greeted him from the mirror, flecks of lighter tones catching the light in his brown eyes; his broad smile lit the room. Dark brown hair framed his square jaw. It had grown long again. It always grew too fast.

His mouth moved, but sound didn't travel through the image. With paper priced too high for anything other than administrative necessities, they'd learned to communicate with rough gestures and signs. Sometimes it left them wondering what the other meant from hundreds of miles away. It was enough to see Bolin safe and healthy in Uduary. It was enough, because it had to be.

Bolin's smile faded, replaced by worry. Xiang offered reassurance. He told him he loved him. Bolin nodded, mouthing the same words. Xiang wanted to tell him they were nearing the Western shores, that he could see the Shei-nam mountains in the distance, that they were still lavender beneath the Starling light. But he couldn't. It would have to wait until he returned home. Xiang would beg Selene to let him see Bolin. She'd relent if Xiang came back with her brother in tow. But if he didn't, well, punishment came in different flavors, and she liked for him to taste them all.

They had to reach Lua before he used his new anchor. She was an odd choice, surely born out of necessity. A thief and woman slender enough to pass as a boy was well below any mage's standards. Anchors were supposed to be robust, strong enough to defend their mage from physical assault while being used as a source for their magic. But the standards for the Moon Oji had always been higher.

Lua must have been nearly dead when the *Requin* found him. It was safe to assume the thief and Oji were anchored, given the circumstances, though it was unusual to find someone willing outside of the Moon tribes. That they'd bonded without the traditional rituals was even more curious. Xiang knew of only one other time that happened, but there may have been others that he was ignorant of.

Bolin's wide grin demanded attention. Xiang pressed his fingers to his lips before raising them and offering an easy smile. The image faded before Bolin could reply.

A fresh scab sealed the cut. Xiang traced the dozens of scars that lined his arm. He'd bleed a new place tomorrow, and another the night after. Forever, until they were together again or one of them died. He stared at the blank mirror for another moment before a shout above pulled him back to the deck.

Fourteen

Audra

The fishing boat sped faster than the dinghy had, careening across the water as Audra dozed and considered giving the mage a watery grave. Would distance break the thread between them? It was tempting either way. But caution held her in check. Ferin would suffer if anything happened to her. Getting to Oxton, then home, was her priority. Only then could she figure out how to dispose of the mage.

Zin might know. She might even deal with him entirely. Audra smirked. He wouldn't know what hit him.

It was early morning when Moon nudged her with his boot and barked her name twice. They hadn't spoken in hours and, over the sound of the hull upon the water, the air between them was thick with mutual resentment.

Curled atop a blanket, a dream fogged her waking brain. It left a quieter feeling than she was used to, the weight of melancholy. She stared at Moon's back, unsure that it had been *her* dream.

She stood and stretched, then startled. To the west were steady voices. All'ights speckled across several piers and dangled from the decks of fishing boats as they prepared to disembark. Behind them, a sleeping city spread out, nestled between shores and the lower reaches of the Shei-nam mountains. This town had been burned and rebuilt numerous times and was where her father and older brother died many years ago.

Moon twisted his hair into a half knot while scowling at the pier. A massive Starling vessel was moored at the closest dock. Its sails were tacked down, but a white flag with a gold Starling burst waved in the breeze.

"You said you didn't want to go to Oxton," she said.

"I want off the sea. This was the closest major port. We can get supplies and head north from here." He glanced at her, arching one eyebrow. "Isn't this what you wanted?"

Audra didn't respond. She gathered the pack she'd taken from the *Requin*. Chon's coins jingled inside. What she couldn't steal, they'd have to buy.

"Horses, blankets, food." Moon's eyes flicked over her. "Suitable travel clothing, and you need boots, or I'll be feeling every stone beneath your feet."

She didn't ask what that meant, too busy forming ways to retrieve the package without an argument. It was a forgone conclusion that he'd be against it. Plus, she'd reconsidered getting Traq involved. It was bad enough she was stuck with this asshole. If Traq found out, he'd break too many Starling rules to help her, even if she told him not to. After five years enlisted and only a three-star ranking, Traq would be no match for what Moon had done so far. And she wouldn't see her oldest friend dead on her account.

She'd wait until Starling was full in the sky to lose Moon. He'd have to hide beneath his robes, and that would draw attention from the locals. Then she could use his vulnerability to her advantage.

"Are you a good thief?" he asked.

She frowned at the disbelief in his voice but nodded anyway. It was unlikely that a writ from Callaway would make it across the sea. For all of Claude Suna's posturing, he wouldn't want the fact that he'd been selling dangerous artifacts spread to the mainland or, more specifically, to the Moon tribe. The islanders strictly avoided negative attention from the other tribes and the Rajav had ordered all the jade destroyed during the cleansing of the Western monasteries. But profiteering should have been expected, and it was likely that both Starling and Moon soldiers had stolen some away to sell to the highest bidders. The jade should never have left the western mountains since there were few left in the world who understood its properties. Auntie Zin being one of them.

Moon hadn't asked what she needed in Oxton, and she'd intentionally neglected to explain further. Confessing to a meeting with a Starling mage wouldn't go well, and it was too early for another fight she was bound to lose. It was enough that they'd made it this far without killing each other, and she'd be more likely to get what she wanted by staying quiet. If the mage knew her thoughts, as he stated, he'd shown no signs of it.

They gave the Starling ship a wide berth and pulled the boat in at the end of the furthest dock. Audra's legs shook with the first few steps on the solid pier. Moon swept past her. A gentle, energetic tug pulled her in his wake. Despite her shorter legs and his long stride, she stayed in step behind him.

"There's an hour until Starling rise," he said.

"The shops won't open until mid-morning," she said.

His sudden stop caused her to nearly run into him. He sneered down at her. "I thought you were a thief."

By the time dawn broke, Audra had snuck through a small window at the back of a clothing shop. She traded her filthy clothes for a pair of dark breeches and two loose linen shirts that hid her breasts, then grabbed a dark green cloak; the color reminded her of the mountain conifers. The fine leather boots she pulled on were supple with strong soles.

Moon hissed her name impatiently from the alleyway. With his tiresome nature, it was no wonder people wanted him dead. After what he'd done to the anglers, she'd add her name to that list.

She considered leaving him floundering in the alley while she darted through the streets to find Traq. But the threat that whatever happened to him also happened to her made her rethink, not that she truly believed him.

Audra shoved the clothing through the window and dropped to the ground below. Moon looked disdainfully at the pile of fabric.

"There must have been other options." He lifted a blue robe made for someone twice his girth. "Is this your petty attempt at humiliating me?"

"It's a common color here and a good disguise," Audra replied. "No one would search for a moon mage in these colors. And it's big enough to hide your robes beneath. Or do you desperately need the attention you're obviously used to?" She threw a set of black pants and linen shirt at him. They were nothing like the finery he was accustomed to, but their darkness might placate him.

She turned away as he awkwardly stripped and changed clothes in the shadows. The blue caught the deeper colors in his hair, cast his light eyes with a cerulean tint. Now he was memorable for different reasons. If he wasn't so despicable, she might not have minded his company.

"Where are the gloves?" he demanded.

He'd mentioned them several times before she'd entered the shop, and his stubbornly persistent lack of faith in her ability to remember the simplest things made her bite back her words. With an annoyed snort, she pulled a pair of black gloves from her pocket and shoved them at him.

"I'll need cover," he said.

"Hats are easy to find once the market opens," she said.

"You're hungry again."

She was so accustomed to ignoring the emptiness of her belly that it was only after he'd drawn attention to it she noticed the rumbling. His sudden grip on her hand made her flush. With the length of his hair tucked beneath the robes, Moon drew his hood up and pulled her into the street.

Scents of cinnamon, mace, cloves, and grilling meats teased her nose as morning vendors hoped to entice those passing by. The intricately formed pastries native to the mountains caught her eye at one stall. The cookies were traditionally shaped into a simplified western script. One for *love*, another for *fortune*, one for *Raia*, and one into a word that neither Starling nor Moons knew—*pangzhufi*. Roughly translated it meant *may the wings bless you*. Selling it here for all to see was a small sign of rebellion that Audra appreciated. She and Traq used to make them for birthday celebrations, and, later, when trying to avoid Zin discovering any plans they might have. Moon followed her eye but didn't inquire.

As the market filled with merchants and urchins alike, an occasional flash of white robes drew her eye, but Moon dragged her into a shadow conspiratorially until they passed.

Traq's Starling vessel was moored in the dock, and, in another hour, his daily route would have him passing their prearranged meeting place. At the right moment, Audra would have to abandon Moon. It would be interesting to see how far their bond could stretch.

That he'd be angry was a given. That she didn't care about his near constant irritability was also a given.

They purchased skewers of grilled lamb and fresh flatbread from separate stalls and leaned against a shaded eastern wall, watching the crowd grow. Several vendors down was a tall stack of wide, flat-brimmed hats with a hole open at the top to allow hair to be pinned through. The flatlands style would complement his disguise.

Moon swallowed the last of his lamb while studying the townspeople.

"You have quite an appetite for someone who said they didn't need to eat much," she said, raising one eyebrow.

His lip twitched. "If my anchor were properly nourished, or her spirit stronger, I wouldn't need it as much."

"Ah, I see. It's *my* fault." She laughed. "Even you must admit that the food here is delicious. I never tasted spices like this until I came here during a spring festival when I was young." The food was her only good memory of the festival. She'd been lost in the crowd, trapped, nearly trampled, when her brother found her. "We should get some wine for the road."

"No wine," he said. "We can't afford the secondary effects."

"It might make you more tolerable."

He snorted. "Doubtful. And it would put more people in danger. Is that what you want?"

Audra gritted her teeth and swallowed her reply. She motioned to the hats before weaving in between moving carts and bodies. Lua hesitated, waiting until an opening in the crowd appeared before darting through. Although he'd tugged his hood over his head before stepping into the light, a hiss escaped his clenched teeth as he followed. Abandoning him here would be perfect.

She shoved one of Chon's gold coins into Moon's hand, withdrawing before that uncomfortable feeling made her flush again. "You'll need this." She pushed him toward the hat stand and, before he could turn back, disappeared between stalls.

She knew Oxton well enough to choose the best routes to lose someone. If Moon found her, then it would support his claims. If he was a liar and whatever she'd experienced was nothing more than a mage's trick, then she'd happily abandon him to his fate.

Fifteen

Lua

The thread chafed Lua's sternum as Audra scurried away. He'd expected her to test him sooner. But the way she'd done it, much like everything about her, was irritating. It didn't matter, she'd be easy to find.

Lua couldn't blame her for her disbelief, really. He'd tested his first anchoring repeatedly, until the distance left both he and Eras dizzy and in pain. He hoped it didn't go that far. But Audra was stubborn and untrained, he should expect the worst.

Beneath the shade of the vendor's awning, Lua tried one of the black hats that was stacked neatly outside. It was lightweight, but the horsehair weaving made it partially sheer and ultimately useless until Audra got stronger. As it was, drawing even a small amount of her energy risked taking too much. She should have been stronger by now, but it was as if something else was draining her. Still, the anglers' lives should sustain him for another few days.

He'd never had to consider disguises before, but Audra's cautions seemed astute. A tightly woven bamboo hat that field workers wore was the most hideous thing he'd ever seen but wide enough to block all of

Starling's rays from reaching his neck and shoulders. No one would expect to find the Moon tribe Oji in such a common and visually offensive outfit.

The vendor tried to sell Lua a finer hat when he saw the flash of gold coin, but Lua held firm. Tucking the silver and copper change into his pocket, he turned to follow the thread. He strolled down refuse-littered side streets, past begging children and thin bodies that slept against stained walls, ignoring the offers of sexual satisfaction that came from haggard men and women alike. A man nearly clasped Lua's shoulder before the Oji jerked away. His magic reached out hungrily, aching for the fool who'd come too near, and it took all of Lua's effort to restrain it. The gloves and clothing helped, but if he lost his focus, the magic would readily siphon anyone who touched him. Lua cursed and spat at the man, which worked to dissuade the others from coming closer. Overt hostility typically kept most people at a respectful distance.

Forcing his little thief to return would take too much energy and sow further resentment between them. Tracking her would prove that he could and perhaps eliminate future tests, though he was doubtful. He'd lied when he'd said he knew her thoughts. Nothing had come to him other than her name and an image of the dagger in her pocket. Obviously, she'd doubted his words. But he could feel her emotions, which was close enough. And right now, she was warm, excited, as if...

"Damn it."

As if she were meeting a lover. No wonder she'd been so set on this town. And he'd caved to her, like an idiot. Another complication he'd be forced to deal with. What would Audra do when Lua had to kill them? He rounded a corner, veering into a cleaner part of town.

Audra sipped from a cup beneath a shade tree of a small, dilapidated restaurant. A squat woman bustled between tables and manned the grill behind a small partition. That his anchor had sought to outmaneuver him so easily was insulting. Lua began to cross the road when a flourish of white robes rounded the restaurant's corner. He paused. A smile broke across Audra's face when she saw the Starling mage. Their embrace lasted a moment too long.

Lua glowered beneath the tilt of his hat and resumed his post with crossed arms. Perhaps she'd say more than she ought to. Maybe she would ask for help. Killing a Starling might make Lua feel marginally better, but that tasted sour.

Audra's happiness was unexpected. It was an emotion he wasn't used to from his anchors. Amusement, yes. Ecstasy in bed, yes. Comfortable, yes. But happiness was rare.

The Starling was tall and broad. Her arms didn't quite reach across his back. His dark hair curled past his shoulders, bleaching at the ends. Only mages stopped cutting their hair after they pledged themselves, whereas soldiers kept regimental short crops. That was true for southern and northern tribes, regardless of gender. The commoners did as they chose.

The plump woman gave them a plate of grilled meat and a bowl of rice to share. They leaned casually toward each other. Lua's scowl deepened each time Audra covered her mouth in laughter or the mage rested his hand on her forearm with too much familiarity. The northern tribe elders would have shamed this outward display of affection.

Lua's jaw tightened. If Audra revealed their predicament, Lua would have to kill her lover. But, he considered, a thief and a mage were a novel enough combination. Maybe they weren't lovers. Either way he didn't like it.

The Starling pulled a small package from the inside of his robes and slid it across the table. She smiled and rested her hand affectionately on his knuckles before pulling the package toward her.

Enough. Lua crossed the street. He'd have to—

He froze inside the restaurant's gate as the object in her hands caught the light. An opaque green stone dangled from a black cord. The relic was tear-dropped shaped, etched with ancient symbols that caught the light. Dragon's-eye jade. Audra turned it over in her hands, wearing a look of relief.

Caution held him where he was, but he tugged on the thread to draw her attention. Audra bit her lip and looked up. She frowned when she saw him and subtly shook her head. With surprising strength, she resisted the summons, remaining exactly where she was. Her impudence knew no bounds.

His skin prickled as he edged closer. The jade should have all been destroyed during the cleansing of the Western monasteries.

"You here to eat or glare?" The restaurant owner startled him. She placed her hands on her hips. "Either sit or leave, but there's no loitering."

Awkwardly, he sat at a small table and faced sideways to watch Audra and her companion. She glanced at Lua. Her irritation brought a thin smile to his lips. The Starling mage started to turn, but she grabbed his hand and his attention.

The woman placed a serving of rice and meat before Lua when the Starling stood suddenly. He moved behind Audra and secured the cord around her neck. Her cheeks flushed at his touch.

Lua yanked the thread again, but she pulled back with equal strength.

Two white-robed figures paused outside the restaurant's entrance. One was an older man who looked bothered by the entire scene, the other was a striking woman with dark umber skin and a long white braid that swung down her back. Her hazel eyes narrowed when she caught sight of the mage sitting with Audra. Recognizing the jealous look, Lua's smile broadened.

"Traq!" The woman's voice was deep.

The man turned, square jawed, and disappointingly attractive in a laborer sort of way. But he had no elegance whatsoever that Lua could see.

"We depart in an hour," she said. When Traq questioned her, she glanced at the patrons. Her eyes paused appreciatively on Lua before she spoke. "Foreign vessel heading toward southern waters and reports of missing fishers north of us."

She was probably more than a seven star, but Lua couldn't be certain. There was something sharper about her magic than her older companion's. She winked boldly when she caught Lua staring, adding a toothy grin. He coughed and turned to his meal, ignoring Traq's quick farewell to Audra. The meat was overdone, and it took work to chew and swallow it.

After the mages disappeared, Audra slid into the chair across from him. Her mannerisms bordered on hostile. "You enjoy spying?"

"Didn't have a choice since you rudely abandoned me so that you could meet with your Starling lover," he said. "You said that you hated them more than the Moon tribe."

Audra's laugh was humorless. "No. I said that I hate you both equally. Difficult to decide if it was your people's assaults or the Starling's opportunistic abuses that have done more damage." Audra glared until he looked away. "Traq's different. He'll always be Western tribe, no matter what colors he wears." She stabbed a piece of meat with her dagger and took a bite. The silence between them lengthened, neither looked at the other.

Finally, she said, "I was going to find you once we'd finished. Just thought it best to keep the two of you apart to prevent misunderstandings like this."

"You should have told me."

She raised one eyebrow. "Really? Do I owe you that, Moonie? Give me your name, then. Let's start there. It's strange that we're supposedly bonded and I don't know your damned name."

Lua pursed his lips. The less she knew, the better. It was bad enough she knew his stars. In the unlikely event that they separated, not knowing his identity might buy some time. Besides, with her obvious affection for the Starlings, he couldn't trust her. That trust worked both ways, that they'd have to rely on each other for the journey, was something he didn't want to acknowledge. His eyes flicked to the relic beneath her shirt, its power pulled at him. "That stone—"

"Is none of your concern. Don't even *think* about it," she snapped. Her fingers drummed on the table. "You're going to have to give me something if you want me to trust you. So far, you've proven to be one of the most arrogant and demanding people I've ever had the misfortune of crossing paths with. That your own people want you dead makes me wonder if they need any reason other than knowing you well."

He remained stoic. She didn't deserve a response. The monks would dispose of her once they reached the monastery. He'd just have to tolerate her until then. But she made everything so difficult.

She threw a disgusted look at him and stood. "Let's find an all'ight and horses before someone recognizes that boat moored in the public dock."

"We don't need all'ight. Moon mages can see clearly in the dark."

"Good for you, but I can't."

"I'll be the eyes for both of us." Forcing her to rely on him might teach her respect.

She cursed and turned away. "You're impossible."

Lua tossed random coins on the table and followed her into the street. When they rounded the corner, Traq blocked their way.

His jaw clenched as he glared at Lua over Audra's head. "Who's this?"

Audra's arms went out, creating a barrier between the two men with her body.

The Starling would be easy to kill. Three stars at most. His life force was thick and siphoning him would bolster Lua's stamina. Yet the press of Audra's hand against his chest stopped him. They had weeks together, and he didn't want them to be more miserable than they already were.

Her words flowed smooth as silk with an alarming conviction. "Traq, this is Chon. He helped me on the *Requin*."

Lua held his surprise in check. That Audra was able to lie so easily to someone whose affections were clear would have unnerved Lua if he hadn't felt the intention behind it. She wanted to protect her friend.

A muscle twitched in Traq's jaw as a hair-fine gold thread wriggled from his hand toward Lua. Lua choked down a dismissive chuckle for Audra's sake. He didn't bother deflecting the thread. Rather, he tucked his magic down and created a barrier so that the boy wouldn't sense anything.

"Where are you going?" Traq's words were leveled at Lua, but Audra answered.

"Nothing's changed," she said flatly. "We're headed to Ferin."

His eyes slid to Audra's. He didn't lower his voice. "You trust him?"

She took Traq's hand. "He saved my life."

Lua watched the softening of her shoulders and the way her head tilted. Had he saved her life, or did she truly believe that he had? Her mannerisms were sincere, and there was something in the way her fingers intertwined with Traq's that Lua didn't like. Maybe he should kill him for good measure.

"Do you trust me?" Audra asked. The tension left Traq's jaw as he nodded. "Then trust my choices."

That didn't sit well, but the boy could do nothing about it. The girl he cared for apparently had differing priorities and emotions. Lua considered there'd been versions of this conversation before. A wound festered behind Traq's eyes, one Lua wouldn't mind prodding.

"Traq!" The white-haired woman from before called from the end of the street, scowling as her eyes landed on their clasped hands. "Now."

Traq nodded to her, catching Lua's eye. He pulled Audra into a hug and whispered in her ear before hastening after the mage.

Lua waited for Traq to glance back before wrapping a possessive arm around Audra's shoulders and turning her away. Sadness shimmied down their thread as they took three synchronized steps.

Audra peeked back to catch Traq's expression. Then, with a curse, she shoved Lua away and stepped out of reach. "Asshole."

Sixteen

Xiang

The Western boats were small, rugged things that looked nearly as worn as the mix of men and women attending them. The villagers wore thin clothes and bamboo hats that shaded their golden-brown skin. They'd been too intimidated by the imposing *Bulou* to flee, and their location was so rural, it was unlikely the Starlings would come looking for them.

"Three men missing since yesterday. A man, his son, and a nephew. They should've returned last night, but there's no trace of them," Galia said. After coming across the grouping of boats with the same fading tribal symbol along their hulls, the lieutenant had rowed out to them to gather more information. The boats waited for the signal to move on.

The *Bulou*'s sails had changed from Moon tribe black to a bland off-white. Though they'd covered their robes, there was no disguising their manners, accents, or complexions. There wasn't a storm to blame, and the sea dragons were further north this time of year. Perhaps something else could be blamed for the loss of these boats, but it would be a difficult stage to set.

"What are they saying?" Xiang asked.

Galia cleared her throat. "One woman whispers of dragons taking them. Someone argued about the Moon tribe, but that was quickly quieted by the elder aboard. He said the Moons hadn't trifled with them in years. He thinks the man drank too much and sank it or hooked something that dragged them into the depths."

From aboard the largest of the boats, three men watched impatiently while the elder scurried around the deck. He yelled at the younger ones. When they ignored him a third time, he slapped one of them on the back of the head with a piece of rope. This drew the other men's attention, and they sprang into action, following the old man's orders.

"What are your thoughts?" Xiang asked, watching the elder.

"I believe them. Even if the youngsters suspect, the older one holds a tight grip on them. They won't defy him."

His eyes slid to hers, waiting. She knew what he was asking.

Galia's voice lowered. "If we kill them, we'll have to kill everyone on these boats. Such a loss would devastate their small community. Possibly doom them without their fishers or boats, especially moving into the colder season. And their deaths would risk an international incident."

"*If* we are caught," Xiang said. "The old man already knows us. You can tell he's trying to carry on like this is normal. He remembers what Moon ships look like. I'm sure of it. Is this all their boats?"

"Yes, sir."

Familiar tanned faces watched him. So much like the faces of his family and neighbors. One of the younger men resembled Bolin. Xiang made a half arc with one arm.

"Take us around," he ordered.

Galia's shoulders relaxed as the captain turned the wheel. She raised her arm, showing that they could go, but stopped when she saw Jayna and Nori standing silently beneath the awning. Soldiers manned the fire cannons, turning them as the ship swept slowly away and came in better view of the six boats. A dozen archers stood at the ready. The sad boats' close clustering made them an easy target.

"Sir?" she asked. "These aren't soldiers. They're simple people. We can't just—"

"Lieutenant, I caution you. Do not deign to tell me what we can and cannot do. My authority comes from our Oja directly. Would you rather risk the lives on this vessel?" he asked. "What will happen if they tell the Starlings that a strange ship visited them with new sails whose crew hid from Starling beneath silks?"

Galia's face fell.

"What will happen if the Starlings capture the Oji?"

Her eyes were glassy. "What of the rest of their village?"

"Be glad they're not here to suffer the same fate." He nodded to a soldier who sent an order down the line. They stuffed the cannons with mud and straw balls covered in oil and, as the ship came in full view of the smaller vessels, a long wand of all'ight was used to ignite each one.

The mages began their spells at Xiang's signal. The wind picked up. The cannons exploded, carrying fiery death toward the defenseless boats. A man dove into the water a moment before his boat burst in half. He reemerged twenty feet away. His limbs kicked furiously toward the distant shore. He didn't look back as people screamed when another volley of fire destroyed the remaining boats.

Xiang watched them burn; his emotions hid behind a stony expression. He motioned to the archers. "No survivors."

A slew of arrows hit people desperately treading water beside the remnants of their boats, but the swimmer was nearly out of reach. A young archer moved out of line toward the rail. She drew the bow, nocked the arrow, and aimed high. It arced against the sky, then fell slowly before finding its mark. The man's death was quiet. The water turned a murky red as he went limp.

Xiang looked back at Galia. "Make sure every board that floats is burned. Each body is weighted, dismembered, or seared. If people want to believe it might be a Western dragon returned, then give them no reason to doubt."

He noted her expression, saw the resignation he'd succumbed to years ago mirrored there, and turned away.

Below deck, Xiang retched into his chamber pot twice before the sweats left him. He splashed cool water on his face from the basin and sat back on his bed, rubbing his eyes. Killing his own people was never easy, but it was necessary.

Damn Lua.

If he hadn't escaped, they'd be close to home by now. These deaths, these things he was being made to do to protect his crew and the Moon tribe, were the Oji's fault.

There was still the mystery of Lua's anchor. The *Requin's* crew insisted the thief had left with him. If Lua'd had to drain three men before escaping, he hadn't fully bonded. Or, Xiang considered, his new anchor was nearly useless.

The *Requin* had been headed for Oxton. But there was no possibility of the *Bulou* simply sailing into port without prearranged authorization from the Starlings, which meant they'd have to take their hunt to land sooner. Jayna and Nori would have a difficult time, but they'd manage. It would be a stretch to blame dragons that hadn't graced the skies in decades, but the ignorant villagers might accept it. The Starlings would not.

After long hours of drunken pleasure, Bolin would often whisper about his mother who had come from a line of Western mages. She'd given up her dragon bond before he'd been born, and surely the beast had left long before the Moons destroyed their village. Xiang once ran his fingers over the red-scaled chest plate Bolin wore but considered them the way one might think of tales told around campfires—history long gone, fanciful and full of romanticism. People loved tales of the dragons and their mages. It gave them hope when there was none. And the culling of the anglers would only aid those stories. If nothing else, it would distract for a while—hopefully long enough to reclaim the Oji.

After returning to the deck, he ordered the ship closer to shore. He'd take a small squadron and the mages and place Galia in charge of the *Bulou*. He worried the proximity to the locals would weaken her resolve, and he couldn't have Jayna distracted by her lover's presence.

Neither of them would be happy about it, but they wouldn't complain. He promised to return Jayna safely to Uduary, but he saw the doubt in Galia's expression. She was losing faith in him. Jayna, at least, would be easier to control.

They understood their duty, just as he and Bolin did. And he understood something they did not know yet. Sometimes, for love to prevail, it needed to be separated. After all, people did terrible things in the name of love.

Xiang paused in his cabin and, on impulse, slipped the bloodstone into his pocket.

Seventeen

Audra

Audra shifted in the saddle, straining to gaze behind them once more. Moon's heavy exhalation lilted toward her. He'd covered the gelding in extra blankets and, even wearing gloves, avoided touching the horse as if it were diseased. It was odd, but the northerners were known to have strange ways, and she wasn't curious enough to question.

"No one's coming," he said.

She nudged her mare beside him, but Moon veered away, keeping several feet between the horses. "You never know with horses. Once they realize there's one missing, they'll be after our heads."

Moon looked ridiculous beneath the bamboo hat, but she kept that delight to herself.

"We paid for one. They won't notice the other until the spell fades tomorrow morning. By then, they won't even know who they're looking for."

"Will a spell that small hold for that long?"

"It depends on the intent behind the spell," he said. "Because you interfered with my original plan—"

"Murder draws attention, Moonie."

"My intention became only to create a little chaos. Releasing the other horses and stirring them up as you stole one. It will take them a while to collect them, and we are already safely away. The horses will be fine."

"Will it last?"

"No. But if a spell hits hard enough, and so long as the mage continues to live, it will work until it's done its job or is unable to continue."

Audra bit her lip. "What was the intent of that thing I dug out of your back?"

"Disable me. Prevent me from casting. Kill me if necessary."

"And when it could not fulfill the intention of its caster, it died?"

He nodded. "It's more complicated than that, but usually the nuances of casting are reserved for theoretical or philosophical discussions, so I'll spare you."

They lapsed back into silence, but it was easier somehow. The road they were on would lead them northwest through a small pass in the Shei-nam mountains. If they made good time, they might miss the first snow.

"Who is he to you?" Moon asked, glancing at her sideways.

"Traq?" She shifted again. "An old friend. We found each other after our villages were demolished."

"Just a friend?" Moon asked. "He acted like more."

She didn't like his questioning, but she was grateful that he'd kept his mouth shut in the street. Not instigating a fight with a Starling was probably out of character for him. "He's more like a brother. It's why he gets so protective."

He snickered. "Brothers don't hold their sisters like that. And what I saw was much more than friendly affection."

Her cheeks flushed. "I doubt you're a great example of what brotherly love is, given our current circumstances." He winced, but the satisfaction Audra had expected didn't come. Instead, the space between them was tense again, and it had been her own doing. She swallowed her apology and remained quiet for a long while. Guilt finally opened her mouth when they stopped to water the horses at a small creek.

"Traq and I were more once," she said cautiously, running her hand down the neck of the chestnut mare. "But Traq's objectives changed when a Starling mage saw something in him. He was young, impressionable. Who doesn't want someone strong to tell them they're special? He filled his head with magic and glory. Told him he'd look good in white armor." She shook her head. "He knew if he enlisted that would be the end of us. I told him, and he knows."

"What does he know?"

"My priorities lie elsewhere." She mounted her horse with a sigh. "He does look good in white armor though."

He cleared his throat. "Forgive me if I disagree."

Audra laughed.

The mountains loomed before them as the terrain changed slowly. Swaying taller grasses were slowly replaced by large stones interspersed beside the conifers she loved. The humidity of the sea had given way to an arid climate. She'd be home soon, and then Auntie Zin could help her figure out this mess with the Moon mage. Zin's tether to all things magic was innate, though when questioned, her answers were evasive or indirect. Zin's undying love for Audra's mother was still strong, and that affection had always extended to her children. She'd kept Ferin well for the last fifteen years, despite the challenges that came with the task.

A pair of argentavas soared above. The huge predatory birds swept one direction, then arced and headed back the way they'd come, casting an enormous shadow over the path before them. They could be a problem if they became overly curious or hungry and had been known to feast on entire families before. The birds' numbers had grown over the last few decades according to Auntie, who said their only natural predator was the western dragons.

"Where is Ferin? I've never heard of it," Moon said. A gentle tug turned her toward him as easily as she steered the mare.

"Ferin isn't a place," she said. They were too close for her to lie anymore. She needed his cooperation. "Ferin is my brother."

He swayed upon his gelding. The subtle change in his expression was inviting.

"He's with our aunt just past the cutoff for Stonetown." She cleared her throat nervously. "The jade is for him."

The connection between them tightened, as if he were probing for truth.

Her chest warmed, and she closed her eyes. A thick rope spun of entwined threads spanned between them. The silvery things pulsed like a living entity. She tapped her surprise down. In her mind's eye, she saw where his long fingers pulled and, reaching out, she pulled back.

His grunt opened her eyes, but she refused to acknowledge what she believed had just happened. The tightness in her chest eased.

"Why does he need it?" he asked.

Audra pursed her lips, deciding what to share. Her voice started softly beneath the weight of his attention. "When your . . ." No, that wouldn't help the strain between them. "When our village fell, a spell struck Ferin."

"What kind of spell?"

She shook her head. "Don't know. He's not been right since, and that was fifteen years ago."

Moon was quiet, contemplative. "Injuries?"

"Stunted growth. Can't speak or communicate consistently. Sometimes he draws; sometimes he gestures. We've tried alternate forms of communication, but he forgets everything soon after learning it. Repetition doesn't help." There was a chasm of sadness in her voice. "It's been like that with everything. That's why I asked earlier about the spells. I guess the one who cast it still lives."

Starling tucked behind the mountains, causing Moon's relief to sweep toward her. "It still hurts beneath the robes and the hat?" she asked.

"Starling burns. I'm at my strongest when both moons are full."

She'd always assumed that the Moon tribes gave greater homage to the smaller Song, who was present thirty days a month, rather than the larger, slower moon whose cycles were almost double that.

He studied the sky. "Most people don't realize that the Moon tribe is divided. Song is more popular, certainly. She's readily available, consistent in her orbits. But fickle. Silence is stronger. He gathers strength in slow, precise movements. Nothing is done without great foresight. You must choose which moon to serve when you get your first star as a mage."

"And you chose Silence?"

He nodded. "His crescent will be rising in another hour. Then we can pick up our pace."

Audra's shoulders and backside ached. "Aren't we stopping for the night?"

He didn't answer, but Audra caught the wisps of magical thread that spun out to their horses, quickening their steps.

His voice strained slightly as he asked, "Which tribe cast the spell that struck your brother?"

Audra stared at the tip of Mount Shi as it blushed in shadow. The image of the pale woman flashed through her mind. "It was a Moon mage."

Eighteen

Traq
Starling Mage

Despite the windowless room the mages shared on the boat, a thin stream of moonlight whispered through the planks above Traq's head and slid onto his pillow. The lower ranks were given the top bunks for situations like these. He should have hung a sheet or scarf just in case, but he'd forgotten. It hadn't been that long ago that the moons hadn't affected him at all. But that was the price of Starling magic.

Durin snored softly below him. Though the older Quinta, five star, exuded a gentleness that drew people in, he fumbled spells occasionally and drifted into stories without end. He had less than a year until he retired to Callaway with his husband. He'd introduced the eccentric man before they'd left the island. Traq hoped to take Durin's place when he retired, even if that meant he had to test for two more stars before then.

Septra Wren was seven stars and the highest ranking in their triad. She slept on a single bunk with her back to them. Her white braid hung off the bed, brushing the floor with the ship's gentle rock. Rumor said she'd begun training in childhood, a documented tenth generation mage from esteemed lineage, but she never spoke of family other than her sister. If it were true, she'd had no other choice in life than this. Although she was only a few years older than Traq, she'd be testing for her eighth soon.

As the boat shifted, moonlight slipped off his pillow and crept across the floor. It danced on the tip of Wren's braid. One of her slender hands reached out and tucked it beneath the covers. Wren's beauty was intimidating, and she had a natural charisma that drew the eyes of potential lovers. Yet in the two years they'd been in the same squadron, she'd only taken one lover and quickly discarded them. Durin whispered that someone already had her heart, but why she didn't pursue them was none of Traq's business.

He rolled over and sighed. Audra had looked thin. He didn't like her hair chopped off, not that he'd ever say something so foolish to her. Hearing her say she didn't care about his opinion would bother him more. He'd hoped after enlisting that she'd come around, but that would never happen. It's not that she'd lied to him, more like he had lied to himself. She'd always been honest with him.

When she'd found him on Callaway before their vessel departed, his feelings and those damn hopes had swayed him. If he'd been caught smuggling the jade for her, Lord Ijion would have ordered a star stripped from him—a painful process from what he'd heard. Being a Westerner in Starling robes was difficult enough as it was, and he shouldn't have risked making his situation worse, not until he found what he was looking for in the southern lands.

He'd always known that Ferin came first to Audra but seeing her with someone else stung. Although Audra had introduced the man as Chon, a typical islander name, the man looked northern, too pale beneath his woven hat. He'd burn pink under the mountain sky. Traq smiled. The man's hair had been tucked beneath his hat and robes, but he looked common enough. Maybe it was only jealousy, but something struck him wrong about the whole thing. He'd been too offended when he caught them together to realize what it was. Audra didn't trust anyone other than himself and Zin. She'd once told him she'd rather travel alone than listen to someone prattle on. Yet there she was, sneaking around with some common man when she should have been waiting for him.

Traq exhaled in self-admonishment. Audra wouldn't wait for anyone. It would be like trapping her in a cage. She'd do anything to get out.

Zin might kill Chon if she met him. Traq chuckled to himself.

"Traq?" Wren didn't bother whispering. It took a couple of hard shoves to ever wake Durin. Being the highest rank, she had the authority to address either he or Durin by their names or titles, depending on her mood. However, both of them were required to refer to her by her ranking.

"Yes, Septra?"

"If you can't be quiet, I'll send you to sleep on deck beneath the silks." She rolled enough to peer at him over one shoulder. "Understood?"

He shifted awkwardly. Sleeping on deck without proper covering would ensure a miserable night since the moonlight would sting every time it brushed over his skin. "Yes, Septra."

The three mages stood beneath a clear morning sky studying the remaining shadow of violence in the surrounding water. Luck had it that there'd been no storms in a couple of days, and the waves had carried some of the wreckage to the shoreline in the distance.

The crew pulled boards from the sea and piled them on the deck. The edges were burned black. After hauling an examination table from storage, they placed a man's torso on top of it. Chunks of flesh had been nibbled away, exposing white, jagged ribs. As Traq stepped closer to examine it, a sea worm wriggled free from the remaining chest muscle and raised its flat head in the light. Wren pinched it between two fingers until it popped. She wiped her fingers on the table's surface before wrinkling her nose at the shifting wind. The fetor of decay wafted over them.

Durin gagged and stepped back. But Traq swallowed his bile and stayed firm. No good would come from showing weakness here.

Wren's gaze moved swiftly across the boards. "What do you see, Tresa?"

Traq held his breath as the wind hit his face. "These ships weren't burned by magic. Maybe the body was attacked, or at least made to look like it." He paused until Wren nodded for him to continue. "The wood might have been hit with a fire cannon, but the markings seem a bit too even, like it was burned after."

Durin scrunched his eyes and leaned closer to the wood. "The damage reminds me of my mother's tales, when the Western dragons attacked vessels for drawing too near their territory in the mountains."

"It was probably made to look that way," Wren said. "Do you detect any magic at all?"

Durin turned away. With his retirement so near, he'd lost interest in reaching for a sixth star.

Traq's thread skimmed over the boards and found nothing. Then it searched the rotting flesh only to find more worms squirming within. As the thread drew back, he paused. A subtle hint of magic drifted in the air, dissipating slowly.

He met Wren's gaze. "On the wind."

She smiled. "Very good, Tresa. Mage wind carried the fire. The bodies were hacked up individually. It must have been gruesome work for whoever did it."

Traq's mouth was dry. All Starling mages were registered, their whereabouts logged with careful detail to prevent anything like this from happening. They'd checked the log before leaving Oxton. No Starling mage had been in this vicinity in nearly a month. "Who could've done this?"

Wren's countenance was reserved as she ordered the captain to take them to shore where several villagers picked through the corpses, searching for their missing.

Sand gave beneath Traq's boots as he followed Wren and a handful of soldiers from one of the row boats. Durin stayed back, it was regimental form to keep one mage with the ship, and he'd been happy to volunteer.

An elderly man with knobby knees leaned on a younger woman as they hunched over part of a corpse, its bloated face was purple and green. Another woman held a small, crying child on her hip as she walked slowly amongst the carnage with tears staining her face.

An old woman reminded Traq of his grandmother, face weathered by salt and starling, revealing a hard history. She was lean, had probably never known a day of rest in her entire life. Her calloused hands turned over boards and sifted handfuls of sand. She looked up at Raia and mumbled a prayer Traq knew by heart, but he kept his lips tight. A moment later, she hobbled into the thicker brush.

Wren was talking to the old man, Traq winced at her attempts at the rural Western dialect. Though the language was essentially the same, the inflection and change in certain words could cause confusion or offense if not spoken thoughtfully. The soldiers spread out along the shore, turning over wreckage and placing those bodies with heads face up for easier identification.

A wail erupted from the brush. Traq found the older woman squatting beside a corpse, fat tears streamed down her cheeks. The body was face down, its limbs half covered in sand. Small crabs had picked at flesh before scuttling away. A black fletched arrow jutted from the base of his neck toward the sky. Only one tribe used arrows so black.

He turned at Wren's sharp intake of breath. They exchanged a small look before the old woman leaned into Traq and sobbed. He wrapped an arm around her bony shoulders and allowed her to beat his chest until her arms wearied. When the soldiers claimed the body, he gently guided her toward the woman with the child.

"We should leave him," he said, watching the men carry the body toward the boat. "Won't the arrow be enough?"

Wren's lips pursed. "It would be best to examine everything intact." She glanced at the old woman. "Tell her we'll give him a warrior's burn when we're done."

Traq lowered himself as he spoke to the woman. Wren didn't know, but Western traditions cared nothing about warrior burns. They cared about their life mattering somehow, and that included their deaths. Life could grow from tragedy by feeding the ground, insects, or animals. No death need be wasted. Everything was connected. But the Southerners didn't understand that, and this wasn't the time to explain.

The old woman begged. This was her only grandchild. She'd raised him after her daughter died. He'd be a father soon. She wanted to take the body home. If they took him, he'd be gone forever. He calmed her by holding her hands and promising to find the killers.

"Do you swear on your life?" she asked.

Even her dark eyes were like his grandmother, who'd buried six children between disease and battles and been fortunate enough to die before seeing all but one of her grandchildren slaughtered during the Moon's last insurgence. "I swear."

The old woman stood on the shore until they had secured their boat to the Starling vessel, watching them raise her grandson's corpse onto the deck. Then she disappeared into the brush, taking her grief with her. The back of Traq's throat quivered with restrained emotions.

Wren stood beside him, distant enough to be respectful. Her voice was thick, tone difficult to discern. "At least we know who we are dealing with."

Traq leaned on the rail and stared out at the sea, wondering if she was right.

Nineteen

Lua

Lua prayed to Silence as it rose above them. His god hadn't spoken to him since the *Mirren*, but absorbing the moonlight left Lua feeling better than he had in weeks. He savored it like a rare wine or a deep kiss. It kept him from drawing on Audra too much. The food over the last few days was renewing her strength, but she'd still be useless if he had to use a larger spell. That would make them both vulnerable.

The argentava that had been stalking them for several hours, circled above. Its twenty-foot wingspan momentarily blocked out the moon before it dove into the trees in the distance, reemerging a few minutes later. Whatever wriggled in its talons was unidentifiable. Another bird rose to meet it. They circled each other, cawing in familiarity as they flew toward the mountain tops. Lua hoped that was the last of them.

Audra dozed on her horse. He'd already caught her from slipping off the saddle twice. The second time, he took the reins from her hand and let her drape across the mare's neck. They'd have to stop soon. The horses were tiring. Though he could force them on, it would be foolish to risk all their lives for his impatience.

It was more than Audra's disposition that frustrated him. That she was equal parts easy-going and demanding and held as many secrets as he did, made their conversations awkward. But when he'd tried forcing the truth from her by tightening the thread, there'd been resistance. It could be her strong will, or possibly the jade.

There were legends that spoke of advantages the Western mages had over the other tribes. He doubted she knew much about the jade or where it came from. Audra would have been a child during the Moon's last assault.

The Rajav had made it his life's mission to destroy the Western mages, their monasteries, and the dragons. And over the course of his long life, he'd damn near succeeded.

There weren't many detailed accounts of the western artifacts. Where the Moon tribe was secretive, the Westerners were downright covert. Their spells were written in ancient script, most of which they'd destroyed rather than sacrifice to their enemies. Even after decades of slaughter, the remaining populace refused to cooperate, either feigning ignorance or choosing death instead of sharing their knowledge.

Audra's need for the relic sparked his curiosity. She'd been honest about her brother. Those feelings were deep and authentic, but there was much omitted. He didn't think the jade could break a spell. His father said that dragon's eye was used to enhance Western magic, not break it. But Lua doubted what he knew.

His anchors spent ten years in study and meditation to strengthen their minds and ability to focus while controlling their emotions before even being considered for the position. Never mind the expected physical training. They'd each been steady, predictable, unwavering streams of energy.

Being anchored to Audra was like breathing beneath a waterfall. She was a constant chaotic rush of fluctuating emotions. How could one person feel so intensely all the time? Severing their bond would be a blessing. He'd never again take for granted the boring anchors he'd grown accustomed to. He tried not to think about what would happen at the monastery. Her fate wasn't his concern or responsibility. A twinge in his gut told him that was a lie.

When the terrain steepened, making nighttime travel more treacherous, they found a clearing between two trees to camp in. Audra curled beneath a blanket as her mare stamped down the grass and nestled into slumber. The gelding stood nearby, swaying. Lua leaned against a trunk and closed his eyes. Only for a moment, he told himself.

Panic ripped him from a dream of fire and beating wings. It took a moment to understand what he saw.

The screaming mare was suspended five feet above the ground. Audra clutched one forefoot, yelling, and cursing as the horse's legs kicked. An argentava's talons ripped through the horse's abdomen. One hoof skimmed the top of Audra's head, but she stubbornly held on. She stood on her toes as the bird's wings threw dust into Lua's eyes. The bird screeched and snapped its razor-sharp beak.

As another hoof brushed the top of Audra's skull, Lua flew toward her. His arms wrapped around her waist as the bird began to pull them skyward. The horse's cries escalated as the talons pierced deeper. Blood painted the ground.

"Let her go," he said, sending a command along the thread. Audra's fingers softened for a second before clutching the leg firmly. "Let go!"

Her body was taut against him. "Save her!"

The horse was doomed. A spell would drain them both. He shook his head. "Audra—"

"Save her, damn you!"

Energy surged into Lua's arms where he held her. Heat coursed through him, cascading over his skin and perching behind his ribs. A silver band whipped from his hand. It cracked, raking the argentava's wing. The bird screeched, one claw releasing as Audra screamed again. A second thread lashed from his fingers, slashing across the bird's neck. The force sent it hurtling backward to the ground. It bounced twice and lay broken in a cloud of dust, unable to rise.

Lua pulled Audra away as the mare crashed down. The horse kicked twice, crying piteously as blood gushed out.

The pulse of Audra's heart moved through him. He held her, the warmth of her body pressing into him. Their threads snugged.

She broke from him and dropped beside the gasping mare, mindless of the blood that stained her clothes. Her hands pressed against the deepest wound, but blood leaked through her fingers and slipped beneath her palms.

"No, no, no, no, no," she pleaded. She looked up at Raia and whispered. Lua knelt behind her. His exhaustion was held at bay only by the rays of both moons upon his skin.

"Audra," he said softly, trying to settle her. Tugging on the thread caused her to turn large eyes on him.

"You can save her," she said. "Please."

"That's not how my magic works," he said simply.

"But thirteen stars. You can. You must."

"There's no saving her." His gut wrenched with the anguish that came from her. Lua held her gaze. "The only mercy now is to end her suffering."

Audra sucked in a breath. "You'd kill her?"

"She'll be dead in an hour," he said, his eyes trained on the downed bird. "Less, if we are kind."

He started toward the bird, trying to block the mix of unfamiliar emotions that suddenly chafed his insides. Foreign tears leaked from his eyes. "I'll let you decide."

The argentava snapped and squirmed at his approach. Long indigo feathers scattered across the ground, shining in the moonlight. One wing was torn awkwardly. Blood blackened the ground, pulsing from a neck wound that closed and reopened as the bird thrashed. Lua placed a steady hand upon the wing. The bird snapped once before Lua pulled the life from its body. Energy coursed through him as the bird stiffened. Feathers fell from its crumbling husk.

He searched for the gelding, who'd raced away when the bird attacked. After a few minutes, his magic found the beast trembling a few hundred yards away, trapped between fallen trees and brambles. Lua reached a tender thread out and coaxed it back.

Audra whispered into the mare's ear. He couldn't hear her words but knew her intent. Mercy. A terrible kindness.

"I can—" It was over before he finished his words. Her blade caught the light as it fell.

The mare's eyes went empty. The blood dripping down the dagger added another crimson layer to Audra's hands. Her lip quivered as she stroked the horse a few more times. Then she stood, the strength of her will suppressing her grief. Lua wondered if she did it to avoid crying more before him, or if it was something she was accustomed to.

A ragged sigh shivered between them. Blood and tears wearied her face. Her expression nagged at him, as if he should say or do something. But for all Lua's stolen years and high education, he had no clue what that something was.

He cleared his throat at the sudden constriction and turned away. "We should go."

Twenty

Audra

They left the mare where she'd fallen. Audra hoped that carrion would make good use of her flesh so that her death wouldn't be for nothing. She should have let the argentava have her, then at least one of them would still be alive.

Audra clenched her jaw to keep her teeth from chattering. Though it had been hours since she'd rinsed the blood from her body and clothes in a small creek, the thinning mountain air forced the remaining dampness into her skin.

Moon subtly kicked stones from her path and offered her water every so often. He was considerate in small, unexpected ways and perhaps not as sullen as she initially took him for. She'd expected him to chastise her, shame her for her impulsivity and recklessness, but he'd barely spoken. She was grateful for that.

After Moon drew the horse back with a spell, the gelding was still skittish. Audra stroked its neck every so often. Petting its stiff coat seemed to bring them both reassurances.

The horse trailed behind the pair as they walked. It didn't need to be said that neither of them had any desire to ride together. Nothing good could come of such proximity. Something strange stirred within her every time they touched. Maybe it was the anchoring, but it caused contrasting feelings of vulnerability and empowerment, edging on desire. After observing Moon's expression for the past few days, she saw it unsettling him too.

Auntie Zin might have an explanation if she didn't try to kill the Moon mage first. Being a creature of magic, Zin knew things that defied reasoning, but her answers were rarely direct. And where Audra didn't trust anyone, Zin damn near hated everyone. It had taken a solid year of Traq sleeping in the barn before Zin called him by his name. Her personality was difficult, but her heart was good. Even if it was wrapped in bitterness and fire.

Ferin would smile and hug her tight, smelling of burnt cedar. If the jade worked the way it was supposed to, they'd both be stronger for it.

"The Heitung pass will put us closer to the border," Moon said.

"It always gets the first snow. It might be covered already. If we follow the Shei road to—"

"We can make it over the pass. That way will take too long."

"These mountains are my home, and I know them better than you do," she said.

He stifled a sigh beneath the shade of his hat. Moon hadn't slept half as much as Audra, and she saw the effects that travelling in full Starling had on him. That he seemed too tired to argue was revealing. She'd grown accustomed to the occasional tug behind her sternum that left her glazed with momentary fatigue, but he hadn't pulled on it all day. That he was exhausted and not using her energy was unusual. But she wasn't foolish enough to mention it.

She looked back at him. "There's a path at the crest and a small cave about a quarter mile east. It's big enough for the three of us to rest in. We could let the light fade a bit."

His eyes narrowed suspiciously as he tested the thread and took a sip of her energy. "Lead on."

An hour later Moon eyed the cave's ancient paintings of flying dragons above the sea before he headed to the deepest recess. Audra settled the horse down to rest and guarded the cave's entrance.

Although they hadn't seen anyone else on the road, it was wise to keep watch.

Moon curled atop the blanket. Exhaustion rolled from him in waves. Audra nibbled on their remaining jerky while trying, and failing, to keep her gaze anywhere other than him. She bit her lip and studied him.

Moon's initial insistence on letting the bird have the horse had been correct. Audra should have let go, but she'd panicked. The mage's sudden compliance and killing the argentava had made him more distant than ever, not necessarily a bad thing.

Audra closed her eyes, searching for the thread she'd caught glimpses of before. It took a few minutes of deep breathing and concentration for it to pulse before her. It was more vivid than the last time she'd seen it. The silvery rope shimmered with smaller yarns and strands of white and gray mixed. Very different from the other—

She startled, sitting upright. A separate fiber was subtly interwoven with the silver. Vibrating shades of green—like the leaves of summer trees or moss on the forest floor or the jade strung around her neck. It snaked through the yarn, glimmering and pulsing with a rhythm different from the silver. She didn't think it had been there before.

Audra reached out, running fingers along the green strand. It thrummed down the length of rope and undulated toward the other end.

Her eyes flew open as Moon moaned. A sheen of sweat dappled his brow as he twitched. Nightmare. She wondered what could scare him; he seemed dauntless. Like he'd been tested so often he ardently believed that failure was never an option. She closed her eyes again, but the threads didn't reappear.

Moon woke less irritable than when he'd lain down, but it wasn't until they'd trekked back to the path that he spoke. "How'd you know about the cave?"

"I needed hiding spots when I first started out," she said.

He looked at her quizzically. "Started out?"

"Stealing was how I survived when I first left Auntie's. Food, clothing, necessities. I'm not proud of it." She shrugged. "But as I got better, I could be more selective about those I stole from. Eventually I got enough of a reputation that people commissioned me. Having places to hide is an occupational necessity."

"Why leave your aunt's?" he asked. "If your brother is still with her, what was your reason?"

Audra slipped on a rock. She landed on one knee and cursed. Sitting down, she pulled up her stained pant leg to reveal a scrape. She hissed at the sting. A trickle of blood ran down her shin.

Moon's expression went strange, as if deciding something. He slowly raised his eyes to hers.

"Do you know why I pulled you away from the horse last night?" Avoiding the Starling light, he dragged up his pant leg. A collection of fine scars crisscrossed his skin, more than she'd noticed in the *Requin's* dim light. Bright blood trailed from his knee, where a scrape that matched hers had appeared. His magic coursed down their thread, jolting her. Her wound stopped bleeding and stitched itself together. His eyes glazed as his own scrape continued to bleed.

"What . . . ?" Audra looked from her knee to his in confusion. When he pulled on the thread, a wave of fatigue swam over her. His wound clotted and healed a moment before his pant leg fell back down.

Her mouth was dry. She remembered when her head swam the first time, when she watched him heal in the brig. "When I cut the bolt out of you—"

"I drew on your strength. Just as I can also help heal you by giving you some of mine." He pulled off his glove and offered her his hand. "It's true that I've done terrible things, but I've never been a good liar."

Audra stared at his hand. Their bond was deep magic, life itself, and she hadn't wanted to believe it. But there was no denying the evidence. "You said we live or die together."

A few strands of black hair slipped from the hat to frame his face. "And we are strong or weak together." The strange emotion in his silver eyes beckoned to her.

She slid her hand into his, the chill in her bones vanishing at the flush of warmth. He pulled her to her feet as the threads between them hummed. They stood inches apart, but neither moved away. His palm was strong against hers.

Moon reached up with his other hand, wiping a spot of dried blood from her brow. The pull between them snugged until the gelding snorted. They drew back, gently pulling their hands apart.

She cleared her throat and hustled past him, moving up the path. "We'll be at Auntie's in another day. Maybe some Western magic can help us."

He paused. "I thought all the Western mages were dead."

Audra did not reply.

Twenty-One

Traq

Though the morning was pleasantly crisp, Traq's mood was somber as he stepped from the *Lightness* onto the dock. Examining the corpse had revealed nothing more than they'd already determined. The arrow had severed an artery; the villager died quickly. No hints of magic at all, just a talented archer.

Traq was almost off the pier, planning the quick route to the barracks when a familiar sigil caught his eye. A small boat bobbed at the far end of the public holds. It had been there when they'd departed, but he'd not paid any attention to it. Wren paused behind him.

"Aren't those the same markings we pulled from the water?" he asked.

She inhaled and brushed past him. "Good eye, Tresa."

According to the guards at the pier, the boat had been there for days, that they didn't know specifics was unsurprising because of their rotations. They'd been waiting for someone to claim it so they could collect the docking fees but were beginning to think it was abandoned.

There was nothing on board, no trace of magic or spell casting, only some half-eaten rice balls left to rot in their palm leaves. This was the missing boat that prompted the villagers' search, only to find their doom.

What happened to the men on this boat remained a mystery. Traq ran a thread over the rails once more and found nothing. Not even the thin sails offered their secrets. If magic were used it had already dissipated.

Wren called him from the dock, white braid trailing over one shoulder. She'd inquired with the local guards about any unusual activity over the last few days. Nothing too out of the ordinary for a port town this size—a few items stolen from street vendors, a horse that couldn't be accounted for, and a finer clothier who reported a break in.

"What was stolen?" Wren asked the shopkeeper, Mirza Hansin. They'd already visited the vendors and were heading to the livery next but had yet to find a lead. Though Wren insisted some of these events were likely related.

Mirza Hansin wore floral-embroidered silks tied at the waist. Her painted lips went thin. "I already went over this when I made my report."

Traq's smile disarmed her. He leaned across the counter, exuding warmth. "Please, mirza. We're trying to help."

She blushed beneath her rouge. "A couple of outfits. Nothing flashy or bold. The most expensive thing they took was a pair of boots, left a rank pair of sandals to stink up the store. I suppose I should be grateful they didn't grab the silks. Probably just urchins, but I'd like some sort of compensation. With the economy the way it's been, anything would help."

"You said 'they.' What makes you think it was more than one person?" Wren asked.

"One set of clothing was smaller, the other larger. Why would one person steal separate sizes?" she asked.

"Colors?" Wren asked.

"Green and blue robes. I've already given a description of the clothes to the man who was here the other day."

"Is there anything else you can think of?" Traq asked. "Anything unusual?"

She glanced between the two mages. "They left their clothes behind.

I tried to give them to the other guard, but he wasn't interested. One set of rags just dumped on the floor, the other in the alleyway out back."

"Do you still have them?" he asked.

A few minutes later, Wren stepped outside with the filthy clothes placed kindly in a linen bag. Mirza Hansin gripped Traq's arm nervously after the door closed, holding him back a step.

"Why are you with them?" she asked.

It was a question he was used to. Enlisting with the Starlings was an act of betrayal. Every Westerner harbored justifiable distrust of both Moons and Starlings, but the southern tribe had been more covert in their atrocities than the northern one. He leaned toward her. "I'm doing what I can."

Her eyes went suddenly glassy. Painted lips trembled. "They stole my mother when I was young. My sister twenty years ago. All dragged south." Her breath shuddered. "Do you know what they've—"

"Everything all right?" Wren asked, leaning in the doorway.

Traq patted the woman's hand once before prying her fingers away. "Yes, I'm coming." He nodded to the woman as he left.

She wiped her eyes and turned away.

Wren spread the clothing out on a long table in their barracks and examined each shirt, a slight furrow between her brows. "Interesting," she said. "Matching blood stains on the sleeves. Anything on the pants?"

He shook his head. "Just dirt."

Wren wrinkled her nose, drawing the bloody sleeves closer. She sent a small magic thread out and watched as the dried blood moved on each corresponding sleeve. Teased by her small influence, drops rose in the air and moved toward each other. A silvery, thin fiber spun between them, latching them together.

She gasped and stepped back.

Traq leaned in curiously. "What is that?"

"A bonding," she said. "Advanced magic, forbidden to even speak of until we get close to our tenth star. Lord Ijion won't even discuss it." Her eyes slid to his. "It's dark stuff."

Something in his gut gnawed. "I've never heard of it."

"It allows a mage to use another's life to strengthen their magic," Wren said.

"Does it kill them?"

She shook her head. "Not necessarily. A bond combines life energies, doubles the impact of every spell, depending on the individual strength of those bound." Her eyes widened as the blood drew toward each other in the air. "I've never seen evidence of one before. This was at least a ten star mage."

Traq chilled. Other than Lord Ijion, he wasn't sure how many other members of the senate held a ten star ranking. "We should tell Senior Monk Altho."

Wren stared at the blood, wearing a strange expression. "You could do a lot with a bond like that. Defeat whole squadrons. Create spells that last for years. Live forever."

"What do you mean?"

"In theory, and this is only what I've read in the archives, a strong bond lengthens the life of the mage well beyond what's natural."

"What about the other one?" Traq wasn't sure what to call the person being used and didn't stop to question why Wren would be researching such a thing to begin with.

Her jaw tightened. "The texts weren't specific about that, but according to a Moon folktale, one mage had seven bonds simultaneously. Do you know who that was?"

Traq shook his head.

"The founder of the Moon tribe. Yueliang himself. Supposedly, he lived for six hundred years. Thank the stars that Taiyang saw the truth and led our people to the light."

Every tribe had different stories about Yueliang and Taiyang. In the north, Taiyang was called *the Great Betrayer*. The Starlings called him *the Great Redeemer*. But the truth of the brothers' division was lost in time. And while Yueliang's life and death was well documented, Taiyang's fate was unknown. The Western monks had assumed he'd perished in the desert sands after teaching the southerners the ways of magic.

Sometimes Wren's words passed devotion into zealotry, but the seduction of power could sway anyone. Traq swallowed. "But each person they were bound to had to die. That sounds sad."

Wren huffed. "Moons don't care about that. They don't feel the way we do. Another monk told me that the Rajav Li-Hun Koray is rumored to have bonded to a dragon once." She shrugged. "No proof, of course, but nothing the Moons do would surprise me. May Starling blaze our path and remind us to be grateful for Taiyang's guidance. Only those that walk in the light have real strength." She saw the look on his face at the second mention of the Starling founder and sighed. "But you should probably tell Senior."

"Me? They'll know I didn't find the bond."

She rested her hand on his. "You'll be testing soon. They'll want to see your ambition. You need to do this."

He didn't pull his hand away, but a nagging question snuck into his brain. "What color did Mirza Hansin say the stolen robes were?"

Her eyes narrowed slightly. "Green and blue."

Traq stared at her, hoping she wouldn't remember the clothing Audra and Chon wore at their meeting.

Wren withdrew her hand and cut her spell. The two drops of blood flew together and sparked green and silver before vanishing. Her voice turned cold. "Tell Senior now. We need to prevent them from killing more innocents."

Traq's throat tightened. "Yes, Septra."

Twenty-Two

Xiang

The small squadron wore muted-colored robes over their black ones. The bland tones of Xiang's native land were uncomfortable. He'd grown unaccustomed to the warmer climate, and perspiration stuck his clothing to his skin.

As they trudged down the road and the terrain shifted from compacted sand to hardened dirt, abandoned structures littered the landscape. The remnants of past destruction, felled ruins of monasteries and villages, were mostly concealed by the greedy climbing vines that had taken over.

In his prior assignments with this triad, Xiang had relied on Nova Verina to act as a buffer between Nori and Jayna. Nori was petty and insecure around the younger, stronger mage, and his disrespectful behavior did nothing but accentuate his weaknesses to the others. Jayna could handle herself, certainly, but Verina often interceded before it escalated. As the soldiers shifted hastily around the pair of mages, it seemed the tension between them was spreading, and Xiang would have to intervene.

Jayna had stopped to empty out her boot. Nori stood beside her with crossed arms. His voice was slightly elevated. Their conversations always looked like arguments and, as usual, the man refused to acknowledge her rank, using her name too frequently.

At eight stars, Jayna was second in command, but she only spoke with authority when angered. The concern on her face didn't seem to spring from Nori for a change. She dusted the sand from her pants and shook her head as Xiang neared. A sheen of perspiration gleamed on both of their brows.

Nori shook his head. "The Oji was at Brav and Elicia's bonding, practically raised Rayan from her second to her sixth star. She adored him. To kill them like that . . ."

"Makes you wonder, doesn't it?" Jayna asked, lowering her voice.

"What made him turn on his people?"

She shook her head. "Why do we want him back so badly that we'll sacrifice so much, and how did he survive killing his own anchor when he was alone? I thought the mage council had to assist with the separation, or it would kill you."

"Best keep that first question to yourself, Octra. It wouldn't be wise to have Oja Selene question your loyalties." Xiang noted the small wince mirrored in the mage's expressions at the Oja's name. "But if you figure out that second part, I'd be much obliged."

He'd counted on Jayna's former association with the Silence monastery being useful. Her training had begun with Silence, but she'd switched to Song after Sharine, the head of the Song mages, recognized the young woman's ambition.

The monasteries didn't like to share their secrets, and Rayan had been one of the few Silence devotees to be sent on assignments. If Rayan hadn't already been on the *Mirren*, Xiang would have chosen her triad instead. But he'd never admit that to Jayna. The young woman often looked at him like a neglected child who thrived on praise.

They'd started down the path again when Jayna asked, "How many anchors has the Oji had?"

"I've only known Dain and Kristo—he was nearing his end when I met him—but perhaps two or three others before that, given his years," Nori said. "The Ojis appear young, but once anchored, years could theoretically be limitless." He shrugged. "Provided the anchors are replaced after being drained."

Xiang listened quietly as the conversation dwindled into theories and conjecture, arguing the semantics of breaking a bond. It was a delicate spell traditionally requiring the aid of other mages. If not careful, the life of the dying anchor could drag the mage into death with them. Jayna believed that managing it alone was impossible.

"Desperation makes anything possible," Xiang said. "Especially with enough stars."

The Rajav had reached fifteen stars before he died and, even though she'd rarely been seen over the last few decades, Raani Amala had been with him for an unprecedented hundred-and-fifty years. Though the Rajav had forbidden the scholars from discussing Amala's longevity, there were rumors that she haled from Western mage lineage. But whether or not that was true didn't ultimately matter. She had no magic, and her body had practically disintegrated in her bed from the constant drain. Xiang hoped the same fate didn't await Bolin.

"And how many anchors has the Oja had?" Jayna asked.

Xiang's step hitched before recovering quickly. His tone chilled. "Four that I know of, but now isn't the time for such questions. We must secure the Oji before he draws the Starlings to our borders. We'll set the silks up soon. Hopefully, we can find shelter before midday," Xiang said. "Any leads?"

Jayna glanced at Nori. It was clear they'd disagreed on something, but for once he deferred to her.

"I think we should head toward Oxton," she said.

Xiang looked between them. "Are we sure?"

Nori's jaw clenched as Jayna explained their conflict. He'd picked up a thread angled inland toward the mountains. But there was also a trace of Lua's magic coming from the city. She said, "It's possible he was in Oxton and moved toward the pass, but that feels strange to me."

When Xiang stopped walking, the others ceased as well. He looked down the road in either direction then studied the sharp mountain peaks as they caught dawn's first rays.

"I trust your judgement, Octra. But I like to think I know the Oji better than you." Xiang's tone was nearly apologetic. "We head to the mountains."

"Sir?" Jayna asked, stifling her disappointment.

"He'll be desperate to reach the monastery and will need to get over the pass as quickly as possible. I'm sure his supporters will meet him there."

Jayna pulled her hood up to hide her face from the morning rays peeking through the trees.

"Will Silence still hold loyalty to him after what he did to the Rajav and Rayan?" Nori asked.

"They will. He's been with them longer than any of us have been alive. Master Fallue will probably paint Rayan as the traitor."

"Should we send a company to intercept him?" Jayna asked.

Xiang kept his voice low, choosing his words carefully. "Our Oja will handle matters across the border."

At the next crossroad, the company turned northwest. Farmland spread out around them, and the mountains greeted them like broken teeth against the sky.

They sheltered during the brightest times of day, making up time quickly as Starling angled toward its winter route. The way was slower than Xiang expected.

On the third night, they'd come across a rundown, secluded farmhouse with a dozen thin horses and slaughtered the small family in their sleep. They'd piled the bodies in the well and rested for the day before riding away. The neighbors wouldn't discover them for several days, and even then would hesitate to alert the Starling authorities, no matter what the crime.

Jayna's looks revealed her opinion in less subtlety than was surely intended, but she didn't complain. She lacked the viciousness that was sometimes necessary, but her obedience made her useful enough. Xiang selected this triad because of their demeanors, and even though Verina was absent, neither of the others had disappointed. Nori was condescending, but he towed the line and had the meanness that Jayna lacked.

Soldiers clustered around shared all'ights when they stopped to water the horses and allow a brief rest. An argentava's mournful cry rang above, drawing Xiang's eye. With a wary look, Jayna motioned to a set of trees in a small field on the opposite side of the road.

"Something happened there," she said.

Nori shuffled up beside her. "I feel it too."

Jayna led Xiang and two soldiers across the stony terrain beneath the yellowy flicker of the all'ight while Nori and the others stayed with the horses. The carcass lay just beyond the trees. Black, gooey decay lingered on some of the bones, while sharp beaks and insects had picked the rest clean. Jayna paused before continuing further into the field.

Enormous dark feathers clumped together in a pile, strung together in an ashy husk. Jayna studied the remains, frowning. They didn't discuss what she sensed. They each knew what a siphon looked like.

"How long ago was this?" Xiang asked.

"Three, four days maybe."

"How weak is he?"

The husk crumbled between her fingers. She lifted a long feather against the moonlight. "Difficult to say. It was injured by magic before he siphoned it."

Xiang pulled Jayna to her feet. "Losing a horse should hinder them."

A thin thread snaked from her fingers to rake over the bones again. Her scowl deepened. "General?" He turned to her, his face haunted by the all'ight. "Could there be another mage with him?"

"Not unless the Silence monks came for him. But even they couldn't find him so readily."

Concern fluttered across her face. "There's something—someone—else here. A trace of magic that isn't the Oji's. But it's confusing."

"How so?"

"It's strange, like trying to determine the exact blend of spices in a ten-spice dish." She released the feather, and it sailed to the ground a few feet away. "I haven't sensed it before."

Xiang gazed back at the soldiers. He couldn't afford to have them lose morale. If Lua had help from another mage, even in his weakened state, their odds would be diminished. "Does Nori know?"

"I don't think so. He's not typically good at deciphering the specifics of spells."

"Best to keep this between us, then," he said. "Let me know if there's anything else."

She gave a curt nod and walked back toward the horses. A lone bird cawed mournfully overhead. It circled above the bones and feathers. Argentavas mated for life, and this one would spend the rest of its days alone. Xiang's chest clenched directly beneath the vials of liger's bane. The swirling wind scattered the feathers across the field.

He looked up. "Best move on," he said.

Soldiers sat, eating their rations and laughing at someone's joke. Nori sat alone, resting his head in his hands. There was time. Xiang propped the mirror on the ground before pulling up his pant leg. He cut a small line across his upper calf while mumbling the spell.

Bolin's face swam before him, dark eyes brightening as Xiang reflected in them. His hair was nearly shaved down to the scalp again. He was animated, clearly trying to share something amusing, but all Xiang could do was smile and nod.

The bleeding stopped too soon, and Bolin faded into darkness. Xiang sat on the cold ground and watched the giant bird come around for another pass. He stood and brushed the dirt from his pants with a sigh. Then trudged back to the road.

"Let's move out."

Twenty-Three

Lua

Lua kept loose hold of the reins to keep the stubborn gelding at a safe distance. His hands may have been gloved, but fatigue caused his focus to slip and, much like his companion, the horse constantly tested him. Whenever it tossed its head, his magic lunged for the beast and Lua worried he'd not be able to restrain it much longer, despite the precautions he'd taken.

Audra stumbled and cursed. Not letting her buy the all'ight had been shortsighted. They would've made better time with more than ring and moonslight. Her familiarity with the terrain didn't make it less dangerous for her in the dark.

Another argentava circled above them for a time. The small warning spell that Lua threw at it left them both spent.

Audra's breath was white against the night sky. She shivered, tugging her hood around her face before rubbing her gloved hands together. Though this was nothing like the northern cold he was used to, her discomfort seeped into him. Back home, a second layer of snow already coated the landscape, with a frozen sheet thickening over the lakes and ponds. Soon the sea would send plates of ice crashing onto the shore as starling moved further away from them. Those nostalgic memories would not spare him from the recent horrors he'd committed when next he entered the castle. Amala was dead by his own hand.

They camped between boulders a safe distance from the road, and he cast a fire with kindling and brush. As soon as the gelding was settled, Audra curled on the ground so near the flames that her cheeks flushed. Her breath was deep and steady though her stomach rumbled. The ache of her tired legs echoed in his body.

He wasn't at full strength and couldn't afford to give much to her. And yet, the fact that he'd taken down the argentava with such little effort was both curious and disturbing. The spell had come unbidden. Twice. He'd searched for a flaw with Audra's thread but found nothing unusual. The yarns were thicker, but that was to be expected, and it pulsed in rhythm with his heart. But there was an awkwardness strung between them, pulling one way then the other. This bond was different.

Audra was too uncomfortable to allow him to sleep, so he reclined beneath Silence's rays and absorbed all that he could. With that, he sent a little nourishment to his anchor. She relaxed slightly.

Audra wasn't the first person he'd looked after. There was his mother, of course, and Eras. Both had needed increasing care before they died.

He'd suffered with Eras, his first anchor, in the end and thought he'd deserved it for surviving. Though the monks separated them and secured him quickly to his second, Eras's life had tried to hold on to him. He'd been forced to cut the final tie himself and watched her twitch on the floor. When he drew a new breath with his second anchor, people cheered. Lua had mourned Eras quietly in the solitude of his chambers for years after.

Memories of Eras came to him more frequently these last few days, perhaps because she'd been the only other woman he'd been anchored with. Committees had handpicked all the others from a pool of soldiers. They discouraged the women or attractive men quickly for fear of another emotional connection.

Brav and Elicia were lucky. Their emotional attachment had come after their bonding. It wasn't always the case. When the pair was incompatible, a mage would often become their anchor's jailer.

Lua rubbed his face. He'd suffered a greater range of emotions over these last weeks than he had in the last seventy years. He wasn't sure if it was because of Audra or everything he'd lost.

Audra rolled onto her back and drew an arm above her head. She was so tethered to everything around her, not just family, but horses and animals. Even the way her eyes smiled at the trees, the taste of wintry air upon her tongue, and the stinging wind against her skin.

He'd never been allowed to feel so alive. Li-Hun's control over his children had been suffocating, leaving no space for anything other than duty. With the Rajav dead, Lua suspected his sister would follow their father's example.

Audra whimpered, dreaming again. Although her waking thoughts were barred to him, glimpses of her dreams flitted toward him. Images of faces or places twisted her memories. But what was dream and what had been real was more difficult to ascertain. He closed his eyes and followed the thread, spiraling into her fear.

Surging heat contrasted with icy air, the combustion of angry spells. Screams as white armor battled black. An occasional flash of green licked out and vanished.

A woman with familiar eyes held his hand, gripping an old sword in the other. Her tears were barely held back by a mother's determination. A small boy clutched to her side while gold and silver spells sailed around them. Swaths of blood painted the ground as they stepped over bodies.

Then the woman set the boy on the ground and told Lua to take care of him. She ordered them to run. He hesitated, looking back once as the woman charged a towering man in white armor. Time had slowed their mother's reflexes; her sword was too long unused. He knew what waited if he stayed, so he ran, dragging the boy behind him.

When the boy stumbled, Lua cursed and tried to drag him. Fat tears rolled down ruddy cheeks. Lua picked up the boy, darting down a narrow street that should lead into the woods. They'd hide in the forest until they got to Auntie's.

An elegant, menacing woman blocked the way. Long, disheveled hair danced around a pale oval face with high cheekbones and cold, gray eyes. Sharp teeth shone in a wicked smile.

"There you are." Dark magic curled between her fingertips. Audra showed no signs of recognition, but Lua knew exactly who it was. In the dream, his sister Selene whispered a few words before the spell raced toward them.

He turned, instinctively angling away, putting the boy in the spell's path.

Lua gasped and clutched his chest to calm his racing heart. His sweat-dotted brow matched Audra's. He cursed and stared at Silence above.

"Is this another test?" he asked. But his moon didn't answer.

Audra twitched, still running in her dream, carrying a limp child into the winter woods.

Lua rubbed the back of his neck. There were spells that could alleviate some of the trauma, but they were complicated and would drain them both. Plus, altering memories was dangerous without specialized training typically reserved for those who chose the healer's path. He'd never considered it before, not after witnessing his father and sister employing those skills too often.

Audra's groan pulled at him. He could give her something of his to focus on instead. He settled on the memory of a spring flower celebration when he was small. The blue poppies broke through the crusted snow around the castle gardens beneath two full moons that traversed beneath the vibrance of Raia. Amala hoisted him higher to better see the festivities from the balcony. Her hair was fixed in a topknot with silver, teardrop-shaped pearls and moonstones dangling from the headdress around her face. She smelled of sweet rosewater and honey. Her eyes crinkled at the corners as she smiled and pointed to the sea.

The water swirled beneath the moonslight. Long figures twirled and writhed as silver backs broke the surface. One square nose lifted, followed by another. Amala called them the sisters. Their mouths opened in a haunting song, ethereal. Everyone quieted to listen, though Lua believed those voices were meant only for him.

He held the memory another moment before sending it down the thread. Audra stilled. A few tears trailed down her cheeks, but she didn't wake.

She had the persistence and passion usually lost when time and sorrow stole them. But given the memories he'd experienced, that felt near a lie. Audra had determination, but for what purpose he didn't yet know.

Selene's face in Audra's dream had startled him and left him with more questions. Another discomfort that—again—he was unused to. But this emotion wasn't borrowed from his anchor like the others, and he wasn't ready to sit with it yet. He and Selene had fought in the northernmost western villages under Li-Hun's order during the last incursion. Audra couldn't have known her face otherwise. If Audra knew who the woman in her dreams was, things between them might deteriorate further. He was already accommodating her by agreeing to deliver the jade to her brother. That would have to be enough.

He closed his eyes and leaned back. He was getting too attached. Especially foolish considering she disliked him so intensely. Audra's death was predetermined, the severing of their bond would see to that, no matter what kind of magic she borrowed from the jade. Nothing could save her. And he needed a stronger anchor if he had any chance of saving his people from Selene.

Audra startled. Bleary eyes squinted at him in the firelight. A hint of concern in her voice. "Everything all right?"

Lua nodded. "Go back to sleep."

She rested her head on her arm, her voice fading. "I had a dream about you in the sea drowning."

He tucked the blanket around her shoulders, her breath softened, and the night was quiet again. Though he fought his fatigue, his eyes closed slowly and he drifted to sleep.

Starling was blushing the sky pale orange when he woke hours later, with Audra's face pressed against his neck. They were entwined with arms wrapped around each other. Though the fire had burned to embers, the comforting heat of her pressed against him. Scents of pine and something wholly Audra flooded his senses. His first thought was to disentangle himself before she woke and misunderstood, but he sighed. It was difficult to pull away from her. The strength of this connection was another thing both disturbing and curious. Even with everything going awry, holding Audra made it feel like everything was just right. Like he shouldn't be anywhere other than by her side. Even if she hated him. With that thought, he jerked away. She *should* hate him, and he should dispose of her as soon as they reached the monastery.

Her breathing deepened as she started to rouse. Lua was poking the charred embers beside the firepit when she opened her eyes and sat up.

Twenty-Four

Selene

"Where is he?" Selene asked into the mirror. Though Xiang couldn't hear her, he was usually good at anticipating her demands. She rested a possessive hand on Bolin's shoulder, leaning slightly forward to meet the general's eyes.

Xiang and his people followed Lua's trail through the western countryside toward the mountain passes. If he made it to the Silence monastery in time for the eclipses, they'd hold a coronation, whether or not the entirety of the Mage Council was present. Master Fallue, the Council leader, was Lua's greatest asset and Selene regretted not getting rid of him and his anchor, Emaline, before.

She'd send word to Sharine to make plans. The Song mage leader could accomplish things without overt detection. Hope for the best but set up preemptive plans for a worst-case scenario. Sharine wanted control of the council, and Selene could give her that. If Fallue attempted the coronation, he and the others had vulnerabilities she'd take advantage of. They'd soon learn that fighting her would only lead to their destruction.

Xiang's image faded. Bolin slumped, his longing pulled on her. The general would reach out again when she wasn't around. Accepting that intentional exclusion always stung. She placed a small kiss on Bolin's brow before leaving him alone. He was smart enough to never say he didn't want her there. Sending Xiang on this mission had been Bolin's idea. If he was regretting it, there was nothing to be done about it. Plus, Xiang had two experienced mages with him, and Lua was weak.

It was unfortunate the third mage had been too compromised to assist. Selene would have to deal with the nine star appropriately. Verina had left her team wanting three separate times while selfishly pursuing attempts at having a child. She'd even delayed testing for advancement since a tenth star would prevent any future pregnancies. Xiang and the others were vulnerable because of her absence.

Selene ignored the bows of passing soldiers as she moved toward the south wing with two guards flanking her. Servants scuttled from her path like nervous crabs, darting into the shadows of alternate passages.

She paused outside Amala's rooms. What was left of her mother lay in a ceremonial coffin inside. Moon tradition demanded a burning at sea, but Amala always wanted to be scattered in the Shei-nam mountains. After Lua was captured and the Rajav's death was announced, Selene would handle the death rites in whatever way she deemed appropriate.

She knocked on the carved door three rooms down. She didn't need to. The Rajav had unfettered access to every inch of the castle. But she remembered when Li-Hun never granted her the privacy she craved. It was difficult enough being a young girl in these walls, Selene saw no reason to make it worse for Dain's daughter.

Grethin, the elderly servant assigned to the girl, opened the door and backed away, giving a wide berth for Selene to enter. The room had been decorated with soft purples and blues, Maya's favorite colors according to Dain.

The girl sat cross-legged on the rug before the fireplace, her hair plaited in two braids that hung down her back. At nine years old, she was too young to know reverence or proper respect and too inexperienced to show the fear everyone else did. It was refreshingly bold. Perhaps that was why Selene hadn't killed her yet. Maya glanced up to

Selene from the scroll she read but didn't stand until Kanata yanked her to her feet. The tutor bowed deeply and forced the girl's head down beside her.

"Apologies, Oja. The girl should know better," Kanata said, keeping her head down.

Selene smiled as Maya peeked up at her. "What are you reading, Maya?"

She pulled away from the tutor's hands. "*The Tales of Yueliang.*"

"That was a favorite of mine when I was your age. Have you gotten to the part with the dragons?"

A shy smile spread across her face. "I'm just starting it."

Selene addressed Kanata. "Has she read *The Love of Raia*?" The woman shook her head. "Just as well. Give her *The Trials of Song and Silence* next."

"Yes, Oja," Kanata said.

"Do you like it here, Maya?"

"I want to go home." A neediness crept into Maya's tone.

"Hm. I'm sure you do. But you must stay here with us for a while," Selene said. She debated keeping her parent's deaths from the girl. No need to torture her before Selene decided her fate. "You can have anything you want to read or eat. Do you like your room?"

The girl nodded. "It's pretty. Only..."

"What is it?"

"I'm worried about Oaklai and Oani. They'll be scared."

"Who are Oaklai and Oani?"

"My ferrets. I've had them since they were babies." Her hazel eyes were wide and imploring.

Kanata continued to study the rug. Only Grethin met Selene's gaze with a look of confusion. The Rajav had forbidden animals in the castle —nothing to get attached to that might suddenly die.

But Selene was the one in control; those old rules needn't apply anymore. "Were they at your house?"

The girl nodded.

Selene turned to Grethin. "Have someone retrieve them and brought here with anything they need."

"Yes, Oja." Grethin bowed before backing out of the room.

Maya's smile was genuine. It touched something in Selene she didn't expect. "What do you want to be when you're older, Maya?"

The girl's chest puffed out. She stood straighter. "A soldier like my father."

Though Selene stood at a distance, her magic ached for the girl's brilliant energy. Gloves might not protect Maya from an unintentional siphon if she moved closer. "Your father wasn't just a soldier, Maya. He was anchored to one of the strongest mages in generations."

Her eyes widened. "He is?"

Selene's lips thinned into a taut line. There was no point in disguising the truth anymore, and the malicious part of her wanted to know what Maya would look like when she suffered. "He was, dear. I'm afraid not anymore."

Confusion swam across the girl's face. She looked from Selene to Kanata. "Wh-what do you mean?"

"Maya," Selene tried to make her voice soothing, but the girl stepped back. "Your father died in service to our tribes."

"Died?" Tears welled in her eyes. Her lower lip trembled. "How?"

At Selene's nod, Kanata knelt beside the girl and wrapped fleshy arms around her.

"His mage killed him."

Twenty-Five

Lua

The horse jerked its head again and dragged Lua's naked wrist from his sleeve into the midday light. He cursed. His flesh had burned tender-pink from the repeated exposure, and he was beginning to question the beast's value.

Between the horse and Audra's incessant warnings about her aunt, the journey was taking its toll. There was an unflinching edge to her voice that, combined with her emotional fluctuations, grated on Lua's thinning patience. Aside from the effect these people might have on their combined energy and health, he didn't care about them at all. Audra quieted blissfully. He sighed with relief.

And then she started again.

The verbal barrage set his teeth on edge and left little space to process what kept happening between them when they slept. He'd disentangled himself before she stirred each time. No matter how serene the moment in her arms had been, Lua wasn't one to take advantage of his anchors. And he didn't want her to misinterpret what had happened. He still wasn't sure.

The horse jerked his arm into the light again, and Lua snapped, cutting Audra's words off. "Maybe *they* should be careful. Surely, you understand—"

She turned on him so quickly he stopped mid-step. The horse tossed his head, forcing Lua's wrist from his sleeve again. He ignored the burn, eyes fixed on the dagger pressed against the pulse of her throat. Cold fury swept toward him. Blood broke through her flesh and trickled down to her collar, the same wound suddenly marring his neck. He held his breath.

"You even *think* of hurting them, and I'll kill us both." She held his gaze, sliding the blade across her skin until Lua winced. With a look of satisfaction, Audra cursed at him so fiercely he nearly blushed. Then she turned and moved steadily down the path.

Lua wanted to say he could stop her from hurting herself if he wished to, but his mouth wasn't so foolish. Maybe the jade would protect her or, more likely, she'd cut their throats just to prove her point. But perhaps she'd already made it.

Beneath the shade of his hat, Lua watched the steadiness of Audra's steps. The line of her shoulders. The cut of her jawline when she turned slightly. She had the beauty of wild things. Fierce and indomitable. Her anger diffused over the course of the next hour, replaced by familiar resentment.

He considered that he'd be rid of her when they reached the monastery and then be bound to someone steadier. Maybe Quin, he'd proven himself to be the essence of dedication and loyalty. But thinking of Audra's death made his breath hitch.

He rubbed the blood from his neck, mildly sorry for provoking her. They'd have to tolerate each other's tempers a bit longer. He sent a little magic down their thread. Audra startled, rubbing her throat as it healed. She didn't acknowledge what he'd done, but her shoulders softened.

The air grew subtly stagnant as they hiked between shrubs and pines, stripping his sense of magic. Something powerful protected this land.

Audra could be leading him into a trap, but her emotions held true; and though she was a skilled liar, he doubted that deception extended to herself.

She scrambled atop a boulder and pointed down the side of the mountain. A wide grin spread across her face as Starling lit auburn hints in her dark hair. It must have been her emotions that suddenly quickened his heart. He stared at her with a sudden realization.

No matter what their futures held, he'd never let anyone hurt her. There had to be another way.

"We're here." She jumped down from the rock. "I'll go first. Auntie doesn't—"

"Take well to strangers." He finished for her. "So you've told me a thousand times today."

"Didn't think you were listening." She scurried down the slope toward a modest house set inside an adjacent hill. The wood construction tilted, reinforced on one side by large stones similar to the ones that littered the surrounding landscape. The east-facing door allowed Starling to shine through the house for much of the day. There was a fenced area with a half dozen goats and chickens clustered together. There were two barns, one huge, the other modest. The few animals didn't justify the size of either structure.

A woman's thick frame filled the home's doorway. Her gaze skimmed across Lua's skin as he coaxed the horse forward. The air tingled with the same anticipation that precedes lightning, skittering down his neck and putting him on guard. Something about her whispered of his father's musings. The Western mages were devious, dangerous. He studied her silver-streaked hair, broad shoulders, and hostile emerald gaze. If this woman were a mage at all, this wasn't the elder auntie he'd expected.

Audra disappeared in her arms. Though she appeared middle-aged, her skin was smooth and lacked the cracked, dull complexion typically earned from living in the mountains.

Audra clutched Zin's hand as Lua neared. "This is Chon. He helped me escape from Callaway."

Lua was prepared for the lies this time, but something told him this auntie would not be so easily deceived.

Zin sighed heavily. "You should have abandoned him before now." She scowled at Audra. "Remember what happened with your last lover?"

"It's not like that." Audra's voice dropped, cheeks flushing with mortification.

"It better not be," Zin warned. Her gaze raked over Lua, pausing temporarily at his neck, then Audra's. "Settle the horse and wash up. No hats in the house."

"Auntie . . ." Audra's words trailed away at Zin's withering look. Grabbing Lua's elbow, Audra twirled him toward the smaller barn. "She'll warm up. It just takes her a little while."

He doubted that was true. There was knowledge in her eyes, and Lua suspected she'd confront him when the time was right. Audra opened the gate and scratched the goats' heads as Lua pulled on the reins and drew the horse inside the enclosure. She settled the horse in a stall while he cautiously retreated from any approaching animals.

He cleared his throat. "What happened to your last lover?" He didn't care, but he was curious.

A hiss whistled between her teeth. "Nothing that concerns you."

He rested a hand on her shoulder. They both froze as energy swirled and tightened between them. "Anything that concerns you concerns me." The words were in the air before he could taste them. Though they weren't exactly as he intended, they held uncomfortable truth.

Audra shrugged. His hand fell away. "I met Kip after Traq enlisted. She was also a bit of a thief. More than a bit, actually. Downright devious to be honest. But she was fun at a time when I'd forgotten how to laugh. We'd been together for a few months. Done a few jobs before we came here. I'd believed what she said to me." She shook her head. "One morning she was gone. Took everything I'd saved and stole some of Auntie's goods as well. Zin hasn't forgiven me for bringing her here."

"Have you had many?"

"Lovers?"

He regretted the question. None of his business. It didn't matter.

She smoothed down the horse's mane. "A few. You?" There was no shame in her voice.

"Not as many as I'd have liked." Damn his mouth, not what he'd meant to say either. But her laughter was contagious, settling in his chest until they entered the house.

Steady flames danced in the fireplace. Zin had drawn the curtains against the light and stood at the small stove beside the hearth, stirring a large pot. Scents of onions and peppers made Lua's eyes burn as he tugged the hat from his head.

"It'll be ready soon. Audra, go tend your brother, he's been waiting for you," Zin said, not turning around. "Your friend can stay with me."

Audra gave Lua an apologetic look before disappearing down the hall toward a doorway at the end. Magic flickered across Lua's arms, not strong enough to be a threat, but enough to get his attention.

Zin motioned him toward the stove. "I won't bite."

He swallowed a retort but moved closer all the same. She was several inches taller than him, with broad shoulders. Her skin was so smooth she might have been forty or four hundred, like his father.

She shoved the spoon at him. "Stir. I don't trust you to chop vegetables since I doubt you've many common skills."

Her tone was like the one he used when speaking to those deemed inferior. He ground his teeth but carefully avoided touching her when he took the spoon. She stood beside him, placing a white vegetable with green leaves upon a cutting board. The sound of the knife slicing succinctly through the stalks made a threatening impression that he took to be intentional.

"Does she know what you are?" she asked.

Lua always relied on his status and power to protect him when magic wasn't an option. Rather than lie, he opted for silence thinking it held more weight.

"How many have you had before her?" Zin asked, her husky voice low.

He startled, tried to step away, but another's magic held him in place. Breaking it would have required pulling on Audra.

The knife crunched through the vegetable again. Zin's tone was dagger sharp. "Don't toy with me, Moon mage. How many anchors have you had before?"

He was neither relieved nor comforted by her clarification. Instead, he continued to stir the contents of her copper pot. Sweat dotted his brow. Though the seduction of a lie tempted him, he chose truth. "Four."

The knife sliced again. "All dead, I'm sure." When Lua didn't reply, she continued, "How many stars are you? I want to know what we are dealing with."

The dawning threat of her, what she was, what she might be capable of, chilled him despite the heat. Her enormous presence engulfed the space, swirled around him and thickened the air. There wasn't any point in fighting her. In his weakened state, she'd easily overpower him, but neither of them would risk hurting Audra.

"Thirteen."

She scraped the refuse into a small bucket before adding the vegetables to the pot. Her face was close to his, breath like the steam that sometimes rose from the poisoned river. "Why Audra?"

He swallowed. His arm burned from the constant stirring, but he couldn't stop. "There wasn't a choice, believe me. The magic lashed out when she saved me. There weren't any rituals or agreements, it just happened."

Zin's jaw clenched. She grabbed another vegetable and chopped it murderously.

"How did you know?" He glanced at her. Most mages couldn't see the bond. It was a subtle, intimate thread usually only revealed during battles and was difficult, but not impossible, to trace.

She sneered. "It was shining in the air before you both came down the hill. It's just one of the reasons your leaders wanted us killed. Don't you know your own history?" Her eyes met his. "Or did you only learn what they told you?"

He bristled at the truth of her words. "We don't have a lot of texts about ..." He let the sentence trail away, wondering why Audra was taking so long.

"I suppose you wouldn't. Li-Hun probably destroyed or hid everything over the last few hundred years." The blade came down again. "Silence, eh?"

With instinctive magic, he dropped the spoon. The handle slid down the inside of the pot before disappearing beneath the stew. Lua stared at her. Most of his own tribespeople couldn't see the difference in magic unless they saw the sigils on the robes or the color of the magic they cast. But the Silence sigil was hidden beneath the blue robes. She shouldn't have been able to tell.

THE MALICE OF MOONS AND MAGES

Her smile was grim. She scraped the orange stalk into the pot. "I spent a lot of time with the Moons in my younger years." With a flick of her wrist, the spoon emerged from the pot, steam rising from the handle. Zin grasped it without flinching and wiped it on her apron. She held it out to him and leaned against the counter. "You've outlived four anchors. How many died of the siphon. Two?" She studied him as she asked. "Three? Four?"

A subtle squint gave him away.

"Three then," she said. "I won't ask what happened to the fourth. I don't care." Her voice lowered as footsteps lumbered down the hall toward them. "You've known too many years, and Audra should have many more before her. Preferably without you. What will you do about the bond? Because I will burn your tribes to the ground if any harm comes to her."

Her eyes flashed emerald. Energy whipped around the room and pulled Lua's hair from beneath his robes. It squeezed the breath from his lungs before he could react.

Zin's spell released as Audra rounded the corner with a tall, lanky boy draped around her shoulders. Their smiles were similar in shape, but his eyes were green, like their aunt's. A sinking understanding swept over Lua.

Zin wasn't her aunt.

Ferin's grin broadened when he saw Lua. He lurched forward with open, welcoming arms, as if greeting an old friend. Lua shuffled backward but the boy was too fast.

"No!" Lua's magic reached out; all attempts to contain it failed as Ferin wrapped hot limbs around him. Silver slicked over the boy's hard skin, sliding away from him and swirling safely back into Lua's arms. The boy laughed without sound.

Audra gently pried them apart. Lua looked from the boy to Audra before meeting Zin's eyes.

"This is Ferin. My brother," Audra said, smiling and running a hand down the boy's arm. Not a boy.

This was all magic and lies.

Lua released a shaking breath. Zin's magic transformed them both to what Lua was meant to see. Audra's home was a den, and her family was made of dragons.

Twenty-Six

Traq

When Traq had taken the evidence of the blood bond to Senior Monk Altho, the old man's face had darkened. An emergency meeting was called with Lord Ijion himself, who'd been visiting from the southern lands. Wren's private meeting with the Starling leader resulted in orders for her triad to capture the murderers and return them for justice for the slaughtered fishing villagers.

Neither Wren nor Traq received any accolades for discovering the bond, only more work. Traq never expected praise, but he'd thought that Wren would have earned something. By the following afternoon, the mages and fourteen soldiers glimmering in pale armor climbed steadily into the Shei-nam mountains atop sturdy bay and chestnut horses.

Durin's normally pleasant disposition was sour. His insistence that a younger mage would serve them better had been overruled when Lord Ijion insisted that Wren's triad not change, offering no other explanation. Durin's irritation tainted those around him, tinging the day with bouts of heavy silence.

Though Wren didn't mention the connection between Traq's friend and the bond, her subtle inquiries about his childhood left no doubt about her suspicions. His answers were direct and without elaboration.

People died in war, and children were no exception. Traq's neighbors and siblings had been cut down during the last incursion while he'd been hunting in the woods, too far from home. If his brother hadn't been injured helping a neighbor the day before, it would have been him in the woods and Traq's throat cut. Wren had looked away at that, guilty expression quickly concealed. He'd barely survived on his own until an auntie in the mountains had taken him in. There was no point in mentioning it wasn't *his* auntie and that, if it weren't for Audra, Zin wouldn't have sheltered him at all. Neither did he tell her he'd only been there a few years when he and Audra left on their first quest, which ended in a broken nose and empty hands. The jade they returned with was always too broken, its magic depleted, and useless at healing Ferin the way it ought to have.

He hoped this jade worked. Ferin hadn't uttered a single word in the entire time Traq had known him, and his movements were often clumsy, like he was out of place in his body.

Perhaps Wren was right, and the Moon tribe's souls were as cold as their gods in the sky, but the Starlings weren't any better. Durin, Wren and her sister, Sechen, were a few of the exceptions.

When the party paused midafternoon to rest, Wren settled beside Traq, leaning back against a tall rock and eating a plum. Liasa, one of only a few other Westerners who'd enlisted with the Starlings, sat nearest to Durin and humored him by laughing at his jokes.

"How long until he retires?" Traq asked.

"Next year." She took another bite. "If you have your fives by then, we can select a two star. Train them right."

Traq knew the implication. Select someone else who was willing to work with a Westerner. That might be more difficult than Wren imagined. "At least Durin's agreeable. Better than some others by far." He watched the old man smile at the attention. Durin always improved with a sympathetic audience. "Do you think he'll keep his magic or give it away?"

She took another bite, wiping the juice from her mouth before she replied. "He'll keep it. You saw how Claude's face lit up on Callaway when Durin performed a simple spell. That sort of pride is difficult to let go of."

Traq smiled. Durin's husband was certainly eccentric, but the affection between the men was pure. "When do you test?"

"When we return. You?"

"Same. Sechen's testing then too." She glanced at Traq with a mischievous smile. "We could ask her."

Traq's cheeks darkened. Wren's younger sister had followed him around for the better part of a month the last time they'd been south. Her unwavering attention had been mortifying. Wren laughed at his expression.

"I'll think of someone else. What do you know about that man with your friend?"

Though her question didn't surprise him, her methods always did. Abrupt. Direct. "I'd never seen him before."

"Hm."

"What?"

She smiled deviously. "He was quite handsome, wasn't he? Surely you noticed."

Traq's jaw clenched.

Wren chuckled. "Oh, you noticed. What was his name?"

"Chon."

She tasted the name on her lips. "It's an island name, isn't it? But so pale. Didn't he look more northern to you?"

Durin settled on a cushioned pallet that Liasa assembled for him. Wren scooted closer to Traq until her thigh pressed against his. Her heat radiated into him.

"What will you do if they are bonded?" she asked quietly.

"We don't know for sure they're who we are looking for."

"But what if they are?" she whispered. Her proximity brought curious glances from others in their party.

Traq stood abruptly. Looking down on her while reigning his emotions. "Then I will do my duty."

A few miles later, a soldier spotted the bones behind a tree, picked clean. Feet had crushed the surrounding grass. Large argentava feathers were strewn atop piles of dust in the nearby field.

Wren studied the area, watching the sky for a mate as Traq sent a small thread out but found nothing.

"What do you think?" she asked. Traq wished she would just spit it out. He sighed. Wren smiled. "They don't have any natural predators, but the ashes still hold a hint of magic."

"So?"

"If our theoretical ten-star mage is weak, he might need to siphon energy from others."

His stomach dropped. "What about the person connected to him?"

"His anchor? She's his lifeline. She might be the only one safe." Wren said with a serious tone. "Lord Ijion said that their connection also makes him vulnerable."

"What do you mean?"

"If we kill the connection, we can kill the mage." She patted his shoulder once before walking away, leaving him pale and ill.

Twenty-Seven

Xiang

Nori lost the thread four days into the journey, but Xiang had already planned their route in anticipation of such an event. The Oji wasn't foolish enough to keep wasting his magic while in a weakened state, and there was only one place he could go. They'd hoped to follow Lua's trail and intercept him before he arrived at the monastery, but they would forge their own path.

Although Xiang had been away from his homeland for many years, the roads hadn't changed. Everything was smaller, dirtier, and more constricted than he remembered. The stark beauty of contrasting sienna and violet hued mountains was diminished with time, and the late blooming shrubs made his eyes water. Only the nighttime cold felt like home anymore.

The stark high desert pass was dotted with too few conifers to allow for adequate coverage against Starling light. Though the all'ights helped the soldiers and horses with the nighttime travel, the search for daily shelter was taking its toll. If they kept this pace, their collective exhaustion would amplify their vulnerability when they reached Lua.

A horse stumbled in the darkness ahead, recovering with a soft neigh.

As if anticipating his train of thought, Jayna said, "We should rest soon."

"There's an old monastery ahead. We can shelter and try to find the thread before we get to the border," Xiang said.

She nodded. "Are you from this area?"

"No. Closer to the Starling border. I fought at Oxton during the . . ." He'd said too much. "Until they consigned me back north."

For Jayna, the last invasion would be an intangible memory. For Xiang it was the end of one life and the beginning of another. He'd been ambitious once too, set on saving his tribe. He couldn't reconcile that youth with the bitter man he'd become. He was proof that love and desperation could make terrible things of anyone.

"The Song monks said the Western mages and their dragons had grown too dangerous, and that was why the Rajav wanted them destroyed. But I've wondered if there were other reasons we invaded the west," Jayna said.

Xiang pursed his lips. This wasn't a conversation he'd willingly delve into. Sometimes he doubted the truth he knew. Every tribe lied to have their version seem most noble and ensure loyalty from the ignorant masses. "I offer no opinion on that. You'd be better served questioning your senior monks."

Her shoulders stiffened at the dismissal, but she kept pace beside him. "I hope Galia's all right," she said.

"The *Bulou* should have returned north by now. They'll be in Uduary soon enough."

Jayna glanced slyly at him. "I know you aren't a mage, but you've seen plenty of ten stars rise and fall. Can I ask you a question?"

He kept his eyes on the road, which turned due north at the crest of the hill. Behind them, the dawning sky was pink and gold. The light would burn her skin soon if she didn't don her hood. "What is it?"

"What will happen to Galia and myself when I test for ten stars?"

He stifled a sigh, considering his answer. "Do you want the truth?"

She nodded.

"Let these words go no further."

She nodded again.

"End it with her now." He might as well have slapped her. "Anchoring complicates love. It makes you vulnerable, easy to manipulate. And, believe me, they'll use her against you." He didn't need to mention Dain or the mess that had come from his secrets. Jayna was observant enough to have her own suspicions about why the Oji's anchor had betrayed him. Dain's daughter was probably dead; Selene hated reminders of failure.

"But Galia is strong, smart, loyal. A perfect anchor," Jayna said.

"True. But because you want her so much, the mage council won't let you have her. They'll choose someone they deem appropriate. Best-case scenario, they'll keep her near so they can use her to manipulate you. Worst case, they'll kill her slowly in front of you as a lesson to not consider anything or anyone more precious than your tribe. It won't matter either way. After ten stars you won't be able to touch her or anything with a heartbeat if you don't want to siphon it. You know that," Xiang said.

Jayna blanched.

He paused his horse to meet her eyes. "Nothing can have greater importance than your tribe, especially not something as mundane as a personal love."

He nudged the horse on, and Jayna joined him a moment later.

"Is that what happened with you?" she asked. "Your devotion to the Oja, I've wondered if—"

"No. Never." He lowered his voice. "My lover has exceptional physical stamina and an unequivocal life force that makes him, unfortunately, an ideal anchor."

Jayna swallowed nervously. "Your lover. He's—"

"You have my advice, do with it what you will," Xiang said, prodding his horse down the road.

In the distance stood a series of buildings that comprised the last of the Western monasteries to fall. It had lasted fifty years longer than any of the others, reportedly protected by dragons until they vanished. Though intricate etchings in the stone peeked through the climbing pothos, the last assault had done irreparable damage. Time and weather had done worse. Two towers still stood tall against the sky, though one's roof was collapsing. Beyond these ruins lay the remains of several villages, including Bolin's childhood home.

Xiang hadn't been here since his sister had pledged herself when he was a child. She'd hoped to achieve greatness, even dreamt of calling a dragon though their numbers had dwindled long before she'd been born. Seeing the monastery in which she died fighting the people he now served brought grief and doubt. His sister had died a brave Westerner, and he would die a traitor.

"We'll camp here until tomorrow eve," he said. With the Song moon absent this night, it would save them from being exposed when they were most vulnerable. There was a collective sigh that lightened the atmosphere. Xiang hoped they could pick up the trail again. The Oji had to be close, and it would be best for everyone if they found him on this side of the border.

Twenty-Eight

Audra

Moon didn't protest when Zin casually dismissed him to sleep in the smaller barn. Audra suspected he'd been glad to escape the house. Given the abrupt change in his manners since they arrived, she thought he finally understood what her veiled warnings had been about. Every tale written about dragons referenced their gruff manners and lethal protective natures, and Zin was a perfect example of those characteristics. Audra couldn't help wondering if Ferin would become that surly when the spell over him finally broke.

Although Moon hadn't cast in days and didn't pull on Audra too often, fatigue wormed behind his eyes. He was perturbed by something she'd been unable to discern yet, but she felt it growing. This thing between them had started to move both ways. His emotions, repressed as they were, slithered down their connection and left her confused.

Against her better judgement, she'd almost begun to like him. Almost. There were layers to him she'd never accounted for.

When the door closed behind him, Audra steeled herself for the wrath that seethed behind Zin's clipped manners. Ferin's snores pulsed through the house.

"Did you think you could hide that he was a Moon mage? From *me*?" Zin demanded.

Audra slunk in her seat at the table, trying to disappear.

"Were you going to tell me?"

Audra caught the insulted glint in Zin's eye and stifled a curse. "Honestly, probably not. I knew you'd be upset."

Zin chuckled darkly. Her magic wavered, red scales glimmered and vanished along her arms. "Oh girl, you cannot fathom the rage that seethes in this heart for that man's tribe." Her talons drummed on the table. "And the bonding? What of that?"

Audra had the good sense to look guilty. Not that she had anything to be guilty about. If it hadn't been for the jade, she wouldn't have been on the *Requin* at all.

She slipped the cord from around her neck. She should have placed it on Ferin as soon as they arrived. The green stone caught the firelight as she laid it on the table.

Zin picked it up and turned it over, her expression momentarily wistful. "What's his real name?"

When she shook her head, Zin's exhalation seared the air.

"The Moons are hunting him," Audra said. "That's how we wound up on the same ship."

Zin's glowing eyes focused on Audra. The dragon turned as still as a snake fixated on a meal. It was intentionally unnerving. Audra hated it when she did this.

"And you *don't* know who he is? I raised you better than that." There was doubt in Zin's eyes. Her fingers drummed on. "He reminds me of someone I once knew. Someone terrible." She quieted for a moment. "What about the bond?"

"He said the monks at the Silence monastery could separate us."

"He's lying. He's only thirteen stars."

"Only? I've never heard of—"

"You won't survive it."

Audra gaped. "What?"

"You'll both die if the monks attempt to sever the bond. They know nothing of western magic." Her voice hitched; the hints of anger replaced by concern. She leaned forward and gripped Audra's hand.

"Would he lie?" Audra whispered. The words were ridiculous out loud. Of course he would. When had she begun to trust him and forgot about the horrendous things he must have done to warrant being hunted by his own awful people? He'd even said as much. But their bond had deepened, the resentment between them diminished. He'd softened toward her. And their lives depended on each other.

"Rather ask, why would he *not* lie? The Moons have never survived on kindness," Zin said. "Do you remember what I told you?"

The words were a bitter sting on her tongue. "Never trust a Moon or Starling mage."

"Especially if they think they have the upper hand."

"What should I do?"

"Remember the scrolls in the monastery's vault?" Zin asked. Audra nodded. "The Western mages could break bonds. Your mother did it. There might be something in there."

"But I'm not even a single star. I still get nothing."

"Stars don't matter. That's the Moon and Starling system. Don't let those labels limit your perception of who you are or what you're capable of. It's a trap that too many fall into. If your mother were here, she'd tell you." Zin's eyes shone. "She never had stars, and she was one of the strongest mages I've ever known. A pity she didn't teach you or your brother more."

Audra bit her lip. They'd never gotten official notice of her older brother's or father's deaths, but, in war, sometimes the only way you knew someone wasn't coming home was when they didn't. She barely remembered their faces anymore.

"Get to the monastery before he wakes. You remember where the vault is?"

Audra nodded. When the Moons felled one tower, the Western mages knocked over another to keep the vault hidden. She'd only ventured there once before when she was barely a teenager and Zin sent her searching for jade. Down in the narrow tunnels and small vault, a noise had frightened her, and she'd abandoned her only all'ight to flee. She'd met Traq, alone and starving, on the way home. How he'd survived all that time in the forests, she never knew.

"Bring back all the scrolls you can carry. Surely there's something in them."

"Won't the bond limit how far I can go?"

Zin arched an eyebrow. "Probably not as much as he lets you think. The distance might cause discomfort, but how else can you discover its limitations? I'll handle the Moon until you get back."

Audra contemplated the jade beneath Zin's hand. "It's not a spell breaker, is it?"

"No. It's a catalyst for dormant magic, Western and dragon specifically. In Ferin's case, I hope it lets him be what he was meant to be. And, theoretically, as he grows, you'll become what you were meant to be."

"Will it work?"

Zin turned the jade over in her fingers, emotion heavy on her face. "If Raia is generous, it will. Get some sleep. I'll wake you before dawn."

Twenty-Nine

Audra

Crisp wintry hints clutched the thin morning air. Raia glittered above. Audra almost tasted fresh snow drifting down from the higher elevations. These mountains suited her better than the desperate streets of Oxton or the greedy island of Callaway. Her ancestors were born and buried here, and even though she enjoyed warmer climates, there was a comfort here she found nowhere else.

The pack jostled against the back of her thighs, empty except for food and a small gourd of water. It was ten miles to the ruins, fourteen if she wanted to visit Pangol. Guilt would settle in her chest whether she did or not. That she and Ferin were the only survivors of that day had birthed a weight that hung upon her shoulders ever since. There should have been more than two scrawny children who scrambled away.

She tried not to think about it as she scampered over dusty deer trails. If she stayed focused, she could be home before the moons rose. There'd be an angry mage to contend with then, but she had already renewed her intent on hating him.

She paused at the peak of a hill, scanning the small valley below. The remaining monastery turret stood against the backdrop of yellowing dried grass and a bright, cloudless sky.

In the far distance, nestled within a dense patch of woods was a clearing trampled down and dark. She stared at it until her eyes watered. There wasn't any point in going there, and not enough time to anyway.

The thread between her and Moon had crossed tender and neared painful. The tightness in her chest and limbs escalated with every passing mile as the bond attempted to turn her around, like a stretched spring waiting to recoil. At some point, the tautness might prevent her from taking another step. She hoped whatever discomfort she was experiencing was triple for him.

Whether or not he planned on killing her at the monastery had consumed her since the previous evening. He'd killed the anglers so casually and insisted it was for their mutual survival. Was that a lie too? She'd grown too accepting of him and should have kept her guard up. But her emotions were raw and muddled.

Never trust a mage was Zin's general rule for everyone save her mother. Audra had always known that Zin and Lorah had been more than friends. The dragon still mourned her, as evidenced by the fact that she'd not left her territory since the night Pangol was slaughtered. Once, when Zin was drunk on rice wine, she'd said she would wait for the call. She had promises to keep. But she refused to answer further questions, which was why Audra was tasked with all the travels. Perhaps because they had the jade, everything could change, at least for her and Ferin. If he could protect himself, he and Audra could have their freedom. Yet, this would bring a new set of obligations they couldn't ignore, matters she'd successfully avoided contemplating for quite some time.

She held onto thin trees for stability, trying not to slip down the steep slope when her nose began to burn. Smoke wisped into the sky behind the monastery. She stumbled and slid to a stop. A horse's neigh echoed toward her. Five figures moved between the stone buildings, covered in ill-matching clothes. Black armor peeked from beneath a colorful sleeve.

Audra scrambled behind a bush, though it would be impossible for them to see her from their angle.

That the Moons might have found them so quickly seemed impossible. Other than the fiasco with the argentava, they'd covered their tracks and made good time. But they'd been on foot, the loss of the horse had slowed them. They'd stopped to rest, whereas this group might not have had to.

Zin's territory had been blocked from detection for decades. It was the reason she and Ferin had survived that night. No one entered Zin's lands without permission. Moon would be safe for the moment—not that she cared.

Though the shared northern border was near, the Moon tribe hadn't set foot in this area since the Starlings claimed it.

She considered turning back, but there were only a few soldiers, and their manners were relaxed. They weren't expecting anyone. If there were Moon mages, they'd not have their full strength until the moonrise, and she had no magic to detect.

The vault sat at the base of the eastern tower, where the last mages had felled it as a final act. Nothing moved at that end, and it would be easy to skirt the perimeter.

It was foolish to consider it. Ridiculous to think she'd succeed. But she'd stolen the jade from a well-locked store and safe and, other than spending a night in jail, crawling through shit, and butchering her hair, had suffered no real consequences.

Unless she counted those events as leading to a potentially fatal bonding with a disagreeable Moon mage. No consequences at all.

Shit. Those scrolls might be her only hope.

Slipping through the tree line around the monastery added an hour to the journey and placed Starling directly behind Raia. The ring's dark shadow chilled the air. Audra followed the toppled tower blocks from the trees to the base of where they'd fallen. Stubborn grass sprouted from the stone's cracks while roots of saplings clawed their way through the leaf-littered ground.

So far, no guards circled this part of the building. Carefully avoiding the dried leaves, Audra scaled the six-foot remains of the crumbling tower's base. She perched along the broken edge as a light breeze swirled dust into her face. Years of leaves and tree litter scattered atop rodent and deer bones clustered to one side, likely left by a liger who'd taken shelter here for a time. But the bones were old, undisturbed. The liger was long gone.

The hatch lay at the bottom of the interior wall that led underground. She never asked how Auntie had known where it was, but her knowledge of things was usually accurate. Zin's connection to the outside world defied human reason, and Audra knew better than to question it. Dragons had their own ways and kept their own secrets. She hoped Ferin would be less secretive when he was well.

Digging through leaves and plying away broken stones, she listened for any movement and was satisfied with the quiet. Her heart picked up unexpectedly. A sharp tug knocked the breath from her lungs. Miles away, Moon yanked on their connection with a rankling tenacity.

His silvery yarn pulsed angrily behind her eyes. The smaller green thread was more interwoven now, intrinsic to the overall shape and strength of the spell. He pulled again. But when Audra resisted, his grip slackened. The green thread brightened as the silver one dimmed.

Let him wait. His mood didn't matter and, given the circumstances, she was glad he hadn't known she would come here. He would have stopped her, waiting to kill her until they reached the monastery. Asshole.

Audra dug through six inches of dirt, insect shells, and small bones when her fingers finally brushed solid wood. The familiar excitement of being where she wasn't supposed to be and the possibility of taking what didn't belong to her made her work faster.

After clearing a small section of the floor, she located a slightly wider space between the boards. When the tip of her dagger slid through without resistance, she pried at the planks. After a few minutes of sweat and silent but passionate cursing, Audra pulled up the hatch. She muffled a cough into her sleeve as a gust of stale air greeted her.

Ten stone stairs disappeared into darkness. Ignoring another of Moon's tugs, she stepped down and followed the tunnel. The passage trailed beneath the ruins, and thin streams of dull light trickled in from above. The tunnel curved south then west again. Paths turned off, but she stayed on the main one until she reached the twelfth hall and veered left.

THE MALICE OF MOONS AND MAGES

Muted voices drifted overhead, disappearing as quickly as they'd come. The lock, stiffened by disuse and time, gave way beneath her skill.

A dim all'ight cast eerie shadows across the scroll-lined shelves. After so many years, she was surprised to find it still barely flickering.

She gently pulled out a dozen scrolls, unrolling the wooden slips to glimpse the characters painted on the yellowing papyrus. Audra tried to be grateful for Zin's sporadic and impatient tutelage on the ancient language. The little bit she could decipher helped her select eight scrolls that mentioned bonds. It would take more time and attention for her to clearly interpret them. Her gaze lingered on several other scrolls, but her bag could hold no more. The rest would have to wait.

The all'ight illuminated her return to the stairs and up into the slanting afternoon light. She extinguished the small flame with the turn of a key beneath its copper base and shoved it into her pack.

She scaled the broken wall and dropped silently to the ground, pausing before darting into the woods. She'd retrace her path, back the way she'd come.

Audra was ducking between low branches when Moon yanked again. His demand lashed painfully around her chest. Her reaction was instinctive. A flash of emerald magic whipped from her hand. It sliced through a tree, toppling it into a neighboring pine with a thunderous crash.

Her stunned gaze alternated between the carnage and her palm. There wasn't time to ponder how she'd stolen Moon's magic. Yells came from the monastery. Boots pounded over dried ground.

Audra ran and leaped over shrubs until her lungs burned.

The ground met her face mid leap, a searing pain snaked around her calf. The pack sailed from her shoulder and disappeared beneath a conifer's lowest bough. She hoped it stayed hidden.

A middle-aged man with cheeks ruddy from exertion appeared behind her. His gray thread spun from a hand hidden beneath long black sleeves and tethered to her ankle. Two soldiers flanked him, swords drawn.

The mage panted. "What do we have here?" Another leash swept toward her, encircling her waist. Audra clawed at the dirt while he dragged her over the sharp ground toward him.

"Nori, stand down." A thick man strode into view, hair shorn close to his head. His coloring was warmer than his peers, closer to Traq's. He frowned in a way that indicated it might be his usual face.

"She took down a tree, Xiang," Nori said. "Aren't the Starlings supposed to be south this time of year?"

Xiang stared at her with a ghost of familiarity in his eyes. "She's no Starling." With one motion to the soldiers, they hauled her onto her feet. He moved close, examining her build and chopped hair. He pinched her chin, turning it one way, then the other before she jerked away. "Could I be so lucky?"

"Sir?" Nori asked.

Audra stayed quiet. She didn't like either of their tones and offering a defense before they asked could lead to more questions.

"What are you doing here?" Xiang asked.

"Ch-checking the ruins," she said. "I grew up near here and was heading back to Stonetown. I only—"

"Where?" Xiang looked more interested than Audra liked. "What village?"

She pulled tears to her eyes and let her limbs soften. Actions that had worked in the past to develop sympathy and lay the foundation for underestimating her strong desire to escape. Sure enough, one soldier's grip loosened slightly. But the man before her was unswayed, waiting patiently for her response.

"You wouldn't have heard of it, only—"

"Say it."

She swallowed. "Pangol."

Xiang chewed on the word. "Pangol. Do you know what it means?"

Her mouth dried beneath his dissecting gaze. "Dragon," she whispered.

He turned brusquely away. "Bring her."

Audra waited until the others turned their backs. Then she dropped from one soldier's grasp and kicked the legs out from the other. She made ten paces before Nori's magic smashed against her cheek.

Everything went dark.

Thirty

Lua

Although daylight cut through the barn roof slats onto Lua's robes, it was the twisting strain inside his chest that woke him. *Audra.*

Where had his little mouse scampered off to? He considered this might be an act of rebellion since they were in Zin's territory, but that didn't feel right. He wondered if being so close to them blinded her to the truth or if she were a better liar than he'd taken her for. He'd expected a surly old woman, not an irritable dragon.

He dragged his robes over his head and darted to the house. The door flew open at his touch. Magic swirled around him and drew him into the shade. Zin sat at the table, scales rippling down her bare arms before disappearing. Her eyes glittered menacingly. Gone were the human fingers from last night, replaced with long talons that raked the wooden tabletop.

"Where is she?" he asked.

A chair pulled out of its own accord as she motioned to it. "Searching for solutions."

He licked his lips before sitting down. His chest ached. "What solutions?"

"How to break your bond without dying." Her claws tapped like dropping knives. "It was my suggestion after she told me you were heading to your monastery. How very practical of you. Kill her where you think her kin can't reach you. As if distance matters to my kind. You cannot imagine what I'll do if anything happens to her."

Zin must have only held this form when Audra or others were around. The amount of ancient magic it took to both maintain hers and Ferin's shapes and protect her territory had to have been daunting.

"I won't hurt her." Lua tasted the truth in those words.

"Can you help it?" Zin asked. "Thirteen stars isn't powerful enough to sever a bond without death as a consequence for one of you. And, correct me if I'm wrong, but you don't strike me as the self-sacrificing type."

He winced as the thread tightened again. "Hurting me will only hurt her."

Her malicious smile was impossibly broad, showing rows of pointed teeth. "I'm not going to hurt you. I'll let Audra do it herself."

Lua frowned. He was missing something important.

"Even after travelling together, bonded and all, you still don't know her, do you? How much has she told you about her mother? Or were you so absorbed in your self-importance that you didn't listen?"

A shiver worked up his spine despite the fire that burned high in the hearth. He didn't remember Audra speaking much about her mother, but he'd seen her in Audra's nightmares. She was ageless in the ways that only magic could influence. How bonds made someone look. Zin smirked at his understanding.

"Audra's mother was yours?" he asked.

"We kept peace at the borders for a long time. My siblings and our chosen mages kept our people safe. You wouldn't know, of course. I'm sure the last Rajav had our dealings stricken from the official records." Her voice eased into a condescending tone of assumed authority. "Did you know he was once bonded with a dragon?"

Lua's breath hitched. "What are you talking about?"

"A history lesson then. Pay attention." She smiled at his discomfort.

"It was before I met Lorah, Audra's mother. There was an old dragon. Honestly, his personality had always been rougher than his scales. Certainly, wasn't the best of us. Damaged goods long before they met. He was with Li-Hun for over a hundred years. Together, they united the Moon tribes. The Rajav was young then, and if he'd stayed that idealistic and good-natured, the dragon might have stayed. But as it often seems to be with humans, power made him cruel." Her smile faded. "I heard he found a more amiable replacement eventually. I've often wondered if he ever mentioned it to his family. I suspect I now have my answer."

A wave of nausea swept through Lua. Their father wouldn't have told Selene. The Rajav trusted her less than the councilors.

There you are, she'd said in Audra's dreams. It made no sense. Why would Selene have been looking for Audra and Ferin?

Zin stared, unblinking. "Make no mistake. That dragon loved him as only a dragon can. From the depths of his whole being. But he learned long ago that love should never be depthless or thoughtless or it is not love at all. And when he saw what Li-Hun was becoming and what he planned on doing, the dragon broke their bond and left him gasping on a castle terrace in Uduary. The Song monks saved him, but Li-Hun never stopped searching for him. Wherever that dragon has gone, I'm sure he felt Li-Hun's death. Once connected, always connected, after all." Her eyes were emeralds beneath a human-like veneer.

Lua shifted uncomfortably. If that were true, it would explain his father's obsession and ensuing paranoia.

"You remind me of Li-Hun. His good looks and confident stride. His short-sighted arrogance and desire to cling to things that don't belong to you."

Lua's fists trembled beneath the table while he fought to control his expression. Her magic brushed across his hands and knees. "I am *nothing* like my father," he hissed.

"Hm, I cannot say. But Audra *is* like her mother. Fierce and loving and strong. Wonderfully good at surviving. Have you felt her coming into her power? Noticed the bond pull more her way than yours since she carried the jade?"

Lua's eyes widened with the memory of the argentava and two bursts of unexpected magic. Zin chuckled at his expression.

"The thing about Western mages that makes them a threat to others, is that they can bond with any other magical creature. Dragons, yes, but Moons and Starling mages too. More than one creature or person at a time. And when their magic bonds, it slowly begins to dominate." Her delight at his discomfort waned slightly. "But there's something else you should know. Your monks will kill you both by trying to force the bond to break. Even if you are healed and standing beneath the light of two full moons that have given their blessings, unless the Western magic is dealt with beforehand, both of you will die. I hope the Western scrolls will provide some guidance otherwise I cannot be held accountable for my actions." She sniffed the air and eyed him curiously. "Of course, there is another way."

He swallowed at the implication. "That would kill me."

She shrugged. "Maybe. But if Audra learns to control her power before then, you both might live."

He closed his eyes. The dragon was right, the alternative she was suggesting was beyond his nature. The thread stretched into the woods and over the mountain. It pulsed painfully, shimmering silver the way it always did but when he examined it closer, there was another color woven throughout. He pulled. Her resistance was stronger than it ought to have been. He winced. "What happened to Audra's mother? What happened to the dragons?"

Her face was full of nostalgic sorrow. "Those are separate questions, and I'll answer only one. Lorah met a good man. At first, it was nothing. She'd taken lovers before. But this common, not terribly handsome man, earned her heart in a way that I could not. Dragons don't like to share, but we are generous in our love. When she wanted things I couldn't give her, we severed our bond. It was painful for us both."

"And you settled here to be near her."

She nodded. "Dragons usually bond only once. Sometimes from necessity—such as injury—but more often for love. Occasionally a dragon might bond more than that, like the one to Li-Hun. But not me. I'll probably die in these mountains, but only after her children are safe."

Claws scraped down the hall as Ferin lumbered into view. He was taller and thicker than the previous day. His face more squared, and his skin had a gold and green sheen that Zin's magic failed to completely cover. The jade glowed beneath a thin layer of flesh upon his chest. He stared from the hallway, astute eyes assessing the mage with less innocence than he'd shown before.

"Children? He's not Lorah's child. And Audra said her brother died years ago."

"Ferin isn't her brother by blood, but they've been family ever since Lorah found him freshly hatched in the mountains after Raia's last storm. His scales were too thin to ward off a Moon mage spell when they were attacked as children. It stole his voice and strength for too long."

Green scales rippled down Ferin's arms before disappearing. Zin's magic struggled to keep them both in these false forms.

There was something off about Zin's words, as if there were meaning in what wasn't said. The way she'd avoided speaking of Audra's human brother bothered him. "But you said 'children,'" Lua said.

"Audra's older brother went missing at the battle of Oxton two years before Pangol was destroyed. But Bolin still lives in the northern lands," Zin said, her eyes searing his skin. "He's not turned out as well as he ought to have."

Lua chilled. "Bolin?" He yanked on the thread, demanding Audra return. They needed to talk. If Selene's anchor was Audra's brother, then this situation was more complicated than he could have ever imagined. The green flash that sailed down through his silver thread struck him like an arrow. It stole his breath. His heart pounded. Zin watched him struggle impassively. "Did Bolin know about the magic?"

"Not entirely. Audra was always the more gifted of the two, but after the spell struck, it's taken years to grow. And Bolin enlisted before Ferin was found. He wouldn't know anything about them now. When your people destroyed the last monastery and met the Starlings in Pangol, it was too late. Lorah fell while saving her children and believed her eldest son had died in Oxton."

He began to speak but winced as the flesh around his ankle burned.

He cursed and knocked the chair over when another strike wrapped around his waist.

"Audra?" The burning eased, but fear swept through him. He tried to see through her eyes, hear the sounds around her, but the way was blocked.

"What's happening?" Zin demanded.

Ferin limped forward, eyes wide with pain. One hand rubbed his side.

"I don't—"

The punch knocked his head sideways, though duller than what Audra received. His vision darkened for a second before his eyes refocused on the surrounding room. Audra was unconscious. That he still lived proved that she did too.

"Tell me what's happening!" Zin growled. Her magic slackened around Lua's limbs.

"She's hurt. I have to go." He closed his eyes, submitting to the taut bond and letting it reel him toward her with little effort.

As his feet lifted from the ground, Ferin leaped forward and reached out, but Lua sailed past him out the door. Lua held the robes about his head as he darted between trees and over rocks, hoping to reach her before anyone figured out who and what she was to him.

Thirty-One

Audra

Audra's waking groan escalated the throbbing behind her cheek. She tried to raise a hand to her face and failed, struggling against the tight ropes that bound her arms to the chair beneath her. Taking in the dimly lit stone room with its curved walls and molding pitched ceiling, dread settled in her stomach.

The room at the top of the remaining tower was only accessible by a steep winding staircase and single door. Audra heard feet shuffling and low voices murmuring on the other side. The room's lone window led to a hundred-foot drop. This would be a difficult place to escape from under the best of circumstances.

There was an old, scarred table before her with a pitcher and two cups placed in the center. Seated across from her was the man from the woods. Xiang leaned back in his chair, assessing her with cool brown eyes that traced over her features before meeting her gaze.

Audra stifled a sigh. It would do her no good to waste energy, and opportunities always favored the patient. She willed her limbs to relax and studied a long gouge in the oaken tabletop while waiting for him to speak.

He tilted his head casually. "What did that captain call you? The western mouse?" he asked.

She looked up with a well-practiced neutrality. Her voice was hoarse. "What captain?"

He huffed. "I see," he said. "It's to be like that, is it?" Xiang poured a cup of water from the pitcher on the table and took a long sip.

Audra swallowed involuntarily before looking away. "Who are you?" she asked. "What do you want with me?"

He settled the cup on the table. "Even a little mouse must know what black robes mean." The narrowing of her eyes at the term made the corners of his lips twitch. "I only want to ask some questions," he said. "Then, depending on the answers, you can be on your way."

She snorted at the lie. If caught on this side of the border, the Moons would eliminate any witnesses. Yet if these were the same people hunting Moon, then she'd be as good as dead if they discovered who she was. "I see. It's to be like that, is it? If you're going to let me go anyway, why not untie me now, and I might be more accommodating."

Xiang smiled, clearly amused. "Would that really work?"

"It's better than lying to me," she quipped.

Chuckling, he pulled her dagger from inside his robes. "You remind me of someone I know from Pangol," he said moving behind her. "Similar warm brown eyes and mahogany hair."

Audra tensed as he unsheathed the blade, but he simply sawed through her binds. She rubbed the deep creases from her wrists, flexing and straightening her fingers to chase the numbness away. Xiang returned to his seat and placed the dagger on the table between them. "You can have it back when we're done."

She snorted. "You mean when you bury it in my neck."

Xiang didn't answer. Instead, he poured another cup of water and set it before her. She cautiously brought the cup to her lips. He waited until she swallowed to start speaking. "This person and I fought together at Oxton. Do you remember anyone from your village? You must have been quite young when it fell."

Her fingers clenched around the cup, shoulders suddenly rigid. She hated talking about Pangol or her family with anyone, but to be trapped in this fallen monastery and subjected to a conversation with a Moon soldier was a new level of insult. If she could give the man something he wanted, there was still a chance he might lower his guard. Sure, a jump from a tall window might kill her but she knew from experience that it might not. "Many people died at Oxton," she replied stiffly, taking another long drink.

"I know. I was there."

His words drew her eyes to him. The warmth of his complexion was deeper than her own and the subtle inflections of a regional accent slowed certain words. He'd been born in western lands.

"Did you turn traitor at Oxton, or were you Moon tribe the whole time?" she asked, failing to constrain her disgust.

Xiang's tone softened. "I betrayed no one. My friend and I were captured together. This young man, his father died there. Killed by a mage while trying to protect his son."

She settled the cup on the table and hid her hands below, but she couldn't help but listen. His words tugged at old wounds.

"He had a younger sister and mother with mage lineage in Pangol," Xiang said. He paused at Audra's small frown. "My friend, Bolin, often wonders if they lived. Where they might be."

Her breath hitched at the name, but she kept her eyes down and bit the inside of her cheek to tap down her reactions. Bolin was an unusual name, and her brother had gone missing in Oxton with their father, Kaul. In all her travels throughout the western lands, she used to ask questions about them but had never learned anything about either of their fates. Cautious hope swelled inside her chest.

"Audra," he said. She looked up too quickly. "I'd like to take you to him. But first, do you know where Lua is?"

Though she'd never heard the name before, she knew who Xiang meant. Some part of her argued that using her brother's memory was nothing more than a cruel trick to gain her trust. Her emotions locked behind a steely expression. "I don't know that name."

"Lua Koray is the Moon tribe Oji."

Audra's mouth went dry as the truth resonated in her bones. Shit. Of course he was. Who else could he possibly be? She licked her lips. "Why would he be here?"

"He's been running." Xiang leaned forward. "Ever since he killed his father, the Rajav Koray."

She inhaled sharply. That fragile unguarded moment revealed too much and she tried to downplay it as best she could. Her jaw tightened. "I don't know anyone named Lua."

"Who helped you escape the *Requin*?" Xiang demanded. "Chon told me about the man you pulled from the water."

Lua's prediction of what would happen to the ship when the Moon tribe arrived came back to her. "What did you do to them?"

"Asked them some questions. Specifically, who removed the constraining bolt from the Oji's back. Then we let them go," Xiang said. The subtle lift of his eyebrows as he spoke knotted Audra's stomach. One liar was usually good at catching another.

She spoke slowly. "I escaped from the *Requin* by stealing a dinghy. There was a man, but we parted ways in Oxton. I never knew his name." She tried to spin some truth with her lie.

Xiang sighed, one hand clenching atop the table. "Lua couldn't have survived long without a bond, not in his weakened state, and you were the only person on that boat to touch him." He glanced toward the window. Starling had already set, and Silence was rising.

Xiang's hand gripping the hilt of the sword strapped to his thigh drew her eye. He would kill her if she didn't say something to convince him otherwise, but her thoughts were slow. Giving up Moon would be damning herself either way. She finally understood what it felt like to be a mouse cornered by a cat.

"Bolin would never forgive me if anything happened to his sister," he said. Audra picked at the scarred table again, determined not to be swayed by such deceit. His next statement stilled her fingers. "The Oja wants Lua alive. If you help us, I can keep you safe."

She traced the deep groove in the oak, wondering if a western mage had made it during the slaughter. Her tone darkened. "If I had travelled so far with someone, why would I betray them?"

"Because Bolin wants to see you again," he said.

The quiet between them was punctuated by her scraping nails on the wood but even that paused when he held something in the air. A black and red stone swung on its leather cord.

"Take this as a promise," he said.

She watched the stone for a moment before laying an untrusting glare on him. "What is it?"

"Bloodstone," he said. "When you're ready to block Lua's power over you, this will help. He won't know your feelings or thoughts, won't be able to track you." He laid it on the table and slid it toward her. "Wearing it over your heart disrupts the bonding spell."

She picked the stone up cautiously, turning it over once before shoving it into a pocket. Whether Xiang spoke truthfully about the stone might not make any difference, but it was better to have it and not need it than need it and not have it. She could determine its worth or value later. Her fingers resumed their tracing. "Why do you want him?"

"If he lives, then Bolin will ultimately die." Xiang's gaze flicked to the window again where cold moonlight was cascading in. His hand remained tight around his sword, as if expecting something.

The dagger on the table was just inches from her hand. These lies were too elaborate to have come up with in the short time since she'd been captured. But if Xiang were telling the truth, she had other questions. "Does Bolin know that our mother, that I . . . ?"

"Later. Audra, where is—" A scream rang through the courtyard, followed by shouts that silenced too quickly. Xiang paled and stood as footsteps hastened up the tower stairs.

The mage from the woods burst in, slamming the door against the wall. "He's here!"

Audra lunged for the dagger. It shook in her hands as she backed away, eying the men before her.

Nori's magic spun out, coiling around Audra's throat as two soldiers rushed inside. She slashed the blade uselessly as the thread cinched deeper into her neck and hoisted her feet from the floor.

"Stop!" Xiang shouted.

Audra clawed and gasped as the gray lash strangled her. Her throat burned beneath the spell. Anger and fear bloomed in her chest. She couldn't die here where so many of her people had met their ends. She struggled without hope before frantically throwing the dagger at Nori. It sparked green, propelled with unusual force and accuracy. It sliced the mage's shoulder and bounced away. Nori's spell lapsed and Audra collapsed to the floor. Her throat was tender and raw. Violent coughs shook her as she tried to rise but her knees buckled with another cough.

Nori cursed. His arms spread, lips moving in a soundless mantra.

"Nori!" Xiang yelled, starting forward. "We need them alive."

Magic swirled around Nori's hands. His sleeves swayed as the spell strengthened and prepared to strike. Audra raised an arm to shield herself and snatched the dagger from the ground with the other. Next time she'd hit his heart.

A deafening roar shook the walls. The roof above them wrenched away in a crackle of silver light. It spun into the sky before crashing on the field below while the tower's upper stones tumbled backward. A dark figure alighted atop the broken wall, robes billowing around him. Audra's chest tightened, the threads pulling her toward him though her legs refused to obey.

A soldier cursed, another yelled for aid. A section of stones toppled inward and buried Xiang's legs beneath them. But Audra saw none of that, her whole being solely focused on the man before them. The Oji of the Moon tribe.

Lua balanced silently. Ebony hair danced around a throat marked with violence, matching Audra's own. Silence was half full behind him, giving its favored child a burst of power that Audra felt shimmering down their bond. His eyes found her, and, in a flash, he was beside her. His fingers lightly traced over her neck and cheek sending a small electric charge into her. He frowned.

"Are you alright?" he asked.

She nodded, mutely.

Nori recovered from the shock and hurled another spell. Lua batted it away and slammed the mage against the wall with a silver whip. Three more soldiers rushed in, swords drawn.

"Hold on to me," he whispered. Audra wrapped her arms around his neck as he lifted her onto her feet. "Look away."

She buried her face against his chest, inhaling the scent of him.

"You dared to touch her?" Lua's voice engulfed the room, one of his arms tightening possessively around her. The Songs had no time to scream. When Audra looked up, piles of black robes and armor, ash, and dust, crumpled to the floor.

Across the room, the rumble of shifting stones drew Audra's attention. Xiang struggled to free himself; his eyes were wide with fear. She tried to turn toward Xiang, but the arm around her tightened.

"After everything, it is you," Lua said, his silver eyes fixed on Xiang.

A silver thread jerked Xiang from beneath the stones. He thrashed as the spell lifted him from the floor.

"Stop," Audra said, though her weakened voice didn't break Lua's concentration. Xiang might be the only way Audra could ever see her brother again.

A darker thread slammed down, severing Lua's spell. A woman dressed in Moon robes pulled her magic back, rushing to Xiang as he fell.

Lua's lips twisted with a merciless smile. "I know you. One of Sharine's pupils, aren't you?"

"Jayna, stand down," Xiang gasped. Lua was too strong, even Audra knew that this woman had no chance against him.

Jayna's arms spread defiantly. "He can't—" Her voice dissolved into a scream. A long, bloody rake bloomed across her chest from Lua's spell. Still holding Audra with one arm, he moved toward the mage.

"Close your eyes, Audra," Lua said lowly. Audra shook her head, fear rising in her chest.

"Moon, stop." Audra pleaded but his jaw stubbornly tightened.

Xiang tried to pull Jayna away, but Lua gripped the woman's arm. A surge of energy coursed through Audra as Lua's magic consumed both Jayna and Xiang's lives, draining them together. Two more soldiers appeared in the doorway and charged the Oji. As they neared, they dried and flaked into husks as his rage engulfed them.

Audra's eyes widened in horror. This was what he'd done to the fishers and who knew how many others. She gripped the sides of Lua's face, forcing his gaze to hers. Her hands warmed on his cheeks.

"Let them live," she begged. "*Please*, don't kill them."

He stared into her eyes, bringing his lips so close to hers that his breath kissed her skin. "Fine," he whispered through clenched teeth. "But only for your sake."

Lua's spell died, spitting green and silver before dissipating. He glared at Xiang and Jayna as they collapsed. "You'll receive no mercy the next time we meet."

Audra briefly met Xiang's gaze as a silver thread lashed upward and a wave of exhaustion swam through her. Lua pulled her close and they rose over the edge of the broken wall into the light of Silence.

Thirty-Two

Traq

Dust kicked into Traq's face from passing soldiers as he pried the rock from his horse's hoof. With the steep terrain, the risk of stumbles and hoof injuries increased as everyone fatigued in the higher elevation. The brisk pace was wearing on the horses.

Wren picked up the other hints of magic first, more subtle than the ones in Oxton. Durin confirmed it, even Traq could taste it here and there. The hope was one trail would lead to the other.

Traq considered visiting Zin to see if Audra had delivered the jade. But Zin didn't like strangers, and she probably didn't want to see him anyway. He was grateful for the years she'd sheltered and fed him, but they'd never had a strong relationship. In truth, she'd barely tolerated him. When he said he was enlisting, she told him never to return.

"What's wrong?"

Wren's voice plucked him back to the side of the road as a small stone flicked from the hoof. She stood so near he caught the scents of sandalwood in her clothing. The soldiers gossiped; even Durin gave them curious glances. Relationships between mages weren't uncommon, though discouraged. Knowing this, Wren's flirtatious behavior was opposed to both of their ambitions. Add in the fact that Wren was a well-respected mage and Traq was a dirty Westerner, and it gave more kindling to the rumor fire. But Traq would be lying if he said he wasn't tempted.

"We should camp soon. It gets steeper in another couple of miles," he said.

"Something's on your mind."

He shrugged. "Nothing I care to share." A couple of soldiers straggled behind them, waiting patiently for the two mages to continue.

"Being here must bring up memories. Coming back home is never easy," she said.

He didn't respond. Wren was still trying to determine if he'd protect Audra or follow orders if made to choose—a question he'd asked himself since Oxton.

Traq climbed into the saddle and looked down at her. The setting light warmed her face, softening the edges of her cheeks, casting an amber hue down her long, pale braid. There was something unattainable about her. It was best for Traq to not reach too high, but their proximity had him considering the softness of her skin a bit too often lately. He nudged his horse into a trot to create distance.

Wren didn't speak to him again until they were seated near each other beside one of the fires. "About your friend..."

Traq chewed a large bite of meat slowly and stared at the flames dancing atop the logs.

"Was she from here too?" Wren scooted closer.

"Pangol."

"Near the old monastery?" she asked. "One of the last villages to fall, I think."

He nodded. Though Stonetown had been rebuilt, there weren't enough survivors of either Pangol or his village to manage the task, so they remained abandoned.

Her brows creased. "Would she go there? Is there anything left of it?"

Traq took another bite before responding. This might be a way to avoid Zin's, which is where Audra probably was. She hadn't visited Pangol in a long time. There would be no advantage to it.

"Where else would they go?" he asked. "Or maybe to the monastery. They'll need shelter as the temperatures drop, and it's on the way to the border."

Wren assessed him coolly. "You meant it when you said that duty came first." She leaned closer, lowering her voice. "If you mislead us, I'll have to report you. Or you'll have to convince me not to."

He squirmed at the proposition. "Do you still have the trail?"

"It's dim but, yes. Though the second trail has gotten stronger."

"Durin has it too?"

The older man sat beneath blankets at the most distant fire. His profile shadowed as he spoke animatedly to an enrapt Liasa.

"I think so. Though he'd likely say anything to return home sooner rather than later. Can't say I blame him." She smiled wistfully. "Island life doesn't sound too bad right now."

Traq cast a sideways glance at him with a pang of envy. Liasa met his gaze with a small nod, one Westerner to another.

Thirty-Three

Audra

Audra inhaled the familiar scents of cloves and vanilla. The combination roused memories of autumnal festivals, spicy soups, and sweet pies. But there was a newly familiar odor too, a combination of night and rain, that made her feel safe.

She had little desire to break from the moment, noticing the warmth of what her head rested on. It rose and fell gently, both comforting and disconcerting. Her fingers skimmed over fine cloth and silky hair as the steady thrum of a strong heart pulsed beneath the splay of her hand.

She startled and tried to draw away. An arm tightened firmly around her. Moon's fingers pressed intimately against her ribs. His blue robes covered their entwined bodies, the sheen of his black ones peeked from beneath. His breath dissipated in the cool air of predawn light. A small frown tugged at his lips with her movement.

Above them was a low wooden roof where spiderwebs had thickened over generations. Old burns blackened the walls, marring the beams from the dirt floor upward. The pattern of it scratched at distant memories.

She couldn't say how long they'd been like this. That neither of them had pulled away was unnerving, and that he continued to hold her was unsettling in ways she didn't want to acknowledge. Audra uncrossed her leg from his thighs and gently lifted his arm away. In response, he rolled toward her. His breath skimmed the top of her head as he draped an arm across her chest. His hair tickled her neck. The thrum of her heart synchronized with his, .

Never in her history of lovers had she slept like this. People were always too warm or moved too much. They snored or didn't smell good. Moon, it seemed, was different. It could only be the bond that allowed their bodies to conform so smoothly together and kept her from rushing away.

Not Moon. Lua Koray. Moon Oji.

Shit.

It was too easy to remain pressed against his warmth when she knew his heart was cold. This was worse than she'd ever imagined. And she was accomplished at imagining terrible things.

He killed his father, Xiang had said. But she didn't care about the division of the Moon tribes, didn't care if they lived or died. Though it seemed odd that something as profound as the death of the Rajav wasn't more widely known. There'd been gossip about it from the guards on Callaway, but she'd been too busy thinking of ways to escape to pay much attention. And even those on the *Requin* were tight-lipped about it. Sailors typically gossiped worse than bitter village elders about each other's children.

The Rajav's death was being kept quiet until they brought the Oji under control.

Audra studied the sharp line of Lua's jaw, the twitch of his brow, the way his black hair held pigments of darkest blue and plum. She'd suspected he was someone of status but wouldn't have believed him if he'd told her who he was or what he was capable of. She felt like a cursed idiot. The truth was, even if she'd known, it wouldn't have made any difference.

Moon Oji Lua Koray, first in line to inherit the supreme seat of power and his father's tyrannical legacy. Lua, whose life and death were tied to hers.

She needed stronger curse words.

His rage had been all consuming, devouring everything in its path, terrifying. He hadn't hesitated to drain the lives of his tribespeople when they threatened her. If she hadn't begged him to stop, he would have killed them all. But Xiang had spoken of Bolin with sincerity, whatever other lies the man had told her, that much had been true.

She should hate Lua for everything his tribe had done to hers, but her feelings were a jumble of horror, awe, and knowingly misplaced admiration that each vied equally for prominence. Never mind the compelling attraction that was more difficult to deny with each passing day. Those recurring thoughts that she should have refused to pluck him from the water all those weeks ago were fleeting and sour. With a huff, she scurried from beneath his robes into the chilly morning air before he could reclaim her.

Lua's eyes slit open like an annoyed cat, before closing again. He rolled away, pulling the robe over his head.

"Why didn't we go back to Auntie's?" she asked quietly.

His breathing altered but he remained quiet. The bag she'd abandoned in the woods lay on the floor beside the base of the warped central supporting column that held up the remainder of the roof. She eyed the two rows of carvings that ran up opposing sides of the column. One set for Bolin, the other for Audra. But hers stopped too soon.

Time had carved its name on every edge of this place. The back of the home had collapsed, its roof scattered down what had once been a hallway to three bedrooms. A soft wind gently rustled the piles of leaves and twigs. The rounded hearth stones had shifted with the cracking mortar. Returning to this broken home gnawed at unhealed wounds.

"Why are we here?" she whispered.

Lua sighed and rose slowly, rubbing his neck. The burn was gone, nothing remained of Nori's spell. "You insisted on coming here after we got the bag."

Audra remembered nothing after they'd leaped from the top of the tower. Leaped? No. They'd flown. But that didn't seem possible. She pressed fists into her eyes to quell the watering.

"You wanted to come home," he said softly.

The heat of him moved closer, and she resisted the seductive tug of his proximity. "I don't remember."

"Not surprising."

"Is that something you do?" she asked.

"What?"

"Alter people's memories? Auntie said that—"

"No." Lua snapped. "I don't. I wouldn't. There's too much cruelty in that spell. You were just exhausted." His voice was pained.

"You killed those people."

"I'll kill more if I must."

"And . . . Did you kill your father?" Her chest wrenched as his expression soured. "Is altering memories worse than that to you?"

"You wouldn't understand unless you've seen or experienced it." He assessed her coolly. "Those mages and soldiers were going to kill us if I didn't kill them first. Their deaths gave us the power to get away and the strength to heal."

She shook her head. "No. Their leader—Xiang, I think—was going to release me."

Lua's eyes narrowed suspiciously. "Why would he do that?"

The bloodstone pressed against her thigh from inside her pocket. She shook her head. "Something about my brother."

The suspicion dissipated. He looked away and cursed. "I didn't know."

"Know?"

"That Bolin was your family," his voice dropped. "Not until Zin mentioned him."

He stepped forward and Audra slid back. "Why would you know? I never told you his name. Why would I when you refused to tell me yours?"

"A fair point." He pursed his lips and had the good sense to look guilty. "Zin knew that Bolin was in the northern tribes. Did she never tell you?"

Hurt bloomed behind Audra's ribs. Zin was always secretive, and Audra had trusted she kept things from her for good reason. Now, she wasn't so sure. The omission cut deep and made her wonder what else she didn't know.

"What do you know of your mother's relationship with Zin?"

"Why?"

"She told me things about your mother, my family. Things she'd seen." He moved closer. "And about the bond between us."

Her eyes flashed dangerously. With the events of the previous day still fresh, she'd nearly forgotten her fury. "You still plan to kill me when we reach the monastery?"

He sighed. "No. Not since before the argentava. I'm sure you've considered your options since this mess began. Maybe debated handing me over to your Starling friend, hoping to separate us."

She scowled at his words, but stubbornness wouldn't let her look away.

He shrugged. "I would have done the same. Perhaps that's why the magic anchored us together."

"Why?"

"Survival at all costs is intrinsic to our natures."

With a sneer she returned her attention to the room. "Pretty sure it's intrinsic to everyone's nature. Maybe we're just better at it than others." Her fingers danced over the central beam's etchings before she stared down the fallen hallway.

Wherever she moved, she was acutely aware of the pull to him, like the orbital force of the moons or Raia's ring around the planet. It was stronger than before, an ache that wanted tending, an itch begging to be scratched. Lua moved with her, staying within a few feet. It was difficult to tell who was anchored to who or whose desire was stronger.

"Is it always like this?" she asked. She could almost feel his breath against her neck, taste his scent on her tongue. Her heart thudded. She hoped she didn't have to explain.

"No," he said, placing his hands gently on her shoulders. His fingers thrilled her skin through her clothes as he turned her around. "It's never been like this."

She stared at his arrogant mouth too long.

"The others . . . I heard their thoughts, felt their emotions. Bending them to my will was easy. But—"

"You don't know what I'm thinking. You never did. What about the rest?" Audra asked.

"I could only control you those first few days. You've resisted every time since then," Lua said. "But I feel all of your emotions."

His cheeks flushed as hers warmed. "All of them?"

He squeezed his eyes shut. "Yes. But I can't tell what's yours or mine anymore. It's damn confusing." His fingers trailed down her arms before falling away. "Did you know what your mother was?"

"She didn't hide it from us."

"And how Western mages bond?"

Lorah had been honest about her mage history, telling them she wouldn't dwell on her past because it led her to Kaul, their father, and to them. But she refused to discuss more than that, insisting she'd tell Audra more when she was older while only sharing childish tales of lore and warnings hidden in nighttime fables. When Auntie had talked about their past on one of their visits, and hinted at Audra's future, Lorah quickly bundled Audra and Ferin up and departed. They didn't go back much after that, not until the night Pangol fell.

Lua retrieved the bag from the floor. "Did you find anything?"

She yanked it from his hands. "Don't touch those!"

"Can they explain how to unravel the bond?"

"I don't know; it's old language. It'll take some time to decipher." Audra clutched the bag to her chest.

He sighed, rubbed his face again. "We don't have a lot of that. Zin said we'll both die if we try to break the bond." Lua stepped back and sat on the floor. "Sit," he said, "please. I'll tell you what she told me."

"Shouldn't we be leaving? What if they come after us?" she asked.

"They're too weak to consider it. We can spare a few moments."

Audra settled across from him but held up a hand before he could speak. "In fairness, I warned you about Zin."

One eyebrow arched. "And do you think you were *completely* forthright?"

She shrugged. "It's not like I could ask if you wanted to meet a hostile dragon hiding in the mountains who'd probably want to kill you." Her smile was mischievous. "You weren't listening anyway. I hoped the shock would give you perspective."

"So, you know what they are?"

"Did you honestly think I was too ignorant to know they weren't human?" She scowled. "To feel a dragon's protective magic and know her feral love." She shook her head. "You really think less of everyone. Your arrogance will get you killed."

Along their shared thread, Audra felt the sting of her words wound him, but no denial came from his lips. Instead, he took her comments quietly, with more introspection than she thought him capable. That awareness drew her to him but instead she leaned away. Her questions could wait until they were moving again. She cleared her throat. "There's something missing from here. I've searched every time I've come back, but with no luck."

He glanced around at the crumbling facade. "What?"

"Something my mother wore for protection. They were here the night the village fell but they disappeared. This might be my last chance to find them."

Cautiously, he took her hand and gently squeezed it. "You'll have more chances, Audra. I promise."

Thirty-Four

Xiang

The weight of guilt hung around Xiang's shoulders as he tended to Jayna where she lay on a pallet on the monastery floor. If he hadn't seen the similarities between Audra and Bolin, and hadn't asked where she was from, then they'd have killed her and moved on. His hesitation had resulted in the deaths of Nori and eight soldiers.

The Oji's wrath had reduced the corpses to husks of double burnt ash sculpted to look like people. Disposing of their remains had caused one soldier to vomit when her lover crumbled in her arms. Some bodies remained more solid—like the one on the *Requin*—with a papery, wasp's nest outer shell. But Nori's remains disintegrated into dust with a single touch.

Lua shouldn't have been that strong. Even anchored, he should still be recovering. Yet he'd tethered to the outside of the tower and killed them all so quickly. It had taken the Oji months to recover when he was anchored to Dain.

Jayna's wound ran from her collarbone to her breast. The situation might have been awkward if she doubted his nature. But their relationship had always bordered on a non-romantic kinship.

Each shallow inhalation tugged her flesh apart while Xiang finished dressing it. Jayna lay silently on her back, watching a ray of Starling inch across the floor. She hadn't spoken in hours. Lua's assault had stolen more than her magic.

"Galia will be waiting for you in Uduary." It was the only solace he could think of offering.

She closed her eyes, her voice a whisper. "What will happen when we get there? I never expected anything, but I hope the Oja won't kill us for our failure."

Xiang fastened her shirt and eased her upright. "It was my decision to bring Audra in. I alone deserve the punishment."

Her lower lip trembled. "Neither Nori nor I knew she was his anchor. And why did he come so late? Anchors are limited by their distance, but I sensed nothing until he was outside these walls. I should have known he was so near. Should have acted faster."

"Then you'd be dead alongside Nori," Xiang said. "I realized who she was, but I hesitated. Everything happened too fast. *I* killed our people."

She squeezed his arm. Guilt, it seemed, held them both.

"Let's get you moving." Xiang pulled her gently up while balancing on a makeshift crutch made by a soldier. It did little to alleviate the anguish in his fractured left leg. They tottered to the door together and stepped into the bright hallway. Starling light streamed through the broken ceiling, reflecting off the cracked stone flooring. Four vacant-eyed soldiers sat around a small fire they'd built in the middle of the hall. They nodded respectfully as the pair passed.

One of the oaken doors at the entrance was long destroyed, the other hung newly askew from its hinges. Stepping into the shadow of the building outside, Jayna took a long breath. A new scattering of large rocks lay where they'd fallen from the tower.

"We should leave," she said.

"We can wait, if we need to," he said. The jostling of the ride would slow her healing. "How do you feel?"

Her eyes squeezed tight, a tear escaped down her cheek. "Empty."

"I should have killed her," he muttered, more to himself than her.

"Brav should have killed him when the constraining bolt was in him." Her hands clenched. "Why didn't they? Why does the Oja want him alive? When people find out what he's done, they'll demand his death and she'll be made Rajav anyway. It makes no sense."

Xiang's pause let her know there were things he couldn't speak of, not even standing alone, bonded in their grief. Rather than offer false platitudes, he shook his head sympathetically. It did nothing to placate her.

"I want him dead," she said.

"Do you want that more than you want to see Galia again?"

She looked away and wiped her eyes. "What do we do now? Half our soldiers gone. Nori." Her breath trembled. "Obviously, we can't take the Oji alone."

"True, but there will be another opportunity," Xiang said. Her eyes slid to his. "At the coronation in the Silence monastery. According to our Oja, there will be a moment during the eclipse when he'll be vulnerable."

"Coronation? They wouldn't without Song approval. Without ceremony? The tribes will be thrown into chaos."

"The Oji only cares for what he wants. And killing his own people won't stop him. He'll even kill his new anchor if she hinders him." There was doubt in those words. The way Lua looked at Audra was revealing. The way he'd listened to her, even more so. "She has the bloodstone."

Jayna turned. "Will she wear it?"

"I don't know, but I think it's possible. The eclipse might be our last chance to stop him."

Jayna wrapped her arms around herself. "We should go."

"You're not strong enough."

"I'll manage. We need to make it to the monastery."

Xiang watched her from the corner of his eyes. "And Galia? You would leave her waiting?"

"Galia understands duty," Jayna said.

Xiang sighed, nodded. "As do we all."

Thirty-Five

Lua

Lua sheltered in a chimney's shadow, grinding his teeth as Audra scrambled over the crumbling stones and rotting wood of fallen homes. She plunged her hands fearlessly into places unseen, and new scrapes appeared across his knuckles. Not that it mattered much. They both healed faster than even a few days ago and with barely any effort. As he watched, the smallest of the scrapes mended and vanished, the larger ones healing a moment later.

Her fervor left him unsettled and in awe of her perseverance. She'd scrutinize some piece of fabric, pottery, or toy, before tenderly reburying it. It was the fact that she cared enough about those long dead to tend to their memory in her own way that garnered his appreciation.

She brushed the hair from her eyes, leaving a dirty smear along her cheek. Her hair was growing fast, soon it might be past her chin. She'd look good either way. And with no small amount of surprise, he realized he looked at her often.

Audra caught his gaze. "This would go faster if you helped."

"I don't know what we're looking for."

She paused, as if considering what to tell him. Finally, she said, "My mother's scales."

He remembered the image of red scales hanging over the hearth during Audra's dream. They were plated together, like armor. "Dragon scales?"

She nodded. "Zin gave them to her for protection. She let it slip once when she was drinking."

"Your mother?"

"No. Zin. It wasn't pretty. Terrible memory actually. She nearly burned the house and barns down with Ferin and I inside. Stopped bringing home wine after that. She still asks for it though."

His eyebrows arched. "How much wine does it take to . . ." He paused, shook his head. "Never mind, I don't want to know. Why did Lorah leave them? Why didn't she place them on you or your . . . Ferin?"

"My brother, don't forget that. I don't know why she grabbed her sword but not the scales." She turned to the next pile. "I don't think about that night if I can help it."

He understood. Lua moved to her side and gently gripped her forearm. The warmth of her seeped into his gloves. "Must you always make things more difficult?"

"What are you doing?" She didn't pull away.

"You need to learn some basics. Consider today your first lesson."

"No, I don't have—"

"You've already proven that you do. What you did at the tower and our spontaneous bond is proof alone," he said.

Audra's breath was suddenly ragged at their connection. "What did I do?"

He ignored the question and steadied her hand. "Wait."

She huffed.

"Close your eyes. I'll lead you through."

"Through what?"

"Close your damn eyes, Audra." Her constant resistance was exhausting. Most people respected or feared him enough to be obedient. But mostly Audra had been frustrated by him. Annoyed, insulted. Angry. It was only lately those emotions had shifted to something softer.

She smirked and said sarcastically, "Yes, Moon Oji Lua." Then she closed her eyes.

Lua chuckled, despite his pride. Maybe he did still want to kill her. "Take a breath. Feel the air on your skin, the beat of your heart. Find the thread, pull on it slightly. Feel it?"

She nodded as energy thrummed gently between them.

"Good. Find the colors of your magic."

"Green?"

"Yes. Now send a single thread into the rubble. Imagine what you are looking for. Give the magic something to find. Do you understand?" Lua asked. He watched her teeth biting her lower lip in concentration. He cleared his throat and looked away. "Careful, like you're helping a chick on its first flight, hold out your hand and see the magic moving forward."

"Should I chant or something?"

"No. Simple spells with single intent don't need it. With larger spells, the vibration of voice and tone can keep them focused."

A single verdant strand spun from Audra's fingers, skimming over the ruins. She gasped as it dove beneath, searching. Her eyes reflected the emerald hue as she watched it take another pass. Her wonder shifted something inside him.

Satisfied, the magic spiraled back into her hand and recoiled around their connection. Her laugh was filled with delight. He reluctantly released her and stepped away.

"Is it always like that?" Her cheeks were flushed. "Like you can do anything?"

"It's probably different for everyone. But, yes, that's what it feels like to me," he said. She studied her hands before closing her eyes. There was the familiar tug behind his sternum. Her magic spun out again, scouring over the next building with increasing speed and snapping quickly back.

"Go slow. Build your accuracy before your speed," he said.

"Why?"

"Whiplash can tear a spell's fibers and those take time to heal. A strong recoil can sever a spell completely. Slow equals strength. At least, that's what Silence believes." He looked away, feeling suddenly awkward. "Try again."

Audra searched through more debris, pulling on Lua's magic for strength when she fumbled. But, as with all bonds, it curled back around, recycling and strengthening each time it returned. He enjoyed the sensations from her as he wandered through the woods from a small distance. When she eventually found nothing, her new skills lessened the disappointment.

"I could've used this all the times I've searched for jade." She settled on a rock across from him.

A skinned rabbit was roasting over a small fire pit beside the remains of her old home. Her eyebrows rose, questioning. He shrugged. "Magic."

"When did your magic come?"

Lua stilled. There was so much she didn't know, and he feared losing her if he revealed too much too soon. He was glad she hadn't wanted to discuss the monastery. He had no desire to tell her that he'd been the one to fell the first tower years ago. That he'd been there when the Western mages were killed. There'd be no going back from that revelation. "A question for a question?" He offered.

She shrugged.

"The Rajav started our training young. I cast my first spell when I was five or six, I think. Destroyed several flowering bushes in the garden. Mother was furious." A rare smile teased his lips before his expression clouded. "If you knew who I was in Oxton, would you have turned me over to your Starling friends?"

"Friend, singular." Audra drew her knees to her chest. She didn't answer right away. Her emotions swayed before she responded. "I don't know. To say no feels like a lie, but I had to get the jade home, and I wasn't going to let you stop me."

Her answer brought him no comfort, but it was honest.

"Do you want to be Rajav?" she asked.

The question startled him. "It's my birthright. My destiny."

She stared at the fire, seeing something far away. "I understand, but just because that's what others have decided for you doesn't mean you need to accept it. Shouldn't you have a choice in your own fate?"

He considered her words. Their meaning extended beyond him, but he couldn't wholly grasp it. "I need to be Rajav for the sake of my people. Selene is selfish, cruel, and shortsighted. She'll follow in our father's footsteps and lead the Moon tribes into desolation. There is no other choice." Something akin to sadness trickled down their connection, but Lua let it go. He rotated the spit, scents of roasting meat permeating the cool air. "What happened between you and that Starling mage?"

She glanced at him. "We were friends, then lovers. I don't know what we are anymore. I still care about him, if that's what you're after, but probably not in the way he wants me to." She took a deep breath. "You had four anchors before, right?"

"Yes."

"What happened to them?"

"That's a different question," Lua said. She frowned, but acquiesced. "What will happen to Ferin if the jade works?"

"There's no guarantee it will. The Moon's spell warped his growth. Zin hoped it would be a catalyst. Get him to the form he should have reached by now. If it works, then his sheer size will overwhelm the spell. In theory, anyway."

"How big should he be?"

She smiled wickedly. "That's two questions."

"So it is." He smiled back.

"What happened with your last anchors, starting from the first? It's still one question, but I need to know."

He turned the rabbit on the spit, eyes gone wistful as the flames reflected in them. "Eras was my first anchor. I was a bit younger than you when I hit my tenth star. She was older, more worldly." His eyes dazzled at the memory.

"You loved her."

"Completely. She was my first love. And my first heartbreak."

Audra rested her chin on her knees, tilting her head. "What happened?"

"The bond takes a lot from an anchor. She lasted almost twenty years." He poked at the fire with a long stick. He didn't want to darken this moment by telling Audra the truth. Magical bonds slowly siphon anchors until they linger on death's doorstep. "Her passing nearly killed me. It would have if there wasn't another anchor at the ready. When our bond broke, the monks tethered me to Jude. He was an ass. Good in a fight but my father's loyalist first. I swear he lasted a long time out of spite alone. Next was, Kristo." Lua sighed. "He was handsome, born to be admired. We were lovers for a time. But he had the luxury of taking others."

"And you didn't?" she asked. Lua ignored the question. "And Dain?"

His jaw tightened. "Dain was a good man. I can say it now, and I can almost believe it even though . . ." He turned the rabbit again, pretending the smoke caused his eyes to water so he could wipe them. "Dain turned the bolt into my back."

Flickering firelight danced across Audra's face as the evening settled around them.

"After sixteen years together, I never suspected a thing. He'd always been a quiet man so when he cut himself off . . ." He cleared his throat.

"Why'd he do it?"

"Selene used his child as leverage. She knew I'd never expect it." The dancing shadows revealed the deep hurt lingering in his expression. Audra lifted the spit carefully from the fire and tore off a steaming leg. She handed it to him.

He waved it away. "It's for you."

"We grow strong together." She shoved it at him. "Eat. Don't make me kick you, Moonie." Steam rose from between her teeth as she took a bite, watching until he did the same. "What happened?"

Lua swallowed and met her gaze. "I siphoned every ounce of magic from the lives on that ship. Then I covered Starling and killed him."

"You covered Starling?" Her eyes widened. A strange expression moved across her face. "How?"

"It's a twelfth level spell. Twelve strings held simultaneously, only possible if there are clouds already available. Chanting helps. I'd only cast it once before."

Her lips pressed thin. She swallowed hard. "And your bond?"

"I exhausted my magic to sever our connection and prevent the process from killing me." Hair had slipped from the topknot and framed the sharp angles of his face. "A few more hours in the water, and

I would have died. But, as chance would have it, a disagreeable thief fished me out."

Audra snorted. "Didn't have a choice. It was rescue you or drown."

They sat quietly until the fire cracked.

"Audra." His voice was full of admonishment. "What does Zin want?"

She looked at him cautiously. "To restore the Western tribes and bring back the dragons."

Dread settled in the pit of his stomach. His father devoted most of his life to eliminating them.

"What does Selene—" Audra started.

"I'm tired." With a swipe of his hand, the fire sputtered out.

"What are you doing? It's *freezing*."

"Then use your magic to make a fire."

"I can't."

"You've never tried," he said. "Either start the fire or get some rest. We should leave soon."

"Asshole," she whispered, but that only made him laugh. "You still want to go to the monastery?" Audra shifted uncomfortably. "Those were your people back there. We should head back to Auntie's."

"Those were my sister's people. My tribe needs me, Audra," he said. A weight settled between them. "I must get there before the eclipses."

"Westerners never fare well in the north," she said softly. "What if they try to separate us?"

"That won't happen without my consent, and I have no intention of giving it." He stopped himself from saying more. Their honesty was too new to risk pushing further. "I swear on my life that I won't let anything happen to you." He leaned toward her, silver eyes bearing into hers. Her desperation of wanting to believe him, the trepidation that her fragile trust might be betrayed, swept toward him. "You're safe with me."

She swallowed and turned abruptly away, poking at the embers with a stick. "On foot?"

"Selene's people would have taken their horses with them by now."

She sighed. "I guess we could go through the spires."

"Spires?"

"Old dragon territory north of here."

"You've been there?"

She shook her head. "No, but no one else will go that way, especially this time of year."

"'Old dragon territory' is not exactly a reassuring image," he said.

"We can pick up supplies in Stonetown before crossing."

He rubbed his chin. "How far are we from Stonetown?"

"A day. Then possibly another through the spires. It would shave off some distance." She rubbed the back of her arms.

That would get them to the monastery with time to spare, let Audra get comfortable before the coronation. He hadn't told her that the alternative to cutting their bond was she'd be made Raani, the official title for the Rajav's anchor. Her dreams of returning the Western tribe and dragons would have to be put aside. It would be best to have that conversation somewhere her reaction could be contained. Then, with the council behind him, he'd determine what to do about Selene. Bolin being Audra's brother turned the situation into a more delicate matter. Together he and Audra might be able to figure it out.

Lua nodded to himself. "We'll leave when the moons are up." He smiled at her as she shivered. "A fire would be nice though."

Thirty-Six

Traq

The rhythmic dance of Wren's braid teased the top of her horse's hips and repeatedly drew Traq's gaze.

The clouds had dissipated in the higher elevations allowing the party to appreciate the bright sky and shimmer of Raia's ring. Durin had taken the quietude as an opportunity to share his knowledge of the topographical and historical regional events.

Traq seethed as the older mage droned on about the Starling-Moon battles and the supposed liberation of the Westerners. He didn't talk about the villages that had been mercilessly butchered or the people who'd vanished under the control of the Starlings. By most calculations, nearly a third of the population had been forced into exile or servitude in the southern deserts after their 'liberation,' never to return. As for those who willingly joined the Starlings, like Traq and Liasa, they had to endure both tribes' hatred simply to survive.

Audra's focus on finding the jade eventually conflicted with Traq's desire to find their missing people. Those differences had divided them. After hearing a few of Liasa's stories about her lost kin, he suspected her reasoning was similar. He was scheduled to return to the barracks in

Siyah, the Starling capitol, after this mission and hoped to learn more then.

Durin had been young during his first battles. He might not have even known why they were fighting. Traq suspected the long passage of time had muddled the Rajav's original motivations for assaulting the Westerners, and that the Starlings had been nothing more than opportunists when they finally intervened. All that mattered in the end was that the Starlings had won, and the Moons had shuttered themselves back in their cold north after the dragons had disappeared.

Until now.

"Did you ever see one?" Liasa asked, riding beside Durin.

His face lit like he'd caught a fish after a long morning with an empty hook. "Once when I was a boy. Magnificent beast. Shining red with enormous wings. It took up half the sky."

"Where was it?"

"North of here, I believe. My mother was a merchant and travelled over borders and seas without restriction. When she was a child, there were dozens of dragons—red, gold, black, and green. She saw the water dragons when she travelled to the islands. With silvery scales, long whiskers, and giant obsidian eyes, she said they kept her ship from being pulled into the edge waters more than once."

"What do you think happened to them? And to the Western mages?" Liasa asked.

"That's the mystery, isn't it? I think—"

Wren cut him off. "They're gone for a reason. Quit speculating."

Traq snorted.

"What?" Wren asked.

"Didn't know that would be the conversation that irritated you," he said. The rest of the group went awkwardly quiet.

"Didn't hear you correcting him about his war details," Wren countered.

He dropped his voice. "I've spent years trying to integrate and learned to hold my tongue a long time ago. People believe what they're told, and they repeat it. I know the truth, and that's all that matters."

"That's like what my father always says," Wren said thoughtfully. "You'll meet him in Siyah when we cast for our stars."

"He'll be attending?" Traq asked.

"He'll be judging."

He wondered if she was joking.

"Lord Ijion must be quite proud of his daughter," Durin said. Stifled gasps escaped from the surrounding soldiers. "I hear Sechen is quite talented, as well. Though she's better known for her charms, isn't she?"

Wren's eyes simmered dangerously.

"Lord Ijion is your father?" Traq had only seen the Starling leader a handful of times. An imposing man—tall and thick with white hair, not that uncommon for the southern tribespeople, but the warm umber tone of his skin was similar to Wren's. And she had the same noble air about her, as if all future success were predetermined. Sechen's complexion was a shade lighter, her hair closer to black.

"He is." The look she threw at Durin would have killed if she'd added magic. "But no favors have been given. I've had to work twice as hard as my peers because old buggers like to dig at my lineage and whisper snide comments." Her tone held an animosity that made the old man stiffen. "I suggest you keep my sister's name out of your mouth, Durin. Sechen has more talent than all of us combined. Do *you* have something to say?" Her gaze slid toward Traq.

"No. I didn't know," he said. It was interesting that neither sister had spoken of their father in the time he'd known them. Wren settled into her seat, shoulders slightly defeated. He cleared his throat. "My parents died with mountain pox before my third birthday. Grandparents, aunts, uncles, my siblings all died in the following years from illness or the last incursions. Everyone who knew them died when our village fell. I've often wondered if any of them were mages." Her eyes shifted toward him. "I wish I knew more about my lineage. I like to think I'd be proud of it."

The corners of her lips twitched upward, but she sighed after a moment. "It's complicated. There were plenty of times I wish I'd been judged on my own merit, not for who stood behind me. And as demanding as he is as a leader, having him as a father is more challenging than you can imagine. There are expectations, inherited responsibilities that I have to accept or they'll fall on Sechen."

"Trust me, it's hard not having anyone in your corner. Having to scrap for every ounce of respect," Traq said.

"But if you fail, you'll only disappoint yourself. You don't have the entire world waiting for you to fall, knowing they'll cheer when it happens. Sechen already gets the brunt of it, through no fault of her own."

He measured his words. "No one of any worth would celebrate either of your failures. You're the best mage I know and certainly one of the strongest. Your father wouldn't risk you if he didn't have faith in your abilities."

Her expression warmed. Though Wren never spoke of gratitude—he didn't know if she knew how—the way she looked at him said more than words could have. Traq's recent consideration of something more between them died with the knowledge of who her status. Lord Ijion was known for his contempt of Westerners, and he wouldn't tolerate his daughter's attachment.

When a scout reported signs of activity at the Western monastery ruins, they'd hastened to the scene. Horse tracks had stamped down the ground, and one tower had fallen too recently to have collected weeds or leaves. Bits of shredded roof and broken stones littered the landscape.

"Traq takes lead," Wren said. Durin looked relieved at the slight to him. Traq and five soldiers circled the ruins and explored the grounds while the rest of their group waited. Instinct moved him into the main building. Eventually, he signaled for the others to join them.

Wren and Durin grimaced as they both dismounted. The stench of decay and rotting eggs spun in the air, but the soldiers were unaffected.

"It's worse inside," Traq said.

They climbed winding stairs to the remains of a broken tower. Behind a battered door was a small room with an overturned table and chairs. Fallen stones scattered across the floor and, though it had been swept, dusty ashes remained. The acrid scent of dark power clung like tar to the walls.

Traq caught a small piece of ash against his fingers. Though every bit of magic in him was repulsed, he brought it to Wren. Her low curse confirmed his suspicions.

Durin's voice was ripe with trepidation. "Who exactly are we after?"

Wren rubbed the ash between her fingers until it dissolved. It stained her fingertips gray. "A Moon mage anchored."

"Anchored? That's illegal. Deadly to both parties."

She arched one eyebrow. "Only illegal for Starlings. But this feels like something more. What happened here?" She examined the broken walls and furniture.

"If I may?" Traq asked, not waiting for a response. "I think we're looking for two separate groups."

Wren nodded. "It would explain some discrepancies we've encountered so far. Two Moon groups?"

"Why would the Moon tribes be warring with each other?" Durin asked. He rubbed his chin.

"This is bigger than us. Powerful forces are at odds within the Moon tribes, and now they're killing their own," Wren said.

"If we can find the second party, the one with the losses, we might get answers before they cross the border," Traq said.

"This is ridiculous." Durin spat. "Let them kill themselves. Send word to Lord Ijion. We should go back. If they'd do this to their own people, imagine what they'd do to ours."

"They've already done it," Traq said. "Remember the fishing villagers? This all started at sea."

Liasa gave a small bow from the doorway. "We've found something. Remains, maybe."

"How many?" Wren asked.

"Four that we can make out. The rest are too . . ." She trailed off with a visible shudder.

Wren nodded. "Don't let anyone touch anything, I'll be there momentarily."

"We should send word," Durin repeated, his eyes flicked between his peers.

Traq's expression was stony. Durin was right: this was more than they could handle. But he wanted to go on.

"I'll consider your council after we've seen the rest, Durin. Even if we send word, it will take a week or more for anyone to reach them, and the Moons will be past the border by then," Wren said.

The implication of her words settled amongst them. Durin squeezed his eyes shut. "You think it better to follow," he said. "Even though they've committed such horrors toward their own people."

Her face hardened. "Can you imagine what they'd do to ours if left unchecked? If this gets out, what happened with the fishing village and here, the international stress could ignite another war."

"But if we manage it quietly," Traq said.

"Maybe we can stop things from escalating further."

Durin muttered a curse about Taiyang's balls.

"We'll still need to send a message though," Wren offered. "Sending an experienced mage to ensure Lord Ijion receives it would be appropriate."

Durin rubbed his face and eventually shook his head. "No. Send a soldier or two. I'm not leaving you." With heavy steps, he turned and left the room.

Traq watched him with a sympathetic heart. He started to follow, but Wren gripped his arm and spun him around.

"Tell me everything about your friend. Where she's from, who her family was. *Everything*."

"There's not much to tell," he lied. But where should he begin? Another orphan, hostile aunt, spell-damaged brother. That she'd spent years reclaiming Western artifacts and was a wanted thief.

Wren sent a little shock into his skin, enough to add weight to her words. "If she and that mage are responsible for this, we're all in danger. Believe it or not, I want everyone to make it home. If your little friend has to die for that to happen, then so be it." She turned to leave, her braid whipping sharply behind her. "Despite your feelings for her."

Thirty-Seven

Audra

The dim all'ight saved Audra's footing through the nighttime woods while Lua searched for any potential threats. A well-fed liger gave them a wide berth. Rodents and winter-coated deer fled at the crunching leaves beneath their feet.

Audra turned the bloodstone inside her pocket. It was sharp-edged, unyielding, and brought a sense of calm that might be either imagined or true. Xiang said it would block Lua's power and keep him from knowing her emotions. But Xiang couldn't know the bond's complexities or that it had and would, she suspected, continue to evolve.

She didn't like that Lua knew her emotions and his feelings had intruded into her awareness over the last week. The unwanted intimacy lowered her guard against him.

Lua wasn't only a deeply wounded man; he was Moon Oji Lua Koray—thirteen stars, murderer—who undoubtedly held significant responsibility for the destruction of her people. Every thought that he'd saved her more than once was countered by the innate understanding that he hadn't had a choice. Yet the frequent heat of his gaze on her skin made something flutter behind her ribs. Hating him had proved to be impossible.

Before the last assault, Stonetown had been a quaint village known for its elaborate festivals and stunning views. Sheltered near the apex of the mountain, the sharp terrain and narrow roads made it difficult for large parties to access, which had enabled its resistance to the Moons far longer than most other northern villages.

The town they stumbled into resembled little of its former reputation. Dark smoke wafted from precariously slanted chimneys as they walked down narrow, neglected streets. A battered inn tilted to one side, already showing signs of stirring in the early morning.

Lua and Audra looked suspicious, from the distinctive color of his eyes and pale complexion to their lack of belongings other than the single, muddy pack flung across Audra's shoulder. Never mind that they looked like they'd intentionally wallowed in dirt.

"Are you hungry?" Lua's breath tickled her skin.

She should have been, but she wasn't. It must have been the bond's doing. Growing stronger together was almost preferable to the years of struggle she'd endured.

Lua's eyes shone brighter too. He smiled more readily when he looked at her. Confiding in him about everything had probably been foolish. But it felt right too. As if there were no one she should trust more. Other than Ferin.

"We'll need supplies," he said.

"I'm not stealing from these people."

He looked at the patched mortar and signs of failing repairs that scarred each building. Generational loss and sadness oozed through the town. "Why would you?"

"In Oxton—"

"I had nothing other than you to sustain me, and we were dying. Oxton is thriving and rich compared to this place." He met her eyes. "Allow me some grace, I don't steal from the poor."

"What about those fishers?"

Lua's jaw clenched. "Kept us alive. I'm not proud of it, but I'd do it again if I had to."

"That man, Xiang, had been on the *Requin*," she said. "He said they'd answered his questions and he let them go. But he was lying."

Lua's lips drew into a thin line.

"You were right. The crew of the *Requin* is dead," she said, "And they made it to the ruins so quickly. How did they track us?"

The inn's door banged open as a hefty, bald man with rolled-up sleeves stepped into the street and emptied a bucket of brown water off to the side. It splattered against the neighboring building. He patted the bucket empty and nodded to them.

"You're welcome if you need a bite. I've made extra," the man said. He propped the door open before disappearing inside.

Lua watched him suspiciously. The silver at his fingertips quelled when Audra touched his wrist. "You'll find that those without much are often the most generous. It's normal to give food away rather than let it spoil, especially if there's a lack of paying customers." Her stomach rumbled as fried hash scented the air. Maybe she was hungry.

His magic vanished, and he gripped her hand. "A good meal and a little rest would do you good."

"Do us both good."

The man, Arn, vanished into the kitchen and returned to the dining room a few minutes later with two plates of eggs, biscuits with clotted cream, small fried cookies twisted into simple script, plum jam, and two cups of salty milk tea. He settled the plates before them with a pitcher of water. The musty room was otherwise empty.

"Long night?" Arn asked. "Probably best to keep moving though, eh? Any problems with the ligers?"

"Saw one, but they let us be," Audra said.

He settled behind the bar, wiping down counters with a yellowed cloth. "Lucky. Never know this time of year. Sometimes the cats get bold."

The familiar food was savory, warming her core in ways she hadn't realized she missed. Lua ate lazily, like a man who'd never known hunger or desperation. Or like one who never considered this meal might be his last.

"Any decent mage with more than a couple of stars can track a spell. Once you get the knack of it, it's easy to find. There's a skill to it, certainly, but magic leaves traces everywhere it's cast." Lua spoke softly, leaning back while watching the innkeeper. "They tracked the bolt to the *Requin*. Then the wind to the fishing boat."

"The wind?"

"Spell fragments would have lingered in the sails. Enough for a skilled mage to find."

Audra bit her lip, thinking of the spell to steal the horse, but the Moons didn't pass them on the road. "Then the argentavas?" Audra asked. "But there were other paths to get to the border and the spell you used at the livery in Oxton—"

"Xiang knows where I'm headed. He'd have picked the most likely route and stuck to it, hoping to beat me there." He shrugged. "He couldn't have expected what happened at the monastery."

The image of the soldiers' and mage's faces dissolving into ash made her push the plate away. "Is that what happened to the fishers?" she asked quietly.

"We needed the fishers to survive. The other was defensive—a choice to kill a moderate-level mage and their companions. I took no satisfaction in the first. The second, well . . ." His voice turned cold. "I told you. I'll never let anyone hurt you."

She stared at the table. There was a possessiveness to his tone. It didn't matter that his motivations were ultimately self-serving. She'd seen the red welt around his neck, the one that matched her own. Protecting her was protecting himself.

"I should have killed them all," he said.

"Why didn't you?"

He leaned toward her, too close. His presence warmed the air between them. "You asked me not to."

They were inches apart. She held her breath, wanting his touch and hating herself for it.

"There's more if you've any hunger left," Arn said, pulling her from the trance.

"You're kind, sir." Lua's voice dripped with uncharacteristic charm. Reminding her of a purring cat that allowed exactly one pet before biting. "Is there a room available?"

He looked from Audra to Lua and winked. "I'll get one ready."

Her face flushed. "No. We're not—"

"Much appreciated, sir."

Arn called a name as he ascended the sloping flight of stairs in the corner.

"We don't have any money," she hissed. "The food was more than enough. To take his generosity further—"

"Money isn't what's needed."

"What then?"

"A solid spell or two to keep this place from falling," Lua said.

"Won't that leave a trail?"

"If I do it? Definitely. But Western magic was always difficult to track. This allows for some good practice."

"No. Absolutely not. I've only picked through some trash. Can't even start a damn fire. And now you think I can seal this place back together? I'm more likely to demolish it."

"I'll guide you. The spells will last as long as we both live." His tone was disarmingly positive.

"Moon, I can't." Her voice faded beneath the sudden heat of his smile. Her heart tugged.

"I like when you call me that. Your lack of reverence is amusing." He brushed the hair from her cheek. Those cool fingers killed the words in her mouth. "Whatever we do from now on must be done together, including this."

She stared at him. Wanting and longing conflicted with a greater sense of duty and the familiar comfort of working alone.

Lua took her hand. His expression was tenderly sincere, as if he knew what she needed to hear. "Audra, I won't abandon you. You're not alone anymore."

Their threads knotted tighter at the same moment Audra realized she was on the edge of being lost to the Moon Oji and his spells. Their fates and desire aligned, even if their goals did not.

Thirty-Eight

Selene

The ferrets skittered down the hall in front of Selene. Their brown-furred bodies slid from the fumbling reaches of the guards who sought to capture them. The creature's annoying chittering bounced off the walls.

It had been a mistake to let Maya have her little beasts. They were surprisingly conniving, and their antics had given the servants more expertise in hunting ferrets than anyone needed. It wasn't just their escapades that annoyed, though. Their stench was assaulting, and they left a trail of destruction everywhere they went. Shitting, shredding curtains and rugs, scratching anyone who caught them. The only one who went seemingly unscathed was Maya. The girl swore the creatures were just overly curious, and Grethin supported her. Still, Selene had begun to wonder if this was the girl's plan all along.

Selene didn't visit Maya daily anymore. Why she'd kept Maya alive, Selene wasn't quite sure. Still, she'd need to be eliminated before the staff grew more attached to the girl.

There were other issues that came first.

Ever since learning Xiang had nearly died, Bolin's worry threatened to overwhelm her. Lua shouldn't have been that strong, and her general offered no reasons for their failure. Xiang's tightly controlled expression was guilt-ridden, and it wasn't like him to withhold information. It annoyed her that there was no way to adequately question him.

Xiang's eyes slid to her frequently while trying to communicate with them, also unusual. Typically, he only looked at Bolin. It piqued her curiosity. She ordered him to bury their losses and return to Uduary.

Sharine, the highest-ranking Song mage on the council was hesitant about aiding Selene at first. After all, executing one's comrades didn't usually increase one's popularity. But the promise of control over future council matters had swayed her, and she'd been aching for Fallue's position for years. Sharine would bring her stock of liger's bane wine to the ceremony and let it spoil before having it served to the anchors. It was more subtle than Selene liked, and the timing would be tough to pull off, but Sharine was convinced that it was manageable.

In any case, Selene and Bolin would have to travel to the monastery, despite her desire not to.

A guard stood clumsily, carefully hoisting the smaller ferret in his hands. The creatures looked so similar it was difficult to tell them apart, but this one was probably the female, Oani. The guard stepped back and bowed to Selene as she made to pass.

Oaklai was further down the hall, busily scratching at a closed door. It chirped at Grethin as she desperately tried to contain him.

The guard gasped as Oani's teeth found soft flesh. The ferret launched from his bleeding hand. Selene turned at the commotion. Her escort flung themselves into the ferret's path—but it was too late. When Oani's claws sunk into the Oja's shoulder, her magic latched onto it. With a soft chirp, a husk dropped to the ground, leaving a clump of ash and fur on the rug. It was over in an instant.

Oaklai squealed from Grethin's arms down the hall. Its nose lifted in the air, catching the dross that drifted toward it from its sibling. The ferret trembled.

Selene ignored the rushed apologies that came from the guards. She caught the servant's eyes, noting the suddenly subdued demeanor of the remaining ferret.

"Return them to Maya's room."

"B-both, Oja?" Grethin looked stricken. "What should I tell her?"

She nudged the corpse with the toe of her boot. "Tell her this is what happens when the rules here are broken. Tell her to keep the other one under better control."

The servant bowed while the Oja passed. That should serve as warning enough, at least until she returned with her brother in chains. After she siphoned all of Lua's thirteen stars, she'd determine what to do with Dain's daughter.

Thirty-Nine

Xiang

The remaining Moon party alternated between restless slumber and riding steadily west toward the Heitung Pass while snow fell around them. Their pace was slowed by Jayna's injuries and Xiang's miserable leg.

When Selene had changed her mind and told him that Sharine would be waiting for them at the Silence monastery, he'd been grateful. The infection-induced sweat that dappled Jayna's skin indicated she wouldn't survive the trip to Uduary. They'd veer north after the border.

The mountain range they crossed wasn't as steep as the Shei-nam behind them, but the wind bit through their clothes and made their teeth chatter. Despite the Moons beliefs that their biggest advantage was an inherent tolerance for the cold, if the situation turned dire, they'd be in trouble. Though, he reasoned, the spare horses could provide another food source.

Jayna's complexion was sallow. She barely ate and was dismissive when Xiang encouraged more. Her bitterness festered like the wound that crossed her chest and refused to mend. Not that Xiang's leg was much better. They needed a healer, and Xiang was prepared to beg for charity at the monastery. If councilor Sharine were there, they wouldn't refuse him. However, if Lua arrived before them, it would be another matter entirely. His magic would want to finish siphoning whatever was left of Jayna's.

Though Xiang may have been Selene's general, his foreign heritage granted him no illusions of loyalty or merit from the Moons. That they'd consistently looked down on the intelligence and character of non-northern tribes had worked frequently to his advantage. And since the centuries old rift between the Song and Silence tribes had never completely sealed, the troublesome antics of the Oji and Oja had taken the focus of both tribes to deal with. That neither house ever overcame the other revealed the juxtaposition involved. But everything was in flux since the Rajav and Raani's deaths.

The soldiers gossiped about it when they believed Xiang wasn't listening. Some doubted Lua killed his father. Yet no one dared speak the other half of that statement—if the Oji hadn't done it, then only one other mage was strong enough to orchestrate it. And no one dared to speak ill of Selene. Lua's punishments were quick, predictable, even methodical. If Xiang were being honest, the Oji was unlikely to make rash decisions that would spiral the country into chaos.

Selene tortured families first, killing innocent children and mothers of offenders before ripping the eyes from their skulls. They took after their father in very different ways.

No matter. Selene had Bolin, and Xiang was at her mercy for it. He didn't care about the tribes or their wars. He only cared about keeping Bolin safe.

A liger cried in the distance. They'd passed occasional paw prints, freshly eaten carcasses, and other signs, but the size of their party should dissuade the cats' attention. The soldiers watched in shifts to protect the horses, just in case. They built three fires in triangulation and kept the horses between them, while the soldiers and mage ate their tough jerky.

"How far to the border?" Jayna's eyes were half open. A green-tinted feverish sheen dotted her brow in the firelight. He'd hoped that sitting beneath the moons might bolster her, but the sky was clouded. Three soldiers had begun to pray to Song for her.

"Not far. After the pass, we'll drop in elevation. It will be easier then."

She squeezed her eyes closed. "And the monastery?"

"Five days, if we're lucky."

"Luck hasn't been with us so far. No reason to think it'll start now."

"We're alive. If that isn't luck, I don't know what is. We could've been dust on the floor like Nori."

She chewed the food slowly before murmuring, "I wouldn't have wished him such an ending."

"Same as Rayan, Elicia, Brav, and all the others the Oji has destroyed along the way. That he allowed us to live is perplexing." Xiang ran a hand over his head, thankful he'd neglected shaving it to the scalp when they'd been in warmer temperatures.

"What can we hope for now?" Her voice was heavy. "We can't win. Even if Nori and I had acted together, we wouldn't have been able to defeat him. It should have taken months to recover from Dain, even with a new anchor." She shook her head. "I don't understand."

The Moon Ojis were bonded to siblings. A distant memory of childish fables told by Xiang's Western grandfather around festival campfires pulled at him. But it slipped like water through cracked pottery. There was no point in mentioning Western tales to Moon tribes. They were never interested in history other than their own.

The horses stamped nervously, ears twitching as the liger called again. The soldiers turned away from the fires, swords drawn. Xiang did the same, leaning on his crutch and scanning the darkness between the trees.

The next roar cut off sharply. Then only the quiet of collectively held breath amidst the falling snow as the party waited for something to happen.

"Xiang." Jayna pointed a finger past the fire, back in the direction they'd come from. Her vision in the darkness far exceeded his own. A small flicker of silver lit her fingertips.

"How many?" he asked.

"At least five. They're in white. One hood up."

Starlings with one mage. Given that it was nighttime and, depending on their level, they could still take them. But Jayna wouldn't survive a battle. Xiang sheathed his sword. They would've attacked already if they'd wanted to, but he didn't order the soldiers to stand down.

"Show yourselves. What do you want?" Xiang demanded.

"A meeting," a woman said, her deep voice crisp in the thin air.

Jayna rose on shaky legs, her hand still extended forward as her lips moved.

"There's no point in casting," the woman said. "Our mages out number you three to one."

Xiang rested a hand on Jayna's shoulder. She hesitated, her spell blooming brighter until a crack of gold beside them stripped a blade from a man's arm, taking his skin with it. He screamed as a dozen Starling soldiers emerged and surrounded them.

A tall, younger mage moved forward. White robe pulled over his tanned features, skin a similar pallor to Xiang's own: a Westerner in Starling robes. An older male mage stood a third of the way around. Beneath the woman's hood were sharp hazel eyes set in a dark complexion. The white of her hair nearly blended in with her garments.

"We don't want to hurt you but will if we must," she said.

Xiang counted blades. There were more soldiers elsewhere, probably tending their horses. Cooperation might ensure survival, and he had no desire to witness the rest of his party slaughtered.

"I suppose you saw our fires and wished to join us," he said casually, as if they were not under threat.

Her lips twitched with amusement. "Just as you say. May we?"

The Starlings ushered the Moons toward the fires as the woman gestured for Xiang and Jayna to resume their seats. The younger mage stood guard as the older one offered to tend to the wounded soldier.

"How long have you been following us?" Jayna asked.

The woman studied her, frowning. "We found your trail at the ruins, followed the scent of your wound the whole way here."

Jayna snorted. "Bad luck."

The woman stooped beside Jayna. "May I see it?"

Jayna protested, but Xiang urged her cooperation, nodding to their remaining group. She pulled the folds of fabric back to reveal the bloody linen bandages beneath. The mages' looks soured in unison.

"I'm Wren, Septra. That's Durin, Quinta, and Traq, Tresa." Her discerning gaze traced the wound. "How are you still alive? This reeks of strong magic." She paused in realization. Her eyes widening in the firelight. "You were siphoned."

"He didn't finish the job, obviously." Jayna tugged the clothes back over her chest.

"You can tell that much?" Xiang asked.

Wren winked. "It's a talent. The siphon was only a guess." She settled beside them on the ground. "We can help with the wounds in exchange for some information."

"I won't accept the aid of a Starling."

"Jayna," Xiang said.

"Not after everything they've done." She gestured to the crying soldier. "And continue to do."

Wren shrugged. "Suit yourself. But we'll still need to know who killed a village of fishers along the coast two weeks ago."

Xiang studied the mage without reaction while Jayna wisely kept her eyes on the fire and shivered. Her fever was worsening. That they'd tracked their party and not Lua could be beneficial. "You're looking for the Moon tribe's most wanted criminal. He's done worse to our own people."

"So you tracked him from the coast to Oxton, then to the ruins?"

"Yes," he lied. He motioned to his leg then at Jayna. "And confronted him. You can see how that turned out."

"Was anyone with him?" Traq asked from behind them. Wren's eyes narrowed.

"A young woman, not one of ours." Xiang said.

"What did she look like?"

"Tresa, enough," Wren warned. "Tell us what happened."

Jayna's eyes rolled back as the small bit of spell she'd wove took its toll. She jerked twice before slumping sideways. Xiang caught her before she hit the frozen ground.

"Can you help her?" Xiang asked.

Wren scowled. "You'd ask for her aid when she's unable to refuse, after she's already made herself clear?"

"I made a promise that she'd return unharmed. Please."

The mages exchanged a look before settling something unspoken between them.

"I'll do it," Durin said. "But you be damn sure she knows it was at *your* behest."

"Anyone forces Moon magic on me without consent, I'd kill them for it," Wren said.

Xiang nodded. Jayna might want to kill him, but he'd deal with that later. In time, he hoped she'd understand.

Forty

Selene

The map's edges curled around the bases of stone vases and small ancestral busts that Selene used to flatten them down. Those stony, stoic eyes stared judgmentally as she leaned over the Rajav's desk, studying the fading inked lines of roads and rivers that trailed across the border between the Western and Moon tribes.

The Silence monastery was marked in the plains beyond the expanse of mountains and poisoned river. Lua had many routes to choose from. She'd eliminated the Heitung Pass for being too obvious, and the southern roads would add time he didn't have. Her eyes lingered on a blacked-out marking just across the border. Her father had obviously eliminated it for a reason, but Li-Hun hadn't left many detailed notes. Based on the state of his affairs, he'd had no plans of dying so soon.

Her only regret was she'd not been able to complete the task herself. She'd planned to siphon him—that would have increased her power far beyond her brother's—but when the Rajav had glared at her with his steel-gray eyes, when he'd ordered her to help him, she'd frozen. Years of obedience and ingrained fear had fought against her rage and desires.

The hesitation had only lasted a moment, but it was enough for him to reach for her. If not for Bolin's sure blade, her father would have siphoned her instead.

She shook her head to clear her mind. Lua could cross the border and river from that blackened mark. Then it would be a short distance to the monastery. They'd need to intercept him before the Silence monks came to his aid.

Selene's fingers drummed on the table while Nova Verina waited patiently. Though the mage's complexion had improved since the healer had attended her, her bloodshot eyes were proof of recent tears. The Oja had planned on punishing her immediately, but given Xiang's circumstances, the mage still had uses.

There were better, more obvious tortures to inflict.

Selene laid her hand on the map. "Here. Take a triad and a squadron. Wait for him on the north shore of the river."

Verina gave a curt nod. "Yes, Oja."

"Keep the element of surprise. Though he's newly anchored, my sources say he's unusually strong. Attack together or you'll have no chance."

Verina nodded again. "Yes, Oja." She raised her eyes cautiously. "What of the Silence monks?"

"Make sure they feel the error of their loyalties if they interfere." Selene met her eyes. "You'll test for your tenth star when you return. I'll oversee it myself."

Verina paled, and there was a satisfying tremor in her response. "Yes, Oja." She bowed stiffly before leaving.

It would take several days to reach their destination unless they ran the horses into the ground, which Selene encouraged them to do. If they failed, only then would she and Bolin intervene. But perhaps she should expect everyone to fail. Lua had always been lucky.

There'd been no word from Xiang in two days, and Bolin's emotions kept them both from sleeping. Something was wrong. There were wheels and parts moving she couldn't see. In the past, Song often warned her about potential trouble and the goddess's quiet since the Rajav's death was poorly timed. The moons waited to see who was victorious, only then would they cast their support. It was understandable, if frustrating.

There was a small rap at the door a moment before Maya was escorted inside with Grethin. Per Selene's specifications, the girl's robes were rich purples and soft blues. She looked like she belonged here. Grethin bowed, the girl followed only a moment behind.

"Maya wanted to give you something," Grethin said. The girl approached slowly with her head bowed. She placed a roll of rice paper on the desk before backing away, biting her lower lip the entire time.

Selene glanced suspiciously at the parchment before turning back to the map. "You may leave."

Maya looked up once before Grethin guided her through the door. Selene waited until the door closed before laying the sheet flat on the table. It was an old, childish poem, one Selene loved when she was young, replicated in Maya's imperfect script. She hadn't read it in years.

> *When the sea meets the sky*
> *And wings fill the air.*
> *When Raia turns her eye*
> *And Starling knows despair.*
> *Silence will roar,*
> *And ready for war*
> *While Song grows quiet,*
> *Preparing for riot.*
> *When mages are bound*
> *To dragons long drowned,*
> *A terrible kindness will call.*
> *Then moons and stars*
> *And mountains will crawl.*
> *Bound together by magic's old scars.*

A small semblance of a sea dragon was drawn along the parchment's lower edge, Maya must have seen the one in the bay recently. Selene read it again. It was odd the girl should give her something after the ferret's death.

There was a soft smudge behind one stanza. She held the paper up to the all'ight and snorted.

Behind the heavier ink-brushed characters was a small figure, delicately drawn in soft gray and nearly invisible. A triangular-faced ferret peeked at her. Selene smoothed the paper back on the table and licked her teeth. Selene could appreciate pettiness, but Maya needed to learn her place and Grethin would have to serve as an example.

Forty-One

Lua

The inn's air was thick with inebriated humor. Audra's laugh was infectious, her thigh pressed against Lua's beneath the table as Arn's latest lewd joke had her nearly choking. She slammed her hand on the table. Lua laughed beside her.

It startled him. He couldn't recall the last time he'd laughed, and the mead that coursed through Audra's system was beginning to affect him. After they'd sealed and straightened the mortar and settled the foundation to last with or without their lives depending on it, Arn had insisted they stay another night.

They should have shouldered away from Stonetown and headed into the spires after a day, but Lua hadn't forced it. Audra liked it here. The customs were familiar but different enough to avoid sad recollection. The people were genuinely kind, despite recognizing him as northern. Still, his presence here put everyone in danger.

Being welcomed so warmly roused difficult truths. These were decent people, and Lua had likely killed their families and friends under his father's orders, not that he remembered much of it. So much of those years were muddled with blood and violence.

Repairing the village had been the right thing to do.

The woman from the clothier shop had given them fresh clothing for mending her chimney so that the smoke didn't get trapped inside anymore. She'd kept the higher windows open for a dozen winters, because every attempt at fixing it had also threatened its collapse. Her health had suffered for it.

Lua slipped into the moonslight to assess the town's well that they'd strengthened earlier in the day, while Audra slumbered between fresh sheets. A part of him knew on a deeper level that these acts of contrition were her influence. The Korays weren't generous with magic or time unless there was an advantage to it. The Rajav taught them nothing should be given without taking something in return.

When Audra threw an arm over his chest while sleeping, the affection slowly rooting inside him bloomed. He'd lain beside her for hours, unsleeping, afraid of ruining that sense of peace she gave him. She quickly pulled away when she woke, and they didn't discuss it. Even when it happened the second night.

He couldn't tell her he longed for those quiet moments together, where they wrapped arms around each other and he could think of nothing else. Even if it was only magic tying her to him.

"Another?" Arn smiled with broken teeth and nodded at the empty mug.

"Yes!" Audra lifted the cup high, slurring the word with complete chagrin.

Lua pulled her cup away. "I think we're done."

She gave him a bleary-eyed look. "Speak for yourself, *Moonie*," she said and roared at her own joke. Arn, thankfully, laughed and didn't question it.

As Lua stood, Audra's inebriation spun through him. He shook his head. "That's enough. We'll set out tomorrow."

Audra's attempt at rising resulted in her draped across the table. Lua scooped an arm beneath her shoulders before lifting her upright. When her knees buckled, he lifted her completely. She sank into his arms, her head resting against his chest. He was on the second step, carefully navigating them around a wooden beam, when Arn spoke.

"It's been nice having you here."

Lua paused, looking back at him.

Arn's cheeks flushed as he spoke. "I thought all our mages were gone."

Lua looked at Audra with her drunk-ruddy cheeks. "Not all of them."

He laid her on the bed, untying her boots and tugging off her socks before removing her outer shirt. Securing the blanket over her, he turned to leave, hoping the waning moonslight would clear his head. Audra's hand found his. Her thread tugged seductively at him.

"Don't go," she mumbled, peering at him from one half-open eye.

"You're drunk. Just sleep it off." He tried to pull away, but she held firm. His desire balanced on a blade's edge.

"Lay down with me."

"I need to clear my head." But his resistance wavered under her pull. She wound her thread around his and drew him down, nuzzling his neck with her lips.

Lua was a mouse trapped beneath her cat's paw, and yet he didn't want to escape. She nipped his throat, then the edge of his jaw. His voice lacked conviction. "Audra, you're drunk."

"I'm not *that* drunk." Her words slurred. She kissed his chin, leaning up on one arm, her mouth moved toward his.

He yearned for her. Their magic entwined. With a force of will, he pushed her away. "Not like this."

Audra's eyes widened at the rejection. "What?"

He disentangled her arms from around him, hesitating at the hunger in her eyes. Gently, he brushed the hair from her face and exhaled slowly. "You don't know what you're doing. And you're too drunk to understand how this might go."

She tugged at his robes to pull him down again. "You could teach me how to light a fire."

Lua leaned forward. Her mouth was so close to his. Her lips parted slightly. Then he tilted his chin up and brushed a kiss across her brow. It was electric, drawing him toward her despite his hesitance. Her arms wrapped around him again.

"*Shit.*" He pulled away and shook his head. "Distance might serve us both better. We can talk about this another time."

He turned and left, glancing back to catch her baffled expression before the door closed.

"You asshole!" she yelled.

Lua rushed past the snickering patrons who'd heard Audra's voice, into the frosty night. He stripped his outer robe and rolled up his sleeves as his breath steamed in the air. The chill quieted the fire that Audra had stoked. Damn if he still wanted to go back. He dragged a hand over his face. He'd have to find another place to sleep.

That he couldn't touch anyone else only heightened each of their moments together. Her touch was more precious to him than food was to a starving man. He'd been unable to explain it to her; it was embarrassing and strangely intimate.

Maybe he should have given in. He longed to taste her scent of honey and pine, to sear it into his bones while wrapped in her ecstasy, to make her breath hitch with pleasure. But once they started down that path, he couldn't turn back. The bond was already too strong, nearly choking him occasionally. If they explored the sexual tension between them, he'd lose himself to her.

If he was a fool for resisting what he wanted, it would have been more foolish to give in so recklessly, especially since she didn't know what would happen. His want for her, his need of her, would become obsessive. It was nearing that already. She was becoming every breath and heartbeat.

It would be different than with Eras or Kristo. His magic had siphoned them a bit with every encounter, until their lives ended too early. Audra's magic could hold its own against him; he could feel it. But what if she siphoned him instead?

He shook his head. Ridiculous. But doubt pricked at his skin.

He prayed for guidance, but Silence only glowed beside Raia's thin ring. Song had already moved on. With the image of desire thick on Audra's face, all his inner arguments were fruitless. He should go back. Maybe she'd sobered a bit. Or maybe she hadn't. He pressed his fists into his eyes and groaned.

A movement startled him. Silver lit his hands as he whirled, but it dimmed as Arn stepped into view.

"You all right?" Arn asked. His bare arms shone from the rolled sleeves of his layered shirts and dirty apron. Heat rose from his uncovered head. "Didn't know if you'd be gone before I caught you in the morning."

"Did you need something?"

"No, just wanted to thank you for helping us. We—myself and the others—are grateful for what you and Audra have done."

Lua waved his hand dismissively. "It's nothing. Fair trade for room and food."

Arn shook his head. "It means more than you know. Before the last incursion, before the Starlings came, we still had a few mages that performed deeds like this. I know you aren't . . ."

Lua met his eyes as the man paused.

"One of us." Arn let the implication hang between them.

Lua kept silent. There was no point in denying it. He'd directly contributed to these people's hardships, and they both knew it.

"But we've seen you helping, and that's what matters now." Arn cleared his throat. "May I offer some advice?"

He sighed and nodded. Advice from a poor man at least a hundred years his junior.

"Hurry through the spires."

Not what he'd been expecting. "What?"

"Audra mentioned you'd be going that way, and I wanted to tell you that just because the spires are quiet doesn't mean they're abandoned. Get through them in one day, and you'll be better for it."

"Something lives there?"

Arn shrugged. "Don't know. Everyone avoids it out of respect. Recommend you do the same. No one's ventured through there in years, even the ligers avoid it. Our last elder swore it was haunted."

"I thought your people believed one's death settled back into renewing the land."

"There are different kinds of death, and not everything settles."

Lua chilled. "Different kinds of death?"

"Just get through quickly and don't anger anything."

Lua lifted his face to the moonlight. "What exactly are the spires?"

"A graveyard," Arn said. "Dragons and mages buried there dating back thousands of years."

"Thousands?"

"Hm. Before we were separated into tribes, when Yueliang and Taiyang were brothers. Back when people and nature were the same and the sisters flew above."

"The sisters?"

"Tales passed down from our elders."

"Myths and children's tales," Lua said. "There's no truth to it." He recalled the childhood fables he'd read, but the Moons had their own historical records. Nothing that spoke of before Yueliang or painted Taiyang as anything other than a fiend, and none had ever discussed it with the seriousness that Arn did now.

"Why would we share the truth with those who seek to destroy us? So many of our people have gone missing. Anyone with a whisper of magic rounded up and taken south, never heard from again." Arn shook his head with a pained look. "Nothing to be done about it now. Come back for the spring lantern festival. It's not as grand as it once was, but we do our best."

Lua gazed at Silence again, noting the alcohol's effects on his emotional control. A twinge of sadness pierced him. They'd never return here. He didn't notice Arn raise a friendly hand to pat his arm. The man's fingers brushed Lua's exposed skin.

The slight touch jerked Lua to awareness. He knocked Arn away, but it was too late. The man paled, his cheeks suddenly hollow. Silver threads darted from Lua's hands to claim sustenance so readily offered.

"No!" Lua tried to tether his magic, pulling it from the man's flesh as it ate at him, but the threads resisted. Arn's eyes widened, his lips moved with unspoken questions as he flailed. Lua fought, but his magic refused to obey.

Green threads lashed through the darkness to cocoon Arn. It wriggled beneath the silver fibers, insulating him. One by one, each of Lua's threads withdrew until Arn collapsed on the ground.

Audra's cheeks were cast in the emerald light that spiraled from her hands. Her face was filled with horror. "You were killing him."

"No! It's not like—"

"You were." Her voice was hoarse.

"Audra, listen to me," Lua pleaded.

"I hoped that I'd been wrong about you. Maybe, you weren't so bad. But you're worse than I ever imagined." Her eyes glistened.

Arn twitched on the ground, but Lua couldn't help him. Audra knelt and lifted the man to a seated position.

"Please listen—" Lua started.

She shook her head. "You're a vile, horrible—"

"I can't stop it!" His voice cracked as his carefully controlled demeanor broke.

"What?"

"I *can't* stop it. The magic attacks anyone who gets too close."

"But we've ... back in the room ..."

He ran a hand down his face. "Only my anchor can touch me. No one else. Nothing that breathes. I take precautions. The gloves, the extra robes, keeping my distance but it still takes effort to restrain." The piteous dawn of understanding warped her expression. He hated the emotions that swept over him. "Arn surprised me. I would never have hurt him on purpose."

"But you didn't stop it," she said.

"I *can't* stop it. I've tried countless times. I tried." He looked at Arn. His eyes were closed but his breathing was steady. At the tower when Lua had rescued Audra, his magic had suddenly withdrawn from the mage. It hadn't been him at all. "But apparently you can."

Audra stared at Lua for a long moment before coming to a conclusion. "Get our things. I'll call for aid once you're back."

He wanted to say something to make her understand, but the tumult of emotions that struck him were overwhelming. He strode into the inn and gathered their few items before returning outside. Arn was propped against a wall, his color mildly improved.

She gestured down a side street that led from town. "Go. I'll meet you there."

"Audra?"

"Can you do what I'm asking without arguing, please? I'll take care of this."

Lua's shoulders slumped. He hoisted the pack and headed into the darkness. From beneath the shadow of a tall pine, he heard Audra's shout. Feet scrambled as people surrounded Arn and carried him into the warmth of the inn. It was a short time later when Audra skirted the corner. She didn't speak, but disappointment trickled toward him as they walked away from Stonetown.

Forty-Two

Xiang

Durin set Xiang's leg with thin, delicate magic, working cautiously like a seasoned sewist to mend both bone and flesh. His pain with the healing had been minimal, but Jayna's screams had shaken everyone. Before the old man treated her, he'd reminded Xiang that Starling and Moon magic were incompatible. By forcing his magic into her, no matter how careful he was, Jayna might never draw from the moons again. But there was no other way to save her.

Moon soldiers carried Jayna by pallet over stone-strewn roads. Her fever had broken, but Wren explained that, aside from the wound's infection, the violent loss of magic had damaged parts of her that were difficult for even Durin's skills to reach.

The Septra asked leading questions about the mage they were following, never offering too much in return. The familiar assuredness to her manners was likely born of privilege, much like the Oja's. Though Wren lacked Selene's conceit. Traq's questions focused on the relationship between the moon mage and his anchor, revealing more uneasiness than curiosity.

Traq admitted to encountering the couple in Oxton and believed the Oji's name was Chon. Xiang didn't bother denying this. If the Starlings knew they were after the Moon tribe Oji, Wren would turn her people around with good reason. But Jayna needed their help, and Xiang could use the Starlings as a distraction when they reached the monastery.

If the Silence monks were busy fighting the Starlings, then Selene's mages had a better chance of dealing with Lua. Though the Starlings had searched each of them for weapons, they'd left him his small mirror. He just needed something sharp and the opportunity to use it. Bolin would be worrying.

Xiang sat beside the fire, rubbing the residual soreness from his leg and watching Jayna's tent when Durin exited it with a heavy sigh.

"She's livid," Durin said. He rubbed his hands together and sat across from Xiang. "Plenty of curses with your name attached. You weren't born Moon, were you?" He didn't wait for a reply before he continued. "I suspected, given your coloring, and that you don't seem to grasp what you've asked us to do to her."

"I understood. But lives have value outside of magic. She'll see that eventually," Xiang said. Durin gave him a discerning look before shaking his head.

Jayna was propped upright on a pillow when Xiang entered the tent. Though her complexion was waxen, she looked better than she had in days.

"How are you feeling?" He knelt beside her, ignoring her poisoned glare. "Durin said you might be ready to ride in the morning, but it seems too soon." He filled a cup with water and pressed it into her hands before she could knock it away. "I know you're upset but—"

"You betrayed me!" she growled. "I'd refused their treatment."

He'd always cared for Jayna more than most other mages. Despite his foreign heritage, she'd always respected him and actively sought his good opinion. She deserved an explanation if he hoped for her compliance. "Do you know why I've served the Oja faithfully? Even after the Moons killed my kin?"

There were rumors whispered behind his back, but he'd never addressed them: that he'd been a spy for the Moons or that he'd saved the Oja's life. Maybe Selene was in love with him. Allowing mysteries to spread often kept the truth well hidden. Offering Jayna a morsel of honesty was rewarded with her softening expression.

"She holds the only thing that matters to me," Xiang said. "I am used and lied to. Perpetually punished. Endlessly manipulated. All so I might earn an occasional hour with him at the Oja's whim. I would do anything to protect him, including killing my people or anyone else's. And I will lie with our enemies if it keeps him safe." She shifted uncomfortably when Xiang took her hand. "I do all this knowing that our love is doomed. One of us will live on without the other. We cannot be together, and I've made myself a villain for it. Yet I can't give him up. It is a torture I wouldn't wish on anyone."

She exhaled. "What does this have to do with me?"

His eyes shone. "You want to know why I insisted they save you? Because I want you and Galia to have something that lasts. They'll have no reason to separate you now."

She stared at their clasped hands, her jaw firm again. "You had no right to make this decision for me."

"You'll live, despite your losses and your pride. If not for yourself, then for Galia." Xiang squeezed her hand once before dropping it. Grief replaced the anger on her face. He'd managed to placate her, which would have to do for now.

She sat forward with a wince. "Where are we?"

"Near the border."

Her gaze darted to the tent flap. "They shouldn't be here."

"No," he said. "I doubt any of them will return south."

"What do they know?" she asked. Xiang repeated the Starling's inquiries and Traq's assumptions about Lua's identity. Her brow furrowed as she listened. "A Starling met the Oji and lived? That doesn't sound right."

"Turns out the Oji's anchor is Traq's close friend. Or was anyway," Xiang said.

"The anchor, the way she spoke to him in the tower, could she have some influence over him? I've only met the Oji a few times, but he seemed different."

Xiang shrugged. Her musings mirrored his own.

"You were friends, weren't you?"

He chuckled. "Friends? The Oji's never had friends. He was helpful when I first arrived, but it was always in exchange for something. Information on his sister's dealings, that sort of thing," Xiang said. "I used to feel sorry for him."

"Sorry?"

"The Rajav's people always surrounded him. Even his own anchor didn't care for him. He's been isolated for a long time under his father's control. Selene had twice the freedom he ever did." Xiang studied his hands. "Like I said, I used to feel sorry for him. I don't anymore."

"Because of Selene?"

"The Oji's conflict with the Oja puts her anchor in jeopardy. Sympathy is an expense I can no longer afford. If we can get to the Silence monastery before the coronation, there's a chance we can still defeat him."

"With their help?" She motioned toward the tent flap. "Do they know why we're headed to the monastery?"

"I've told them that there is a festival for the eclipses."

"A festival?" Her voice was incredulous. "And when we get there?"

"Wait and intercept. If these people can be useful, maybe he can be subdued again," Xiang said.

"Reinforcements?" she asked.

"I haven't been able to get any messages through since you collapsed."

Jayna rubbed her temples. "Kill his anchor. That's the only way."

Xiang's expression darkened. "Audra might cooperate. I saw her waver in the tower."

A stiff wind blew in with Wren. The thick white robes drawn up to her chin matched her pearly teeth. Her gaze flicked between them. "We'll break camp in the morning. Hopefully, it won't be too difficult to ride in the daylight for you."

"I'll cover well," Jayna said.

Wren smiled disingenuously. "I'll ride beside you. I can help if you fatigue. It will give us a chance to get to know each other." That the Starling leader wanted Jayna close spoke more of respect than distrust. Plus, it would keep their soldiers from thinking of rebellion.

Jayna grimaced and pulled her robes around her. Xiang helped her onto unsteady feet. "Won't that be nice?" Jayna said, meeting Wren's smile with one of her own.

The Septra tilted her head, gaze flicking suspiciously between the two of them. "I'm certainly looking forward to it," she said, holding Jayna's gaze for a moment before departing.

Forty-Three

Audra

Audra paused at the hill crest before the trail dropped into a long valley, pulling her hood up against the sudden snow. She'd always thought this place was named for the mountainous peaks surrounding it, but that wasn't it at all. Naked, white trunks soared into an overcast sky as far as she could see. Some curved like ribs, creating fractured archways. Others were hinged, dangling at odd angles. The rest jutted into the air like sharpened spears. A boneyard.

Stubborn juniper shrubs dotted between the bones, its pungent scent mixed with the musky decay that lingered beneath everything. She shivered, her feet refusing to move. There was an archaic, intangible presence here, a subtle magic that spider-danced across the nape of her neck.

Lua secured his hood against the muted daylight before launching down the slope. They'd only spoken a few words since leaving Stonetown; the tension between them was painful. Her questions were stuck in her throat. She'd been insulted at his rejection, confused as to how she could have possibly misinterpreted his signals. Then alcohol-fueled rage had pulled her from the bed to confront him. The shock of seeing Lua siphoning Arn had sobered her quickly.

The magic had reacted instinctively to her will. Her wits had been so slowed by mead and emotions that Lua's words hadn't registered at first. But she'd thought of little else since. Why he refused to touch horses or people, why he kept most of his skin covered even when the air was warm, it all made horrible sense.

The wave of shame that accompanied his confession made her understand for the first time the enormity of his isolation.

Lua could only have contact with his anchor. And she was his fifth. By her calculations, he'd not been able to touch more than one person for over a hundred years, and only two of those had been lovers. It didn't sound terrible at first, yet the more she considered it, the more pitiable it was.

Audra wasn't prone to physical expressions of emotion. She'd never hugged people she wasn't close with. It wasn't her nature. But she *could* hug if she wanted. Or hold someone's hand. Or brush against them in a crowded market. She could flirt and fuck casually and tend to animals and the ill without gloves. Lua could do none of that. Still, he should have told her about his limitations before.

He peered up from beneath his hood at the bottom of the slope, waiting. Her boots slid as she descended, but he steadied her. His touch sparked inside her chest, and the sudden withdrawal left her aching when he turned away. The threads between them wrenched, as if their magic didn't want to be separated.

The deeper snow was a day or two old, but the slight melt and refreezing gave it a crust that snapped with each step. The snow stopped as they moved forward. There were no bird calls or other signs of life, which only stressed the wind's whistle and the crunch beneath their feet —and a sense of being watched.

Audra's gloved fingers brushed the stone in her pocket again. Xiang said it would cut Lua off, but that was before one of his mages had tried to kill her. It would be foolish to trust Xiang's words. Zin would say not to trust anyone, yet she'd lied about Bolin. It made Audra wonder what else was kept from her.

Lua cut a path deep enough for her to easily follow. The only person

Audra was inclined to trust was the one whose life depended on hers. Despite his shortcomings, she wanted to believe in him. But that could be the lies the magic spun between them.

Halfway through the valley, they perched atop a boulder in the narrow shade of a rib bone and shared the last of the jerky. They hadn't been able to collect the food that Arn had prepared for them. Audra foraged winter berries before they entered the valley, but nothing grew in the spires. Maybe they'd be able to hunt on the other side.

"I'm sorry," he said softly.

Audra startled. "What?"

His unblinking gaze was unnerving. "I'm sorry about everything," he said. "I didn't mean to hurt your feelings."

"My feelings? What does that have to do with Arn?"

"Before Arn. In the room."

"Oh." Heat bloomed up her neck to her cheeks. She cleared her throat. "It's fine." It wasn't. "I misunderstood. I guess it was just the bond that—"

"No."

"What?"

"It's not the bond. If that were the case, then I would have been lovers with all my anchors. The connection doesn't necessarily equate to attraction or intimacy," Lua said. "I wanted to. I wanted you."

"You walked out. I threw myself at you and you left."

He shook his head. "You don't know what could happen to me. To us. And you were drunk. To put you in that situation without talking first would have been shortsighted and selfish."

She examined his vulnerability along their thread and closed her eyes. He took a deep breath in response.

"Tell me," she said.

"It consumes me."

"What does?"

He studied his hands, his words hesitant. "Magic feeds on desire. The more it has, the more it wants. It's gluttonous. And it won't . . . No, *I* won't be able to let you go. You should know this." He rubbed his face. "I won't be able to resist if you do that again."

Vulnerability shivered down their threads. He was the loneliest, most formidable man she'd ever met, and that mix of contrasts encouraged her to believe that her feelings might be deeper than desire, feelings that might be more powerful than the magic strung between them.

If she gave herself to him, would he fight for her? Or fight to control her? She already cared for him. Knowing someone's feelings from the inside would break anyone down. Lua was all kinds of wrong and deep wounds and damn if she didn't like the thought that this broken, dangerous man needed her. But she wondered how long it would last. Nothing in her life lasted, and the temptation that this might be different was both intriguing and terrifying.

"I know you've done horrible things," she said. "Things we haven't talked about yet, but I feel their weight on you."

He held his breath. His guilt swept over her.

"But the feelings I get from you aren't malicious. Maybe you're not terrible. Maybe you've just been broken too many times to remember what being whole is like." She paused until his eyes drifted to hers. "But I doubt you are irreparable. However, since we are stuck together, I need you to do better. To *be* better."

"For you?"

"No, Lua. For you and for us. If there is to be an us."

Hope gleamed in his eyes. "For us."

An icy gust jerked his hood back. Loose hair waved around his face as he hissed. Audra winced. The wind shifted, swirling and ricocheting from the opposite direction. Securing the hood, he stood protectively in front of her as the musky odor increased.

A shadow moved behind a row of spires. When Audra turned, there was nothing, only tall, stark bone that gleamed in the light. She shivered as ancient words whispered in her ear, coaxing, mocking.

"Did you hear that?" she asked.

Lua clutched her hand as if it were priceless, refusing to alter his pace for whatever lurked around them. His mannerisms were born of a life that had convinced him he was stronger than any threat. Audra envied that confidence. She eyed the cut of his stubbled jaw as energy poured between their hands. She didn't pull away.

"Zin said dragons once lived here," Audra said. "That this was their chosen resting place."

"Arn called it a graveyard." Lua turned sideways when another gust yanked his hood. Audra caught the fabric's edges before it was pulled away. Flurries danced around them.

Lua's eyes were winter storms. His lips parted as if a question lay just inside. Their threads pulsed in sync with their heartbeats.

"Audra," he said. Beneath the hesitation and doubt, desire shadowed his features.

A sound between a purr and snarl whipped into their ears as a sharper wind kicked snow into their faces. With a shuddering breath, he wrapped an arm around her shoulders.

Movement pulled at the corner of her vision. That same feeling of being examined brought her sharply back to focus. A sudden squall blocked out the afternoon Starling shine, forcing them to squint as they moved forward. Audra recognized the pungent scent and shivered. Occasional whispers followed them until Lua and Audra scrambled up the hillside and left the spires behind.

Dark clouds blotted out the expansive sky as the wind attempted to topple them backward. Before them was an expanse of flat grasslands turned muted white and gray in the twilight, segmented by a wide river that split the land like a gaping wound. She'd never seen the blood river before.

Lua stood behind Audra. The thud of his heart pressed against her back. He pointed to an enormous structure looming on the horizon. It was too dark for her to see clearly.

"There," he said with relief. "Only another day or two."

"What'll happen when we get there?"

"Then we can build the life we want."

Audra stared uneasily at the horizon. He was lying to himself, but she allowed it. Having a life with someone was something she'd never considered. Would he help to rebuild her tribe after what his had done? She turned to him, yearning for a future unimagined, a future she wanted to believe in.

His expression was full of tentative want. "Audra?"

"Lua. Shut up." She stood on her toes and wrapped her arms around his neck. Her lips were an inch from his. She waited.

A moment fraught with surrender and desire lingered between

them. Lua's hand found the base of her skull. His mouth crashed into hers. Audra pulled him closer as her lips parted, demanding.

Another gust pulled the fabric from Lua's head, but they ignored the sting of wind. Everything in the world was forgotten, save for each other.

His heat pressed into her despite their layers of clothing. One arm wrapped possessively around her waist. As their threads knotted together, they dissolved into their intertwined magic in a shimmer of green and silver that insulated them from the wind and snow.

And Audra knew there was no going back.

Forty-Four

Traq

Traq and Xiang rode near the front of the party as they traipsed down sloping, winter-hardened paths. Several starlings scouted ahead, while the rest encircled their captives. Jayna was under Wren's care somewhere in the middle, while Durin took up the rear with Liasa.

The weather and landscape had changed when they crossed the border the previous evening. Empty plains with snow-covered, leafless trees and shrubs had replaced the tall peaks, thick conifers, and rocky terrain. Occasional squalls forced them to find shelter and slowed their pace.

The Moon's propensity for deception was notorious and studying them had confirmed Traq's suspicions. Too much was hidden in a myriad of lies. But the random questioning by he and Wren revealed no new information.

"Will the Silence monks welcome you?" Traq asked.

Xiang shrugged. "Not likely, I'm not welcomed anywhere outside of Song monasteries. I'll always be a foreigner. In that, I suppose, you and I share some similarities."

Traq bristled, felt the darting glances of the surrounding soldiers. "We're nothing alike. I haven't betrayed my people."

"You must have been a child during the last battles, but you enlisted with your oppressors as soon as you were old enough. If that's not betrayal, I don't know what is. But, please, try to convince me of your moral superiority," Xiang said with disdain.

"I've tried to protect my people as much as I can. Can you say the same?"

Xiang's voice turned heavy. "No. In that you are correct. I've killed my tribesmen. Also, Moons and Starlings alike, as the situation demanded."

"You have no loyalty."

"Only to myself and those I love. The rest of this tribalism is divisionary tactics to keep people under control," Xiang said. "Perhaps when you're older, you'll see it for what it is. What would happen if they ordered you to kill your tribespeople? Would you be an obedient Starling or be labeled a Western rebel? How long after you protested would they strip your stars and slit your throat? Or I hear there's an even more gruesome end for Westerners in the southern sands."

Traq held his words. It was foolish to be goaded so easily. Xiang was taking his measure, hoping to use them to subdue Chon, but what he planned after that was uncertain.

Xiang promised that the Rajav would be grateful. They'd send an account of all that transpired, stating the Starlings were responsible for capturing the mass murderer to Lord Ijion and the Starling Senate. Wren responded too quickly, but she'd always needed to prove herself. That Xiang noticed that tendency and sold it to her with just the right amount of desperation in his voice was a testament of his skills.

They rode in silence through the dormant fields for a long time before Xiang spoke again. "Let me ask this. It's obvious you have some sentiment toward the western girl. But what does she really mean to you?" Traq pursed his lips as Xiang continued. "What will you do when your Septra orders you to kill her?"

"She wouldn't." Doubt thickened his voice.

"And if that's the only way to prevent catastrophe?" Xiang asked.

"That girl is anchored to our greatest criminal, which makes her his most vulnerable point. Best you consider what that means."

Tension settled behind Traq's eyes. He knew what it meant.

"Everyone will want to kill her at the first opportunity."

"And you?" Traq asked.

"I don't want her dead. If she cooperates, then perhaps Chon can be subdued," Xiang said.

Something in his tone nagged at Traq, but he didn't reply.

Hours later, after Jayna slid from her mount in exhaustion, the convoy made camp, building fires and erecting tents as Xiang and Durin tended to her. She'd grown stronger since the infection cleared, but she wasn't healed completely. She hadn't drawn more than a trifling of magic since she'd woken. Between the siphoning and Durin's healing, she probably wouldn't ever again.

"It'll take years for her to acquire more than a star or two, if she ever does." Wren sat with Traq beside the fire, watching the shadows move inside Jayna's tent. "She'll be useless unless we use her as bait."

"Bait?"

"Chon might want to finish her off."

"We sacrifice her?"

"They're waiting to do the same." She nodded to the Moon soldiers, nibbling their rations and mumbling to each other in their sharp dialect. "They might kill us once our usefulness has run its course."

"Then why are we taking the risk? Why help them at all?"

"I might be wrong. Maybe we can foster a positive relationship with their Rajav through this one act. If we can guarantee peace for our countries, wouldn't it be worth it?"

"What about the adage 'never trust a Moon'?"

"I still abide by that, but I'm willing to consider that thinking might be outdated."

Traq shook his head. "Xiang wants Audra alive. To use her to control the mage."

Wren scowled. "I assumed they'd want him dead."

Traq leaned toward her. "What do we really know about Chon? He's a powerful mage, but their words are formal. Practiced respect.

The soldiers don't speak of him at all. Have you noticed? Not one word."

"You know I get lost in their dialect." She scooted close, her shoulder brushing his. She dropped her voice. "When Jayna was slipping into delirium, she mumbled something about an Oji."

"Oji?"

"The Rajav's oldest. Oji for firstborn, Oja for second. Father fought them both in the last incursion. Said they slaughtered all the monks and several villages before they were stopped."

It was both white and black robes that killed his people, but he knew well enough to hold his tongue. Audra strapped to someone who represented everything she fought against made his teeth grind together in anger. She'd prevented him from knowing the danger she was in. No. It was more likely she'd protected him, and he'd been too hurt to see it.

"Why the monastery?" he asked. "I know there's an eclipse soon, but why go there?"

"He's relying on the Silence monastery to protect him." Wren rubbed her neck. "Something's going to happen during the eclipse festival."

Xiang exited the tent and settled beside the fire, looking as dour as ever.

Wren winked at Traq. "Traq and I just made a bet."

Xiang rubbed his hands together before giving her a droll look.

"Is the Oji going to the monastery because of the eclipse, or does the eclipse just happen to be occurring at the same time?"

Xiang's gaze turned hard. He cleared his throat. "What do you know of the Oji?"

"Not enough, apparently. Enlighten us," Wren said. A gold thread whipped from her fingers and encircled his throat.

Xiang stilled, staying within the small net of magic to prevent unintentionally connecting with it, as if this were a familiar experience.

All eyes turned to the golden glow of Wren's magic. One of the Moons shouted, the others rose to their feet where they met the Starling's drawn blades.

"Tell us about the Oji."

Xiang's face tightened.

"He won't tell you anything." Jayna stood in the tent flap; a slender arm draped around Durin's shoulders. "But I will." Xiang's eyes darted toward her, but she shook her head. "We need their help. The best thing we can do is ask for it properly."

Wren's magic withdrew slightly, leaving a single gold fiber encircling the general's throat.

"I knew you were the smart one," Wren said.

Forty-Five

Lua

Audra's chest gently rose and fell as she dreamed. Her warmth seeped into Lua's side beneath their shared blanket. They'd walked cautiously into the night as the clouds parted to allow the ring and moonlight to guide their way.

Lua prayed for guidance, but neither moon spoke—not a whisper since the sea. Their neglect was unnerving, as if they were waiting to make a decision.

Audra and he had shared deep kisses and tentative hands that had eventually settled in slumber. He'd wanted more, but it was too new and raw. He kissed the crown of her head, inhaling the scent his soul had grown to crave.

Lua feared disturbing anything between them. Who he was, the things he'd done, would horrify her. It wouldn't matter that he'd had no choice or couldn't clearly remember. He wouldn't blame her for hating him if she knew everything. Even if he wasn't the man he used to be.

Audra sighed, shifting in his arms before resettling. Her dark hair lay across her cheek. He should tell her about the coronation. There would be a moment when both moons were eclipsed that the tether between them would thin. The moons would withdraw his magic until they shone again. Then he'd receive their blessing and his reign would begin: Rajav Lua Koray and Raani Audra Shan. He wouldn't allow anyone to dispute it. With their combined power, even Selene wouldn't be able to usurp him.

Selene had kept Bolin on a leash so tight it nearly strangled him, but now Lua understood why Selene's power had grown over the last seventeen years. Bolin had the blood born of Western magic. Lua wondered if Selene knew what she had or if she intended to do to him what Li-Hun had done to their mother—use him until there was nothing left but dying flesh and agony.

Lua had never openly disobeyed his father, not even when the Rajav's paranoia and obsession intensified, and he demanded that all remaining Western mages be eliminated. Lua thought it had been only about the dragons, but he understood more after Stonetown. Audra's magic had controlled his even when he could not. Even though she was inexperienced, she'd undone his siphon instinctively. If they weren't anchored, she would have been a serious threat.

His chest tightened. She would plead for her people, and, for her alone, he would go to war and liberate them. He'd gladly slaughter the Starlings and drive them back south. After everything, it was the least he could do.

The dragons were a different matter, though. Audra would have to understand. He bit his lip, wondering what would happen if Zin and Ferin interfered.

Although they hadn't spoken of it, he was certain she'd acquiesce on this. She was reasonable, after all, and her emotions had begun to match his own. He didn't care if it was love or the mutual cravings of their entwined magic. Every fiber of his being longed for hers. He wanted her to need him the way he clearly needed her. To be her world, her everything. He didn't care if that was selfish.

Her fingers toyed with the ends of his hair. No, he would never give her up.

When they rolled up the blankets and resumed their journey,

Audra's smile was as cautious as his own, but she reached for him more often and he responded. Each glance she spared him left him feeling awkward and vulnerable, but he didn't mind it. She was the warmth that bloomed inside his frozen veins. A new home for his scarred heart. But he wouldn't say those things to her until after the coronation.

The blood-red river shone bright against the muted winter landscape, turning the snow covered shore a lighter shade of pink. Wherever the river leached into the ground, nothing grew. Audra's eyes traced it warily toward the mountain on the northern horizon. "What's wrong with it?"

A vague memory scratched at him, but he shook his head and gave the only answer he knew. "The minerals from the mountains keep it from being potable." Lua explained. "We'll have to stick with snow."

She searched the shoreline. "Where do we cross?"

He flashed an arrogant smile and pulled her close. His fingers interlaced with hers as he tugged on their magic. Silver and green swirled around them.

"What—?"

His lips brushed her temple as he lifted them from the ground. He no longer cared if his magic left a trail. Nothing could stop them now.

Threads reached out, latching into the air as they floated upward. She clung desperately to him. Halfway across the river, a thread slipped. They dropped a foot before Lua sent another yarn across and latched onto thick tree branches. Using their combined magic was like drawing fingers through still water: easy. They could have flown for another mile, but Audra's nervousness was contagious. She'd have to learn control quickly. Her magic was like a stumbling foal and more powerful than she realized.

When Lua steadied her on the ground, the exhilarating thrum of her heart coalesced with his. He rubbed his thumb across her lower lip before his mouth met hers. She softened into him with a small moan. Green and silver spun around them, insulating them from the chill for timeless minutes.

He pulled back with a breath, admiring the brightness of her eyes against her skin. Audra was everything beautiful he'd neglected noticing before. She was moonslight on water, red-feathered birds on gray days. She was the first taste of rain after a long drought and blue poppies breaking through spring snow.

A subtle energetic shift caught his attention. Lua shoved Audra behind him. His magic whipped wide to meet two streams of gray that arced toward them.

"Songs," he hissed, Selene's people. Three mages stood on the horizon, lined against them with a dozen dark soldiers. Their hands formed mudras as lips moved soundlessly.

Audra gasped as the spells wove together like a giant fishing net made of lightning. Lua gripped her hand and a counter spell slashed through the Song's tapestry, tearing it into small pieces that dissipated in the air.

Two mages hurled another spell at Lua, while another targeted Audra. Their spell burst apart as his silver countered. His fury surged with his magic, but he didn't know if it was his emotion or hers.

A silver spike impaled Audra's attacker into the ground. The two remaining mages worked their way to opposing sides as soldiers raced forward with drawn blades. A spell broke into smaller barbs raining down around Audra and Lua, but he turned the shimmering shards back at their soldiers. Three fell, ice freezing their blood before it could stain the grass. A few others stumbled.

A hint of familiar magic caught Lua's attention. One of Xiang's usual mages, Verina's voice echoed around them, but he couldn't make out her words. If she'd been with him at the monastery the fight might not have gone as quickly as it did. Xiang had been foolish to leave their most powerful mage behind. But Verina wasn't on the field before them. It was a diversion.

He conjured a razor-edged defensive shield and hurled it outward.

"Lua!" Audra yelled. She shoved him sideways, a sharp stream of gray magic flying from the left. An emerald barrier surged from Audra's arms. It shattered the gray magic like glass. Her cheeks flushed as the barrier turned wire thin and snaked toward the source of the attack. She grunted. Their power swelled as a row of trees toppled, shredded, revealing Verina's shocked face.

Audra met Verina's next spell with a chorus of curses and magic. Green and gray collided in the air. Lua was tempted to pull her back, but Audra seemed to handle her own.

Lua blew back another volley of spikes, but the soldiers dodged and dove down the hill. Ten blades shone as Starling burned through parting clouds.

Audra cursed again as another gray thread whipped past her cheek and struck the ground behind them. She clapped her green-glowing hands together, blowing the mage's hood off. Verina stumbled, shrinking back and raising her hands against the light. Audra's next lash sliced Verina's throat. Crimson scattered across the snow.

Three Song soldiers raced toward them, only twenty paces from the couple. Lua gripped Audra's hand, yanking her back to his side. Their magic rose between them, focused and furious. Horizontal and blade sharp, the spell split the soldiers into halves, their torsos falling mid-step as they screamed. The shimmering crescent continued, severing heads and limbs before striking the mages full force. They disappeared in a cloud of gore and blood.

All was quiet save for the sound of Audra and Lua's gasping breath. Audra stared at the horror spread across the landscape before dropping to her knees and retching. She quickly dissolved into empty heaves and hiccups. Lua knelt beside her, until her shaking arms wrapped around him.

Too many years had passed since his first kill, and her emotions were too intense. He didn't tell her that he was proud of her, which he was. Nor that he knew they'd be unbeatable. That the magic came so readily to her, that she'd protected him, was proof of the legacy they would build together. Instead of words, he held her quietly, and that seemed to be enough.

"Oji!" A familiar voice rang from behind the carnage. A row of Silence soldiers atop glossy black horses were framed along the horizon. A soldier called out again while raising a salute. Even across the distance, Lua could see the broad smile on Quin's face falter as the party moved closer. Quin had trained for years to replace Dain as anchor, he'd be sorely insulted by Audra's presence.

Anjing, a wiry, middle-aged ten star and the second highest ranking

Silence mage behind Fallue, rode beside him. They trotted forward, heedless of the death beneath their hooves. Audra wiped a hand across her mouth as Lua helped her to her feet.

"We're safe now," Lua said.

She stared at the soldiers, trembling. Her disbelief sang between them.

Forty-Six

Xiang

Jayna told the Starlings who they were tracking: the Oji Lua Koray, thirteen-star mage of the Silence tribe, first in line to the throne, and, supposedly, over a hundred and fifty years old.

Certain details she conveniently omitted, like the fact that the Rajav Li-Hun Koray and his Raani were murdered six weeks ago. Instead, she reinforced what the Starlings had already determined. They were after the Moon tribe Oji who'd attempted a coup and murdered innocent civilians on his quest for power, conveniently omitting that he had taken out an entire ship of mages and soldiers while fighting a constraining bolt. The casual references to the upcoming lunar eclipses and sacred festivals didn't mention the coronation. They'd find that out if they managed to get inside the monastery.

Wren and Traq asked random questions, occasionally rephrasing them hours later, but Jayna's answers were steady. Xiang kept his responses either evasive or hostile, hoping to paint a picture of division and elevate the perception of Jayna's trustworthiness. They would need that trust when they reached the Silence monastery.

Xiang had half hoped for Selene's troops to intercept them, but the roads were clear. Likely, she'd already sent people to monitor other routes to the Silence monastery in anticipation of Lua. Either that or her spies had caught sight of Xiang with a group of Starlings and held themselves back.

No matter. Xiang was determined to turn this situation to his advantage, even if the Starlings fell.

Jayna was growing too soft toward Durin as his questions leaned more personal, asking about her relationships and upbringing, offering his own experiences in return. Durin's face lit up when he spoke of his childhood and the tales his mother told from her journeys. There was a desperation to be heard in his voice. Xiang's grandmother had gotten like that in her later years: trying to impart wisdom to those who didn't wish to receive it.

Wren occasionally quieted Durin's ramblings with a sharp word, while Traq looked almost sheepish. It was an odd grouping, but they seemed cohesive. There were disagreements, annoyances, but ultimately, they worked well together. Their tolerance of each other's irritating qualities was affectionate, familial.

Without Nova Verina, Jayna and Nori had never gotten along. When the nine-star had miscarried two days before they sailed out on the *Bulou*, there'd been no time to select another mage, even though they were always strongest in threes. It was Xiang's misplaced faith in Selene's bolt and the *Mirren*'s crew that had let them embark without proper formation. He'd been a fool and, as they passed into northern lands surrounded by their enemies, he'd had plenty of time to consider his errors. If they'd had a third mage, Nori might still be alive. With Jayna's injuries, there was the distinct possibility they'd be facing the Oji without any Song mages.

"You're sighing," Liasa said, riding beside him. She'd been stationed closer to Xiang since the incident around the fire, haunting his steps with an expression that bordered on irritatingly cheerful. Her cropped reddish-brown hair was peppered with silver. There were lines around her eyes, but the warmth of her complexion gave her a youthful appearance. "Anything you care to share?"

His next sigh was pointedly aimed at her. Liasa chuckled.

"What part of the Western lands did you come from?" she asked.

His eyes flicked to her. "It doesn't exist anymore."

"Family gone too, eh?" she asked. "I was one of seven children. All lost except for a sister that was stolen south after Oxton fell. Heard she'd birthed a soldier's child and couldn't return. Don't suppose I'll ever see her again."

"But you're a Starling now, should give you some options," Xiang said.

She shook her head. "It was either join or risk following my sister's fate. Kind enough of them to give me an option, I suppose. But it's like what you said the other day—I'll always be a foreigner." She shrugged. "It's all right, though. I carry my home with me." She thumped her chest once.

Liasa's tone coaxed him to share, but his past was long buried. Not looking back was the only way he could keep moving forward. She asked, "Do you have any Western affiliation left?"

A frigid gust stung his cheeks; he squinted at the bite. "All my loyalties lie in the north now."

She studied him as they rode and eventually shook her head, as if she'd been searching for some redeemable quality and been disappointed. "Pity."

Bits of Durin and Jayna's conversation drifted toward them.

"Never quite grasped the concept of relationships when I was always gone," Durin said. "But met a fine man a few years ago. He runs a store, museum of sorts, on Callaway. I'll be retiring there when this mission is done."

"What's his name?" Jayna asked.

"Claude. He's a good man, despite his peculiarities." Durin's voice was reverent, reminding Xiang of the way he spoke of Bolin. "What's their name? Your someone."

"Galia," she said. "She's waiting in Uduary. But I doubt that I'll make it home."

Durin smiled gently. "There were many battles I shouldn't have survived. And each trial made the next days sweeter. Just focus on getting through today, then tomorrow, then the next day. That's all we have anyway, isn't it? Right now. And I'm glad to have met you, Jayna."

Xiang rode behind them, stoic and wordless as the highest tower of the Silence monastery loomed on the horizon. He and Jayna hadn't needed to speak of what would happen when they reached the monastery. The Starlings would be sacrificed, and old men didn't fare well in battles.

Forty-Seven

Selene

Maya's screams were louder and longer than Grethin's death had taken. The servant's husk crumbled on the floor. Motes of dried skin drifted in the air.

Selene dipped her hands in the water basin atop a table, before drying them on a towel. Kanata held Maya, trying to turn the girl's face away from Grethin's remains. The ferret trembled from its cage in the corner.

"I warned you about respect," Selene said, while donning her gloves. "You brought this about."

Maya's lip trembled. "I don't understand." Her voice dissolved into sobs.

"I thought the poem was kind at first, an apology for your pet's behavior. On closer examination, I noticed your little rendition of the beast." Selene laid the towel next to the basin. "Was it meant to inspire guilt? Try to manipulate me again, girl, and it won't be your servant in ashes."

Maya shook her head, two braids danced around her shoulders. "I just wanted you to have something of her. Grethin didn't do anything. She—"

"You were under her supervision. All your actions are a reflection of her, Kanata, and myself." Selene glanced at the tutor, whose eyes remained downcast. Maya continued to cry. "I suggest you remember that in the future."

Maya's sobs followed Selene down the hallway as the door closed. The sound bothered her more than it should have. Still, better the girl learn that disrespect would not be tolerated.

Bolin leaned against the wall outside her rooms, chatting with the two guards stationed there. One guard looked more interested than she liked. Dark circles ringed Bolin's eyes. "Where were you?"

"Dealing with the girl."

The guards opened the doors as Bolin shadowed her inside. She tossed her gloves on a table. "Why haven't you killed her by now?"

"I'm still considering it."

"You've never hesitated before. What's different this time?"

She shrugged, annoyed she didn't have a decent answer. Perhaps she was growing sentimental. "Is everything ready?"

He nodded. "I selected the mages myself, two ten stars, the rest all four to nine stars. Two squadrons and horses to spare. Plenty of provisions. But the cold—"

"No word yet?" She knew the answer, even if she didn't know his every emotion, the despair etched on his face told her. She gently cupped his cheek. "Don't worry. We would have heard if something had happened."

"I shouldn't have let him go."

"I allowed it." She stared at his mouth, considered tasting his lips, but it wasn't the time. "You had no say in the matter."

He pulled away and wiped his eyes. "We should leave soon. No point in wasting time."

Her hand lingered in the air before retracting. "Make it so."

Bolin left without a backward glance. His heart had always been Xiang's, and she'd hoped he would come to her if the general suddenly vanished. But if Bolin's heart broke, she would suffer with him. And that was the last thing she wanted.

They'd push the horses and troops through the higher elevations. A risk this time of year but taking those roads might give them the element of surprise. Sacrifices would have to be made, but that had never stopped her before.

Forty-Eight

Audra

Audra tried the handle for the tenth time, but it remained stubbornly locked. The shadows beneath the door shifted when she cursed and kicked it. The two men guarding her didn't respond. In fact, beyond a servant delivering a tray of food, she'd been ignored.

It was strange. Audra was usually comfortable being on her own. Not that she'd ever really been alone, but these weeks tethered to Lua had made solitude unfamiliar. She could see their green and silver connections when she closed her eyes.

Kindling waited to burn in the fireplace, but there were no matches to strike it and her all'ight was too weak. She poked the braised, undercooked lamb and frowned. The food was bland. Even the seasoned vegetables and dense flat bread were nearly tasteless without the warming herbs of Western fair.

Slanting evening light entered through a small arched window and provided a view of the surrounding landscape. Past the dull, patched roofs of the small village that surrounded the monastery, snow-carpeted fields spanned as far as she could see.

She fumbled through the scrolls but was too distracted. When the script eluded her, she shoved them back in the bag. She supposed she should have been grateful that Lua had insisted they leave her and her things untouched.

Being cold and bored wasn't anything new. Stealing took patience, and conditions like these were expected occasionally. But being locked in was nothing she'd ever grown accustomed to. Despite Lua's fondness for this drab place, she wasn't impressed. The monastery wasn't the gleaming symbol of dark power she'd expected. Though it was tidy, the place was worn and run down, the air stale, as if its time had long passed and no one dared to mention it.

The Moons had fawned over their Oji, bowed respectfully, and cast their eyes away from him before ogling her with unnerving curiosity. But once the monastery doors closed behind them, the soldiers practically carried her up to this room. Hours had passed, and Audra was trying not to doubt Lua's reassurances. That she'd not been interrogated yet was probably the result of his protection.

She closed her eyes. The thread was as it had been, green and silver entangled with knots. She reached out, searching for something of him, and found annoyance, frustration. Whatever he was dealing with, he was nearly as unhappy as she was. That brought her some measure of warped satisfaction. She would have been angrier if he'd been content. Which made her wonder if, in fact, her annoyance was her own or a result of his. It was difficult to tell where she ended and he began.

The window shook beneath a frigid wind that wafted into the room. She shivered and pulled her robe tighter. A decent host would have lit the fire, but the Moon tribes were especially harsh to foreigners. How had Bolin survived all these years here?

She held the bloodstone up in the fading light. It was unimpressive when compared to the precious stones she'd stolen. Even broken, the jade was always warm with life, but this remained cold no matter how long she held it.

Another gust hit the window. Her teeth chattered as she shoved the stone into her pocket. Lua made her practice lighting fires more than once, but she'd struggled to complete it. Every spell she'd created so far had been born of a strong immediate desire. Or instinctive, like Arn or during the fight. The image of blood spraying across the ground waited for Audra every time she closed her eyes.

She rubbed her hands together and stared at the wood waiting to be burned.

Audra wasn't sure she could manage a spell on her own. Maybe Lua's magic acted as a catalyst to hers. She didn't have any training. All she had was a bit of green thread as temperamental as her emotions.

And excuses. She seemed to have plenty of those lately. Zin would say there was no point in complaining if you weren't willing to try. Lua had said nearly the same.

She allowed the frustration to coil inside her, hating the dreary room. Cursing the cold that slithered beneath her robes and into her boots. Damning the mages and soldiers that locked her in. Hating—

Green energy leaped from her hand, and the kindling burst into flames. A log popped, sending chunks of smoldering wood onto the threadbare rug. It smoked and glowered, eating away at the aged fabric before Audra doused it with the pitcher of water.

The fire popped again, sending a wave of warmth onto her cheeks as she stared at the burned rug. Maybe no one would notice. Or they'd start a fire for their guests from now on.

The door opened sometime later, waking Audra from near sleep on the hard couch. She wiped her mouth as Quin, one of the men who'd greeted them on the fields, entered. He was stocky and might have been attractive if he could wipe the hate from his face. He examined Audra with disgust, as if she were shit he'd accidentally stepped in and hadn't figured out how to scrape off his shoe yet. But she suspected he was working on it.

"Come with me," he said.

Audra rubbed her eyes. She wanted out of this room, but she didn't mind watching him squirm. "Why?"

His contempt deepened. "Master Fallue has summoned you."

"He's not my master. Where's Lua?"

Quin flinched. No one used Lua's name so casually, she'd noticed.

"Our *Oji* waits with Master Fallue."

The irritation in his voice made her move slower. She stood and stretched before nodding casually to the floor.

His eyes darted between the burned carpet and her face. "What did you do? That was original to this wing. How... No, why—"

"There weren't any matches." She shrugged, tugging her robe around her shoulders. "You could have started it before leaving me to freeze to death. What did you think would happen?"

He seethed. "It's unfortunate that suffering in silence is apparently not in your nature."

Audra's laugh made his jaw clench. She grabbed her bag and followed him out the door. They walked down twisting, stone corridors to a set of stairs that curved around a massive foyer and plunged down a hundred feet into the center of the building. Quin nodded to passing soldiers as they descended.

At the main level, his pace quickened down another hall, forcing Audra behind him until they reached a pair of plain oak doors. He knocked once before leading her inside.

The elderly Master Fallue was gaunt and pale. He sat at the end of a large table, his wispy beard trailed down his black-robed chest, rustling slightly with each breath. His silver hair was tied in a formal topknot. Lua sat beside him, donned in his worn black robes, hair half down. Her chest tightened at his smile. Desire pulled her a few feet forward before she stopped and tried to remember her anger.

"Audra?" Fallue asked, forgoing any formalities. "What is your surname?"

"Shan."

Fallue's tone was low. "A terribly common Western name."

She bristled though Lua still smiled, like he hadn't heard the intended insult. "There's nothing wrong with being common," she said.

The old man studied her with a frown. "How are the accommodations, Audra Shan?"

"Drafty."

Quin cleared his throat. "There was an incident, Master."

Fallue's white eyebrows rose like caterpillars trying to crawl off his face.

"The Westerner burned the rug that Mistress Onia wove," Quin said it matter-of-factly, but there was a hint of satisfaction.

"Burned?" Fallue's eyes narrowed at Audra. "Ah, well. It was quite old. Probably only took a spark to ignite. Have it taken to the weavers. Perhaps they can mend it."

Quin's cheeks flushed. "Yes, master."

"Leave us, Quin. I'll send for you if you are needed."

The soldier gave a small bow and threw a venomous look at Audra before he left. Lua motioned toward a chair beside him, pulling it out as she approached.

"The Oji and I were having a debate," Fallue said. "It would seem that he won."

The chair lacked padding, confirming to Audra that the Moon tribes loved their misery. "Is that why I've been locked in that damn room for hours?"

"Audra, don't be rude," Lua said.

Fallue pursed his lips. "It is. He wanted to prove that your magic could start a fire. We kept waiting for word from the guards."

Lua looked almost guilty as Audra spoke. "Matches would have been simpler, and you wouldn't be short a rug."

"You managed it, didn't you? I knew you could," Lua said quietly.

"A one star could do that." Fallue shook his head. "And look how long it took her."

"Western magic isn't like ours. There are no stars with—"

"We still don't know for sure that she *is* a Western mage and, if she is, how do you think *that* will be received?" Fallue's voice urged caution. "Did you see Quin or the others? After everything they've done for you, you come home anchored to a foreigner. How does that make you any different from the Oja?"

Audra shifted uncomfortably. Every retort she considered died before it left her lips. Maybe she should ask to be locked back in that room. It was probably warmer than where she was now.

Lua's eyes narrowed. "You didn't see what she did when the Songs attacked us. Or how she stopped an accidental siphon. It's new to her. She doesn't have control yet."

"Better to sever her now before she gets control."

"I trust her." Lua's voice rose above Fallue's. The old man quieted, eyes narrowing as Lua gripped Audra's hand and stood. "You don't know her yet."

"Wait," Fallue said. He rose gingerly, bracing himself against the table. "Don't be like this."

"I am about to be made Rajav, and you would still deny me what I want. How much longer did you think you could control me with my anchors?"

Fallue's mouth snapped shut. "I've only tried to protect you."

"By catering to my father. But he's dead now." Lua pulled a little on their thread before continuing, "You want to protect me? Then teach her. In that way, you can help us both."

Lua tugged her through the door. Two guards hastened ahead of them, down the hall and up the winding staircase to the third floor. The Oji didn't acknowledge those who bowed as they passed, and Audra didn't look at anyone. The gasps as they saw her hand in his were more than enough attention.

The guards opened a set of arched doors and swiftly closed them behind the couple without a word. The room was bigger than Zin's cabin. A fire danced in the large hearth, and steam rose from a copper bathtub where sprigs of lavender floated atop the water. The largest bed Audra had ever seen sat against the farthest wall. Its black oak frame was draped with ebony curtains.

Lua gripped Audra's hand and drew her close. They were alone, and they were finally safe. Her feelings might be muddled, but she knew what she wanted in that moment.

Despite his shell of arrogance and entitlement, he'd been insecure when speaking to Fallue. Lua feared disappointing him and his people, worried about failing everything he'd been raised to value. Against all of that, he'd defended her, fought for her, and she knew he'd do it again.

"Are you all right?" she asked, brushing the hair from his face with tentative fingers. The connection sparked through them. His expression was cautious, mixed with shuddering need.

Their mouths collided in a frenzy of desperation. They stumbled backward, kicking off boots and frantically tearing at clothing until their naked legs met the bed. The overwhelming arousal of his flesh against hers consumed her.

He paused, panting, and cupped her cheeks. "Are you sure?"

Audra shoved him down onto the soft mattress and straddled his hips, feeling his desire beneath her. She leaned over him, inhaling the scents of road and lust, cloves and night, and stared into his pale eyes. She considered her usual flippant responses, thought about telling him to shut up again, but that wouldn't do. Not now. She could speak truth, and he wouldn't leave.

"There's nothing I want more."

Audra savored his mouth, kissing his neck and chest as his fingers worked through her hair. He groaned, rising, and flipping her onto her back. She opened to him, biting his lip as they became one.

The silk curtains reflected green and silver as their magic entwined. It rose and fell in undulating waves, dissolving before rising again until it exploded with dazzling brilliance, causing the sturdy bed frame to shift against the wall.

She lay in Lua's protective embrace, a sheen of sweat glowing upon her skin. His eyes were closed, breath deep and satisfied. Audra traced the lines that crisscrossed his chest. She counted them, remembering the marks she'd seen on his back on the *Requin* and those on his legs from the road. So many scars.

"Where did they all come from?" she whispered.

"Hmm?"

"Your scars."

His body tensed slightly but he kissed the top of her head. "It doesn't matter. Nothing matters before you."

Her chin rested on his chest. "I want to know your pain."

Silver eyes slitted open. "In time, I'll tell you everything if you want, but for now, I only want my thoughts to be here with you."

She smiled dreamily; a euphoric, nearly drunken emotion warped her senses. That feeling that she might dissolve into him nagged at the edges of her awareness until she remembered what Lua had said to Fallue.

"You said that you were about to be made Rajav."

His jaw tightened. "The coronation is in five days, during the dual lunar eclipses."

"Coronation?" She pulled away from him. The impact of Fallue's words hit her. The Rajav was dead, of course Lua would be the Moon tribes Rajav. "Even though you killed . . ." Her words trailed off; they'd not spoken of it. Bitterness swarmed toward her at the mention of his father.

Lua rose onto one elbow, frowning. His voice was barely a whisper. "Audra, I didn't kill my father."

"But—"

"Selene and I . . ." He bit his lip, trapping truth inside him for a breath. "I just made him easier to kill. Selene did the rest."

Audra stared at him, understanding what he could not say. "You killed his anchor."

Sorrow and shame swept over her. His silver eyes turned glassy as he looked down. He'd cut people down without flinching, spoke of killing Dain with less emotion than he showed now.

Something warned her to let it settle, but the strength of his emotions coaxed her tongue. "Who was the last Raani, Lua?"

Lua's throat bobbed and it took him a long moment to respond. "My mother."

Audra's vision blurred, tears slipping from her eyes. Lua turned his attention to her shaking breath and wiped his thumb across her cheek. A hundred questions cluttered her mind while gnawing distrust encroached on the bliss they'd shared only a moment before.

"My mother was the kindest person I've ever known," he started.

"But you killed her," she said with a horrified breath.

He licked his lips, shaking his head. "It's not like that. Not exactly."

She sat up, drawing the blanket up to cover her breasts as her words turned threatening. "Then you tell me what it's like, Lua. You tell me right fucking now."

He reached for her, but she pulled away. "You remember what I said back in Pangol about the anchoring bond taking a lot from an anchor?"

She nodded, stealing herself.

"Amala, my mother, should have only lasted twenty to thirty years at most. Just long enough to see Selene and I out of our childhoods," Lua said. "But she was different, her aging was slower than it should have been. When her body finally turned against her, father wouldn't let her go. For decades, mother begged anyone who came near to kill her." Lua's voice was steady though immense grief held his expression.

"To say that she suffered doesn't give the whole scope of what she endured. Her joints were warped, body too weak to leave her bed. Her anguished cries echoed down the halls for years and no matter how much we pleaded for father to release her, he refused and forced the healer to keep her alive. Whatever had allowed her to last longer than the others, had also enabled his magic to flourish. They made draughts that kept her pain at bay while also trapping her in sleep. But when her pain became too strong for him to deflect, he'd put a stone around her neck, and it would diminish the connection for a little while." Lua cleared his throat.

"When her bones began crumbling to dust beneath her skin, the healer came to me because she feared the Rajav's response. Selene and I agreed that helping our mother let go was the right thing to do."

Audra was rigid, stuck between empathy and sickness. She licked her lips. "How?"

He shook his head. His voice was low and tremulous. "You know how. I held her in my arms and drew the life from her myself. The last thing she felt was the arms of someone who loved her."

The wave of sorrow that had clung to Lua for weeks crested and crashed over them both. Audra pulled him down onto the bed and held him in her arms.

The fire in the hearth was sputtering low when new worries woke her. The fear that her fate might be the same as his mother's weighed on her. But Lua lay beside her, studying her face with raw emotion. Trapping her here would be the same as being locked in that room upstairs. She had goals, obligations that had nothing to do with the Moon tribe. None of that changed despite her feelings for him.

"What if the same thing happens to me?" she asked.

He shook his head. "Mother had no magic, Audra. She had some Western blood, but nothing like yours." Lua tucked a lock of hair behind her ear. "I won't let anything happen to you, I swear it. You will be made Raani, a holy position."

"Will they accept a common Westerner in that role?"

"Fallue didn't mean that."

"Yes, he did."

"There is nothing common about you. You're a mage," Lua said.

"One star."

"A one star wouldn't have been able to do what you did in Stonetown or against that mage today."

She scooted to the edge of the bed, where his touch couldn't distract her. "What about Zin and Ferin?"

"What about them?"

"When can I go home?" She asked.

A crease formed between his brows. He clutched her hand before she could escape, kissing her palm. His voice was soft. "Audra, you are home."

Forty-Nine

Xiang

Xiang slipped into the tent in a rare moment of opportunity. Jayna sat beside the fire, answering the Starling's incessant questions with half-truths. Traq asked about anchoring while the others listened aptly. Anchoring wasn't taught to the southerners, so, naturally, they were fascinated. As Jayna spoke, Wren listened quietly, biting her lip as if she had her own opinions on the matter.

He clutched the small mirror that had gone unused for days. It had been too long since he'd contacted Bolin and, though they grew closer to the monastery, Xiang struggled with a solid plan. The Starlings kept close watch on him and Jayna. Understandable. If their situation were reversed, he would have done the same.

No. He would have dismembered their bodies and dumped them in shallow graves long ago. It was a fundamental difference in perspective. Mercy would be their downfall after Lua was defeated. Theirs would be a welcome sacrifice, and Xiang would not sorrow at the loss.

He propped the mirror on the floor and took out a small, dull knife he'd managed to hide during a meal. He closed his eyes and chanted the short mantra while drawing the blade across the back of his forearm. It took five attempts before an adequate amount of blood surfaced and the mirror's image rippled.

At first, the view on the other side was only an empty chair with a blank canvas wall behind it—a tent. They were travelling.

Bolin slid into view with a relieved smile. There were tears in his eyes as they use practiced gestures and pantomimes to communicate. Selene's angular face peered behind him, quickly taking in his environment. Xiang told them what he could, hating how Bolin worried since there was nothing to be done about it.

Selene wanted to know how far from the monastery they were.

He held up two fingers.

She made a gesture that was commonly rude toward the Starlings, then held her hands wide and counted fingers. *How many are with you?*

Xiang showed the three mages and ticked off the number of soldiers. Her expression was grim. She rested a placating hand on Bolin's shoulder. Selene managed to indicate a higher-ranking mage, maybe a council member, but the purpose of the mention was unclear. After a round of reassurances to Bolin, his wound clotted, and the image faded. His own haggard face stared back at him.

He stuffed the mirror into his interior pocket and pulled down his sleeve. If Selene went to the monastery, Bolin would be in jeopardy when she confronted Lua. Her actions were a direct result of Xiang's failure to capture the Oji.

Laughter trickled from the fire outside, but their humor was lost on him. They'd asked him to join them, but he wouldn't waste time on those who didn't know they were about to die. Despite his promises of retribution and cooperation, Selene wouldn't render mercy unless there were advantages to be gained.

He wondered how Audra fared with Lua. If the monks demanded them separated, the way Lua had swept in at the ruins made Xiang think they'd have a difficult time. Whatever was happening with the Oji and his anchor made him unpredictable and elevated the risks before them.

Whether Selene or Lua was stronger had long been a source of quiet debates for many years. He held more stars, but she was more conniving. That their anchors were siblings would only come into play if Bolin recognized his sister, and that was unlikely given he'd not seen her since she was a child. Xiang wouldn't tell him. Knowing Bolin, it would only confuse his sense of self-preservation. If Xiang could save Audra for Bolin's sake, he would. But he'd willingly sacrifice her if it came to it. If she wore the bloodstone, there was a chance she could survive, but nothing was guaranteed.

Xiang closed his eyes at another round of laughter. He curled on his side, pulling a blanket over his head. He hoped to dream of Bolin's soft lips and tender touch, but his nightmares were filled with the bloodied faces of those he'd killed.

Fifty

Lua

Lua left Audra with three attendants who'd been instructed to make her more presentable. Though he'd grown accustomed to her foul vocabulary, the veracity of her curses made the servants flinch. He gently encouraged Audra's tolerance, reminding her that she had to make a good impression on members of the mage council. Only minor appearance changes, nothing she couldn't throw off after the coronation and monthlong celebrations in Uduary.

Her sudden lapse into silence worried him, but he'd address her concerns later. All that mattered was they were together. The scent of her lingered in his hair, consuming him. He tasted her on his lips. He debated returning to her, dismissing the servants, and locking the doors behind him. But there were obligations he couldn't avoid, and they had years before them.

The house of Silence had waited generations for this coronation, and preparations were hastily underway. Fallue leaned against a table while Anjing barked orders at the bustling workers. The younger mage bowed nervously when Lua entered; he'd been trying to strengthen their relationship over the last few years in anticipation—or hope—of becoming the head of the Silence mages when Fallue retired. But Lua suspected that the man might be too easily perturbed to hold the position when it became available.

Workers tested the ceiling's panels repeatedly, oiling hinges when they caught and inspecting the ropes that would hold them open during the ceremony. They'd arranged the tables in spiral patterns around the center dais where the ceremony would occur. A dozen formal chairs for the joint council members were positioned around the throne on the stage. Lua expected half those would be empty. He frowned when he noticed a chair missing.

Fallue's cane tapped rhythmically across the floor toward Lua.

"Where's the Raani's chair?"

"Can we continue our discussion from yesterday without you becoming emotional?"

Lua swallowed a retort that would have only proved him right. "If you're going to repeat that I should give her up, you can save your breath. I won't."

"And what will happen when the rest of the council arrives? They'll have better arguments, and you can expect less respect than I have shown," Fallue said.

"Then we'll replace them."

Fallue's calm demeanor vanished with a huff of outrage. "Oji?"

Anjing, the servants who lingered in the corners, and even the workers above paused at his tone. Lua raised his voice slightly. "Anyone who speaks against my anchor, speaks against me and shall be dealt with as I see fit."

A murmur spread through the room, low enough to keep the words indistinguishable but loud enough to ensure that they'd heard him. Gossip spread faster than any decree would.

Fallue lowered his voice, leaning close like they'd once done when toiling over the scrolls in the lowest vaults. Back when they appeared the same age. Fallue hadn't gained his tenth star until much later in life. "The council is made of both tribes equally. You can expect cooperation from Silence, of course, but the Songs will surely balk at this. And the ministers—"

"Selene's anchor is Western. The ground they stand on is mole ridden."

"Selene is not becoming Rajav. If she were, it would be our council members raising concerns. And rightly so," Fallue said. "This spits in the face of tradition."

"Raani Amala wasn't wholly northern either."

Fallue looked away. "There was never proof of her heritage either way. As long as she denied it to the council, they couldn't refuse her. But your Audra Shan." He shook his head. "I doubt she'll be as complacent."

Lua smirked. "No, probably not. So, I suggest the council attempt to adjust their demands and expectations unless they seek an early dismissal."

Fallue hissed. "Don't be like that."

"Like what?"

"Like your father."

Silver lit Lua's fingertips. "Watch your words, Fallue. Our history doesn't supersede respect."

Fallue caught the eyes of a few servants until they scuttled back to their tasks. "Walk with me, Oji. Anjing, carry on." The mage gave a curt nod as they exited through the door toward Fallue's office. Two guards walked behind them at a respectful distance.

"I can see that you are already attached to this one, certainly more than with Dain. But this bond is unpredictable. Unstable at best. There are reasons the Western mages kept to themselves. Their magic is difficult to control and, if memory serves me right, so are their mages. And their dragons—"

"You don't know that."

"Listen to reason, Lua. Your father was so convinced of their danger that he spent countless wars wiping them out. And now you've brought one home as your anchor, with plans of elevating her to one of the most powerful positions in the country." Fallue's voice rose. "Besides, the relationship of anchor is meant to be with those without magic. Protocol and history affirm that two mages bound will only create a power struggle and eventually, someone must lose."

"How long were my parents anchored?"

"That's not—"

"How long?" Lua demanded.

"One hundred and fifty-three years."

"An exceptionally long life for an anchor. My father chose Amala for the very reason I choose to keep Audra by my side. If a hint of Western magic could allow the last Raani to live for as long as she did tethered to my father, imagine how long Audra and I will have?" From his rooms above, a soothing sensation shimmied down their thread in response to his heightened emotions.

Fallue shook his head sadly. "But look what it did to Raani Amala. The torment and suffering she endured, so much so that she begged—"

"I'd *never* hurt Audra," he said. "You don't understand what we have. You don't know her."

"And you do? How deeply can you know someone after only a few weeks? We don't know what she's capable of. Or what her magic could do. I doubt even she knows."

They glared at each other while Lua chewed on a response. His words would hold little meaning here. Even though he'd be the Rajav soon, he'd spent a lifetime beneath his father's control. His single act of rebellion—pledging to the less popular Silence moon—had widened the rift between the tribes. The council wouldn't trust his judgement, even after he'd helped rid them of their oppressor. But he couldn't avoid Audra standing before them for scrutiny.

"Will you train her if she's accepted?"

Fallue rubbed his beard and sighed. "*If* she's accepted."

Lua stifled a gasp when Audra entered the room. He'd only ever seen her in travel-worn breeches and dusty robes, but the woman who stood before him had transformed into something sleek and dark.

The traditional black tunic had been tailored to accentuate her shape. Thirteen silver stars were sewn down her right sleeve, while the left sleeve was blank. Her robe was black, its glittering interior lining matched his own. Form-fitting breeches were tucked into elegant, tall boots laced to her knees. They'd cut her hair at a sharp angle that followed her jawline, and her skin glowed from the scrubbing she'd endured. Dual kohl stripes painted from above the arch of her eyebrows, down her eyelids, to the middle of her cheeks to symbolize the revered status of Raani and her full lips were stained a deep crimson. Audra looked exactly like Lua had instructed, and he didn't care how presumptive it was.

She stood before the council's five men and three women, meeting their scornful gazes one at a time before seeing the look on Lua's face. Her cheeks flushed.

Fallue cleared his throat. "Audra Shan, you stand before this council, as all potential anchors must, to submit to questions that will determine your compatibility with the role of anchor to the Oji Lua Koray. Do you swear to answer honestly?"

Audra swayed nervously. Lua responded to her quickening pulse by sending a small reassurance toward her. She took a deep breath. "I do."

He'd prepared her for some of the questions, the ones about her parentage were easy. The council exchanged nervous glances when she spoke of her mother as a Western mage. They'd openly frowned when she recounted her healer father who'd died fighting the Moons in Oxton. That drew questions about her loyalty to the Moon tribe.

"I have no loyalty to the Moon tribe," she stated flatly. Anjing raised his voice in outcry. Sharine, the head of the Song mages, sneered. The woman's rich brown hair had auburn hints, her complexion was pale as milk. Audra regarded her casually. "My loyalty is to Lua."

They quieted at that. Lua smiled. It was the answer he yearned for.

Who did she worship? What was her daily ritual of prayer? Audra had no such rituals or worship. She held nature to the highest regard and hoped to be returned to the ground someday or left for animals to eat, rather than burned at sea like their tribes preferred. Would she consider converting if asked? Her glance at Lua revealed her answer. She wouldn't like it, but she'd play along if she had to.

What about the rest of her family? She skirted around her aunt and adopted brother, briefly mentioning her older brother, who'd gone missing in the same battle that killed her father. Lua had warned her not to mention Bolin at all. When the questions turned to situational theorizing, Audra held her ground. Some answers struck well, others fell flat.

"Fallue said you are a mage in your own right," Sharine said. "Do you have control over your magic?"

Her eyes darted to Lua again. A sheen of perspiration dotted her brow, smearing the edges of the kohl as the hours had worn on. "I didn't think I had much magic until recently."

Sharine's smile was tight. "Our mages train at an early age. How is it your magic only just arrived?"

"Maybe because all the Western monasteries were destroyed and our history stolen from us during years of Moon and Starling assault. There wasn't anyone left to learn from." Audra's glare was unflinchingly hard.

Sharine cleared her throat and exchanged uncomfortable glances with several other mages before she spoke. "Historically, Moon mages haven't been allowed to bond to each other as we deem the connection too volatile. Would you be willing to give up your magic in order to keep the bond?"

Audra frowned, confused. Her eyes found Lua's. "Is that possible?"

Sharine's tone was condescending. "Magic can be gifted. Many mages pass theirs on to subordinates when they retire. But it cannot be taken or coerced unless—"

"Unless someone over ten stars demands it," Lua said. Audra held his gaze for a long moment before turning back to Sharine. He didn't want to hear her answer. Lua moved to her side and gripped her hand. "These questions are at an end."

"Oji, we aren't done," Sharine said.

Lua silenced her with a raised hand. "I am stronger with her beside me." He tugged on their threads, a rope of green and silver swept above the council members' heads as they gasped. It sliced the wall sconces in half and scorched the stone. The rope spun around the room while encapsulating himself and Audra in a sphere of silver and emerald. Then he added two more spells: a shield before them and a platform beneath their feet that raised them a foot above the ground.

"Audra defended me without hesitation when Selene's loyalists attacked us after we crossed the river. If she gives up her power, you will say she's not physically suited for the job, that she'd be a liability and unable to protect me." He shook his head. "Do not expect me to tolerate these games. Audra *will* be my Raani, and she won't give up her magic. Not to you or anyone."

The council shifted between open hostility and nervousness as the spell lashed inches above their heads. Fallue alone sat unflinching, his expression resigned.

Audra clenched Lua's hand. "Stop. I can answer their questions."

His anger surged as he regarded the council members, sitting in their high-backed chairs, dressed in the finest robes with their anchors safely roomed nearby. The former Rajav had allowed most of them to choose their anchors in exchange for favors. But Li-Hun was dead, and no one would dictate who Lua could have anymore.

His magic blazed toward Sharine. She jerked backward, raising a shield before her, but it cracked beneath the ferocious assault. His thread stopped inches shy of her heart and hovered, licking hungrily toward her.

A thin green strand curled around the silver, winding from Audra's hand to the tip of Lua's magic. The pleading tone of her voice reached him.

"Stop, *please*."

Emerald brilliance surged down Lua's thread, forcing it to retreat and spiral backward. As her magic sputtered in the air, Audra yanked her hand from his, glaring accusingly. The platform beneath them vanished, and they dropped to their feet.

The council erupted in shouts. A few people looked sick, others nervous, but it was Master Fallue who spoke calmly. "Now we see the power of Western magic."

Fifty-One

Audra

"*What the fuck was that?*" Audra's voice echoed into the hallway before the door of their room finished closing. She didn't care that anyone heard her. "I was supposed to make a good impression. Are you trying to get us killed?"

Lua scowled and crossed his arms. "I don't like your tone."

"I don't care! I'm not the one prone to violence. We were supposed to impress them, not try to *kill* them. What were you thinking?" Her cheeks were flushed.

A muscle in his jaw flexed, but he only huffed. Audra flung her robe on the bed, sliding away when he reached for her. She wouldn't let his touch confound her.

He'd just attacked a council member, and the hostility thrown at them when they left was justifiable. The interview had gone well until then. Lua moved closer, but she stepped back.

"Answer me," she said.

"I didn't like the way they were treating you."

"So you attacked them?"

He ran a hand through his hair. "I didn't mean for it to go that far."

"What would have happened if I hadn't stopped you?"

"You did stop me."

"Play along. What if?" she asked.

He studied the ground. "I don't know."

Her anger slowly waned, morphing to an understanding that wormed its way into her brain. All their time together, she'd reasoned his occasional violence was due to his weakened state. After all, he'd never directed his anger fully at her.

Because he couldn't.

She wiped her eyes, smearing the kohl's lines further. He'd been showing her exactly what he was capable of the entire time, and she'd chosen to deny it. "Is this who you really are?"

He'd started to reach for her, but his hand paused in the air. "What do you mean?"

"You'd kill your allies along with your enemies."

"Of course not."

Audra swallowed, tasting the bitterness of his lie. "Then what was that?"

"The magic took over. I'd only wanted to give them a hint of what we could do."

"Oh, you definitely did that."

"But then I thought about their anchors and how unfair it was that they should question you." Lua's eyes narrowed as he spoke. His magic tugged hungrily at hers, but she held it back.

"You mean question *you*," she breathed. "This had nothing to do with me. I've dealt with worse before. You used my presence as an excuse to assert your authority."

"No, that's not—"

"And what did you prove to them? That you'll turn on them if they make you uncomfortable."

"Audra—"

"That you can't be trusted."

Lua froze, his eyes full of wounds as her words found their mark. Insecurity crept into his voice. "Do *you* trust me?"

She bit her lip. He couldn't hurt her without hurting himself, but that didn't equate to trust. She cared for him. True, it could be the magic making her feel things that she confused for something genuine. Trust might be a wholly deeper issue. She shouldn't trust anyone. It was only now that she remembered.

He stepped closer. Worry marred his handsome face. "Do you honestly think I'd do anything to hurt you?"

"No." An honest answer to a simpler question.

"Do you think I would hurt your family?"

She shook her head. He'd have a difficult time trying to hurt Zin, and Ferin was still a dragon, even if he wasn't grown yet. But there was someone else and Audra's worry extended past her own wellbeing.

"What about Bolin?" she asked.

"What of him?"

"Will you protect him?"

His head dropped a moment before he ran a hand through his hair again. A slew of emotions raced toward her—anguish, sorrow.

"That is complicated."

"Promise you won't hurt him."

He groaned. "I can't promise that."

She stepped forward, forgetting about the desire that such proximity brought. "Why not?"

"Do you want to know where he's been?"

Dread settled in her chest.

He met her eyes. "Just like you, Bolin was an unfortunate victim of being in the wrong place at the wrong time."

"What does that mean?"

"I hadn't put it together until I spoke with Zin about Western mages. I don't think anyone else has yet either."

"Lua—"

"Our father delighted in sending Selene and I into battles to prove what we could do. She gained her tenth star decades ago, just after I did. But she grew stagnant. She was sent to Oxton with her anchor." He grasped Audra's hands, connecting their energy, calming her as he spoke. "She was reckless—instead of keeping her anchor safely on the ship, she brought her into the fray. A soldier killed Selene's anchor in the battle. He didn't know what he'd done, of course. From what he told me later, no other mages were near enough to save Selene. She should have died. I wish she had. But there was a young Western soldier nearby. When her anchor died, Selene's magic latched on to him."

Dozens of questions became dust in Audra's throat.

"It shouldn't have happened so easily. Like I said before, there are rituals and procedures that are normally followed. When she returned north with two Western soldiers, she said they'd aided her, demanded they be given protection by the Song tribe, and refused to have her new anchor severed."

"Two soldiers?"

He nodded. "Xiang killed Selene's anchor. He wouldn't abandon Bolin to her. They've been beside her ever since."

Audra's vision blurred. Any hope of having her brother returned was lost. Lua's sister, his greatest enemy and, according to the whispers she'd caught in the halls, the greatest threat to the Moon tribe's cohesion, was anchored to her brother. Bolin could never come home. And given what the last Rajav had allowed his Raani to endure, Audra doubted that Bolin would ever be free again.

"You see, I cannot guarantee your brother's safety. All I can do is try to ensure yours." He pulled her into his arms.

She breathed in his scent, let the warmth of his touch envelop her as she quietly broke. Later, lying crumpled in his arms, his heart beating in sync with her own, his words echoed in her mind. *Do you trust me?*

And Audra had no answer.

Fifty-Two

Traq

Traq picked at the black thread of his borrowed robe. He didn't like how it looked against his skin. They'd erected the somber Moons' tents outside the small village near the towering monastery. Beneath the black fabrics, they blended in with the dozen other campsites and soldiers, but that did nothing to ease his mind. He was finally in agreement with Durin. They shouldn't be here.

He hated hiding beneath the colors of their enemies but, more than that, he hated relying on the intel of traitors. Xiang's recent warmth was insincere, and Jayna fed them half-lies. They all knew it, but Durin seemed to like the Moon mage. Of course, he liked anyone who lent him half an ear.

The only thing they agreed on was that Lua must be dealt with. But how and what would happen to Audra were points of disagreement. She was nothing more than a pawn to everyone else. Expendable. A necessary loss.

Xiang insisted his Oja was working on a plan to hinder the Silence mages, and they'd have reinforcements when they entered the monastery.

They'd adjusted their schedules. Moon mages were nocturnal by nature and, other than the laborers, the commoners by tradition. They stayed up late, avoiding the moonslight, then secretly basked in Starling's warmth.

Despite years of dedicated training, attuning to Starling had never come easy to Traq and the measly three stars he'd managed weakened in the cold north.

Using Jayna as cultural interpreter, Traq and Durin scouted the village and monastery's exterior, leaving Xiang with Wren. They wouldn't reveal Selene's general until they needed to enter the monastery. But Jayna had other ideas for that.

Jayna wouldn't talk about Xiang directly. Her loyalty to him outweighed her anger, and Traq could respect that.

According to the Moons, Lua would be most vulnerable during the eclipses, though they hadn't explained why. Maybe they didn't know or, more likely, they didn't want to tell them.

Wren wasn't foolish enough to trust the Moons, nor to sneak into their monastery without a plan of her own. While Xiang and Jayna still slumbered one afternoon, she called Durin and Traq together.

"If we can secure Audra, the Oji will come," Wren said.

"And then?" Durin asked.

Wren's mouth was a hard line as she stared at the fire, flames dancing in her eyes.

"She'll kill her if he's not cooperative," Traq finished.

Durin sighed and rubbed his chin. "There must be another way. From what I've gathered, she's a victim of circumstance. If we kill her, we're no better than them. And it would give them even more justification for cutting us down. Then what would our Starling leaders have to do?"

"If you have a suggestion, I'd love to hear it." Wren's voice was heavy. "As it is, I'm regretting this entire enterprise and am especially sorry for dragging you along."

Durin waved his hand dismissively. "I could have refused. You aren't *that* intimidating, and I'm not as foolish as I like you to think. Plus, I'm the only one here who's fought the Moons before. Their style differs from ours. Their mages are grouped the same way we are but don't work together like us. We should strategize with that in mind."

Wren's hand rested on Durin's forearm. "You could still leave. No one would think less of you if you took Liasa and headed south."

"Shut it, Septra," he said with a wink. "You won't get rid of me that easily. I've still got some spells in these hands." He looked at Traq. "Have we considered that Audra might help us?"

Wren huffed. "She's more likely to have us killed."

"Not if it's an old friend," Durin said.

Their attention settled on Traq. "It won't work. The Oji will remember me from Oxton."

"It's possible to avoid him. I know the Silence protocols and routines. It's not difficult to navigate the monastery." Jayna drifted into view a few feet away. Xiang shadowed behind her. "And, believe me, I have no desire to run into him again. I began my training here. I know my way around."

"You remember the layout?" Durin asked.

"Well enough. I can get in and out a few different ways," she said. When Jayna caught Wren's suspicious look, she shrugged. "I was sixteen. The inns in the village were a lot more fun than the monks and my studies."

"He'll kill you both if you're caught," Durin said.

"Yes," she said. "But it's a risk I'm willing to take if you think Audra can be swayed."

"It's feasible," Xiang said calmly. All eyes turned to him. "She hadn't known who he was until the ruins."

"She could have been lying," Wren said.

"You didn't see her face. Her reaction was genuine. If I were her, I'd be questioning everything," Xiang said.

Traq would be entering a liger's den with one of their own beside him. It could be a trap. Worry clouded Wren's face as she stared at him. But, once caught, she looked away.

"And you're sure you can avoid the Oji?" Wren asked.

Jayna nodded slowly. "It's three days until the eclipse. He'll be busy, and I doubt a Westerner would be allowed to attend the preparations. Even if she's anchored to him, she's still an outsider. She's probably sequestered under guard. Meals being delivered. Almost everyone will be sleeping if we go in after Starling rise," Jayna said. "We can blend in with the servants and have a message delivered with her first meal."

"I think I know a way. Can you cook?" Traq asked. Tender memories of shared secrets with Audra tugged at him. He needed to get her away from the Moons, away from all of this or their years of hard work would be for nothing.

Jayna gave him a quizzical look and opened her mouth to reply, but Xiang cut her off.

"You said she's been arrested before," Xiang said. Traq nodded. "And she escaped custody?"

"Yes, several times. Audra hates being trapped."

Wren eyed Traq. "Now she's anchored to the future Rajav. Isolated, surrounded by enemies. This is a more elaborate jail than she's been in before."

They were quiet for a few minutes.

"How good is she?" Xiang asked. "Could she escape if she wanted to?"

Traq rubbed his hands together. He nodded slowly. "I don't think there's anywhere she couldn't get out of if she put her mind to it. Either through manipulation or sheer stubbornness."

"Then let's challenge that. We can get a note to her with instructions on where to meet us," Jayna said.

"If your relationship is as you've implied, seeing you may inspire her to join us," Xiang said.

Traq kept his concerns to himself.

"What about the Oji?" Durin asked. "Won't this be putting Audra in jeopardy?"

"He won't hurt her," Xiang stated. "I think he has feelings for her."

Traq's hands clenched until he caught Wren's look. He'd rather try to rescue her but had to be realistic. If Audra was under the Oji's power, they might all be doomed.

When he joined the Starlings, Audra had made it clear there'd be nothing more than friendship between them. He'd wasted years foolishly holding onto the notion that her opinion might change. He'd clung to the idea of her out of loneliness. But he doubted that he even knew her anymore, and letting the hope of her go felt like a deep breath. His gaze lingered on Wren's slender fingers twirling the end of her braid.

She caught his eye and smiled. He was still a fool. Traq wanted someone like the mage sitting beside him. Lord Ijion might have Traq flayed at the first rumor of something between them, but the way Wren flirted with him like all she wanted was a small sign of interest in return gave him hope. Traq nodded to Jayna. "I'll be ready when you are."

"Two things," Xiang said. "Don't reveal too much unless she agrees to cooperate and remind her to wear the bloodstone."

The Starlings exchanged a look. "Bloodstone?" Wren asked.

"She'll know what it's for." Xiang turned and retreated into the tent, leaving Traq and the others glaring at his back.

Fifty-Three

Selene

Icy wind flicked loosened hairs from her braid into her eye with a sting. Selene's curse caused the nearest soldiers to flinch.

Bolin leaned toward her, rocking atop his winter-coated mare. "I'll redo it when we camp."

She didn't reply. Sometimes she hated that she needed him. Tending to her hair seemed a simple thing, but she'd never been good at it. If left on her own, she'd leave it loose and wild. The tangles never bothered her until she tried to comb it out. Bolin was adept at plaiting hair and used metal crimps to hold it in place. The western look brought a sense of empowerment.

After the general's last communication, it was apparent he was hiding information. It was bad enough he'd been captured and their time was limited, but restraint held him back.

She considered that Xiang's reticence might be related to Bolin. Perhaps he'd uncovered something while traipsing through the old monastery, but she'd made sure there was nothing left of Bolin's old life to return to. Even claiming the dragon scales that had hung above their family hearth. He'd only worn them once before, and the red was a striking contrast to his black attire.

They settled for a few hours when Starling rose. Thankfully the light was lessening as the season tipped toward winter solstice. After the eclipses, the Moons would be at their strongest until spring. The Starlings wouldn't dare come for them until then, which left time to prepare, if needed.

They camped in a flat area that could accommodate the party. After raising their tent, Bolin filled the copper censer with campfire embers. The tent warmed quickly, and after whispering their Song prayers together, he'd faded into a deep sleep. He propped the mirror beside him, waiting for Xiang's image to appear.

She watched the rise and fall of his chest. His lips puffed with each exhalation while resisting slumber. It was moments before morning twilight that the mirror glimmered. She gently reached across Bolin and claimed it before racing outside and drawing her robes around her.

Xiang startled at seeing her and checked her surroundings. They were alone. He looked relieved, but his mannerisms were rushed. She mouthed Bolin's name, and Xiang nodded.

Selene knew most of the gestures frequently used but she struggled with others. Xiang repeated or altered the movements until she understood. The gesture for Western tribe was easy, his movements meaning Bolin were understandable. But then he mentioned Lua and gave the symbol for anchor, and another symbol she didn't know.

Xiang's frustration was evident in his tightly controlled expression. He licked his lips and gave the symbol for brother. Then repeated the symbols together.

Western, Bolin, brother, anchor, Lua.

Lua's anchor was Western? Xiang nodded before repeating Bolin and brother. The image edges faded as his wound began to clot.

She frowned. Bolin didn't have a brother, and his sister was dead. Selene handled Pangol herself after learning of Bolin's mage heritage. Her spell struck true; she was sure of it. They'd lost them moments later when the Starlings interfered, but the girl was dead. She bit her lip. But they hadn't found a body, not even of the little one the girl had carried.

She signed *Bolin, sister, Lua, anchor.*

Xiang nodded and rubbed his face with a grimy hand. As the image faded completely, he gave a last symbol, one she knew from their work with Dain. *Bloodstone.*

If Bolin discovered that his sister was alive, if he spoke to her, then he might find out that Selene had lied to him. When she promised to find his family, he'd expected her to bring them home, not kill them. And it seemed she hadn't completed that either. She'd get another message to Sharine and see if she could contain Lua's anchor before they arrived.

Sharine's contacts were supposed to be sending the liger's bane wine as a celebratory gift. When Xiang messaged again, she'd give the order. If the girl couldn't be secured, make sure all the Council's anchors met similar ends, including Lua's.

Fifty-Four

Audra

Audra's fingers wrinkled in the lavender scented bath. Lua had left to meet Fallue an hour earlier, he hadn't slept for more than a few hours since Stonetown and had been pulling on their connection to sustain him. Transitioning leadership took more planning than Audra had ever considered, selecting new ministers to head the different economical and agricultural branches made for long nights and late days.

There'd been no formal announcement of the Rajav's passing yet. She couldn't imagine how they'd spin that. The traditional mourning period would normally prohibit the coronation of a new Rajav, but the tension between the tribes was too tumultuous to be left without clear leadership. As Lua explained it, he'd disassembled all his father's committees to build his own. She'd hoped that by "disassembled" he hadn't meant murdered, but she hadn't trusted his answer enough to ask.

He'd selected new advisors from both Moon tribes after scrutinizing each candidate's history and alliances. But there was still Selene and her loyalists to contend with.

Audra was grateful she wasn't allowed at these meetings. That they'd tolerate her as Raani was enough for Lua, but her feelings were unclear. She'd never had many choices in life, especially since Ferin's injury, as if their fates were controlled by forces unknown. She reached out, felt the comforting reply, and sighed. Their path should have gotten clearer after she found the jade, but everything was increasingly complicated.

The luxurious apartment reminded her of Callaway, though with more resentful guards and better plumbing. Occasionally she'd half-heartedly study the scrolls before rolling them up again. Then she'd be insulted by Fallue during basic practice sessions. He muttered that even a one star shouldn't struggle with the minor tasks set before her. But her magic remained unpredictable until she grew angry. Then it did whatever he'd asked with such force it destroyed several workstations.

Her longing for Lua was like a youth in lust's first entangling. And they were entangled, their threads knotted and coiled even more than their limbs were these days. She couldn't die like his last anchors. And between the wearing the jade for a time and Lua's bond, she was stronger, healthier, than she'd ever been. As if she could handle anything. Perhaps his confidence was rubbing off on her. Or his magic.

Audra had finished dressing when the usual servant set her meal on the table nearest the fireplace. The woman gave a small bow though Audra had repeatedly asked her not to. Normally she left straightaway, but she hesitated.

"Mirza," she began.

Audra winced. There wasn't an official title for her until Lua was made Rajav, so this was what they called her. That most of the servants delegated to her care were twice her age made the formal address worse.

"One of our cooks tried to make a traditional Western meal for you. She hopes it pleases you." She bowed again before backing toward the door and leaving.

That someone had attempted anything on her behalf made her curious. Maybe they'd eventually accept her.

Beneath the tray's cover was a cup of salty milk tea, yogurt, biscuits with clotted cream, the small cookies twisted into elaborate shapes, and winterberry jam. Arn had made a version of this in Stonetown on their second morning, but this smelled different, familiar. It brought back memories of her father's cooking, and later of Traq standing over Zin's stove trying to recreate his grandmother's recipes and meticulously shaping the cookies into Western script. But that was a long time ago.

She hoped the Starlings were treating Traq well. The pretty white-haired mage in Oxton looked like she wanted to, but Traq had always been slow in that department.

Audra was nibbling on a biscuit when she noticed a corner of parchment folded beneath the pastries. One word hastily scribbled in Western script: *Remember.*

A suspicion—unrealistic and wholly unreasonable—came to her. She spread the cookies on the table in a row and released a long breath.

The snow hit her face like shards of broken glass, sharper than it had ever been back home. Though the traditional winter furs trapped in heat and the shearling lined gloves insulated her hands, her cheeks chafed in the frigid wind.

Audra darted around a corner and waited. No boots crunched on the frozen ground in search of her. The guards grumbled when she'd insisted on going outside and losing them was too easy. They knew she couldn't go far.

If she'd interpreted the message correctly, Traq would be in the fourth cold storage area past the next building. If not, then he'd be on the opposite side in a barn somewhere. The storage room seemed less likely to be disturbed than a barn would be. The doors were flat on the ground, stairs disappeared into the underground rooms used for salted meats and root vegetables. As she reached the bottom, an all'ight flickered on.

Traq's face was chapped, but his relieved smile spread warmth between them. He rushed toward her and wrapped her in a hug, lifting her feet from the ground. She pushed him away and gaped at his appearance.

"What are you doing here?" she asked. "Wearing *Moon* robes now?"

"I-we came to find you."

A tingle rippled down Audra's spine as another presence tugged at a recent memory. With Fallue's coaching, her ability to discern between lesser and greater stars had improved. Traq was nearing four stars, but what she detected was something much less than that. "Who's here?"

"We met at the ruins," a woman said, stepping into the light. Tall and pale, her black hair pulled back in elaborate braids that sat on top of each other and trailed to her lower back. "We didn't get a chance to talk then."

Audra glared at Traq. "You brought her here? Did she tell you they tried to kill me?"

The woman held up her hands apologetically. "That was Nori, who the Oji killed by the way. Admittedly, Nori was an ass, but I'm Jayna, I only want to talk."

"You're working together?"

"It's not like that, Audra," Traq said. "Please, I meant it. I came to find you."

Somewhere in the monastery, Lua tugged on the thread. Her heart quickened as she sent a small reassurance back to him. She doubted she'd be able to protect Traq if Lua discovered them together. The guards had probably informed him she was alone on the grounds. They had little time.

"Why are you here?" She knew what they were going to say. Only one thing could make the tribes work together: a common enemy. "You're here for the—"

"The eclipse is tomorrow." Jayna cut her off too quickly.

"The *coronation* is tomorrow." Audra corrected. Traq's face changed subtly. "That's why you're here, isn't it? Did she tell you she works for the Oja? That they've been trying to capture and kill Lua to prevent his ascension?"

"There's more to it than that," Jayna said. "You don't know the atrocities he's committed against his own people, let alone yours."

Audra bristled but attempted to quell her defensiveness. Something in her words wrung true. "What're you talking about?"

"Has he told you what he did at the behest of the Rajav to the Western mages?"

Audra huffed. "Selene's no better. You think I don't know what she's done to my family? To my people? Just ask Xiang who he was before he sold himself to her service."

Jayna pursed her lips. "You don't know what Xiang has sacrificed."

"Sure, I do. His country, his people, his morals." She winced as Lua's thread pulled taut in her chest. He was searching for her. Again, she let him know that all was well but knew that wouldn't satisfy him. Her emotions were too raw. She glared at Jayna. "You know nothing about your Ojis." She turned to Traq. "And you should leave as soon as you can."

"Please, Audra," Traq said. "What about the fishing village he killed?"

She stared at him. "He didn't."

"Audra—"

"I've been with him since the *Requin*, Traq. He killed three men so we would make it to Oxton, but that was it. We never came close to any villages and no other deaths except when they attacked me in the ruins. They've been lying to you."

Audra turned to leave, but Traq stopped her. "What happens after the coronation?"

She looked back at him, hesitating. Her deepest fears whispered in her brain.

"What about Zin and Ferin?" he asked. "What about all the things we-you've been working toward?"

Lua was on the grounds now, moving slowly, giving her time to come to him, like a liger searching for a rebellious cub. But a shiver of worry and insecurity ebbed from him.

"None of that has changed."

"Do you honestly think he'll let you restore everything his tribe tore down?" Traq asked.

Audra started up the stairs. "He'll help me." She couldn't hide the uncertainty in her voice.

"Have you asked him?" Traq asked. "I don't want to see you trapped here."

She shoved the door open and paused, looking back. "Lua will kill you both if he finds you. May the wings bless you, Traq."

"Audra, the bloodstone—"

The door slipped from her fingers, cutting off Jayna's voice. She raced across the grounds and met Lua as he rounded the corner. Beneath the shade of his hood, he broke into a relieved smile. His arms engulfed her, wrapping her in comforting scents of home.

"Where'd you go? The guards are in a huff."

"Just needed some air. I'm not used to being stuck in one place, let alone one room." She gestured at the frozen landscape. "Besides, where could I go?"

He slipped his hand in hers and they turned back toward the monastery. "Is that what you're worried about? Being trapped with me?"

"No, not with you." Traq's words still echoed in her ears. They were far enough from the cold storage. She pulled him into a corner. "I need to ask you something."

His gaze skimmed over her face, softening. "Anything."

"When the coronation is over, will you help me?"

"With what, my little mouse?" He kissed her fingertips.

"Restoring my tribe. Rebuilding our monasteries."

She felt the chill in him, the pause that took a moment too long. Then he smiled reassuringly and brushed the hair from her eyes. "Of course."

"What about the dragons?"

The thread coiled tight between them, but he neither released her hand nor pulled away. "No one knows where the dragons went."

"We can find them together."

He sighed, letting something heavy waver toward her. "We'll discuss it once we are settled."

She returned his small smile, despite a sudden awareness of the constricting tether around her. He couldn't let her go, and his help would be perfunctory.

When their bedroom door closed behind them, his lips stole her breath. The heat of their entwined bodies consumed her. She hated how much she wanted him. Their passion was demanding, leaving them both wanting for more as their magic engulfed them. A knock at the door drew Lua from the bed and back to his meetings too soon, leaving Audra alone to contemplate her situation.

Lua believed it was love, but she wasn't sure. It was magic built on desire. And magic, she was learning, was greedy, shortsighted, and terribly addictive. Even now, the ache for him was wholly distracting.

Pulling the bloodstone from the depths of her bag, she ran her fingers around its blunt edges before slipping the cord over her neck with nervous fingers. Though nothing in the room changed, everything seemed marginally duller. For the first time in years, her internal world was quiet. She tugged off the stone and the connections came rushing back. Checking the threads confirmed that all was well.

She'd have to be careful when she wore it, time it so that she could make reasonable excuses but dulling the connection between them, at least temporarily, might let her remember who she was outside of Lua's dizzying influence. That was her hope, at least.

She wrapped her worn green robe around her and sat cross-legged on the couch. With a resigned breath, she closed her eyes and found the mass of tangled threads, equal parts green and silver. After deciphering a scroll she'd previously overlooked, she could finally make some sense of it. She stared at the connection for a long time, then she reached up and untied the first knot.

Fifty-Five

Xiang

The venomous tones hurled between Traq and Jayna were dampened by the falling snow. Xiang and Durin sat alongside the fire, warming their hands like old men, surveying the emotional undulations of the young. The Moon soldiers were sequestered in a tent with several Starlings ringed around it, awaiting Wren's orders.

Traq's cheeks were flushed. "We should have slit your throats ourselves."

"There *is* a celebration," Jayna said.

"That's a bit more than a celebration," Wren snapped. "You were going to escort us in as a special tribute to your new Rajav."

Jayna glanced at Xiang for support, but he took another sip of water and held his stoic countenance. Though he'd hoped to delay it a bit longer, this scene had been inevitable.

"He'll never be Rajav," Jayna said. "That's why we wanted you with us. We need to stop the coronation before—"

"What happened to Rajav Li-Hun?" Wren asked.

Jayna licked her lips. "He died six weeks ago."

"How?"

It was clear Jayna wasn't sure what to share or hold back. She paused for too long. Jayna couldn't see the gold thread uncoiling from Wren's hands behind her back, nor the all'ights in several of the Starling soldiers' hands, waiting to engulf the Moon soldiers in the tent.

"They killed his anchor in her rooms on one side of the castle. The Rajav's remains were found a short time later on the other. It was calculated and concise," Xiang said finally.

"You want us to believe that the Oji killed him and yet they would ordain him the next Rajav?"

"Believe what you want," Xiang said. "But only his children would ever have been capable of killing a man that powerful. And the Rajav was universally despised."

"You said someone killed his anchor first, which would have made him vulnerable. How many stars was he?" Wren asked.

"Fifteen."

The Starlings gasped.

"Impossible," Traq said.

Xiang levelled his gaze at him. "Just because other tribes don't allow it doesn't mean it doesn't exist. Blame your limitations on your own leaders." His eyes slid to Wren and she glanced away.

"What happens to a fifteen star when their anchor dies?" Durin asked, small eyes sparking in the firelight. "If the Oji is thirteen and survived a short time without an anchor, what does that mean for the higher ranking?"

"I'm not sure. All I know is when Raani Amala was killed, he was vulnerable."

"Raani?" Traq asked.

"The Rajav's anchor. It's what Audra will become if the coronation takes place," Jayna said.

"Who was this Raani?" Durin asked. "It must have been difficult to be trapped with such a man."

"By all accounts, Raani Amala was calm, kind, and rational. Perhaps that's why she lasted so long." He noticed their curious looks. "Being anchored to a powerful mage causes premature aging. The anchor's life force is used as fuel for the mage's power. The mage strengthens the anchor but also slowly drains them. Eventually the siphon kills them as the mage remains hardy. Most anchors die within thirty years of their pledge, but Raani Amala was different from the others." He didn't want to say more, that the rumors of the woman's western heritage had been downplayed. The Starlings were known for their own abuses of western power and blood.

"How old was the Raani?" Traq asked.

Jayna's voice lowered reverently. "Ancient. Her body broke well before I was born. She could only be fed soups or yogurts. Hadn't left her bed in decades. There were rumors she begged for death, that people heard crying outside her rooms."

"But the Rajav refused to release her," Xiang said.

Durin wore a sympathetic look. "Did he love her so much?"

"Not at all. The man had no love for anyone. She was a tool for him to use. Something about their bond enabled his magic to flourish. He feared losing his power, nothing more," Xiang said.

"So her death was a mercy, and the Rajav's was an opportunity," Wren said. "But who killed them?"

"Maybe we should ask who killed the fishers," Traq said. Durin and Wren looked at him. "Audra insisted the Oji didn't kill those people."

"And you believed her?" Xiang asked. "She's bound to him now. She's not the person you remember."

"As if I would believe the words of a traitor." Traq's hands glowed, golden threads wove between the fingers of his clenched fists.

"A mage can control their anchor. Make them say things. Do things they wouldn't normally do. The Oji used to force his prior anchors to kill for him. Who's to say he didn't do that this time?"

"Audra's no fighter, and she'd never murder her own tribespeople. Unlike you." Traq's gold thread slashed the flesh above Xiang's brow.

Jayna started toward him, but Xiang raised a hand to stop her. Blood dripped into his eye, cascading down his cheek to his chin. He licked it from his lips and chuckled. "I wonder what else he makes her do for him. I wonder if she likes it."

Durin's shield blocked Traq's whipping thread from its killing stroke.

"Enough." Wren stepped before Traq. "Stand down."

Xiang wiped his sleeve across his brow and met Wren's gaze. "We won't be going in alone. The Oja will be here with Song mages and soldiers." Xiang's teeth were pink.

"Then you don't need our aid after all," she said. "Just as well, I'm tired of these manipulations. It must be exhausting living with those wasps between your ears."

He scowled at the insult. "They're a day away. We'll need help delaying the coronation until she arrives."

"What's in it for us? Betrayal then death? "No, thank you," Wren said.

"Glory, accolades. The new Rajav indebted to the Starlings for their service. There are many rewards if you stay and only disgrace if you leave empty-handed."

"What about Audra?" Traq asked.

"Her fate is tied to the Oji's," Wren said without malice. She turned to Xiang. "How do you plan to hold off the coronation?"

Xiang licked his bloody lips again. Though he thought of Selene's promise of Liger's bane wine to subdue the council's anchors, he said, "We get hold of Audra."

Fifty-Six

Lua

Lua leaned back in the unforgiving chair, absorbing the Mage council's bickering about insignificant ceremonial details. What words should honor the late Rajav—whom everyone hated—while praising the new one—whom they feared.

Selene's absence since leaving Uduary was of greatest concern. Though the Silence scouts hadn't found her party on the passable routes, it was understood she was headed to the monastery. He'd already developed a strategy with the Silence mages for when she might appear at the gates. He couldn't risk sacrificing all the lives in the monastery for Bolin, and it was unfortunate that he was Selene's biggest weakness. He would need to conceal that from Audra.

The council had droned on for hours, with Sharine casting occasional furtive glances at him, when he noticed a sense of absence. The awareness came slowly, quickening his pulse. He closed his eyes and examined the thread, but it was the same. Silver and green entwined with some places thicker than others.

Studying the people seated around him made him wonder if he was becoming as paranoid as his father. A coronation should be celebrated with friends and family. Yet Lua doubted the few friendships he had, other than Fallue, and his only living relation was Selene, who'd bought Dain's betrayal with his daughter's life.

If not for Audra, he'd be utterly alone.

Perhaps that was why he'd forgiven her earlier deception. The guards had ceased following her, because they feared what Lua might do if they forced her to return. He could almost sympathize with them. And Audra was right, she couldn't go anywhere without him knowing. But her omission of who she'd met with wounded a scar still tender.

Maybe it was nothing, but the guards reported two Moon soldiers exiting the grounds soon after she met him. They returned to a camp on the fringes of the village, and Audra hadn't left their rooms since. Lua would deal with those soldiers after the coronation. He'd have to set a precedent. Boundaries had to be clear. No one had access to the Raani without his permission.

That she didn't grasp the complexity of her request was clear. The political battles that would come from aiding the Westerners and another war with the Starlings would test all of those who professed their loyalty. He didn't know where the funds would come from. It would be difficult to expect his tribe to carry the burden of reparations when each winter brought their people to the edge of starvation.

He could hear the arguments, see them unfolding with vigor and contention, but the look in Audra's eyes and the pull of her heart held greater influence over him. The Moon Rajav shouldn't help her, but Lua couldn't refuse. The atrocities committed against her people deserved attention. That he'd been a part of those events left him ashamed and committed to doing better for her. Soon, he would tell her about the things he'd done and hope for forgiveness. There was still so much to say, but they had time.

He strummed their thread and waited. Her reply didn't come. Another strum went unanswered. His sudden grunt brought nervous looks from those around the table.

"Do you disagree, Oji?" Fallue looked drained. The demands of the last week had taken a toll. Fallue had declared only a year ago that he'd die with Emaline, his anchor. Rajav Li-Hun had argued with him, but Fallue would have none of it. He didn't want a life without her, and Lua understood. He'd wished for death after Eras, but with Audra, he wanted to explore centuries.

"What's left to discuss?" Lua asked. He tugged again on the thread. The connection shivered, as if it were blocked. Suspicion grappled with his restraint, though his voice remained calm. "Everyone is tired. Let's deal with the remaining issues tomorrow. Be prepared to quickly argue your points and make concessions."

"But we still have—" Fallue started.

"Tomorrow. You need rest."

Lua didn't wait for the parting formalities before exiting the room. He hastened his pace halfway down the hallway. The guards struggled to clear the servants from his path as he took the steps two and three at a time.

He threw the bedroom doors open and rushed inside. Audra lay curled on the couch atop a pile of scrolls that Fallue had given her to study. Her brow furrowed at the cool breeze that entered with him. A fire still burned; shadows danced low across the walls.

The thread purred between them again. She must have been sleeping dreamlessly. It had been foolish to doubt her.

Scooping her gently in his arms, he carried her to the bed. Pulling off her green robe and outer layers before covering her with the thick blanket, he sighed with relief. She curled against him when he slid into bed beside her, throwing an arm across his chest.

"It's late," she mumbled. "Or early."

He kissed the top of her head. "Bureaucracy takes time."

Her eyes slitted open. "Everything all right?"

"It's nothing. I was just worried."

"About?"

"You."

"Me?" She leaned up on one elbow.

"I reached out, and you weren't there." He licked his lips. "It reminded me of what happened with Dain."

She stiffened. "What happened with Dain?"

"I've told you."

"No, you've only told me a little. Tell me the rest, from the time he was anchored until his end."

He swallowed nervously. "I don't know if you want to hear it."

She curled a lock of his hair between her fingers. "You need to say it, or it will be a wound that continues to bleed."

The Moons discouraged any talk of one's feelings or failings. Tight regulation of one's emotions was expected but since he'd met Audra, his feelings were tumultuous, and he still felt exposed from discussing his mother. He hesitated.

Audra brought her face inches from his. "Speak, Moonie."

He laughed, and the words poured out, tentatively at first. Dain wasn't his first choice, nor his second. But the Songs insisted Elicia would be a better fit for Brav, and the other anchor declined at the last moment. Dain was a quiet man but ferocious when he needed to be. He became like a brother. They laughed at each other's jokes, pulling pranks, and sharing hard truths.

Anchors aren't allowed familial attachments. Their entire existence was dedicated to their mage. No marriage, no children, unless it was with the one they were bonded with, like his parents. So when a woman came forward claiming that Dain had fathered a young girl it was handled quietly. Lua kept them well fed and homed, gave extra money to keep everyone quiet. If Li-Hun knew about them, they'd have been killed straightaway.

Selene had used them to turn Dain. After his parents died, he and Dain had gone to the isle of Shuray, east of Callaway. Selene was supposed to join them. They would strategize before standing together before the Council and help their people find a new way forward.

"But Selene never showed," Audra said.

He shook his head. "The *Mirren* arrived with those I'd thought loyal to me. As I killed them—in self defense—Dain took advantage of my distraction. He'd been distant since we left Uduary. His emotions and thoughts normally so open, were cut off, but I didn't have time to wonder. It wasn't until he twisted the bolt into my back with only a wince that I realized my foolishness. He carried me onto the boat himself, took my robes and wiped my brow. All without a word."

"How?"

"A relic the Rajav kept. Bloodstone."

Audra paled. "But the bond?"

"It was still there. I could draw energy to live, but it took days of doing nothing to cultivate enough strength to fight the bolt."

"And then?"

"Then I siphoned everyone I could until I was able to sever the bond and sink the ship. There was no other way." Lua's voice was strained.

Audra brushed the hair from his eyes, cool fingers smoothed the creases of his brow. "You had no choice. But that doesn't mean you still can't hurt from it. His betrayal was brutal, but he knew what might happen. So when you couldn't find me earlier . . .?"

He shrugged. "It's foolish."

"Go on."

"I thought that somehow Selene had gotten to you." The words sounded small and vulnerable.

She rose to her knees and kissed his forehead. "We've been tethered together all this time and yet you still question my stubbornness?" Her smile was gentle. "But there is something you must understand."

His chest constricted.

"I want things in this life that don't involve this unchosen role of anchor. My tribe, my family. The dragons. My goals have not and *will not* change," she said. "But I am desperately and stupidly loyal. I won't betray you."

He pulled her close, breathing in the scent of her hair. Their hearts thrummed together. They each had their secrets, but their connection was true. She loved him, even if she hadn't said it yet.

"I need to tell you something," she said. "But you must promise you won't be angry."

He pulled back. "I can't promise until I know what it is."

"Promise to try." She slid from the bed, taking her warmth with her. Rummaging through the bag that lay crumpled on the floor, she clutched something before returning to him. A black cord dangled from her fist.

Lua chilled. "Audra?"

"Xiang gave it to me at the ruins. I didn't truly believe him. Didn't know what had been done with it." The bloodstone was dull in her hand.

Slowly, he took it from her, running his fingers over the edges with a look of disgust. "You've had this since the ruins?" She nodded. Her worries and fears trickled toward him. "You wore it today."

Her cheeks flushed. "For the first time."

"Why?"

"Lua, I can't give up everything I've been working toward."

He fidgeted with the rock, attempting to hide this fresh pain from her. "And you wouldn't give these up for me? To stay by my side. I promised to help you."

"But there are limitations on how you'll help. I felt what you didn't say. If there were another way, then maybe." Her shoulders slumped. "Would you give up being Rajav for me? Or give up your magic to stand beside me if I asked?"

He stared, dumbfounded. He had no answer to give her. If he did either of those things, he'd be powerless, useless to her.

"You wouldn't," she said. "And I wouldn't ask you to. So, please, don't expect the same of me. I'll stand beside you through the coronation and celebrations. But after that, I must find a way to help Ferin and Zin. There is still so much to do."

"You'd leave me?" His voice was weak in his ears.

"It's not like that. We can find another way to make this work."

"The bond won't let you go far."

"There are teachings in the Western scrolls that might make it possible," she said. "That's why I wore the stone. I didn't want to worry you. But I guess I did anyway. I'm sorry. I didn't know what had happened before."

The stone was heavier in his hand than it had any right to be. He bit his lip, staring at the greenish-black surface, studying the flecks of blood red. He thrust it back at her. "Keep it." His snapped. "Wear it when you want. Block me if you must."

"Lua—"

"If this is what must happen to keep you with me, then so be it. Do what you want." His voice was hard as he shoved the covers off and stood to leave. Being near her bruised his heart.

"Stop," she gripped his hand, her magic staying him. He shook his head, though his feet refused to move. Gently, she tugged him back onto the bed and cradled his face with her hands.

"I'm here now. I am *with* you."

He looked into her eyes, the insult slowly waning.

She smiled tenderly. "Do you hear me? I am talking about this because I want to be with you and still manage to be me. Not just your Raani, but Audra, a foul-mouthed Westerner."

Every other anchor had lived for him, but Audra was nothing like them. It was daunting and confusing, spitting in the face of everything he'd known. But when she looked at him like that, his soul bowed to her. He'd never been so sure he wanted to live as he was when with her.

She kissed his forehead. "Don't leave like this."

Her touch sang through him, coaxing their thread and drawing him close. Their lips connected as his hurt dissolved into passion. He pressed her onto her back and stared into her face.

"I'll never leave you, Audra Shan." Lua's breath trembled. "You are everything to me. I love you."

Fifty-Seven

Xiang

Bolin gestured swiftly with the understanding that their time was limited. Selene loomed behind him. Xiang remained stoic while receiving the disappointing news, acutely aware of Wren's scrutiny from the other side of the mirror as she watched for signs of betrayal.

A blizzard had struck the higher elevations, blocking most of the roads between Uduary and the Silence monastery. Selene was pressing the party forward, but they'd be lucky to arrive before the ceremony started.

Sharine's liger's bane wine would arrive too late for the coronation. Without the wine, they'd need another way to subdue the council's anchors, and he doubted the Starlings would go along with outright murder. He'd told them that abducting Audra was their primary goal, but Selene wanted to use the wine on the council either way. With the council's strength, the chances of stopping the coronation were slim, even with Sharine's aid. Killing Audra might be the best chance they had, but neither Traq nor Durin would tolerate it.

Selene met his gaze through the glass. He understood her gestures only because he knew her mind so well, but he conveyed none of that to Wren. Instead, he nodded and gave a last farewell to Bolin before the image faded.

"What news?" Wren asked.

Xiang tucked the mirror in his robe's pocket, his fingers brushing the vials of liger's bane he carried. All emotions were hidden behind a flat expression. "The snow has delayed them, but they should be here by the eclipse."

She took a deep breath, looking suddenly weary. "You're sure she's coming?"

He nodded. "She has supporters in the monastery already, but their hands are tied until she arrives."

"Audra is the key then." Wren rubbed her neck. Traq, Durin, and the Starling soldiers would blend in well enough with Xiang's remaining troops. Everyone knew the general's Western heritage and wouldn't question those around him if they looked foreign. A few of the Starling soldiers would be draped in full robes and gloves to cover the darker hues of their skin. But Wren's appearance was an exception, she was too striking to be overlooked if she attempted to enter through the front gates. After seeing how understaffed the kitchen was when they'd made Audra's meal, Jayna believed they could get in with the extra staff that had been hired. Wren tried darkening her hair with magic, but it hadn't held. So she'd coated it in layers of dark ashes. It would have to do.

Once inside, the women would head for Audra's room. Wren would take care of the guards, then they'd convince or coerce Audra to wear the bloodstone, if she still had it. Jayna knew of a place for Wren to hide until Selene arrived. "What happens if we can't get to her?"

"We can still weaken the council's mages," Xiang said.

"How?" Wren's tone was suspicious.

"It's nothing you'd want to be involved with."

Wren's expression hardened. "Try me." Xiang had overheard a few of the Starlings discussing Wren's father. She might have been reared with a deeper understanding of costs and balances of politics than her peers.

He'd carried the three vials for years, hoping to never have to use them. This wasn't their intended purpose, but it might let them survive the night. And Wren might be the only Starling amenable to the proposal. "Poison."

Wren assessed him cautiously, her demeanor unchanging. "You'd kill them?"

He shrugged. "Some might survive."

Her stare was unnerving until laughter at the fire startled them. Wren turned back to him. "Then what?"

"We attack when the Oji is most vulnerable," Xiang said.

"During the eclipse?" she asked, considering. "It would put us on equal footing as the remaining mages, I guess. Until the eclipse passes."

"It's the least dangerous solution I can think of."

She lowered her voice. "And where would we get it?"

"I've carried it with me for nearly twelve years." He met Wren's eyes in a challenge.

She gave one small nod. "We never had this conversation." Wren rose and moved back to the others. He understood her lack of inquiry and that she wouldn't tell the other Starlings. Deniability was a powerful tool. That she didn't want to know why he had the poison meant that she wanted no reason to have sympathy for him. That way she wouldn't hesitate to kill him if it came to it.

They'd bought all the eggs from a local farmer that morning, several loaves of bread from a baker, and links of lamb sausage from two separate villagers. A feast compared to what they'd been eating since the *Bolou*. Steam rose from the plates of the mages. Xiang settled closer to Jayna after taking a plate that was begrudgingly offered to him.

Jayna picked at her food, looking sullen beneath her robes.

"You should eat," Xiang said.

Jayna shook her head. "I'm too nauseous."

"You need sustenance."

"He's right," Liasa said, "Don't know when we'll get a chance to eat again."

"Or if," Jayna said.

"You'll live through this," Durin said. "Moon mage in a Moon monastery. But us—" he looked meaningfully at the other Starlings— "our chances are slim."

"Why didn't you leave?" Jayna asked softly.

"It's a terrible trait that Starlings have. An overbearing sense of justice combined with an inability to admit when we've made bad choices. And that one comes from generations of those factors." Wren smiled sheepishly from across the fire as he nodded to her. "So here we are. Conspiring with people who'll probably sacrifice us at the first opportunity."

Gazes flicked to Xiang. He took another bite and chewed slowly, offering no reassurance. Whatever happened to them after the eclipse would be decided by the new Rajav.

Liasa patted Durin's shoulder. "I'll be beside you the whole time."

He smiled at her. "And we shall blaze a path to glory."

She chuckled nervously. "I'd rather blaze a path home."

"Same, Liasa. Same," Durin said.

Liasa rose a moment later and joined the other soldiers, strapping knives to her thighs and securing a sword to her hip.

Jayna's tone was heavy. "Those weapons won't mean anything if the Oji gets close. And there are probably a dozen other ten stars in that monastery."

"But your Oja will save us, right?" The sarcasm was rich in Durin's voice.

Xiang stood. "She'll be here before the eclipses. You have my word." He caught the worry in Jayna's eyes. He said to Durin, "You could stay here. You don't have to go in."

"Abandon my friends when they might need me most?" He shook his head. "I'd rather die beside them than live with that burden on my soul."

"But Claude is waiting for you," Jayna said.

"He understands the risks of what I do," Durin said. "I'm grateful for the time we've been given. Honestly, it's been more than I deserved."

The soldiers looked like they were enjoying a last meal. Their laughter was a little fuller. They threw affectionate arms around each other's shoulders. It was much warmer than Moon soldier behavior. It reminded Xiang of his first battles in Western colors, and he found himself thinking of those long dead.

Durin leaned toward Jayna. "You should tell your Galia that you love her. Say it often, so she doesn't doubt. Put more of yourself into it

THE MALICE OF MOONS AND MAGES

than you think you're capable of. That way, when you're gone, she won't doubt what she meant to you."

Xiang swallowed the food in his mouth then walked away, abandoning a mostly full plate. Ducking into a tent, he pulled the mirror out and sliced his arm again. Bolin jostled atop his horse, Selene beside him. Xiang pulled out a vial of the liger's bane from his pocket and tried to explain what they would do. Selene's surprise at the poison faded quickly, but Xiang knew there would be repercussions the next time they were alone. He told Bolin he loved him before the connection died.

It was late afternoon when Wren called everyone together. Starling would set soon, then both full moons would glide across the starry sky. The huddling soldiers listened intently to Wren's orders, each of their nervous breaths wisping white in the air.

Xiang would lead Traq, Durin, and the soldiers into the monastery through the main gates. Wren, Jayna, and the liger's bane would go through a servant's entrance.

It was difficult to determine who was which tribe. There were minor differences in build, coloring, hair textures, and general manners, but similar features peeked from beneath each robe. Nervousness shifted their feet and tensed their shoulders.

"Say your prayers to whatever gods you call to," Wren said. "Make peace with the ones beside you. And, if we are lucky, perhaps we will see a new day dawn. May Starling blaze our path and Taiyang watch over us."

The soldiers echoed quietly back to her. Traq's lips remained sealed, though Durin said it a little louder. "May Starling blaze our path."

One Moon said softly, "Let Song guide us." The others murmured the same.

Xiang and Jayna stood quietly beside each other. An eerie calm swept over the combined group, and, with no more rhetoric, they marched toward the monastery.

Fifty-Eight

Audra

Audra clung to the sheets, holding on to the last vestiges of Lua's fading scent. He'd drawn the bed curtains to protect her from view while attendants carried in hot water and prepared his robes. No one other than his anchor could help him dress, but he hadn't asked her to yet. He kissed her passionately, had one hand already wrapped in her hair, when a voice outside the door called to him.

The frustration in his eyes told her he didn't want to leave. He cursed and kissed her forehead. "I'll see you at the ceremony."

Audra knew what was expected of her—wear the traditional dress and kohl. Walk behind Lua, but not too far, and remain silent in her seat. If anything should happen, protect the Oji with her life. Audra had laughed at that. She'd protect him, but not because they ordered her to, nor because their lives were intertwined. But because she couldn't imagine an existence without him.

When she was little, her mother had said some people were made from the same starlight. No matter the time or place, they'd always be drawn together. Audra wasn't romantic, but it felt as if they'd always known each other. Two lonely souls anchored together against the world.

The bloodstone tumbled from the bedding when she rose, skittering across the floor. She wouldn't wear it, not now anyway. Its presence hurt Lua too much. She tossed it in the bag with the scrolls. One more thing to figure out together later.

Audra had quietly untied the rest of their knots after he'd fallen asleep beside her. The threads were strong and smooth, and untangling them was the right thing to do. With the knots undone, things felt simpler. Clearer somehow. It wasn't their magic that made her heart race when he touched her. No matter how smooth those threads were, they would always be hopelessly entangled.

The scrolls spoke of untying the knots and severing strings one at a time, but there was a veiled warning in the words she was missing. If Zin were there, she would have known. Of course, if Zin needed to be there, then most of these people would be dead. Something she understood well enough was to leave some strings attached. The fewer the strings, the further they could stretch. But for how far or how long was unclear. And what toll it would take on them both was unknown. Still, it was the only option she'd come up with so far.

Despite the distance, she was sure the jade had worked for Ferin. The bond was strong.

When the servants brought a tray of food, Audra checked for another note and left it covered. Seeing Traq had left her worried. If he had any sense, he'd be miles away by now. Neither he nor the Starlings belonged here. *She* didn't belong here.

After bathing, she bided her time perusing the scrolls until the attendants arrived and insisted on moving her to another room as a precaution. Rumors circulated that Oja Selene's people had infiltrated the guards, and extra measures were being taken to ensure Audra's safety. They escorted her down two floors to a smaller, dusty room.

They braided her hair in small, swooping twirls before securing the ebony and silver ceremonial robes around her. Her face was painted with kohl, her lips stained the darkest red. It was heavy and hot, but she didn't complain, if only because she remembered Lua's previous reaction.

A skittish young servant brought another tray with a small jug of wine. Audra inhaled the oaky aroma longingly then decided against it. She needed to keep her wits. Besides, she was too nervous to eat. What she wanted most was for the night to be over.

A month ago, she crawled through shit for hours on Callaway. Now she was about to be given a seat of power in a country she hated with a man whose love threatened to consume her and who was likely the most despised person in four tribes. She should prepare for anything. Slipping her dulled dagger into the folds of her pocket was absurd after killing someone with her magic, but having something familiar to hold brought a sense of security.

Starling faded along the horizon, casting Raia in a thick shadow along the opposite edge while dual full moons rose. In a few hours they would overlap, and the world's shadow would steal their glow and restrain their magic.

It was evening when Quin and four guards entered her room.

"Where's Lua?" she asked. Those within earshot shifted uncomfortably.

"The Oji is waiting for you," Quin sneered. The guards surrounded her when she stepped into the hall.

"Fallue didn't mention an armed escort."

"*Master* Fallue owes you no explanation. You shouldn't think you warrant any."

Audra's jaw tightened as the air whispered caution. Something wasn't right. They passed the main stairwell to the end of the hall and took a small, winding set of stairs down. Chanting echoed against the stone walls. Strange words that hearkened back to ancient times chilled her bones. The voices drowned out their footsteps as they descended into the dim light. She steadied herself with one hand against the damp stone wall.

Quin's face morphed into a contemptuous mask in the sconce's warm glow at the bottom of the stairs. He gripped the hilt of his sword. The other soldiers had disappeared behind them somewhere in the darkness, safeguarding the entry.

Audra found the dagger in her pocket. It would be useless against a trained swordsman. She skirted along the wall as he mirrored her movements.

"We're alone," Quin said. "Time to be honest. If that's even possible for a southerner."

"Westerner, idiot. If you're going to insult me, try to get it right. Otherwise, you sound ignorant and unobservant." The thread tugged in response to the sudden quickening of her heart.

"You're all southerners to us," he said with loathing. "Your kind should be dead."

"Did I do something to you? Personally?" she asked. "This kind of hatred usually comes *after* I've done something."

His fingers twitched around the hilt. He wanted to act, but because of his Oji, he wouldn't. She saw his hostility for what it was masking—jealousy, envy, sadness.

"Oh, I see, Dain was with him for many years, right? He must have been getting close to his end. You were supposed to be his next anchor." Quin's face darkened as she spoke. "Is that it? You blame me for whatever you think you lost."

He hissed. "I should be beside him, not you. I've trained my whole life to protect him. You are *nothing*. Less than nothing. A foreign parasite here to confuse him. You ruined everything. You stole him."

"Well, she is a thief." Lua emerged from the shadowed tunnel behind Quin, midnight robes flowing around him like star-littered water. A silvery thread snaked from Lua's hand and wrapped around Quin's neck.

The guard's eyes widened. He tried speaking, but each movement caused the magic to blister his chin. A sickly, burning stench permeated the room. Lua pulled her to his side protectively.

"Let him go," she said.

Lua's jaw clenched stubbornly. The thread pulsed closer around Quin's throat.

"He wasn't going to hurt me," she said.

"I heard the threat in his voice."

"He wouldn't. Hurting me would hurt you." Her magic thrummed, aching to reach and calm him, but she held it at bay. She needed to see him try to withdraw it on his own. "He's loyal to you. Please stop."

There was a slight tug along their thread. Lua's magic sizzled, bright and blinding, before dissipating. Quin gasped and rubbed the welts around his throat.

"I'll deal with this after the ceremony," Lua said. "You should thank your Raani for sparing your life."

The look Quin gave her could have been many things, but gratitude was not one of them. The chanting reverberated from beyond the corridor into her bones.

With a last look at Quin, Lua guided her gently into the dark hall. They stopped outside a massive, ornately carved arched entryway. The Silence moon god sigil—composed of bluest abalone and obsidian—was split in half across the doors.

The chanting voices inside had dropped into soft prayers. Their vibratos made Audra pause as it kindled memories of the Western monks' ceremonies she'd attended as a child. But the incense that drifted through the doors was different. These words were unfamiliar.

Quin's sentiments haunted her ears. She shouldn't be here. And Traq—

"Forget him. You belong with me." Lua kissed her knuckles while his other arm held her waist. Their bodies pressed together, breath in sync.

"Lua—"

His mouth met hers. Audra dissolved into the sensation of being seen at the deepest level and desired anyway. Both fierce in their visceral longing to be half of the whole they were creating.

The chanting beyond the doors resumed and swelled. Lua held her, kissing her forehead. Nervousness shimmered toward her. He wanted to be the Rajav, but his need for her held him in this moment. Audra held him, knowing that everything was about to change.

"I need to tell you something," she said.

He smiled. "I know it's difficult for you to say."

"You know?"

"You love me."

Lua frowned at her hesitation. She'd been a fool. He would have shown Traq mercy if she'd asked him to.

"Yes. I love you. More than I've ever loved anyone. And I don't care if it's magic or being your anchor or whatever it is. You are mine and I am yours," she said. "But there's something else I should have told you yesterday. Traq is somewhere on the grounds, and the Moon mages from the ruins. They're together and—"

The doors creaked open, casting Lua's features in stark contrasts of shadows and all'ights. The chorus overwhelmed Audra's small voice. She desperately gripped Lua's hand.

Fallue motioned them forward, but Lua hesitated, holding her gaze for a long moment. A small furrow marred his smooth brow. His jaw jutted subtly to one side. Lua's worry deepened.

The cheers that rose from the room were like a wave calling to the sea. An electric thrill pulsed in the air. He brushed the fallen hair from her eyes and tucked it behind her ear. He embraced her a final time and whispered into her ear. "I'll always protect you."

Fallue shot her a reticent look before formally saluting the Oji. With a small squeeze of her hand, Lua pulled away and started into the room. Protocol held Audra back a pace, breaking their hands apart. She clung to his obsidian wake, momentarily overwhelmed by the lights and engulfing noise.

Fifty-Nine

Selene

The blizzard stalked Selene and her Songs over the narrow mountain passes and across the icy flatlands. Six horses had fallen over the previous three days, and two soldiers had died in their sleep, their lips blue in the pale starling light, fingers frozen shut. A few soldiers grumbled at not performing proper funerals, but there was no time.

Bolin tried reassuring them that leaving the bodies for the animals was the right thing to do. A good death meant contributing to the continuation of life around them. His Western beliefs did little to appease most of them, but a few had nodded politely, pretending to understand.

The moons were nearing their conjunction when they finally rode past the empty tents and village outside the Silence monastery. The combined illumination made those last few miles easier on the soldiers. Despite the frigid temperatures, Selene pulled back her hood to absorb as much Song light as she could. She prayed like she always did, but the stubborn moon refused to acknowledge her.

Bolin had been solemn since Xiang's last message. Selene wished he'd looked more surprised when the general revealed the vials of liger's bane. She wondered how long Xiang had been planning her death. She'd keep a tighter grip on he and Bolin moving forward.

A thick crowd of commoners gathered around the main gates, trying vainly to gain entry for the coronation. The people parted when Song soldiers ordered them to give way with the points of their sword. There was no need to announce her. By the nervous looks of the guards, and the two Silent mages, seven and nine stars, that blocked the entrance, they'd been expecting her. She slid from her horse and approached the main gate. Bolin blended in with the soldiers behind her, but his anticipation bled into her.

The nine star mage was a large, middle-aged woman with a steady confidence that probably intimidated anyone other than Selene. The seven star was a thin man with boyish features who nervously licked his lips and gave a slight bow.

"Open the gate." Selene said.

"Apologies, Oja. Under orders of both the Oji and Master Fallue, no one is allowed entrance until after the eclipses," the woman said. Fear hinted in her voice. The man was still as a rabbit.

"Stand aside. I won't say it again," Selene's patience had thinned over the days of travel. Posting these weaker mages here was an intentional insult. The shifting shadows of a squadron beyond the gates caught her eye. Her hopes of lessening the casualties were dwindling.

The woman bowed again, deferentially. "I cannot do that, Oja. I beg your forgiv—"

Silver lashed from a third mage hidden atop the wall. It sliced Bolin's cheek as he jerked sideways. The magic skidded across his scaled armor, careening into a neighboring throat. The soldier fell, gurgling on steaming blood. A shout from above sent a volley of arrows arcing toward the Songs.

Blood dripped down Selene's jaw. With a furious scream, her magic spun toward the nine star. The woman conjured a shield, but it shattered beneath Selene's attack.

Another lash from above cut down two soldiers beside Bolin.

Whistling arrows lodged into shoulders and eyes before shields could be raised.

Two Song mages wove a wind spell that sent the next wave of arrows spiraling into the crowd of innocent onlookers. People screamed and scattered; four fell to the ground.

With a tug on Bolin, Selene's cheek stitched together. She rushed forward as her shield absorbed another whip from above. The nine star stumbled back. The seven star man leaped between them, trying to catch the Oja.

Selene spun away, but the nine star's thread encircled her ankle and threw her off balance.

The seven star's thread aimed for her throat. But it fizzled, faltered. The spell died in a scream as the mage's hand tumbled to the ground. Blood spurted from his wrist as Bolin's blade drew back and pierced the man's chest.

Selene's magic captured the tether around her ankle, encircling the thread and yanking the nine star toward her. Bolin lunged forward, cleaving halfway through the woman's torso as she screamed.

The remaining mage targeted them again, but Selene was faster. Her spell dragged the mage from the wall toward her. Her hand caught his face, magic consuming him, then dropped him in a pile of dust and robes.

Selene pulled on Bolin. The next blast hurled a dozen Silence bodies from the wall. Bolin's small wounds healed. His cheeks flushed, and pupils dilated. A smile twisted his lips. The thrill of a fight surged between them.

Song soldiers rallied behind them as Selene pressed the gates open.

Selene, Bolin, and five soldiers moved stealthily down the winding passageways. Her forces would head for the ceremonial hall when they were done outside. She'd ordered them to kill anyone who stood against them, no matter what tribe they claimed loyalty to.

Anchors rarely shared the same meals with their mages outside of their homes. That way if one were poisoned the other could give their companion enough energy to sustain themselves. However, if they survived, any poisoning would weaken both parties for a time. It wouldn't take much of the liger's bane to diminish them. If Xiang had managed to poison the anchors' wine the results would be in full effect during the peak of the eclipse. But in case that plan failed, Selene would visit Master Fallue's anchor, Emaline, first. The death of the Mage Council and Silence monastery's leader would create chaos that could be advantageous.

And considering how vocal Emaline's animosity toward Selene had always been, how she'd spread rumors about the Oja, that decision was easy to make.

Emaline had once been a renowned fighter with a keen mind, but the anchoring had taken its toll. The woman was weak and blind, not that Selene was prone to pity.

A terrified servant had quickly given up Emaline's location. Selene siphoned the two guards stationed outside while Bolin knocked loudly on the thick wooden door. The Oja wiped the dust from her hands.

"What does everyone want?" Emaline's throaty yell cracked with annoyance. Another voice tried to calm her.

Bolin opened the door slowly. "Beg your pardon, Mirzas. Would one of you fine ladies be Emaline?"

Selene shoved past him, slamming the door against the wall. "Quit playing games, Bolin. We're on a schedule." She entered the room in a flurry of ebony robes, eyes glittering with stolen life.

A familiar woman sat beside Emaline on a small couch and held a cup of wine near the woman's lips. The hint of magic that wafted from the young woman was sickly, mostly spent, barely even a star. A plate of soft foods and assorted cutlery was scattered on the table before them. The mage paled at seeing Selene and placed the cup on the table.

"Emaline, it's been too long. Unfortunate that I'll miss seeing Fallue, but it's you I'm looking for," Selene said.

Emaline's milky eyes narrowed. "Who is this?"

The younger woman shifted nervously and whispered, "It's our Oja, ma'am."

The older woman cackled and shook her head, graying hair dancing across her face. "Not *my* Oja. I don't have a damned Oja. She should have been smothered in her crib as the Rajav wanted."

Selene's smile didn't waver, but her eyes flicked to the mage. "Aren't you one of Xiang's?"

"Jayna, Oja."

"Of course. Best to move out of the way, dear."

The edge of Jayna's tunic twisted desperately in Emaline's gnarled fingers. "You'd let them kill your senior mage? Weren't you mentored in the house of Silence?"

Gently, Jayna undid the old woman's fingers before backing away. She shook her head. "That was a long time ago. I can't help you."

Selene stepped forward. Bolin sauntered behind like a shadow waiting to breathe. Emaline flinched as the light shifted across her eyes.

"Have you spread any more rumors lately, Emaline?" Selene asked.

"Not rumors. Facts."

"And what facts are those?"

"The Rajav never wanted you close to the throne. Every time he sent you to war with an incompetent anchor, he hoped you wouldn't return," Emaline said. "He knew you were damaged from the moment you drew your first breath."

Selene's laugh was high and light. "Thank Song for Amala then. But no, I'm talking about the more recent rumors surrounding my poor father's death."

"Ha! Your *poor father*. Those words should make your wicked mouth bleed." Emaline spat.

An insincere frown marred Selene's delicate features. "You know, I can make this hurt. Draw it out so the whole assembly witnesses Fallue wither and suffer. Hacked to pieces slowly while knowing his beloved anchor suffers the same fate. Or we could just wait for the poison to work, right, Jayna?"

Emaline froze as understanding took hold. A moment later, her fingers found the glass of wine. Slowly, she brought it to her lips and took a small sip. She resettled it on the table and snorted. "Special vintage, my ass."

Metal glinted in Emaline's fist, a small dagger slashed toward Selene. Bolin yanked the Oja backward. His sword whispered through the air. Emaline's head landed at Jayna's feet while her body crumpled to the ground.

Selene sighed with disappointment. "Too soon, love. I could have used her energy."

"She attacked you," Bolin replied. "You said we were on a schedule."

Selene stared at the old woman's face wistfully. "So we are." She glanced back, sharp eyes laying Jayna bare. "Come along, dear. You're in too deep to go anywhere else."

Sixty

Audra

Audra followed Lua through a cloud of incense that wafted toward the large open panels overhead. Raia's vibrant emerald glow was muted by the brighter tones of the full moons. Silence loomed against the dark sky; its bluish hints contrasted by Song's yellowy cast. The smaller moon inched slowly before the larger one, nearly in line.

The hundreds of people that filled the room quieted at the Oji's entrance. Those of higher status sat at round tables near the dais, but others lurked in the perimeter as ominous faceless shapes.

Audra flushed beneath the kohl. The amount of constrained magic in the room caused her head to spin when she curiously reached out, searching for Traq. She clutched the insides of her robe as the memory of the only other time she'd been surrounded by so many people flooded her brain. Lost and alone, pressed between bodies. Trapped. That fear had never quite resolved.

Being held in small cells was bad, but this was worse than any jail she'd ever been in. As her heart ticked faster, Lua's steps slowed. He glanced back at her. A steadying swell filled her chest, a calming reassurance that everything would be all right. That she was safe with him.

Audra followed him onto the dais where Anjing, Sharine, and the remaining council members stood before their chairs and bowed at his approach. Three chairs reserved for Song tribe council members remained empty.

The Oji stopped before the black oak throne in the middle of the stage. Its back was carved with two sickle moons interwoven, cut in opposing directions. Like most chairs she'd experienced since entering the northern territory, it looked hard and unforgiving: intended to keep its occupants miserable.

Lua flashed a knowing smile at her and motioned to a smaller chair beside his. Though still austere, a thick cushion filled its seat, embroidered with a small green dragon. The surprise of it caught in her throat. Throughout Audra's life, her comfort had gone largely neglected due to either circumstances or by her own denial. A small, tortured part of herself believed that because she'd survived death many times while others had not, she didn't deserve care or comfort or love.

He'd seen her discomfort, knew her façade of strength covered deeper pain, and repeatedly sought to alleviate all of it in his own way. His actions meant more than she could voice. This was what she'd imagined love was. Not grand gestures or proclamations, but small acts of consideration done only because he wanted to take care of her. And no matter who he'd been before they met, she loved Lua more than she'd realized. He winked at her, his smile warming her insides as she bit her reddened lips.

The crowd waited for the Oji to sit before doing the same. The speeches would come after the ceremony. As Fallue spoke, the all'ights dimmed, the room lit only by Raia's glow and the dual moonslight that streamed in from above. The mixture of blue, yellow, and subtle green blended across Lua's pale skin and ebony hair, turning him ethereal and beautiful. He glanced at Audra once, offering a small smile before he closed his eyes.

The council members stood and spread their arms, chanting prayers with their unfamiliar words. Their voices vibrated through the air.

Lua took a shuddering breath and gripped the throne's armrests. He closed his eyes, whispering the same prayers he said each night. He gasped, chest thrusting forward at the same moment sharp pain cascaded into Audra and burned her insides cold.

The cascading light changed with Song's transit over Silence. Raia was lost in darkness, emerald hues only visible further away from the apex. A sliver of Silence morphed from blue to dark red as the planet's shadow spread across its surface. With every passing inch, Lua's magic was wrenched away, like skin flayed from muscle.

Audra's green thread spanned between them, untouched, but Lua's silver thinned as he offered himself to the moons. She gritted her teeth as his anguish flooded through her. Fallue said Lua would be vulnerable until the eclipse passed and the moons returned his magic, but she'd not realized entirely what that meant. This was supposedly the surest way to gain the blessings of both moons and their tribes. The responsibility of the Raani was to ensure their Rajav survived the process. But she couldn't have anticipated how painful it would be, like talons shredding through their flesh.

As the shadow crept over Song's edges, Lua convulsed. One by one, each of his threads vanished, leaving only a single fiber between him and Audra's green threads.

She didn't know how long she could feel his pain and not react defensively. What little of his magic still coursed between them was raw and frail. Instinct demanded she do something, but protocol insisted otherwise. She thrummed her magic into his remaining thread and gave him what she could. Her head swam, dizziness threatened her consciousness, but she resisted. Lua needed her.

Sanguine shadows engulfed both moons and the temperature inside the room plummeted. Darkness fell, save for the sparse scattered all'ights and the amber glow that streamed from above and encapsulated the man on his throne. Lua was too still. The pain from him had vanished as quickly as it had come, as if he were suddenly empty. Or as if he did not exist. The moment stretched in agony.

Protocols be damned. Audra scrambled over the side of her chair and clutched his cold hand. Her heart beat alone. Lua wasn't breathing. She flooded more of herself down their remaining thread, but the energy recoiled back into her. Her breath hitched on the edge of panic.

"Lua?" Her shaking voice echoed through the silent hall. Her breath a white swirl in the darkness.

A stream of bluish light struck his hand. Lua sucked in a breath, and Audra with him. The council members resumed their chanting, but their voices were strained. A sickly sheen of sweat dotted their brows. They muttered, choked. Anjing collapsed and writhed on the floor, followed rapidly by three others.

Fallue swayed on his feet, staring fixedly upward. He continued his prayers until a red line bloomed across his throat. Blood spewed from beneath his beard and cascaded down his chest. When his body crashed on the stage, his head rolled away. His lips uttered one word.

"Emaline."

Sharine alone stood unaffected. She eyed the unconscious Lua still slumped on his throne while shocked screams rippled through the room. People stood, unsure. Guards rushed toward the dais, but Audra didn't know if they intended protection or assault.

She climbed to her feet and stood before Lua, daring anyone to come near. Fallue insisted that Lua would wake when the eclipse passed. But the Mage Council leader was dead. His glassy eyes stared at the sky above. Somewhere in the room's dark recesses, someone screamed her name. But a harsher voice rang out.

"Now!"

Sixty-One

Traq

Traq exchanged confused glances with Durin and Liasa as the Moon council members toppled to the floor. The room morphed into chilled chaos that pulled the Starlings away from their position along the back wall. The shiver that worked down Traq's spine had nothing to do with the frigid atmosphere.

Well-dressed people knocked each other down in a panicked rush toward the doors. Soldiers sped toward the dais, but it was impossible to differentiate who was who. When the first council member fell, Xiang raced away from Traq and Liasa before they could question. The general slid through the scrambling attendants, cutting down those in his path with a terrifying focus.

The remaining Moon mages brought weakened gray or silver light to their hands. They'd still be vulnerable until the eclipse passed completely. Wren's orders to her people had been absolute: no casting unless they were out of other options. A hint of gold would give the Moon tribes a common enemy, and there were powerful mages in the crowd just waiting for their magic to return. Only when they reached the dais should they consider casting to capture Audra.

Traq shoved through the throng, hauling people from the floor before they were trampled, while keeping his eyes on Audra. Donned in midnight robes with her face painted, Traq hadn't recognized her at first. It was the way she moved that gave her away.

The reddish hue that encapsulated the throne was slowly transitioning to blue. Audra stood before the Oji, blocking him from view while she glared at the remaining council member. The small blade in her hand caught the light. But the tall woman who approached her looked unconcerned.

"Audra!" He called her name again, but he was too far away. Even if the mage lacked full strength, Audra was no match for a ten star. One touch would kill her, and Jayna said not even the bloodstone could prevent a siphoning.

He drew his sword and muscled through the crowd, ducking blades and fists of those still cast in shadow. It was impossible to tell enemies from allies but, other than their own soldiers, it didn't matter. If they could capture Audra or incapacitate the Oji, they'd have enough leverage for when the Oja arrived.

"Traq!" Wren gripped his shoulder, holding him back. Her hood had fallen, darkened braid dangling over her shoulder. She panted, breath visible between them. "She doesn't have it."

"What?"

"They moved her before we could get to her." She sucked in a breath as she shoved something hard into his hands. "Found this in Audra's rooms." Wren shouted over the escalating noise. "She's not wearing the bloodstone."

The rock was cold and flat. He looped the cord around his wrist and met her gaze.

"Go," she said.

"Wren, I—"

"Go! Before it's too late." She pointed at the dais.

Traq caught her arm. He kissed her.

Wren shoved him back. "Now? After everything? You've the absolute worst timing."

"I didn't want you to think—"

"Go. That's an order, Tresa. I'll be right behind you."

Traq shouldered his way toward the dais. Song was nearly free of the eclipse. Silence would follow soon after. Then the Moon mages would have their power back, including the man still slumped on his dark throne.

Audra yelled at the council member, but her words were lost. The taller woman was more ornately dressed than the other mages were. She remained calm, holding her hands up in supplication as she approached the throne.

Xiang's blade swung viciously through the air as he neared the platform. Though his expression was placid, his assault was nightmarish. Each hit connected with either block or blood. Every determined step carried him through those in his path. Audra and the Oji would die when Xiang reached them. And Traq was too far away to stop it.

Sixty-Two

Lua
Rajav

Lua was ether, existing between life and death, between something and nothing. He basked in the light of the two moons while the surrounding space reddened. In this space, he was laid bare, open and vulnerable. Here there was only truth and no way to deceive even if he'd wanted to.

"*He must make his choice,*" Silence whispered.

"*He's like the rest of them.*" Contempt ruled Song's tone.

"*No. He's already shown his differences.*"

"*Killers. Destroyers. Betrayers. Mark my Song, he'll be the same.*"

"*He must choose,*" Silence said.

"*It won't matter. They never change.*"

Lua doubted where he was for a moment. Weeks had passed without hearing Silence, and Song had only spoken to him twice in his life, the last time in the sea. His fate balanced on the blade of their blessings. But their tones were disturbing, as if disappointment were a foregone conclusion.

Silence answered Lua's worries before he could speak. *"The dragon mage is fine. With some care, she'll yet live through this night."*

"But you might not. Everything depends on your choices, little Oji."

Without a voice he struggled to form a cohesive response.

"He doesn't know the truth," Song said.

"He wouldn't. It's been too long. Words and bones have ground to dust."

"If he wants our blessings, he must choose. Just like the others."

"What don't I know?" Lua asked.

"There he is."

"He's been here. You would know if you listened. There is strength in Silence."

An ethereal sigh. *"Then let me guide him. Lua Koray, Oji of our Moon tribes, son of Li-Hun Koray and Amala Shirav. Direct descendant of Yueliang, will you right the wrongs of your ancestors?"*

He was trapped in confusion.

"He doesn't know. Why would he?" Song said.

"What choice?" Lua's voice was barely a whisper.

"Do you see her defending you? As if you didn't take part in the slaughter. As if your ancestors didn't steal the power from hers? She should kill you while you are cut apart. Losing you won't hurt her now."

Audra shimmered before him, worried eyes blacked with kohl, lips crimson red. A single green thread, thin as a spider's silk, spun from her hand into his arm. It nestled in his chest before soaring toward him. It lashed around his essence and attempted to reel him back. Below his body gasped, but above he resisted.

"What choice?"

Their voices merged into a painful chorus. *"Will you right the wrongs of your ancestors to mend all that was broken?"*

The wrongs of his ancestors? The destruction of the Western tribes—or something more? So much history was erased. Where would he stand in the future if he denied this request? He tried to say as much, but the words failed again.

Song's voice was thin. *"I am nearly uncovered. In a moment, the connection will disappear."*

"I will," Lua said, too loudly.

Song's color changed to blinding ivory. *"Return the world to how it was meant to be. Let me guide you."* Her voice faded as she moved beyond the shadow.

Audra's pull grew tighter, pleading. He tasted her fear.

Silence filled his mind. *"Few of your ancestors have dared to challenge the shame they've inherited, and those who did failed the task now set before you. Indeed, Li-Hun nearly made it irreparable. You must make it right."*

"But Li-Hun had your blessing."

"No. Not mine."

"His magic?" Lua was sure Li-Hun had spoken to both moons. His father made sacrifices, public prayers, bragged of his connection. But his magic had only ever been gray. Only Song's. Lua had questioned his father on many things over the years, but his magic or claim to the throne had never crossed Lua's mind. The realization sickened him. To be made the true Rajav demanded the blessings of both moons, and his father had never had it. He'd lied to everyone because he could, and no one dared to question him.

"You come from thieves and liars. Remember the vows you've made, and I will give you strength. Seek the sisters when all is lost. They will aid you. They have their own regrets."

"Wait!" Lua cried, the moonlight blinded him.

"They've been waiting. We've been waiting."

Pain jolted him into consciousness. The roar of battle assaulted his senses.

Sixty-Three

Xiang

X iang knocked a mage to the ground, slamming his sword into her chest as he passed.

Thirty feet until the steps. Fifty more and he would cut Lua and Audra open. Bolin might hate him for a time, but eventually he would understand. There was no other way. Xiang had been swayed by Audra's connection to Bolin at the ruins. Seeing her painted as the Raani now, he regretted letting her live.

Councilor Sharine stalked across the stage, her hands raised in a placating manner. But Xiang knew their orders were the same, either incapacitate or kill Audra. The Oji remained ensnared in the moons' trance, unconscious, with only his weak anchor for protection. That he'd survived Dain's death meant Xiang had to ensure he didn't survive Audra's.

The dagger in Audra's hand looked incapable of doing more than peeling fruit, but she stubbornly held her ground, crouching before Lua. Audra's snarl revealed everything that made her Bolin's sister: passionate, wholehearted, and unyielding. It was a pity that she had to die.

The room was a blur of violent shadows. No magic called yet, but the air tingled with anticipation. Somewhere in the chaos, Traq yelled Xiang's name. But as magic flickered in Sharine's hands, Xiang had no time for distractions.

A blade forced him back as his foot touched the first step. The soldier's sword swung again, but the general met it. Her next swing was too loose, easily blocked. Xiang's parry swept under the woman's blade. He pressed her back, but her footing held sturdy. She grunted and, as his strength overwhelmed her, she spit in his face.

"Traitor," she hissed.

That voice had offered easy camaraderie to the mages and soldiers regardless of their tribal affiliation. Liasa had even tended to Jayna when she was near death.

He stepped back. "Stand down, Starling."

Her cheeks were flushed. "I'm from Oxton, remember?" The sword drew up, blocking his path again. "You can't go up there."

"Step aside."

"I have my orders." Her voice and sword were steady.

"Orders get people killed, Liasa. They'll never take the Oji south or hold him accountable for the crimes he's committed."

Her shoulders squared. "That might be the first true thing you've said."

"Then why are you in my way?"

"Those are my orders. Once we hold you captive, your Oja will let us go."

"And the Oji?"

"The Septra has a plan for that too." Liasa stood before the steps. In this light, she appeared older than he'd taken her for on the journey. Where he'd thought her naïve, he recognized she might just be pathetically optimistic. That somehow life's traumas hadn't ruined her.

His blade swung up. "So be it."

Their metal clashed and sang with determination. Hit upon hit, she parried and blocked. She grunted, cursed, but held him back. Yet her strikes scraped down his armor and left him unscathed.

A spark of silver reflected in her eyes, countered by a blast of gray. Magic lit the surrounding room.

Song was uncovered. Silence grew stronger. The window to kill the Oji was fading. A gray blast struck the floor beside them. Liasa startled, and Xiang knocked her blade aside before his sword gutted her.

She gasped, gripping his shoulders while her sword clattered away. He laid her on the floor and withdrew his blade. Xiang closed her eyes and sighed. In that other life he often dreamed of, he would have enjoyed calling Liasa a comrade. Behind him, Traq darted through the crowd, Wren close on his heels.

He stood and with a resigned heart, started up the stairs.

Sixty-Four

Audra
Raani

Despite the chilled air, sweat had smeared the kohl down Audra's face. A pulse echoed through her veins like a question, closer, clearer than it had ever been before. With a tug, she answered it, though she knew she didn't need to. She crouched defensively in front of the throne as Sharine stopped a dozen paces away. The other council members were scattered around the dais. Two still writhed, while the others lay lifeless.

"You did this?" Audra asked. She was more surprised at the brutality inflicted on the other council members than she was at the betrayal. The mages had trusted Sharine implicitly, and she'd let them die.

"I don't want to kill you," Sharine said. "You saved my life before. I don't forget such things. Still, a bargain had to be made."

"With Selene?"

Sharine's jaw tightened. "Best you use her title, or she'll kill you sooner than later."

"You're one of hers. Of course, you're here to kill me," Audra said.

"I'm not. But you are the easiest way to control the Oji."

Audra muttered. "Shit. You people are the worst."

"Not as bad as your Oji."

"Lua is better than all of you combined."

Sharine laughed incredulously. "He's exactly the villain he was made to be. Look how well he's convinced you otherwise? He was ruthless during the last invasions. More brutal than his sister by far. I doubt he told you what he did."

"Shut up." Audra knew there were things Lua had been too ashamed to confess, but she refused to be swayed by this woman in this moment.

Gray glowed from Sharine's fingers. "I apologize for what I'm about to do."

Magic spun forward. Audra ducked. A green shield erupted before her. An emerald shining in a sea of night and storm clouds. A collective hush spread through the hall, followed by quick exclamations. She knew some of them would be thinking that it wasn't possible. The Western mages should all be dead. And if there was one left, there was a chance that a dragon would answer her call.

Sharine's blow cracked hard against Audra's shield, and she stumbled sideways. The next blast struck the floor near her feet. Oak splinters darted through the air, catching Audra's forearm. Behind her, Lua rustled in his seat, but his eyes remained closed.

Sharine hammered Audra before she could cast any stronger defensive spells. One blast skimmed past Audra's head, careening into the throne. It knocked Lua sideways in the chair.

Audra spun, screaming. Lua's sleeve smoldered. At seeing his raw, burning skin, a frenzied anger coursed through her.

Emerald fire erupted from Audra's hands. Sharine's shield flickered beneath the assault. Audra snarled and advanced a few feet, leaving a gap in Lua's protection. Sharine grunted and fell back a step. Audra's spell wormed into the moon mage's shield and broke it down one inch at a time.

Audra didn't notice a lone figure racing up the stairs behind her.

Sharine retreated, screaming as the emerald magic seared her hands. A blade jutted through her chest from behind. It lifted upward, pulling the councilor's feet from the floor. She choked, blood spewing from her mouth a moment before the blade yanked free. Sharine's body hit the ground with a thump.

Audra's magic dissipated in a shimmer as Quin's reddened face came into view.

"Quin?" Audra asked.

"Protect him!" Quin yelled.

Audra whirled. Xiang stood before Lua with his sword drawn back, its metal glinting in the celestial light. The primal fury still coursing through her surged, darkening the edges of her vision. With a guttural roar, emerald streams propelled her dagger toward him.

Xiang's sword froze mid-swing. Rippling green threads held it still. The man went rigid, muscles locked tight as the small blade pierced his throat. He opened his mouth, his expression one of disbelief as verdant fire engulfed him.

Blood gushed from his lips. Audra watched in horrified fascination while her magic wriggled between the plates of his armor. Slithering into each opening, searing his flesh before boring deeper, reaching for his bones.

Xiang fell, writhing in agony beneath Audra's fury. Somewhere in the shadowed room, a man screamed Xiang's name. The mournful sound drew her attention away from the scene. She turned.

A gold blast crashed into her, hurtling Audra across the dais. The green fire dissipated, leaving Xiang in a charred heap.

A moment before her head hit the floor, her Rajav opened his eyes. Then all went dark.

Sixty-Five

Lua

Emerald shine flickered through Lua's eyelids a moment before they opened. Smoke blurred his vision as he tried to make sense of the surrounding disorder.

A body smoldered at his feet. Its skin crisped black, unrecognizable save for the blade clutched in that hand. Audra's dagger jutted from what had to be General Xiang's throat.

"Audra?" He reached for her, but the connection was thin as spider's silk. He rose, wincing when he leaned on his blistered arm. Twitching or lifeless figures lay scattered across the platform. Lua choked when his gaze found Fallue's body.

Nothing made sense. Where was Audra?

Lua's shining thread snugged around Quin's throat as he stood over Sharine's lifeless form. The Rajav struggled to stand even as his magic surged. "What have you done?" His voice was hoarse.

Quin gasped. "Sh-she attacked you."

"Where's Audra?"

Quin motioned to a crumpled figure behind the throne. Lua released him and stumbled toward her. Again, he found only the thin connection she'd spun when he was unconscious. As he reached for her, a golden net enveloped her.

"Stop." A woman spoke from the front of the stage. "I don't want to hurt her." Her face reminded Lua of another time, many miles away. The Starling from Oxton wore Moon robes, her hair had been dulled dark. She stood behind Traq who'd made it halfway across the stage and seemed to be waiting for Lua to move.

Lua sneered. "You're not strong enough."

Wren's magic dragged Audra across the floor like an empty sack. Traq moved forward, reaching for her.

The white light that burst from Lua's hand punched Wren's chest before she could react. It encircled her, winding its way down her limbs and shifting the gold that clung to Audra toward Lua. Her magic changed, shimmering as it dissolved into him. Wren screamed.

"No!" Traq cast a weak shield before Wren, but it shattered into fragments.

With a flick of his wrist, Lua sent Traq flying down the stairs. He reeled Wren forward and gripped her throat.

"You shouldn't have threatened her," he said.

Wren thrashed, prying at his fingers while his magic consumed her. Her eyes were wide, terror filled.

Audra had warned him. But he'd never considered an assault on the council. Nor that Traq would turn on her. He'd savor their deaths, bask in their suffering.

"Lua?" Audra's eyes opened. She whispered. "Please."

His grip tightened in frustration before releasing Wren. His magic protested, licking out at the dying woman before he swatted her away like a gnat. Wren skidded across the stage and tumbled from the dais. She'd be dead soon. He'd taken enough to insure it.

He cradled Audra to his chest. "I'm here. I've got you."

Kohl and dust smeared her cheeks. Her fingers grazed his face, but their connection didn't change. Their touch should have re-anchored them. All his studies had said so. Fallue had confirmed it. But the threads were slow in forming. It wasn't right.

"Stay." Her words slurred; voice weak. "Everyone always leaves."

He kissed her forehead, staining his lips black. "They'll have to kill me first."

"That's not as difficult as you make people think. Father's death is proof of that." Selene prowled onto the platform.

Bolin rushed onto the stage, falling to his knees before Xiang's corpse. A wail tore from his throat as he clutched his lover's remains.

Lua lifted Audra as he stood. She gripped his robe, pressing her face into his chest. A pulse rippled around them. His heart or, hopefully, hers.

The tears that wet Selene's eyes matched Bolin's. "I *might* have let her live." She glanced at the bodies around them. "None of this would have happened if you'd just come back on the *Mirren* like you were supposed to. You've made things so difficult, especially for me. We could have ruled together."

He held Audra closer. "You were always a better liar than I was. And if it weren't for Dain, I might have believed you."

She shrugged. "It wasn't difficult to convince him. Everyone knew Dain wasn't a good anchor. He was soft. All too willing to sacrifice you for a useless child."

The pulse strengthened, grew louder. The air swirled. A shadow blotted out the moonlight above. "You killed his family."

She rested a tender hand on Bolin's heaving shoulders. "And your anchor killed Bolin's."

Lua's retort stuck in his throat. Xiang hadn't told them about Audra. He considered his words, glancing once pointedly at Bolin's weeping figure before continuing. "We are each guilty of atrocities. You still have Bolin. Audra is mine. We need not do this. I have the moons' blessings. They will never accept you now."

Bolin lifted his tear-streaked face, eyes finding the figure in Lua's arms. "Audra?"

A gust of wind blasted through the panels above, carrying a familiar and unnerving scent. Audra's gaze shifted upward with a shuddering sigh of relief.

Enormous, dark green wings blocked out the sky. The dragon landed on the rim of the panels, thick talons crunching the metal frame. Chunks of ceiling rained around them. A long, squared nose jutted into the room, nostrils flaring. Sharp, emerald eyes landed possessively on Audra.

If it had been full grown, flames would have already engulfed the room.

"Ferin?" Lua said.

Bolin's robes blew back as he stared upward, paling. The red scales that glittered across his chest drew the dragon's gaze. Ferin snorted, a hot breath of steam lilting through the cold air. The sound broke the shock in the room. Mages and soldiers stampeded toward the doors. Selene covered her eyes as the buffeting wings spun dust in the air.

"A choice," Silence whispered.

He had to get Audra away from here, save what he valued most. Lua's magic shot upward, wrapping tightly around one of Ferin's wrists. Lua hauled them skyward.

Ferin launched into the night, hoisting them through the panels. When his talons gently engulfed Audra, Lua relinquished her without hesitation. He reached for the other front limb, but a gray whip nearly sliced off his fingertips, ricocheting off Ferin's chest.

Selene screamed from the battered stage below. She gripped Bolin's shoulder and hurled another blast with her other hand. Audra's shield flickered and fell beneath the assault.

"No!" Lua's magic went wide as he swayed with the pulsing of wings. He missed Selene by a foot.

Selene's next spell skimmed past Lua. It struck Ferin's arm, inches from Audra's head. But instead of dissipating like the others, the thread recoiled and encircled Lua's thigh.

His magic reacted, trying to consume Selene's energy, but her spell tightened. Still connected to Bolin, she yanked hard on the thread. White and emerald were both sucked down the line. He felt the drain of his power and, looking at Audra, saw the siphon drinking greedily from her. Lua's lash around Ferin weakened. The dragon's wings faltered. As he flung another blast downward, a dizzying wave of fatigue disoriented him. His magic dimmed.

"Lua!" Audra reached a shaking arm toward him. She was pale, the color dulling in her eyes. Selene's magic devoured the western magic through their frail bond.

"She might yet live through this night," Song said.

Audra croaked his name again. Lua met Ferin's eyes. In a moment, he understood what he'd refused to acknowledge before. If Audra died, the three of them would perish together.

"Losing you won't hurt her now."

Someone else could protect and sustain her. And trying to keep her would kill her.

Everything coalesced into a clear understanding. If Audra died, all hope for her people died with her. The truth Zin had spoken clearly—Western mages could sustain multiple bonds, and that dragons protect their own if they are able—was now perfectly obvious.

His breath shook. There was no other choice. Audra had to live and, with her, the youngest of the remaining dragons. To right the wrongs of his ancestors.

"Take her," he whispered to Ferin.

His spell rose, glittering beneath the light of two moons and Raia's ring. With a small prayer, it slashed down, severing their bond and snapping Selene's tether.

Audra's anguished scream ripped through him. Blood trickled from the corner of her mouth as her eyes found his. "No!"

Ferin's talons tightened around her. His other claws grasped for Lua, but the mage was already gone.

Lua studied the curve of her cheek as he fell away, longing for a life they would never know. With a shuddering breath, he unspooled the last of his magic. It rose hungrily, coiling into Audra until there was nothing left inside him.

His heart slowed. Each muscle cramped as if every bone were suddenly breaking with the loss.

"Lua!" Audra cried. Silver and green threads lashed around Lua's torso from her hand. She jerked him toward her, but it was too much, too fast. The threads snapped and recoiled. Her scream echoed toward him.

Then the Rajav Lua Koray plummeted to the ground, watching giant wings fly away.

"You've done well, little Rajav."

Sixty-Six

Selene

Selene's blast barely missed the dragon. The beast vanished into a sea of ring and moonslight, taking the Western mage with it.

A golden thread slowed Lua's descent, but he landed hard. His breaking bones fractured the stunned silence. He bounced once and didn't move.

"Who did that?" Selene whirled around. An older Starling mage stood at the top of the stairs. She snarled, drawing magic into her hands.

Jayna rushed before him. "He helped us."

"He's a Starling."

"He saved me. Maybe he can save the Oji too." Jayna's voice was desperate, her eyes latched onto Selene's.

Selene studied the old man with a scowl before turning to Lua. "He's probably dead already."

Lua groaned. Selene huffed. "Shit. He's always been stubborn." She looked back at Jayna. "Fine. Keep the old man if you want. Maybe he'll be useful or maybe I'll change my mind tomorrow." Magic teased her fingers. "But first, let's find out how weak my brother's become."

"No!" Quin rushed forward and threw himself protectively atop

Lua's body. He grimaced, expecting death. Nothing happened. No magic reached out to claim him. Lua was less than ten stars, if there was any magic left in him at all.

Her vision blurred again. "Bolin?"

He pulled his tearful gaze from the sky, tracking the dragon's flight while Xiang's corpse crumbled in his arms.

"Grieve later," she said. "Remove the guard for me."

Bolin gently laid Xiang's head on the ground. Ashes clung to him, dusting the air as he stood. Quin rose without struggle, his face dour with disbelief.

When Selene nudged Lua's ribs with her boot, his eyes flicked open. She wasn't disappointed he still lived. Perhaps he'd reveal what the moons said, and she could use that to regain Song's blessing. "Hello, Brother." Her prodding turned to violent kicks until the Oji's groans ceased completely.

"He'll wish he were dead," Selene said. She nodded to Quin. "Since you're so devoted, you can care for him. Secure them together." She ordered before glancing at Jayna. "The old man too." The Oja searched the upturned tables and broken bodies, gaze landing on a Western man holding a dark-skinned woman whose gasps were fading. "What about them, pet? Worth keeping?"

Jayna bit her lip, taking caution with her words. "Traq knows Audra. He might be useful in finding her."

"And the woman?"

Wren's chest shook with each shallow breath. Traq's frame shuddered as he stroked her cheeks.

"Her father is a powerful Starling lord of some kind," Jayna said. "Keeping her would start a war."

"I suppose we'll have to deliver her and the other Starlings back to them. We'll send condolences and thanks. Make sure they know it was the Oji who did this," Selene said. "And congratulations, Jayna. You've just been promoted."

Jayna's bow obscured her expression. "Thank you, Oja."

"Is there anyone you hope to celebrate with?"

She hesitated. "No, Oja. I've no one."

If it were a lie, Selene would find out soon enough. "Best keep it that way. I'm tired of my people being distracted."

Traq's sobs wrung through the room as Wren went limp. Selene sighed at the display. She looked away, but death was everywhere.

"Audra." Bolin studied the sky. Silence light gave his features a bluish tint. Selene felt the sharp sting of betrayal reflected at her. "My sister's name."

She drew her robes around her before turning away. They would address this matter in private. A small moan drew her eye to Anjing. He twitched slightly. He could be useful. "Gather the highest-ranking mages left. We'll need to form a new council. The house of Silence has fallen."

"You lied." Bolin said softly. "All these years, after everything I've done for you, you lied to me."

She paused. Tension crept into her shoulders and jaw. His sorrow and devastation grappled her heart. "So what if I did? It made no difference. Your knowing would not have changed anything."

"It would have changed *everything*. You said they died. That you saw their bodies when the Starlings raided Pangol." He wiped his mouth.

Her tone changed to near sympathy. "Well, we must find them now. Before that dragon gets much bigger." Her eyes rested on Xiang's body. "Take time with your grief. And then we will plan a reunion."

"Selene—"

"We'll find them. I promise." Selene walked away, not stopping to wipe the unwanted tears from her cheeks until she was in the hallway. Stunned mages and soldiers idled past, either Song or Silence, it no longer made a difference. Under her reign, they'd be united once more, whether they wished it or not.

Sixty-Seven

Audra
Western Mage

Pain blistered behind Audra's eyes. She must have been unconscious for a long time. Her mouth was dry as sand. Each breath caused her ribs and head to protest. But beneath the physical pain and exhaustion was something worse—absence.

She reached for Lua and found nothing. Her small thread spun outward, but it slammed back into her chest. The way wasn't blocked; it was gone. A road washed violently away without a trace.

A dark canopy draped around her to the warm ground. Dim light slipped beneath the edges. Something wriggled in the dark beside her.

A thin mouse raised its whiskers an inch from her nose. It stood on its back feet to get a better view of her.

"You left me," she whispered. It squeaked and scampered beneath the edge of the canopy, disappearing into the light. "You said you wouldn't."

Sobs rolled like waves trying to drown her again. She curled into a ball, gasping until she could barely breathe.

The light shifted. The canopy rose a few inches. One edge angled up, allowing a fresh breeze to meet her wet cheeks. She studied the enclosure's warmth, the gentle rise and fall over her. It wasn't a canopy after all, but an old friend whose wings had blessed her.

Her fingers trailed over the leathery flesh, tracing his scales where they overlapped. She could tell Ferin was awake by his breathing. Though he sheltered her beneath one wing, he offered her privacy in his own way. He'd always been good at that.

They'd been bonded since Pangol. But he'd never been strong enough to leave Zin's protection before. When the moons' spell struck him, he'd needed a mage to survive. The child who carried him had to do. Neither of them had ever had a choice in it. And she'd searched for ways to heal him ever since. Now she was the one who needed care, and Ferin could do nothing except protect her while she cried.

She patted his side softly. "Can you speak?"

When the wing lifted, Starling light blinded her. Ferin stared down with shining green eyes, his response trickling down their connection.

"Not yet." Audra leaned against him for balance as she struggled to stand. He was bigger than she'd ever imagined he would get but still only half the size of Zin in her true form. The jade was nearly invisible beneath a verdant scale along his throat.

They were perched on top of a tall cliff. The shoreline below was ringed with reefs and sand bars, making it practically inaccessible by boat. She wondered how close they were to the edge of the world. The blue-green Empyrean spread to the horizon beneath a partly cloudy sky. The thickest part of Raia rotated slowly above. Audra wasn't familiar with this island, but Ferin must have brought her here for a reason. That thought knotted her stomach.

She was glad they hadn't gone home. Zin's deception had served its purpose, but the next words Audra had for her would be filled with anger. And Ferin probably needed to stretch his wings outside of her territory.

She leaned against him, heard the familiar beat of his heart. Her voice shook. "I had him. I could have saved him. But I wasn't . . ."

Ferin nudged her gently. Tears threatened to consume her again. She breathed in the sea air, let the shine warm her face. "He's alive. I know it."

They watched the sky change colors as Starling slipped behind Raia's ring. A shadow covered the island and surrounding sea. When the wind changed direction, it brought a hint of thick, acrid musk, like the spires or the barn Zin slept in. Another dragon was near. Where there was a dragon, there might be another Western mage.

Dark clouds wove together in the distance. She could taste the storm's approach. Lua said he'd drawn the clouds together. It sounded impossible at the time, but something told her it was within her power now.

Silver and emerald rose to her fingertips, spiraling together and reaching up.

"No." She pulled it back even as the silver resisted. Somewhere in the wintery northern lands, Lua was powerless and alone. Determination bloomed in her chest. "Maybe all that thieving was just practice." She wiped her cheeks and took a deep breath. "After all, how hard can it be to steal a mage?"

Sixty-Eight

Lua
Fallen Oji

Durin was gentle, though he would have had many reasons to hurt his charge. The old man's voice was steady and calm as he mended Lua's bones, even when Lua wordlessly resisted. He hadn't needed a healer since he'd been a nine star, but this was different than he remembered. No matter how kind the Starling was, his wire-thin magic burned beneath Lua's skin, raking steely claws that scarred his insides.

Still, he preferred the pain's distraction to the deeper rending of his heart.

Quin coaxed food and water into his mouth. Occasionally Selene would observe, Bolin staring behind her, as she made barbed statements. She'd frown when Lua didn't react. All questions went unanswered. Attempts at conversation were unacknowledged. Lua took shelter in silence. Let everyone else fill the air with empty words; he was broken with no hope of ever being whole again.

He was free to indulge in his misery. Memories and sorrow were all he had left of Audra, and he wouldn't let anyone steal that, not even with good intentions.

It wasn't until Selene was convinced of his powerlessness that they headed away from the monastery. Lua lay on a pallet with his eyes closed as the wagon rocked beneath him on the road to Uduary. They'd shorn his head to the scalp and dressed him in drab homespun cloth. Selene burned his elegant robes in front of him. No one called him Rajav or Oji unless they were mocking.

A stream of Starling whispered through the wagon's side and struck his face. He winced, but it didn't burn. The warmth was pleasant, like an embrace he'd never expected to feel again. He couldn't recall the last time he'd enjoyed Starling's light.

Lua's thoughts were full of the way Audra had been when they first met: butchered hair cut so close to the scalp he swore he saw nicks—like his was now—her cheeks too thin, rich brown eyes that assessed and dismissed him before he ever uttered a word. A smile that managed to be sarcastic, and a warmth that reached into him. He'd underestimated her repeatedly until he'd fallen too deep. He'd assumed he knew her, but even then, he'd been mistaken.

When they arrived in the capital, Selene would do what she wanted with him. There would be no trial, and with his magic gone, he posed little threat.

It should have killed him. From severing the bond to giving his magic away, he should have died. He wished he had. It hurt to think of Audra, and the moons wouldn't let him be. But he didn't answer them either.

Edging on the cusp of sleep, he reached out the way he always did, searching for her. As a dream reached up to claim him, a spider's silk of green glinted in the darkness.

Acknowledgments

This manuscript bloomed late one night when a particular scene rooted in my mind and refused to let go. The world then grew around these characters and their trauma. I've always drawn inspiration from the unwavering determination of the human spirit and the longing for both validation and connection. As a history lover, I studied the rise and fall of several civilizations for reference while drafting a world with both fading and vibrant cultures. But getting this story polished and published required a team and I'm incredibly grateful for those who've given their attention, time, and love to this tale.

I am incredibly grateful to everyone at Cursed Dragon Ship Publishing, but especially to Kelly Colby for laughing with me during my one-eyed pitch. I also want to express my deep gratitude to S.G. George for fully embracing the vision of this book and working through each round of edits with dedication and consideration. I appreciate you more than you know.

This book might never have been written without the late David Farland, my first writing mentor when I returned to the craft after a thirty-year hiatus. His teachings and generous critiques laid the foundation for bettering my storytelling and confidence.

To the Writers of the Future Contest judges and coordinators who helped me believe in my writing and gave me the priceless gift of the best peers from around the world including, but not limited to: Azure Arther, M. Elizabeth Ticknor, Michael Gardner, Chris Winspear, Kate Julicher, JL George, Ryan Cole, Rebecca Treasure, Leah Ning, Michael Panter, J.A. Becker, Z.T. Bright, Desmond Astair, and of course, Mike Jack Stoumbos. Go read their stuff.

To everyone at Superstars Writing Conferences but especially Kevin

J. Anderson and Rebecca Moesta. Truly, SSWC is a phenomenal group of supportive writers and I'm grateful to be part of the tribe.

To every editor who took the time to provide critiques that helped me grow as a writer. Especially B. Morris Allen of *Metaphorosis* whose guidance pushed me to craft something beautiful from pain.

A thousand thanks to those friends who've suffered through some truly awful stories and been brave enough to tell me the truth. I hope this makes up for some of it. To my beta readers (Julia, Becky K., Christopher, Paul, Morgan, Dustin, and Robert) who provided insightful and often hilarious feedback on that first pass. Thanks to my friends who've endured my emotional roller coasters and happily strapped in for the ride. Julia Ashley, Julia Vee, Azure Arther, Rebecca Treasure, and Hardeep Chahal, your friendships are worth more than gold. Thanks for the many conversations that kept me grounded.

To Gena, whose unrelenting love, strength, and firm conviction that we are each responsible for making a better world continues to inspire me. Though your spirit lives in every story I write, you are forever missed.

To my dad who spent long hours at a typewriter crafting sermons or stories. My mom for passing on her love of reading and never corralling my unusual interests. To Chris, Cathy, and Duane, I love you. To Alexa and Brit for making me a better person.

Paul, my husband and biggest fan. Thank you for encouraging me to find my voice and for loving me through all my chaotic incarnations. I know it's not always easy.

And, most importantly, to you, dear readers, for putting up with my tales. The best is yet to come.

~N.V.

About the Author

N.V. Haskell returned to writing in 2019 after many years away. Since then, she's published numerous short stories and won the Writers of the Future contest. She lives somewhere between suburbia and haunted creeks with her long-suffering spouse, rescue dog, and generations of birds, groundhogs, and squirrels that she can't help but feed.

After many years in healthcare, she remains stubbornly optimistic. When she's not hiking or staring at a screen, you can find her incognito at Comic Expos or Renaissance Fairs.

Make sure to check out her website for more information: www.nvhaskell.com.

- facebook.com/nvhaskell
- instagram.com/envyhaskell
- tiktok.com/@nvhaskell

Join the Cursed Dragon Ship Newsletter

Want more just like this one? Sign up for our newsletter so you don't miss out on the adventure. You'll get:

- A free book for signing up
- Advanced notice of new releases
- First word of books on sale
- Opportunities for free books
- Most up-to-date information on author appearances.

We're busy and know you are too. We won't send more than one newsletter a month.

Register below.

Want more Romantasy? We have a suggestion.

LIGIA DE WIT

BRADAI'S PLEDGE
TOUCH OF FAETE

Ryanne and Titus are fated to change the destiny of the fae and the pirates, whether that means destruction or salvation depends on their choices.

If you're in the mood for more fantasy

MISPLACED ADVENTURES

ONE GOOD EYE

HETTIE STORMHEART
BOOK ONE

JEN BAIR

What happens when you drag your magic-wielding siblings into a war they want nothing to do with? You get a family feud of epic proportions.

Made in the USA
Columbia, SC
02 April 2025